DISTANT ECHOES:

RICHARD III SPEAKS

BY

JOANNE R LARNER

Dedicated to: -

Lynne Lawer

My sister and friend. You are unique.

Also, to the hero in this book:

Richard Plantagenet

Duke of Gloucester and, by the Grace of God,

King Richard III of England and France and Lord of Ireland.

"Loyaulté Me Lie"

DISTANT ECHOES

With very best
wishes

Joanne
Larner

Also by Joanne Larner:

The 'Richard Liveth Yet' Trilogy:
>   Richard Liveth Yet: A Historical Novel Set in the Present Day
>   Richard Liveth Yet (Book II): A Foreign Country
>   Richard Liveth Yet (Book III): Hearts Never Change

With Susan Lamb:
>   Dickon's Diaries: A Yeare in the Lyff of King Richard the Third
>   Dickon's Diaries 2: Another Yeare in the Lyff of King Richard the Third

Contributing Author:
>   The Box Under the Bed: An Anthology of Scary Stories
>   Grant Me the Carving of My Name: A Collection of Stories about Richard III

Quotation

"...Where distant echoes still resound
That which is lost may still be found."

From 'Sheriff Hutton' by The Legendary Ten Seconds

Table of Contents

Prologue

Bosworth Field, August 22nd 1485

Mars, the God of War

He tried to force a way through the pike men to reach his enemy, but there came a sharp, ringing pain on the top of his head, so powerful that it forced him to his knees in the mire. His vision blurred and time slowed down as he fought to rise. He had to – it was his duty to defend his realm. A rough hand jerked his head backwards and a searing pain sliced along his jaw, as a dagger cut the leather strap and his helmet, with its crown, was carelessly tossed aside. Furious, he struck backwards with the point of his elbow, feeling the shattering of his adversary's nose and it gave him an instant to rise, swaying and panting with the exertion. Another blow glanced across his scalp and he felt the blood seeping from the wound even as he twisted round, leading with his sword arm to slice off his attacker's arm. He swung again and again, his teeth gritted, feeling no pain as the adrenaline coursed through his body, giving him the strength of desperation. Bodies piled up around him, but more kept taking their place, one of them the traitor, Rhys ap Thomas. "Treason! Treason!" he yelled and lunged towards him, blood and sweat blinding him. Then he was falling forwards, sprawling on his knees.

He felt a sickening blow from behind to the back of his bowed head. "Trea– !" His voice was cut off at the moment the second strike from the halberd crashed into him and his life was extinguished.

Chapter One

London, Twenty-first Century

I'm So Excited

Eve fidgeted with her feet under the desk and tapped her fingers on the hard edge of the wood. The letter was ready and now seemed to be a good time to deliver it personally to David Quigley; he was in a genial mood for once. Well, he wouldn't be once he had read the contents and found out his Assistant Director of Technology was leaving Future Tech. But then again, it was a step over the precipice, into the unknown for her as she had no new job to go to and the economy was still rather volatile. Who knew these days whether they would have a career from one day to the next? Perhaps she shouldn't leave after all. But she knew that she couldn't bear the boredom any more. Constant drudgery and no thanks for it, tedious work, belligerent bosses and irritable colleagues. And James had a well-paid job. They could manage on his salary until she found something else. Right! Let's get it done, she thought as she pushed herself up to her feet, her legs trembling despite her resolve.

"Eve! Have you heard about the new project?!" Rupert bounced into the room, beaming, his grin igniting a fire in his eyes that she had seldom seen of late.

"What project?" she asked, smiling back, unable to resist his infectious mood.

"'Fly on the Wall' – the new project commissioned by the Boss Man. Its aim is to track suspects or spy on people using their unique DNA sequence." He perched his long frame on her desk, swinging his leg like a kid. "It's only a prototype at the moment of course, but if we can bring it to market, we'll have a revolutionary new product, a highly original and unique – infallible – way of monitoring criminals on probation, suspected terrorists, wandering teenagers – the sky's the limit!"

"I don't know anything about it," she said. That was a lie; she had overheard David talking about it on the phone, but she hadn't been informed of it officially.

"Really? You surprise me. David was only just saying you will be transferred to it as Deputy once it's up and running – next month, apparently."

"Well, I might not be here by then; I'm handing in my notice," she said.

His face fell, his mouth still open in readiness for the next word and then he flushed a deep red.

"You can't go!" he shouted. "Who will I tease if you go – you're the only one with a decent sense of humour in the whole place! Not to mention the lovely cakes you bring in."

She snorted. "Thanks for such a glowing vote of confidence. That's all I'm good for, eh?"

But, even as she uttered the words, she knew she was being unfair. Rupert was the least sexist man she knew and always kind and encouraging.

"Of course not! David needs you – he may not admit it but you are the life blood of this place; he'd be lost without you."

"Oh, really? Why doesn't he ever say so, then?"

He winced, his eyes serious and sad. He looked down at his shoe, as he pushed the waste paper basket underneath the desk with his toe, his dark brows frowning, and bit his lip.

"He thinks it'd show weakness, I s'pose. But he would, though. Be lost, I mean. So would I," he muttered under his breath, glancing up and then down again. "Couldn't you just wait until it starts and see if things improve? Just give it a chance."

His eyes had now transformed to those of a cute, starving puppy. Eve sighed. If only she had been more decisive, it would now be a fait accompli and she wouldn't be feeling so torn. She liked Rupert and, if she left, she would miss him, but…

"OK, then," she sighed, her resolve melting in the face of his puppy dog expression. She reluctantly returned to her computer and began to work.

The time dragged, as usual, but at around two, Rupert and Eve were summoned into David's office and she saw immediately that this was no ordinary meeting.

David was deep in conversation with a tall, slim man with long, straight, blonde hair and blue eyes, peering myopically through a pair of fashionable spectacles. He was younger than David, who was now nearing fifty and looked it. Eve guessed the new guy was about mid- to late-thirties. And he was fitter-looking too (in every sense of the word). Not only was he slim-waisted and broad-shouldered, he was also very cute. *Stop it,*

Eve! she admonished herself. *You're taken!*

"Ah, Eve, Rupert," David said as soon as they entered. "I'd like you to meet Stellan Andreasson, our new boy. Stellan, this is Eve Pritchard – I've told you about her – and Rupert Williams, our programming whiz kid."

Eve reached out her right hand and Stellan shook it firmly, his grip strong and warm. He smiled as he made eye contact and, stupidly, she felt herself blushing. His gaze was a confusing combination of reserve and flirtation and when he smiled, his teeth were white and even and an adorable dimple appeared on his left cheek. Then Rupert also offered him his hand, a slight frown on his face.

"Stellan is the brains behind a fantastic new technology which has the potential to make millions – and he has agreed to work with us on its development for market. Our reputation has obviously gone before us and he has travelled here from Sweden because we are the best. He will need an assistant to perfect the programming and testing and a manager to project manage the whole thing. That's where you two come in." David looked at each of them in turn, his gaze boring deep into theirs as if trying to ascertain how trustworthy they were. "I am assigning you two, and only you, to this project. It may sound melodramatic, but this needs to be kept top secret until it is properly developed; we wouldn't want any of our rivals to get a whiff of this, that's for sure!"

He gave his characteristic snigger, then continued.

"I hope you don't mind, but you will both have to sign a confidentiality agreement," he continued. "Yes, yes, I know!" He stopped any protests even before they could utter them, by waving his hand and acting as if he had no choice in the matter. Eve capitulated, as usual, and they both agreed to sign the agreement – hopefully Rupert would be more circumspect in the future than when he had revealed it all to her!

David spoke again, once the documents had been signed.

"Well, I suppose you would like to know how it all works, so I'll hand the meeting over to Stellan."

He waved his hand in Stellan's direction and the Swede stood up and cleared his throat. The presentation on his laptop began with a click of his remote control and the title appeared: 'Fly on the Wall'.

There was a picture of the machine on the screen – it looked like a large printer or scanner, but it had speakers and could be connected wirelessly to a PC.

"I am pleased to present to you my invention, 'Fly on the Wall', which is a new technology through which individuals can be tracked through space and time and their conversations accessed.

"This is done by the use of DNA sequencing – we need a complete genome to be able to home in on the individual. As you know, suspects arrested by the police are now routinely DNA tested and many witnesses to crimes are also – in order to eliminate them from the enquiry. These samples can be used to track them. So, for example, if a suspected terrorist is questioned and released, the police can use their DNA sample to keep track of them. Criminals on probation can also be traced and the police could see whether they are keeping to their parole conditions. As for other uses, parents could provide their children's DNA and then if anything happened to them, or if they ran away from home, they could be found. There would be no more cases of children being hidden in the cellar of a paedophile – they would be found."

"How does it work?" Rupert asked.

Stellan clicked onto the next slide. It showed a depiction of a DNA sequence showing the pattern made by the different nitrogenous bases: adenine (A), thymine (T), guanine (G) and cytosine (C), the sequence and ordering of them being unique for each individual.

"This is my DNA. The sequence is programmed into the machine, which has a very powerful computer integrated into it. It analyses the DNA and converts the sequence into a wavelength. You know how a radio picks up the wavelengths of the different radio stations? Well, the 'Fly' identifies the individual's unique wavelength from their DNA and then scans a given area – obviously the greater the area to scan the harder it is for 'Fly' to locate the 'station' as it were, but in theory it could scan the whole world and find the exact location of the subject. It can even scan a given place and time to see if they were there at that time and what they were doing at that particular point in the past. This means that suspects can be pinpointed to the scene and time of a crime. It doesn't mean they were 100% the perpetrator, of course, but the chances are narrowed."

"Wow!" Eve said. "Is that even possible?"

"Clearly, yes," he said and clicked to the next slide, which showed a map of Sweden. He pointed with his laser pointer to a red dot in the centre of Stockholm. "That is where I was a day ago. I programmed in my DNA and it correctly pinpointed me."

He moved to the next slide. The red dot had moved to a different location.

"Then I added in the time element – you choose a specified location, date and time and 'Fly' follows the DNA trail and finds if you were there at that time. This is my birth date and, as you can see, I was born in Gothenburg."

"How can you prove it is the right person's trail?" Rupert asked.

"Well, as you know, every person's DNA is unique (except for identical twins). Therefore, there is no possibility of 'Fly' getting the wrong person. Although, at the moment this wouldn't stand up in court, of course. But it could still be used to prevent crime and possibly find lost children, even if not yet to convict criminals."

"That's amazing!" Eve said.

"And that's not all," he continued. "Fly can follow the DNA of someone and 'tune in' to their voice vibrations so that we can overhear whatever they say."

He clicked his remote and the sound of a baby crying was heard filling the room.

Eve looked at Rupert and he had the same puzzled frown she had on her face.

"It's me crying, as a baby," Stellan said, smiling and showing his attractive dimple. "Thirty-eight years ago."

Eve looked back at Rupert and he laughed. It was unbelievable, yet Stellan seemed to be entirely serious.

"But that could mean cold cases could be solved. The police could see whether the suspect was actually at the scene of a crime at any given time and overhear what they said. It could convict them by their own words," Eve said.

"That's the theory, yes," he said. "But we need to do some more research and trial it thoroughly before it can be brought to market. That's where you come in. We can test it with your DNA and refine the techniques. Are you agreeable to that?"

"I suppose so," said Rupert. "As long as you delete the details afterwards. I don't want you spying on me when I don't know about it."

"You will be in total control of the data," Stellan said.

Moments

So it was that, for the next few months, Eve had started enjoying work again, even if it meant she was working longer hours and arriving home exhausted. Luckily, and somewhat surprisingly, James was understanding about the whole thing, because David was pushing them to finish testing, so they could bring the device to market. She and Rupert got to play with 'Fly' and test it out. It was amazing!

After they had sequenced Eve's DNA, she programmed in the date of her seventh birthday and the location of her home at that time, in London. When they switched on the sound, they heard a child's voice:

"Stop it! Stop it! Leave Katy alone!" followed by a piercing scream and then a wail and the sound of a child sobbing so hard they couldn't stop. There were no other voices to be heard, but the child's voice gradually stopped sobbing and said: "OK, Mummy, but don't let her get my Katy again, will you?"

"Oh my God!" Eve said. "That was my seventh birthday party and my so-called friend, Sharon, snatched my doll, Katy, from me and punched her up in the air. My mum took it from her and put it up on a high shelf. I remember how upset I was by the whole incident. I used to anthropomorphise my toys in those days."

"You still don't like it if a cuddly teddy or baby animal toy is 'ill-treated' though, do you?" Rupert teased.

"Ha! We still have to investigate your DNA – that should be revelatory!" she laughed. He went quiet then.

She changed the date and location in the programme and homed in on her very first date. She remembered the details of it as it had been such a disaster. Georgie, the boy concerned, was two years older than her and had asked her out to the cinema. She was only thirteen and she was surprised, now, that her mother had allowed it. Maybe it was because she knew Georgie and perhaps trusted him. But Eve wasn't really ready for dating boys and, when he called for her, she panicked and asked her mum to tell him she'd changed her mind. And then, hearing the disappointment in his voice, she relented and called to her mum that she would go after all.

"I'll meet you outside the Chip Inn," he had said, as she wasn't quite ready to leave. Then, when she arrived at the said chip shop, there was no one there, although she could see a figure with his back to her, looking in the window of the electrical shop next door. She wasn't sure if it was Georgie, so she sidled round and tried to peer at him from the side to check, but he turned also, at that moment, away from her, leaving her standing behind him. She had tapped him on the shoulder and he almost jumped out of his skin when she suddenly appeared there out of the blue!

From there it just went from bad to worse. They had gone to the Odeon, the local cinema, and he had talked about motorbikes the whole evening, during any breaks in the film. He hadn't tried to have a snog, thank goodness, but she worried about it the whole time, flinching at any slight movement he made, in case he was going to try something.

Then he walked her home and carried on the motorbike monologue – she was bored senseless. The final humiliation came when he asked her if he could put his arm around her. She thought the fact that he asked her was the worst thing. If he had

11

just done it, it would have been more natural and less cringe-worthy. Of course, she said 'No' and she never saw him again.

The episode as heard by 'The Fly' was rather difficult to understand, as it only relayed Eve's side of the conversation. At first, she thought it must be wrong or faulty, but having been reminded by Rupert that only her DNA would be 'overheard' she remembered how shy she had been in those days and realised that she would have let Georgie do most of the talking…talking about motorbikes, of course! No wonder she wasn't saying much. But it was both embarrassing and fascinating to hear her, very young, voice snapping out 'No!' when he must have asked to put his arm around her. It brought back all the embarrassment of that time.

When it was Rupert's turn, he keyed in a date and soon after, they heard his voice saying: "Yes, Sir! I'll do it!"

Then: "What do I need to bring?"

"It's when I volunteered to make a Vernier scale for the school open day," Rupert said. "I had to stay behind every day for several weeks. Mr Miller, the physics teacher, wanted it made from wood, finished, varnished and perfectly accurate – it was a pain!"

Eve smiled. It would have been so much clearer if both sides of the conversation could have been heard, but still, it was pretty miraculous to be able to hear anything at all, through time.

"Do you understand how it works, Rupes?" she asked.

"Well, it's a visual aid to take an accurate measurement reading between two graduation markings on a linear scale by using mechanical interpolation."

"No, not a Vernier Scale!" She pushed him playfully on the shoulder. "Fly on the Wall!"

12

"Not really, at least not all the technical stuff, but Stellan explained it to me in a simplified way." He frowned as he attempted to replicate Stellan's explanation. "Basically, everything is made of energy and our voices are the same – sound waves. The energy emitted never dissipates completely, it just sort of drifts outwards. It is linked precisely into our DNA – don't ask me how – so the DNA of each individual has its own unique frequency and it means a computer can pick up this trail and reverse the energy drift virtually, so that the sound waves come back together and we can re-hear what was said at any given time and place. We have to know those as accurately as possible so that the computer can distinguish that pattern of energy. Like an echo, I suppose."

"Hmm! I suppose that sort of makes sense," she laughed.

They continued their testing and refining their technique of homing in on their 'vibe' as Rupert insisted on calling it, recruiting paid volunteers who were only told the minimum of information. The machine seemed to work perfectly.

Unfortunately, when, finally, the technology was presented to any company for sale, including Governmental Departments whom one would think would find it invaluable, they all shied away from it as 'violating the human rights of the subject'. David was angry and disappointed, but above everything, he was resourceful and so he then took his idea to parents and schools as a way of keeping children safe. They all seemed interested, but delayed in order to check the implications of 'monitoring' children. In the meantime, David called another meeting, again with Stellan and they all gathered in the board room again.

"Right, I have called this meeting, because we need to brainstorm a way to make up the shortfall caused by the lack of

13

interest in the 'Fly' of the Government and Police departments. We have spent a lot of time and money financing the testing of the machine and we have to recoup that somehow; interest from parents and schools is all very well, but we don't even have a definite 'yes' from anyone yet, so we need to think outside the box. What other uses could it be put to? Stellan?" He looked at him over the top of his glasses, the top of his pen pointing at his chest.

"Hmm, well, how about for mountaineers, explorers and the like – they could be tracked if they get into trouble."

"OK, yes, a possibility. Rupert?"

"Would it work for animals, dogs, cats, etc?"

"I don't see why not," Stellan replied.

"Then it could act like a microchip, but with the possibility of tracking rather than just identifying."

"Good, yes, that's a good idea, Rupert. What about you, Eve? Any bright ideas?"

Eve was a bit put out that he had asked her last, because she had also had the pet idea – she guessed great minds think alike. She had nothing else.

"I can't think of anything at the moment, but give me a while – sometimes it takes me some time to have my brainwaves – they don't come at short notice."

"OK, fair enough – but let me know if you think of anything else, all of you. And in the meantime, explore the ideas you have just suggested. This could work after all!"

And they were dismissed.

Goodbye To Love

That evening, Eve was planning to brainstorm for ideas about the invention, but it all went out of the window when she walked in and found the note.
All it said was:

Eve (not even 'Dear Eve')
I'm sorry, I can't carry on like this. I'm not in love with you any more. I've gone to my mother's. I'll collect my stuff another time.
Sorry.
James

She sat down heavily on the sofa and just stared at it, her head spinning and feeling 'out of it' as if she wasn't really there, that this couldn't be happening to her. Although she had sensed that they were going through a rough patch and she'd suspected James wasn't happy, she'd had no idea it was this bad. In her family, people stuck together and at least tried to work things out. Then she began to panic. How on earth could she afford to pay the mortgage and the bills with just her small salary? She would have to move. But thank God she hadn't quit her job! She bit her lip and put her head in her hands. Now she had a headache – God! Bloody James! It was typical of him to act without even discussing it first. And his timing was immaculate! Why now, just when her work had become more interesting – and demanding?
She so needed to concentrate and see if she could come up with an idea – a great one preferably – so that she could justify

asking for a pay-rise. Her first instinct was to call someone and cry on their shoulder, but normally that someone would have been James. She considered her father – no, he would only say 'I told you so' – he had never liked James and her mother was ill. She had no siblings, so it was either a friend or colleague. Not a colleague – she didn't want them knowing her personal life. She finally rang Lucy, her oldest friend.

"Oh, hi Eve, how are you?"

"Fine, thanks – actually, no I'm not fine. James has left me! Can you believe it?"

"Has he? Oh no! What are you going to do?"

"I don't know – I might have to move; the flat is too expensive for me on my own."

"I suppose so, yes. I think –," Lucy began and then Eve heard her gasp and giggle and a muffled male voice. "Sorry Eve, I've got to go. I could ring you later?"

"Who is it, babes?" said a voice she recognised. It was James.

"No, don't bother, I can see you're… busy!"

And she hung up, her chin wobbling as a wave of self-pity enveloped her. Food! She needed food. And distraction – something to take her mind off her troubles.

She ordered a takeaway to be delivered so she didn't have to cook, and took a notebook, intending to write down any ideas. But it was useless – she only ended up with some doodles which she was sure a psychiatrist would have had a field day with, especially as they were smudged by her tears. So, she decided to try to forget about work and watch TV – take her mind off everything, get absorbed in something else. She flipped through the main channels; there was nothing riveting there, only reality TV shows and soaps, nothing that would make her concentrate and forget her problems. So, she turned to the channels lower down the list and stopped at the History channel.

There was a repeat of a documentary about an archaeological dig in Leicester. She had seen it when it was first aired, a few years ago, but it had been fascinating, so she turned to that channel and settled down with a glass of wine to watch it again. The documentary was about the rediscovery of the remains of Richard III, the last English King to die in battle and the murderer of the 'Princes in the Tower', at least according to Tudor propaganda – she remembered the documentary had questioned the latter and piqued her interest at the time, but she had not had a chance to do any further research and had forgotten all about it. She'd remembered it again later when the mediaeval king's remains had been re-interred at Leicester Cathedral – there had been some coverage of it on TV and a couple of debates about whether he was a good or a bad king and she hadn't been sure either way – she liked to do her own research on such things and make up her own mind – people always debated by cherry-picking the points that supported their arguments, so you couldn't really rely on them. And she never had found the time to research it – life had got in the way. But it would be just the thing to distract her tonight.

For most of the documentary, her strategy worked. Then came the part where they were trying to identify the remains for sure and using carbon dating, etc. They had managed to extract enough DNA to get a 'Y' chromosome, proving that the skeleton was indeed male, and some mitochondrial DNA with which they compared a descendant of his sister, traced through the female line all the way from the 1400s to the present day, a feat in itself.

At the end of the programme, they added some updates to their research – they had identified his probable hair and eye colour, ascertained that he had had a high-status diet and that he had eaten more lavishly in the last two years of his life – when he had become king, so no wonder! And they had now managed to sequence his whole genome.

She felt her heart lurch and the words echoed around in her head:

"We have managed to sequence Richard's complete genome – no, that doesn't mean we will be able to clone him!" the technician had said.

But maybe the Fly would be able to track him in some way. She tried to remember if Stellan had said anything about whether the trail had to be fresh, but she couldn't.

Still, at least she had something to suggest when she went into work the next day.

The King in the Car Park

She decided to sound out Rupert first. He would be honest, she knew that, and if her idea was flawed, impracticable or stupid she wouldn't have shown herself up to 'the Boss man'.

"So, let me get this clear, you are suggesting that the 'Fly' could try to track a person who has been dead for five hundred years?"

"Yes, Richard III – The King in the Car Park. Did you see that documentary about how they found him? It was repeated last night and it gave me the idea; they have his complete genome."

"But what would be the point – he isn't going anywhere, they know where he is."

"Yes, I know that. But what if the 'Fly' could pick up on his

18

words, could listen in to his voice, to things he said?"

"From five hundred years ago!? I doubt it would be possible and, even if it were, what would be the commercial use for that?"

"Well, I'll ask Stellan if he thinks it would be possible; if it is, well, haven't you ever heard of the mystery of the Princes in the Tower?"

He made a face, screwing up his nose as if there was a bad smell wafting up his nostrils.

"I'm not that knowledgeable about history, I'm afraid. It rings a bell but... no, you'll have to tell me."

"Richard III was the brother of Edward IV, the first Yorkist king in the Wars of the Roses. When Edward died, unexpectedly, his son, also Edward, who was aged about twelve, should have been the next king, Edward V." She paused, taking a sip of her coffee. "And he had a younger brother, Richard, who was nine years old. Well, their uncle, Richard III, who was Duke of Gloucester at the time and living in Yorkshire, was named Lord Protector in Edward IV's will. But the widowed queen, Elizabeth Woodville, and her family had the young prince in their care and they tried to cut Richard out of the picture by 'forgetting' to inform him of his brother's death and rushing young Edward to London to try to have him anointed and crowned immediately, before Richard arrived. Then they would be able to control the new young king and Richard would be powerless to stop them. But another noble, Lord Hastings, informed Richard and he managed to intercept the royal party and take control of the prince."

She took another drink and Rupert frowned, trying to follow the complicated story.

"Everything seemed to be going ahead for the coronation, with

Richard confirmed by Parliament as Lord Protector, when suddenly things changed. Richard declared the princes illegitimate, saying that Edward had been bigamously married to Elizabeth, and took the crown himself. When Hastings seemingly objected, he was executed on the spot, without a trial, and the princes were kept in the Tower, from where they disappeared, never to be seen again." She paused and took a deep breath as she collected her thoughts. "Richard was only king for two years and then Henry Tudor invaded and defeated him at the Battle of Bosworth. No-one really knows what happened to the princes. It was the standard story for centuries that Richard had had them murdered to keep his position secure, but lately many have denied this and say it could have been Tudor who had them killed. There are two main camps on the issue and they will never agree, but nothing can be proved either way." She gave a swift grin. "Imagine if we could get to the bottom of the mystery – straight from the horse's mouth, so to speak?"

He was still frowning, but then he nodded.

"Yes, I suppose a solution to a five-hundred-year old mystery would be a commercial proposition – we could make a TV programme and sell it to the highest bidder."

"Exactly! And it would be much more interesting than eavesdropping on errant spouses or wayward children."

Stellan was out of the office until the afternoon, so she was fidgety all morning and when he finally arrived back, she grabbed him before he could get involved in anything else.

"Stellan!" she said and shoved him into his office, closing the door behind them. He looked at her in surprise at her strong-arm tactics. Then she continued:

"I have an idea of how we could use the machine – can you

tell me if it will work, before I approach David with it?"

"Of course, what is it?"

She explained her idea and had to go through all the explanation about the princes in the Tower again because he hadn't even heard of Richard III.

"Hmm, well I have obviously never attempted to track anyone that far back in time, but in theory, I don't see any reason why it wouldn't work. Yes, go ahead and put it to David – see what he thinks. But how are we going to get hold of the genome? Presumably not just anyone would be able to access that information?"

"No, that's true. I haven't worked that out yet, but maybe the Richard III Society would be able to help – they should have some clout when it comes to projects about him."

She requested to see David as soon as possible.

As she put her idea to him, he sat in his leather swivel chair and regarded her narrowly from above his spectacles. Somehow, he always made her feel like a schoolgirl hauled in front of the head teacher. He let her speak without any interruption until she had reached the part about solving the mystery of the princes in the tower and then his eyes began to glitter; she could almost see the pound signs in their blue-grey depths.

"Excellent! Now that's what I call thinking outside the box. I knew you would come up with something original. I am putting you in charge of this part of the project – first you need to access the DNA of course. Do you know anyone who belongs to the Richard III Society? Or the archaeological team?"

"Well, not the archaeology team, but I have an old friend who belongs to the Richard III Society. She's obsessed with him. That's how I saw the documentary in the first place; she insisted

I watch it with her – it was about the twentieth time she'd watched it – and to be fair it was fascinating. So much so she joined the Society, so she might be able to help."

"Great! She must agree to keep it confidential. Is she reliable?"

He looked at her as she nodded.

"Can you email her a confidentiality form. Then speak to her. Tell her we will pay her a consultancy fee. Start from there and, once she is on board, tell Stellan he is to prioritise this over the other prospective uses, OK? And you might also try to find out the locations and times of significant events from Richard's life so that Stellan can triangulate the co-ordinates for the 'Fly' once we get his DNA."

"Sure, will do!"

She left his office and whizzed an email over to Sue, with a brief explanation. She checked her mobile to see if she had Sue's phone number stored; she did, so she immediately texted her, asking her to check her email and then call her.

Then she went onto the internet and began researching the time-line of Richard III's life, noting down any key events that might be relevant and checking them against other sites to verify the information as much as she could. There were some dates which were pretty certain, like his birth, his death and his coronation. But others were vague and disputed, such as his marriage, the birth and death of his son and his exile in Burgundy when his brother had been briefly overthrown by the Lancastrians. She realised it might not be an easy task. Then she discovered that there were some extant examples of letters he had written at different times – most of these were dated and the locations where he wrote them given, so that might be a good way of locating him in place and time. She was up for the challenge.

It wasn't until the next day that Sue phoned her and Eve was just on her way out heading for work. She went back inside, closing the door and switching the kettle on as she flung her car keys on the work surface; David would forgive her being late if she had made some headway with the project, she hoped.

"Hi Eve, I'm curious – what can I help you with?"

"Hi Sue, thanks for getting back to me. I have a rather strange request. I was watching that Richard III documentary – you know, the one that converted you to a Ricardian? – and it gave me an idea. I'm working on a special project involving DNA and I wondered if you knew anyone who has access to Richard III's genome sequence. I assume you read the agreement? Basically, we are hoping to use a new technology to track him through time and that can listen to his voice. It's pretty exciting and it might even shed some light on the mystery of the princes in the Tower."

"Really? That would be fantastic! But I don't know anyone with access to Richard's DNA – I could make some enquiries though. I do know lots of Ricardians and some of them have contacts."

"Brilliant! Thanks for that – you can pass my mobile number on to them, if they can help. Don't tell them the details, though, OK? In the meantime, what news do you have? How're Roy, Lukas and Abbie?"

"They're fine – Roy is working hard, Lukas has just started an apprenticeship and Abbie is choosing her University for next year. They are growing up so fast. And how are you and James?"

Eve paused long enough for Sue to realise something was wrong, and as she explained the situation, she found there were tears on her cheeks – dammit! Her mascara wasn't waterproof. But it seemed that Sue had opened the floodgates and she found herself pouring out all her woes and worries, resulting in her being nearly an hour late for work.

"Sorry, David," she said, glancing at his thunderous expression as she made her way to her desk and feeling, as usual, like a naughty child. "I had an important phone call just as I was leaving. My friend Sue. She is on board, so I thought it best to talk to her and try to get the ball rolling on sourcing Richard III's DNA; I have a possible lead for that now."

His expression softened, very slightly.

"OK, but don't make a habit of it," he grunted and, turning on his heel, marched back into his office. She breathed a sigh of relief. She didn't know why she found David so intimidating. Maybe he reminded her of her old teacher. Rupert caught her eye from the other side of the computer island unit and made a silly face. Translated into an emoji, it would have been the one with the tongue out winking. She shook her head, rolled her eyes and bent to her desk.

Later that day, Stellan announced that he had contacted one of his old colleagues who had studied and worked alongside Cherry Keen, the scientist who had managed to isolate Richard III's DNA which had enabled them to positively identify him. He had managed to get an invitation to a charity ball which was being held in Leicester Guildhall, located next to the cathedral where Richard was now buried.

"I have two tickets – who should come with me?" he asked David. "Would you like to come?"

"No, I'm not one for those sorts of events, Stellan. Everyone trying to impress everyone else with their posh clothes and eating poncey food. I'd much rather have a curry and a pint of beer in the local Indian. Take Eve."

"What?" Eve said, startled that David would just assume she would want to go – that she could go.

"You don't mind going out for the night with Stellan to meet Cherry Keen, do you? Free meal and the company will pay for the hotel."

"Hotel?" she said, frowning.

"Well, you won't want to drive home after the ball, will you? It will be late and if you're driving you won't be able to drink. Stay overnight and come back the next day."

He looked at Eve's stunned expression with guileless eyes. "What? What's wrong with that?"

She sighed. "Oh nothing, I suppose. It's just – I might have had plans."

"Well, have you?"

"No, but..."

"Well, then, that's settled. Don't worry, I will pay you overtime."

Well, at least that was something. She pursed her lips in annoyance. She hated that kind of event as well. Still, at least she would be going with Stellan. He fascinated her and she certainly found him attractive, so it might not be too bad.

"What about my cats? I can't leave them alone for nigh on two days."

"Put them in a cattery. I'll pay for it."

"But they've never been in a cattery. I –"

"Don't worry, Eve, I'll drop in and feed them. Check they're OK," Rupert said. He looked annoyed.

"I don't want to put you out," Eve said, concerned he had felt obligated.

He smiled. "It's fine, really, I love cats."

"OK then. Thanks, Rupes."

Make It Happen

Two days later she was driving to Leicester with Stellan, dressed in a hired ball gown and feeling uncomfortable. She hated wearing dresses at the best of times, let alone any so formal and feminine as this! She felt more at home in jeans and an old T-shirt. She only hoped she wouldn't be expected to dance! He had suggested they make their way to Leicester together – one car would save fuel and it had seemed churlish to refuse. She watched him drive out of the corner of her eye, his long fingers stroking the wheel and his right arm resting on the side of the open window.

He was playing classical music on the radio – not her usual fare, but she found she was quite enjoying it.

"So, have you met Cherry before?" she asked, filling the slightly awkward silence between them.

He paused, glancing in the mirror as a car pulled out to overtake them, then braked slightly to let it back in.

"Yes, a couple of times, but I doubt if she will remember me though."

"Your friend – what's his name?"

"Alex."

"Alex, yes. Is he on quite good terms with her then? Do you think she will let us have the DNA sequence?"

"I think they were quite close at University. He said they often worked on projects together. He even helped out a bit on the Richard III project; he has been part of her team for several years. He thinks she will help us. He has a flat quite close to our office in London, but his main home is in Leicester."

"Does he know what the project is?"

"No, not exactly. I just said we are studying DNA sequencing and hoped to compare some of our samples with Richard's – he thinks it is something to do with genetics and ethnicity, since that's what I was involved in before."

When they arrived at the nearest car park to the venue, he gallantly helped her out of the car and they walked through the shopping mall to the Guildhall, where they entered the lobby and were shown into the Hall itself.

There were about ten tables with elaborate centrepieces of white roses and foliage – for the House of York, she realised. Cutlery was laid out for a sit-down meal and while this was going on, there was some entertainment in the form of a live jazz pianist. The meal was excellent – worth it even if this proved to be a wild goose chase, although she was meant to be on a diet – oh what the hell, she had only herself to please now. James had always preferred her slimmer version and couldn't resist making snide remarks when she had started to put on a few pounds a year or so ago. She had always battled with her weight. As long as she exercised, she stayed slim no matter what she ate, but lately she had been so busy with work that the gym had been side-lined and she could no longer get away with eating on demand – she had to really watch the carbs and she loved her desserts too. Well, tonight it was banoffee pie, her favourite, so the diet could get stuffed! Or she could. Literally.

Alex was already there when Eve and Stellan walked in through the door and he wandered straight over to them, his gaze on Eve. She realised immediately who he was from Stellan's description. He looked immaculate in an expensive Italian suit, bow tie and shiny shoes. He was shorter than Stellan, and darker, his skin tanned a golden brown.

27

"Ah, this must be Eve – you never told me she was so beautiful!"

What a smooth operator! She thought. She was pretty, but she had never thought of herself as beautiful. Before she could say anything, he bent over her hand and kissed it, as if he were a courtier and she a lady. How over the top could you get?

"Nice to meet you, Alex," she said.

They were seated and served a sumptuous meal before the dancing began. Alex sat one side of her and Stellan the other, but Stellan was a quiet man and seemed preoccupied with his own thoughts, so she ended up speaking more with Alex, who was a witty and entertaining companion. As the evening wore on and things became less formal, Alex finally steered them over towards Dr Cherry Keen and her entourage, if one could call it that. She was surrounded with smiling admirers who hung on her every word, nodding and laughing.

"Hi Cherry," said Alex, squeezing past a rather large lady wearing a flowered gown and a chunky, sparkly necklace, who glared at him as he caught Cherry's attention.

Dr Keen raised an eyebrow, but looked quite amused as she excused herself from the conversation she was having with a tall man in a blue suit, and turned towards Alex.

"What are you up to now, you devil?" she said. Her brown eyes twinkled as she smiled at him. The smile really lit up her face and made her look ten years younger than when she was being serious.

"I'd like to introduce you to some people," he said, smiling back. This is Eve Pritchard, and this is Stellan Andreasson. They work for Future Tech – an IT company – and they need your help. I'll let them explain," he finished, leaning in to give Cherry a swift brush of his pouty lips on her cheek before ushering Eve and Stellan forward to speak to her.

"Hello, Dr Keen," she said, suddenly nervous; Cherry Keen was almost royalty as far as the DNA world was concerned and a lot depended on how this went. Maybe even her job.

"Hello, Eve, Stellan," she answered. "Please, call me Cherry. Well, what can I do for you? Look, let's go over here out of the way, shall we?"

And she led them off, out of the main hall and into a small private room off the corridor outside.

"Ooh, that's better," she said. "I was hoping somebody would come and rescue me from that bloody man!"

Eve smiled as if she knew what she was talking about. Stellan licked his lips and put forward their proposition.

"Well, our company is investigating a project which could tie in nicely with your own one – when you sequenced Richard III's DNA. Are you still investigating it or have you discovered everything about it now?"

"We have finished our investigation and published all our findings in peer reviewed journals. We also contributed to another documentary. Perhaps you saw it? We analysed samples from the skeletal remains of Richard – from his femur and one of his ribs to compare the composition – that way we can tell if his diet changed because the rib bones are remodelled more quickly than the femur. We could tell his diet became richer in the last two years of his life – and he drank more wine. We could tell where in the country he was brought up and lived at different times. Also, we analysed his DNA more closely and found out that there was a 96% probability of his having blue eyes and a 77% chance he had blond hair as a child."

"Really? I always thought he was dark haired," Eve said.

"Many people do, mainly thanks to Laurence Olivier's

portrayal of him in Shakespeare's Richard III. His hair did probably become darker as he matured, but it was almost certainly fair in childhood. A lot of people think he was older than he was too, because of Olivier – he was actually only thirty-two when he was killed at the Battle of Bosworth."

Stellan nodded.

"I see. Well, as regards his DNA, I have invented a new kind of computer which can analyse a DNA genome sequence and 'tune in' to the individual's unique pattern. Alex may have told you I am interested in ethnicity, in particular. We wanted to use Richard's DNA to experiment to see how much can be picked up from ancient DNA. We would pay a fair price for your help, of course." He did not reveal the exact aim of their project and had not actually lied, Eve noticed.

Cherry nodded, her frown of concentration etching soft lines across her forehead, but said nothing for a few moments.

"Hmm, it certainly sounds interesting. But I'm afraid I don't have any of Richard's DNA material left – we put all the samples in his coffin with his remains at his reburial in 2015."

"Oh, yes, of course, but we don't actually need the DNA itself, just the sequence – the computer programme does the rest."

"I see – well, it does seem very interesting, but I would have to OK it with the University and the Richard III Society, etc. It could take a while, but give me your card and I will see what I can do."

Stellan took out a business card and gave it to her with a nod of his head.

"Well, Stellan, Eve, it's been very interesting meeting you, but I'm afraid I'd better get back to the ball. I'll be in touch," she said with a smile.

And she walked sedately off down the corridor and into the

Hall, to return to her admirers.

As Eve and Stellan entered the Ball again, the noise of the music, raucous laughter and loud voices raised owing to the reduced inhibitions of excess alcohol, assailed their ears. Eve felt her heart rate rise – she had never enjoyed being in crowds of people, especially drunk ones, and loud noises gave her a headache if she had to suffer prolonged exposure. She was about to ask Stellan if they could leave when Alex appeared, saying:

"So, how'd you get on with Cherry?" He didn't wait for their answer, but continued: "She's great, isn't she?" He leaned in to whisper in Eve's ear: "I think she has a bit of a soft spot for me, you know – she always let me get away with murder where she was quite strict with the others."

From most people this would sound arrogant, but the way Alex said it, with a big grin and a self-deprecating manner, made it amusing. And Cherry had seemed more than tolerant towards his abrupt interruption of their conversation with the man in the blue suit. Maybe she did fancy him. And she had to admit that his easy-going way was rather attractive, even if he did have enough confidence for about three men.

"Eve," he said. "Here, take my card – in case you have any questions or…?" He raised his eyebrows questioningly, his eyes dancing with merriment.

"I don't really think…" she began, but seeing the exaggerated disappointment on his face, sighed and accepted it. "OK, then, just in case I have a question," she said.

She put the card in her silver clutch bag and turned to follow Stellan out, but Alex called out to her:

"Eve, have you seen the tomb yet?"

She looked at him, puzzled for a moment, but then realised he meant the tomb of Richard III, which was in the cathedral, next door.

"No. No, I haven't," she replied.

"Would you like to? It's open from 10.00 am tomorrow. I could give you the tour. And Stellan, of course."

"Yes, please. That would be great," she said.

"Brilliant! I'll meet you outside the front gates at... shall we say eleven?"

"Sure. See you tomorrow."

My Prayer

Alex was waiting for them when they arrived at the cathedral of St Martin's the next day. He didn't seem disappointed that Stellan was there too, but spoke animatedly about the excitement in the lab when they found they had a match for Richard's DNA, meaning they were 99.999% sure it was really him. His enthusiasm was infectious and she felt excited as they made their way solemnly into the cathedral and round to the right where Richard's place of rest was located.

There was a stand of votive candles just before the entrance to the area where the tomb was located and, for some reason, she felt she ought to light one.

"Wait!" she called as she rummaged in her bag for some change and took a candle from the rack.

"For Richard," she said softly as she placed it in the sand. Why had she done it? She couldn't say, other than she felt compelled, somehow. It made her feel peaceful.

They walked through to the tomb and she stood in awe beside the structure. It was a large angular shape, set on a black base and it had a narrow, incised cross which went almost halfway down into the stone. She couldn't say she loved the design – it seemed much too modern for a mediaeval king – but the stone itself was beautiful, full of tiny fossils. She said as much as she stepped forward and placed her hand on the stone. It was smooth and cold to the touch and she shivered as a rush of emotion swept through her. It was an overwhelming sadness and... regret? No, disillusionment. She also felt strength... power and a longing for... something; she couldn't tell what. Disorientated, she stepped back and the feelings receded. How odd. Had she just experienced the forceful personality of Richard Plantagenet?

Say What I Feel

So now they had a long waiting period while the Richard III Society and the University of Leicester discussed the details of handing over the genome of Richard III. Life went back to being boring and, with the inactivity, Eve found herself getting weepy for no good reason. One time she was watching a silly game show, one of her two cats on her lap. A young couple were on trying to win some money for their upcoming wedding. She could tell immediately that they were not the brightest two bulbs in the chandelier. They had to answer questions while the money in the pot gradually dwindled and dwindled – it was obvious they were going to run out of time. It wasn't even exciting as they answered hardly any questions. When the money ran out and a loud buzzer sounded, Eve began sobbing.

"They shouldn't have been allowed on there – it was obvious they were never going to win. It's just humiliating for them, it isn't fair!" she sobbed. She was more upset than they were! She realised she must be depressed. She had never felt this way before but, in a sudden flash of inspiration, she recognised it was because her grief at her failed marriage had come to the surface, despite her attempts to suppress it.

James had called round the evening before to pick up some of his clothing and Eve had wanted to go to him for comfort, as she had always done before, but she couldn't. He wasn't nasty or cruel to her, but he was distant and wary – a stranger. So, taking her cue from him, she behaved the same way, calm, cool and unemotional. But the emotions had been there, hidden away, and the young couple, just starting out on their life together, had triggered them to come to the surface.

She had rung Sue and they had a long chat. Sue suggested she should go out, join a club, keep busy in some way.

"I don't want to start dating again!"

"I didn't say that, did I? Just get out and do something different – take your mind off things."

She was right, of course. Perhaps, she could find out some more about Richard so that, when they got the DNA sequence, she would more easily identify the situation. Yes, she could join the Richard III Society and do some research.

She had not been listening to Sue while she was considering her way forward, and she had to ask Sue to repeat what she had said.

"I said me and my mum went to see a medium a couple of weeks ago and got a message from my dad. It was amazing that she was so accurate – she knew things that nobody else could have known. And she told me that I'm psychic and should go to development classes. So, the other day I joined one. It was very interesting and I'm really enjoying it. They do loads of different stuff like Tarot cards, Angels, spirit guides, past lives and crystals."

"How do you know if you are psychic then?" Eve asked, intrigued.

"Well it could be a lot of different things, depending on what area of it you have an aptitude for. I've always felt very connected to nature, animals and wide-open spaces – Sharon says that's because I'm a Shaman."

Eve wanted to laugh, but stopped herself as Sue sounded so sincere and she would have hated to hurt her feelings.

"She also says everyone is psychic to a greater or lesser degree and it's like painting – everyone can be trained to paint a picture that others can recognise, but some people are special and have a gift like a Da Vinci or Picasso. You just have to find which type of psychic you are. She gave us a questionnaire for homework, you see, and the answers point you in the right direction. Do you want to see what area you're right for?"

Why not? thought Eve. *It might keep my mind off James.*

So, Sue read the questions over the phone to her. They were things like:

'Have you ever been immediately attracted or repelled by a place or person, for no obvious reason?'

'Have you ever had an out of body experience?'

'Do you often know who it is before you answer the phone?' and

'Have you ever picked up information about someone from holding something that belongs to them?'

In all, there were about twenty or thirty questions and, strangely, Eve could answer 'yes' to quite a few of them.

"It seems like you must be very psychic, Eve," said Sue. "According to the results, you are an Empath, with Psychometric skills."

"What does that mean?" Eve asked.

"Well, an empath is someone who can pick up on other people's emotions and psychometry is the ability to pick up information about something through touch. Like if you hold something belonging to someone, you can 'know' certain things about them. You should see if there is a psychic class near you – it would do you good, get you out and about again – keep you busy."

"Hmm! I don't know. It seems a bit far-fetched to me."

But even though she consciously thought the idea was preposterous, a small part of her knew that she was psychic, because she had had the occasional strange experience, like her feelings in the Cathedral at Richard's tomb.

The earliest such occasion she remembered had been when she and her family were on holiday and they were trying to get to the other side of a church. The gate was closed, so her father had led them through the churchyard part of it and she had felt they were trespassing and was worried they might get into trouble, although maybe that was partly because she had mistakenly thought the 'Trespassers will be prosecuted' sign meant 'Trespassers will be executed.' No wonder she felt uneasy! Then she had touched the crumbling old wall and suddenly had the feeling she wanted to run out of that place, that there was something there she didn't like.

The second time, she was in a queue in the newsagents as a child when she 'felt' someone was behind her – nothing unusual in that – she was in a queue after all! But this 'someone' must have been an evil person, because she'd had such an overwhelming feeling of horror and evil emanating from him. She'd turned around surreptitiously, and was amazed to see a perfectly ordinary-looking middle-aged man. He

36

wasn't even in her personal space. But she 'knew' he was an evil person and she also instinctively knew he hurt children. Of course, she couldn't prove it – she wasn't going to ask him after all! But a year later she had seen him on TV – his name was Fred West, the evil man who, with the aid of his equally evil wife, had tortured and killed numerous children before he was caught. She remembered the shock of recognition and the revulsion and horror of knowing she had been standing just in front of him!

Nevertheless, she decided to take Sue's advice and try to find a psychic development circle locally. Perhaps it would help if she could control her abilities better. There was one only fifteen minutes' drive away and luckily someone had dropped out of the circle after only two weeks, which meant there were still eight weeks left and she could join in without being left too far behind. A week later, she attended her first ever circle. It was held at the premises of a very famous psychic medium, Terry Southwell, although he only actually taught the advanced level classes and Eve was very much a beginner.

Her tutor was Linda Roberts, a lovely lady who encouraged her students without pressurising them too much and she made the classes fun, resulting in the whole class feeling confident and relaxed. There were also whole day courses on at the weekends and Eve noticed that one of them, two weeks later, was on the subject of Psychometry. As Sue had said, this was where you held or touched an object and tried to 'pick up' on its origins, energies and any information you could. She signed up for the day with eager anticipation. Everyone had to bring something for the others to practise on, something which had belonged to somebody who was now deceased or to themselves or a member of their living family. Sitting in the customary circle, they passed their objects around to the left and then they each wrote down all that they could ascertain from that object, repeating it until everyone had worked with everyone else's object. At the end, the class discussed their efforts and Eve found that she had been the star pupil for this task. She had been useless at scrying, rubbish at runes and terrible at Tarot, but she had found that each time she held something and tuned in to it, particularly if it was made of metal, she could really be transported into a 'zoned out' state where all the emotions associated with the object came flooding in.

One lady had brought in a ring which had belonged to her aunt, now deceased. When Eve held it, she suddenly felt overwhelmed by a wave of grief. It was like a punch to her solar plexus and she began to tremble, then sob as tears stung her eyes and spilled down her cheeks.

"All I can get is 'I miss her, I miss her!'" she told the woman. "Do you miss her?"

"Well, yes, of course, but not to that extent – she was quite old and ready to go. She was suffering, so it was a relief really. I wonder why you are so emotional – even more than I was when we lost her... Oh! Hang on! I know what it is! My aunt had been very close to my mother, her sister, who died very young. It's my aunt's ring, not mine, so it's *her* emotions you must be feeling and she was really distraught when my mum passed away, she definitely did miss her. They were best friends as well as sisters."

Eve was pleased with this result, although the emotion was very powerful and a bit scary. Jayne, the teacher for this class, told her that the feeling in her solar plexus was because that was the chakra area which corresponded to the emotions; it was where the expression 'gut feeling' came from.

The next thing she tried was a silver cigarette case which had belonged to a man's late father.

"I feel happy!" Eve told him. "So happy, I just want to laugh."

He nodded. "This cigarette case was his retirement gift from his work. He couldn't wait to retire – he hated work. Odd really; most men's lives revolve around their jobs, but he would much rather have been at home or on the golf course. He really loved his retirement, so the happiness makes sense."

Jayne praised Eve's efforts.

"However, you need to get a bit more than just emotions – though that's a good starting point. You need to go deeper, let yourself go a bit more and note whatever comes into your mind. Don't be afraid to make a mistake – it doesn't matter, that's how we learn. But you have real talent for this and you can develop it much further. Here, try this."

And she handed over a very old-looking ring. It was battered and a dark brown colour. When she looked closely, she saw a delicate pattern engraved on it, but it was unrefined as if it was hand made. When Eve took it into her hand a rush of emotions overwhelmed her.

She began to speak, closing her eyes to concentrate.

"I feel fear, and I have the sense that this is the wedding ring of a working-class person but that the lady, she's definitely a woman, had not really wanted to marry. She was young and afraid." She paused as new emotions came flooding in. "I just 'know' that the woman has grown to love her husband, who is quite a bit older than her, but kindly and generous. I 'know' there are five children, three sons and two daughters and that the birth of the fifth child was the most difficult of all, that the woman nearly died. Now I feel grief and the sense that her husband has passed away well before the woman and that she mourns him. I also feel the woman has to work hard, something to do with an inn. That she enjoys a gossip and flirts with the customers. That she isn't beautiful, but striking looking and loves her family more than anything."

She said all this as she sat there, the ring clenched in her hand, then opened her eyes.

"Do you get any idea of what time it dates from?" Jayne asked.

Eve closed her eyes again and tried to let her thoughts roam wherever they wished.

"Fourteen hundreds? No, surely not, that's far too old," she said, embarrassed.

"No, you are right, Eve," Jayne said, smiling. "It's a mediaeval pewter ring, found in Yorkshire by a metal detectorist. Experts agree it dates from the late fifteenth century, so you are spot on. However, I can't say if the other information you picked up is right or not, obviously, as no-one knows. Although I will say I have also studied it and I also sensed much of what you said – the woman owner, her marriage, being widowed and working hard. So, you have done brilliantly, well done!"

Eve felt encouraged and resolved to practise her skills at Psychometry whenever she had the chance. It seemed to be her 'thing'.

Don't Give Up

It was not until four weeks after their meeting with Cherry Keen that they received the DNA sequence from her.

"Thank goodness, they agreed to let us use the sequence. For a price, of course. Let's hope it was worth it. At last we can try the machine!" David said, his expression one of relief and elation. They all trooped in to Stellan's room.

The first attempt came with a sense of suppressed excitement. Even Stellan, who knew the machine's capabilities, had an air of eager anticipation about him. The machine was set up in his office, in the middle of the table and they all gathered around it, as if it were some pagan god they felt compelled to worship.

Stellan entered some co-ordinates into it – they were for Fotheringhay, the birthplace of Richard – he had decided to start at the beginning, which seemed logical and would make it easier to keep track of the different attempts they made.

When he set the values and scanned in Richard's DNA sequence, you could have heard a pin drop. Then the machine started to whirr and Eve's heart rate increased even as she was wondering why she was so tense and excited. There was a minute of noise before the machine displayed the disappointing words: 'Unable to find subject.'

Eve let out the breath she hadn't even realised she had been holding in a sigh and Rupert said: "Holy crap! That's a bummer!"

David was frowning and Stellan was shaking his head in annoyance.

"I will try again and call you all if and when it happens," he said finally, but nothing happened that day. He couldn't work out why, but finally decided it might be because he didn't have the genuine DNA of Richard – only the sequence – and although this had worked for modern subjects, perhaps five hundred years was too far away for it to be feasible.

"Of course, it could be that it isn't possible at all and my theory is wrong," he added. "But I don't really think so."

His self-confidence was admirable, but David wasn't too pleased. Although he said nothing, Eve felt waves of frustration and annoyance emanating from him.

41

The rest of the day was uneventful, unfortunately and, later at home, Eve had just fed the cats and was musing on what to cook for her own supper, when she had a sudden idea and went to fetch her clutch bag that she'd had at the Ball. She fished about in it for a few moments and then pulled out Alex's business card. Before she had second thoughts, she dialled his number and his smooth voice answered on the second ring.

"Hi Alex," she said "It's…"

"Eve!" he interrupted her. "I'd know that lovely voice anywhere." She was rather flattered that he had realised it was her. "What can I do for you?"

"Well, we got the DNA sequence today but, unfortunately our test results are… disappointing. Stellan seems to think they would work better if we had an actual DNA sample, rather than just the sequence…"

"And you wondered if I could help out? Didn't Cherry tell you all Richard's DNA samples were interred with him? As far as she knows, anyway…"

Eve felt her heart rate increase. Could he mean he knew of some of Richard's DNA that was in circulation somewhere?

"Look Eve, have you eaten. I was about to send out for a takeaway, but I'd much rather eat out. As long as I'm not alone, of course?"

He made it a question. Well, she hadn't eaten yet, so why not?

"Yes, I'd love to come out with you for dinner, as long as we go Dutch."

"Sure," he said. "What's your address? I'll pick you up."

Help Yourself

When they were settled in the rather posh restaurant Alex had taken her to, she decided not to wait.

"Look, Alex, I want to be straight with you – I've arranged to meet you on the off chance that there might be the tiniest bit of Richard III's DNA still lurking about. Our experiments are not going well and, as I said, Stellan thinks the actual DNA might be the answer. Will you... can you help?"

"Oh damn! And there I was thinking it was my charm and charisma," he laughed, not seeming to be too bothered by her revelation.

To her surprise, he rummaged around in his pocket and produced a test tube labelled 'R3 – DNA sample'. He proffered it to her with a courtly flourish.

"Your wish is my command, Madame," he smiled.

"This is Richard's DNA sample?" she asked, taking it gingerly and squinting at the contents, which appeared to be a dark cream coloured powder.

"Yes, from a tooth."

"Wow! How come you have it? I mean, I thought you said all the samples were buried with Richard." She suddenly felt quite emotional, a bit dizzy.

He glanced at her and grinned, his eyes twinkling with mischief.

"Well, while Cherry was analysing Richard III's remains, I was one of her 'inner circle' so to speak, so that meant I was trusted with access to the remains as well. We all had to help to get the research done in time – they wanted to announce the results quickly to keep people's interest in the project. Well, a small sample from Richard's tooth got 'lost' during the process.

I 'found' it."

She stared at him, appalled. That counted as theft, surely. But he was unfazed and simply chuckled at her shocked expression.

"Oh, come on Eve! I'm sure I'm not the only one who has a small piece of 'Richard' in his possession."

"Really? Well, I don't want anything to do with it. I don't approve at all!"

"Ah! But what about your boss?"

She frowned. She didn't like it at all, but he was right. David would definitely put his financial interests before any scruples, if the question arose.

Alex continued: "And I don't think Richard will miss them. You see, I was sure that in the future it would be a useful thing to have, that there would be more research to do, I just didn't think the opportunity would arise so soon."

"Opportunity?"

"Well, although as a friend of Stellan, I am happy to help him, there are two conditions. One, I want to be in on the project, part of the team and credited along with everyone else. And two, I want you to come on a proper date with me, one where you haven't come just for Richard III – makes me quite jealous."

She rolled her eyes.

"Seriously, I want to get to know you better. You are a very unusual creature, Eve. Intelligent, beautiful, natural."

She laughed shortly.

"I'm nothing special."

As she said the words, she was horrified to realise that she had tears pricking her eyes. She blinked and took a quick swig of her wine hoping he hadn't noticed. But of course he had. He reached over and gave her hand a little squeeze, saying nothing.

That was both the best and worst thing he could have done, and she bit her lip desperately as the tears began to spill. She didn't want to have to tell him how her boyfriend had deserted her after only five years together. Hell, they hadn't even managed to reach the notorious seven-year point. Alex released her hand and gently wiped the tears away with his thumb, but still he remained silent.

"I'm sorry," she said. "It's just that –"

"No, you don't need to explain. We all have difficult times."

He looked down and pushed his starter around with his fork, his expression thoughtful and wistful. Then he met her gaze and shook his head.

"Let's not be sad – tell me something more about yourself. What do you like doing in your spare time? Do you prefer dogs or cats? Where's your favourite holiday place?"

She attempted to smile through the tears and, taking out a tissue, dabbed at her eyes, hoping her eyeliner hadn't run.

"I love reading and painting. I like dogs and cats, but I think dogs just edge it for me, although I can't have them at the moment, as I'm working full time… and my favourite holiday place is Scandinavia. I love the snow and the Northern Lights. But I also like Italy, especially Venice, Florence and the Amalfi coast. And what about you?"

He smiled, broke a bread stick and took a bite.

"I like eating out, deejaying – I do a gig once a week in my own time. I like dogs too, big ones, preferably. And I also like Venice and Amalfi, but I've never been to Scandinavia – I think I'd enjoy it though, as I do like cross country skiing."

Eve was pleasantly surprised at how easy he was to talk to and how genuinely interested in her he seemed. All in all, the meal was a resounding success and she was mildly tipsy by the time he dropped her home. She wondered if it would still be her home in the near future. Maybe she could manage to buy James out of his share and keep up the repayments on the mortgage.

She didn't ask him in, but he kissed her goodnight, his mouth tasting of the brandy with which he had finished off his meal. It felt alien, kissing someone who wasn't James, but not unpleasant and she went off inside, having agreed to a date the week after. She felt a lot lighter than she had when she'd got up that morning.

She decided to change into her pyjamas straight away; the smart clothes she had worn for the dinner were not the most comfortable and the pyjamas were very cosy. She slipped her furry kitten slippers on and made herself a cup of hot chocolate. Then she picked up her bag and took out the small vial of yellowish powder. She held it up to the light and stared at it in wonder – this had come from the mouth of a king!

As the thought entered her head, she felt a pull of emotion in her solar plexus, a strange, subtle feeling of agitation and something else she couldn't place. She again felt the powerful 'presence' of a masterful personality. Was it really the spirit of Richard or just her own imagination? Suddenly, on a whim, she rushed into the bathroom and searched the medicine cupboard. She finally found a small, unused sample bottle, unopened and sterile, and put on some latex gloves and a face shield from the first aid kit. With trembling hands, she removed the stopper of the little vial and tipped the tiniest amount into the sample bottle, replacing the stopper immediately and then the lid of the sample bottle. She didn't know exactly why she'd done it, perhaps because she thought she might try to 'tune in' to Richard's essence again, to try to understand the last Plantagenet king a little better, using her psychometry. She replaced the vial in her bag and put the sample pot in the drawer of her computer desk.

History

When she told Rupert about Alex on Monday, to her surprise, he made a 'Pffft' noise and when pressed, waffled that Alex sounded like 'a right plonker'. She changed the subject and showed him the little vial of Richard's DNA.

"Wa – hey!" he whooped and snatched it from her hand, pretending to take it into David to claim the credit.

She threw a pen at him and then felt bad when it caused a small cut on his head from the impact of the metal clip.

"Bloody hell, girl, you nearly had my eye out!" he said, his voice rising up the scale in his alarm.

In the end, they went in to see David together and he immediately agreed to Alex joining the team in return for the sample, provided he signed the same confidentiality agreements as the others had. He summoned Stellan and got his agreement too, asking him to arrange for Alex to come in the next day, when the sample would be ready for another attempt.

By that time, Stellan had scanned Richard's DNA and correlated it with the sequence from Cherry. They had a list of locations and dates to triangulate so that it would be easier to home in on Richard's 'wavelength'. They again chose to start at the beginning – his birth on 2nd October 1452 at the castle of Fotheringhay in Northamptonshire, since that was pretty certain as to date and location.

The machine was ready and they all waited with bated breath for the result. The 'Fly', appropriately, buzzed as it digested the information and the lights on its interface console flashed impressively, but after a period of about fifteen minutes, the dreaded words 'Subject not found' reappeared and Stellan sighed.

"Sorry, guys, it isn't working. I'm not sure why – I have carefully put in the right date and the co-ordinates of Fotheringhay castle – we know exactly where it is – or was – so that must be right. Is it certain that Richard was born on that date?"

"Oh yes, he wrote the date and place of his birth personally in his own Book of Hours which is still in existence. My friend, Sue, told me all about it."

"Well, it might be an idea to check if there could be a mistake, just in case."

He seemed rather despondent. Alex looked worried and David looked about to blow a fuse. Rupert sat on his chair, with his long legs splayed out and his hands linked behind his head, frowning, his lips in a pout of deep thought. The chair looked miles too small to support his large frame.

"OK," Eve replied. "I will check again with Sue."

So, she telephoned Sue immediately the unsuccessful meeting had ended and Rupert followed her to her desk to watch her while she did it. He had been unusually quiet in the meeting and she had picked up that he was feeling down. She had noticed that she could often pick up on people's emotions ever since she had begun her psychic development. She supposed she always had been able to do this, but had now become more aware of it in a conscious way. She smiled at Rupert as she spoke to Sue, asking if she had any suggestions or whether the birth information might have been incorrect. He gave her a rueful smile in return and began doodling on a scrap piece of paper.

"Did you factor in the difference in the calendar?" Sue asked. Eve's attention was immediately drawn back to the phone. "What difference?"

"Well, they changed the calendar not long after that period, something to do with the timing of Easter and so they changed from the Julian to the Gregorian calendar. They 'lost' several days which meant that all the dates moved forward by the same number of days. I think we would have to add about nine days to the date of Richard's birth, so that it would be on what we know today as the eleventh of October."

"Brilliant! I'm sure that's what it must be – thank you, Sue."

Rupert was staring at her with an inquisitive look in his eye, so she explained it to him as soon as the conversation with Sue had ended.

"Righto!" he said. "Let's get back in to Stellan and tell him what he needs to do."

"Hold on, I have to recheck it first, so we know the number of days we have to advance the date is accurate."

Eve Googled the change of date and found a site where you could enter the Julian date and it gave the Gregorian equivalent. Sue was indeed correct and Richard's birthday would be October 11th using the Gregorian calendar. She shouted over to Rupert and they made their way back to Stellan's office. She knocked on the door and he answered, a deep frown creasing his brow.

"I have found out why it didn't work," Eve said. "It's because of the change between the Julian and Gregorian calendars. Because the Julian calendar wasn't accurate enough – they had too many leap years which made it go out of sync with the solstices – they changed to the Gregorian calendar by omitting ten days from the old calendar. In Richard's year it would only have been nine days, so that means his birthday wasn't on October 2nd by our calendar today, but October 11th."

"Of course!" he shouted, slapping himself on the forehead. "Come in, come in and we will try it again. I will call David…"

When David arrived, they all sat down again in the seats they were occupying before and waited yet again while the 'Fly' buzzed, whirred and flashed as it calculated its parameters.

Then the buzzing stopped and the flashing lights stilled. Instead the machine displayed the message: 'Subject found'.

They all looked at each other and then Stellan stood up and raised a finger ready to press the 'Play' button.

"Ready?" he said. They all nodded and he pushed the button.

Eve jumped at the sound that emanated from the machine – it was a screaming, animal sound and very eerie. Stellan fiddled with the controls and then suddenly the unearthly sound mutated into the soft mewling of a baby. A baby whose cries had first been heard over five hundred years before. A baby who had lived and then died thirty-two years later; Richard Plantagenet, son of Richard, Duke of York and Cecily Neville, brother of Edward IV of England, and the future Richard III.

Chapter Two

London, Twenty-first Century

The Voice

They stared at each other, and then David began to laugh, patting them on their backs and shaking their hands, while Rupert whooped and Stellan and Alex both grinned. Eve just felt stunned. When she had heard that little cry something pierced her heart and she felt very protective. She wanted to hold that little baby, to rock him to sleep, to protect him from harm. She knew it was said babies are programmed to make us want to protect them, but she had heard them cry before without this feeling. It was very strange. She remembered the previous occasions she had 'felt' something odd. Was this, too, her psychic ability? Was she somehow 'tuning in' to Richard Plantagenet?

"Was that really Richard III as a baby, crying?" she asked Stellan, trying to cover her confusion.

"Well, provided that was his real DNA, then yes," he said. He was still grinning.

"So, what happens now?" she asked. "Have you recorded that?"

"Of course – the Fly automatically records and backs up all overheard conversations – or in this case, noise! I suppose now we need to decide what date and time to focus on next. I think you, with the help of your friend, would be the best person to decide that. I mean, should we immediately try to locate him in 1483 when the princes disappeared? Personally, I think not." He gave her a smile that made her insides quiver. "For one thing, it would be difficult to locate him 'cold' like that – it would be much easier if we can move chronologically and allow 'The Fly' to refine its scanning each time; it learns how to focus on the individual by adding to its information – the vibration will vary as the child grows, for example, or it can subtly change if the person is feeling a different emotion. Also, it would be easier to prove and validate that it is really Richard if we have several examples of his conversation at specific events, which were known to have occurred at a given time and place; the evidence will carry more weight. Do you agree?"

She swallowed, nodding. "It sounds logical to me. I'll draw up a list with my friend, Sue, and bring it in as soon as I have verified it."

David also asked Eve to write up an account of all the research they had done so far, record their progress and now, transcribe any verbal content they discovered. She agreed as she had decided that would be a good idea anyway, but first she had to ring Sue.

Singing You Through

Again, Sue helped her out.

"Well, there are some books which specify Richard's whereabouts at different times, though they aren't all certain. For example, it is thought that Richard was in Ludlow when the Lancastrians sacked it, with his mother, brother George and sister Margaret. They were traditionally supposed to have waited for the enemy to arrive at the market cross, but that may just be legend. Also, it was thought that he went with his brother, Edward, to the Low Countries when he went into exile, but some think he didn't go there with Edward but separately, slightly later, and met up with him then. Other dates are uncertain, too."

"OK, I see, so perhaps it would be best to try to find the more certain dates and times first and then try to locate the others. I'm not sure how much leeway the machine could cope with at such a great distance in time. Thanks for the suggestions."

Eve spent the next weekend going over her research into late mediaeval history, with particular emphasis on the life and times of Richard III (or the Duke of Gloucester, as he was known for most of his life).

She found out that his life held several mysteries. For example, it was known that he fathered at least two illegitimate children, seemingly before his marriage, but it wasn't known who their mother or mothers were.

He declared Edward's children illegitimate, but did he bribe or threaten the Bishop of Bath and Wells to back up his invented story of a previous marriage? Or was he shocked when the Bishop revealed his brother's secret first wedding and so acted simply through conscience? Did he scheme and plot for years to be king, as in the Shakespeare version of his story, or did he accept the throne reluctantly and out of a sense of duty? And did he murder the princes in the Tower, the two sons of Edward IV, or did they disappear because he moved them to a place of safety?

There were so many enigmas and riddles surrounding Richard and most of the events that were questioned could be interpreted in two entirely different ways, as could the actions of some of the other major players of the time.

For example, when Richard took control of the new boy-king, Edward V, why did the dowager queen, Elizabeth, rush off into sanctuary? Was she so afraid of Richard because he was evil, vengeful and ruthless or did she have a guilty conscience because she had been plotting to bring him down?

Perhaps the Fly would be able to answer some of these questions, but first, it would probably be wise to eavesdrop on other, more straightforward conversations, those that were uncontroversial.

They decided between them to move the time forward a few years, to keep the co-ordinates of Fotheringhay, since it was quite probable that Richard spent a fair amount of his early childhood there, and so they tried a Sunday about six years after his birth in the Church at Fotheringhay. The machine gave its usual whirring and buzzing sound and, when Stellan pressed the button, they heard a voice; it was certainly a child's voice and Stellan had told them that they wouldn't be able to hear any other people to whom Richard might be speaking, but they didn't need to anyway. For the young voice was singing. It was a religious hymn by the sound of it, although Eve couldn't understand the words. None of them could; it seemed to be in Latin. But the voice was so sweet and pure it brought tears to her eyes as it soared heavenward. It was certainly a song of praise to God and spoke of faith in God's goodness and wisdom. It was full of optimism and hope. Could this really be the voice of the murdering usurper, Richard III? That notoriously ruthless and evil tyrant? It sounded more like the voice of an angel.

"Wow! Rupert said. "It's bloody amazing, Stellan. You're a genius! And who would believe that angelic little voice belonged to an evil, child-murdering tyrant?"

"Oh, so you've already made your mind up have you?" asked Eve. "What evidence do you have for that viewpoint, may I ask?"

"Well, I saw Richard III at the Old Vic a few weeks ago – he plotted and murdered his way to the throne and killed those poor little boys, his nephews, when he was meant to protect them. Your archetypal wicked uncle."

"Shakespeare! Really?" Eve looked at Rupert out of the corner of her eyes, her lips pursed. "I would have thought you could have done a bit more proper research rather than basing your opinion on a work of fiction! Shakespeare makes no end of errors and compresses the action that took place over years into a few weeks. He has people being in places at certain times, when it is known they were miles away – for example Richard was not at his brother's deathbed. And he wasn't at the first battle of St Alban's either, at least not unless he was very precocious, because he was only about two at the time!"

Rupert frowned. "Really? But surely Shakespeare based his story on fact – OK he might have embellished it a bit, but there's no smoke without fire, as they say. There must have been some truth in it – after all, he was right about him being a hunchback, wasn't he?"

He leaned back in his chair, linking his hands behind his head, triumphantly.

"Apparently not, actually. Sue has a friend who's an osteopath and she says he wouldn't have had a hunchback." She smiled smugly.

Rupert scratched his head. "Well, what was all that stuff in the documentary then? Yes, I've seen that too. The spinal expert said he was a hunchback."

Eve sighed. "Not really, he said they might have called him a hunchback, but after he explains more fully you see that Richard didn't have the kind of deformity that we would recognise as a true hunchback, in other words a forward curvature of the spine. He had a sideways curve."

"Same difference, surely. He was still deformed."

"OK, but his deformity wouldn't have been obvious at all to anyone who hadn't seen him undressed. Only the body servants and his close family would have known of it. When he was dressed the only slight sign would have been one shoulder higher than the other."

"So why did they call him 'Crouchback' then?" Rupert was grinning and staring at her challengingly.

"They didn't. At least not until after his death – don't forget he was stripped naked and flung over the back of a horse. Sue's friend says that a sideways curve twists in that position and then it does seem more like a hunchback. That must be when the rumours started."

One Step Forward

Their next 'stop' was Ludlow: The Market Cross. They waited in their usual places for 'The Fly' to digest the co-ordinates that Stellan had entered. They were on tenterhooks because this time would be the first time, hopefully, that they heard Richard's speaking voice and his own words. Of course, they had thought this the last time, but it had turned out to be his singing voice they had heard.

Eve glanced at Rupert and saw his right knee jiggling up and down in anxious anticipation. David was still, but wore a deep frown of concentration on his tanned face and Alex was twisting a pen between his long, slender fingers. Stellan was the only one who seemed calm.

Then they heard a child's voice… but try as she might Eve couldn't understand a word of it. It sounded like a foreign language but none that she knew. The 'r's were rolled, though not as much as Italian and the vowel sounds were open and strange. She began to wonder if Alex had given her the real deal – could he have substituted someone else's DNA, someone foreign? Or had he been mistaken when he took the sample? Or had it been contaminated? Perhaps it was the machine malfunctioning. She looked at Stellan.

"The machine is working correctly," he said, as if reading her mind. "But I don't recognise the language. Richard III spoke English, didn't he? His time was later than the era where the monarchs all spoke French?"

Rupert and David were both nodding, but she had a sudden thought.

"Of course! He did speak English, yes, but it was Middle English, not Modern English as we know it today – it was even

57

a bit different from Shakespeare's language. So, it would be unintelligible to us."

"Well, what do we do? How do we... translate it?" asked David, looking at her.

"I don't know anyone who can understand Middle English," she said. "My friend, Sue, might have a contact though – she has been telling me the Richard III Society has been asking for help in researching old archives and they would be written in Middle English, so someone who can understand that might be able to understand it spoken too."

"OK, it's down to you again, Eve," David said. "Stellan, can you make a copy of the recording so that we can send it to whoever Eve finds?"

Stellan nodded. Eve stood up resignedly and made for her desk, ready to phone Sue again. Rupert followed her and sat down next to her as she called her friend.

"Hi Sue, it's Eve again. Listen, do you know anyone who would be able to understand spoken Middle English?"

"Not off hand, but I could ask on the Facebook groups. I'll make enquiries and get back to you."

It took her three days to find Mary Mander, a staunch Ricardian who was involved in the archive project. Project 'Fly on the Wall' was certainly experiencing a lot of delays and setbacks. She hoped this was the last.

Mary had degrees in mediaeval history and linguistics and had studied under Professor David Crystal, who was considered one of the foremost linguistic specialists in the world. Eve rang her immediately and, without actually telling her that it was Richard himself who was speaking, she asked her if she could possibly translate the words spoken on the tape into modern English. When she confirmed she could, they set up a meeting and she was hired as an associate, having signed a non-disclosure agreement. While Eve was waiting for Mary to complete the first session, she read up a bit more about Richard, so she could more easily identify whatever 'eavesdropping' they heard, by its context.

When Mary had sent her the translation, they listened to the recording again, with a copy of Mary's translation each, so they could know the modern meaning.

Mama

"Mama, I am afraid of the nasty queen. George told me her soldiers are going to kill me because I am the runt and that Papa cannot save us. But he can, Mama – he is a great warrior, is he not? Mama? Mama? No! Mama!!!!"

The pitiful little voice sobbed and sobbed, tearing at Eve's heart, until after several minutes of soft whimpering, the sobs gradually subsided. Then:

"Meg, hold my hand? Will it be well? Will we be safe? You are shaking, George! Do not fear, if we stay together, we will be safe. Hold my hand, too. See, that is better. They will not hurt us, Mama said. She never lies – not like you, George! See, there she is, she is coming back to get us. Why is she crying? She never cries. Mama!"

Then there was a little more muffled sobbing.

"Yes, Mama, I will be brave."

Long pause.

"Where are we going? Will Papa be there?... Why not?... Will Harry be there? I do not like him. He and George always tease me because I am smaller than them."

Pause.

"Really? Papa was like me when he was my age? But he is a great warrior. I am going to be like him then, when I am big. I will keep you all safe. I will, George, like Papa. When I am grown, I will never be afraid. Like Papa…"

House of York

This was the one-sided conversation when Richard was eight years old, at the co-ordinates of Ludlow. Eve had discovered it was a time when England was in turmoil, the dynastic struggle now known as the Wars of the Roses was in full swing, the pendulum of power swinging from one camp to the other, as battles were won and lost, strategies succeeded or failed. The Lancastrian army, headed by the Queen consort of Henry VI, Margaret of Anjou, had attacked Ludlow not knowing that the Duke of York, Richard's father, along with the older two of his four surviving sons, Edward and Edmund, had already fled, leaving his wife and, with her, the three youngest children, Margaret, George and Richard. He was trusting that the Lancastrians would not harm women and children. Eve explained all this to the others.

"Luckily, he was right and Cecily and the three children were sent to her sister, Anne, and brother-in-law, the Duke of Buckingham, where they were treated with scorn for being on the Yorkist side. Cecily was descended from the Lancastrian branch of the family and they were all descendants of King Edward III, but she had married into the House of York."

Eve gestured with the pen in her right hand to emphasise what she was saying. "Cecily's husband was Richard, Duke of York, the surviving heir of both the house of Clarence and York and one of the richest nobles in the land. He had finally tired of

60

being dutiful to his king, Henry VI, with no reward. He had even had to pay for the army required in France to try to hold on to Henry's inherited lands there. The crown owed him thousands of pounds by this time and he was having to resort to selling off some of his property to stay afloat. The amount amounted to several million pounds in today's money, an astonishing sum."

She took a breath, looking into the faces of each of her colleagues in turn, as she attempted to gauge their thoughts. David was nodding sagely as if he had already known all of this. Stellan was meeting her gaze keenly, his eyes intense as he concentrated on her words, Rupert was fidgeting with his pen while swinging on his chair, a frown on his face, and Alex was making notes. She continued:

"Not only that, but Richard of York had been named Protector of the Realm during Henry's periods of insanity or catatonia, when he was to all intents and purposes in a vegetative state. Then, just when York had started to get the state of the country into some sort of order, Henry would revive and York's power would again be removed and the country thrown into disarray." She emphasised her words with a firm nod and then added:

"He had finally had enough and openly claimed the throne, but Parliament denied it to him, unwilling to depose an anointed king. However, they did decree that, on Henry's death, York and his family should be the rightful heirs to the throne. Since Queen Margaret had a son, not much younger than York's youngest, Richard, she was hardly willing to agree to this and that is when the see-sawing battles between the two camps began."

She checked her notes and gave Stellan some co-ordinates and dates for a few months after the sack of Ludlow, on the coast of southern England, where Richard and George had been sent, under escort, to escape the wrath of Queen Margaret, following their father's and brother, Edmund's, deaths at her hands.

'The Fly' commenced its whirring, or, as she liked to think of it, buzzing. Then they heard Richard's voice again. Still, they could barely understand an odd word here or there, so the recording was sent to Mary once more and the returned translation read by each of them, as they listened to it again.

Cast Your Fate to the Wind

"George, do not fear. Mama says it will not be for long, that Edward will avenge father's death and become king. George! Stop crying. We will be safe in Burgundy and then Edward will send for us." Pause.

"I do understand. I am afraid as well, of course, but we are sons of the great Duke of York and we must not show it. That's better. I will sing to you, to cheer you."

His plaintive voice, high and pure and yet strong, poured out from the speakers and she felt her heart swell again at the courage of a small boy, torn from his homeland, having only recently learned of his father's and brother's deaths and heading into unknown dangers, and yet comforting and reassuring his older brother. In her head she heard the word 'steadfast' and knew it was an apt description for him.

'The Fly' had tracked his journey across the sea (where they had again heard some soft crying and a fair bit of vomiting) until the boys arrived in Burgundy.

"My name is Richard, son of the Duke of York. It is a pleasure to make your acquaintance, Sir. My mother, Duchess Cecylle, sends her heartfelt thanks for keeping us safe at this difficult time."

It had been there they had paused.

Propaganda

"Well, he was quite the diplomat even at such a tender age!" said Stellan.

"Yes, and how brave, considering all he had gone through in the last few months," she added.

"Are you turning into a Ricardian?" Rupert laughed, as if it was the worst thing in the world.

"Don't be silly!" she said, but his words stayed with her for the rest of the day; perhaps she had started to favour the Ricardian view of Richard. That evening, she Skyped Sue and asked her why *she* had become a Ricardian and what it really meant.

"Well there are various interpretations of the term. Generally, it refers to those of us who believe that Richard was wrongly vilified and that his bad reputation was all because of Tudor propaganda. Some are just open-minded and think there isn't any proof either way. Some think he did kill the princes in the tower but that he was still overall a good king and he was just a product of his times. And there are some who think he was something of a saint. The Richard III Society feels that these have undermined the Society's credibility, but they feel the Society has gone too far the other way, because they refuse to be seen to be pro-Richard any more, in case they get accused of beatifying him."

"And which camp are you in?"

"Well, I think they should defend his reputation, and so what if they are seen as biased? The ones on the other camp certainly are! That's what the Society was founded for in the first place – to defend his name. And in more recent times they have found evidence which tends to lean more towards him being innocent, although there is still no agreement and others interpret things differently."

"So why do you remain a member?"

"Well, one – to keep an eye on them! Two – because they still have a lot of interesting trips and talks going on and three – because I have a lot of friends in the Society."

"OK."

"But I'm also a member of the Richard III Loyal Supporters who are definitely pro-Richard. Why do you ask? Have I converted you?"

She laughed and Eve joined in.

"Well, I don't know about the matter of the princes, of course, but I am absolutely intrigued by him. I have been reading a few books and it certainly seems plausible to me that the Tudors blackened his character in order to justify their taking the throne. I mean, how could you trust Henry Tudor when he was so sneaky as to date his reign from the day before the Battle of Bosworth? By doing that he could confiscate land and property and execute anyone he thought was a potential threat to his reign. He was the usurper!"

"Exactly! And we also know that Richard brought in many good laws in his single Parliament, some of which form the basis of our laws today.

"Yes! Why doesn't that get more publicity? Why is it only this bloody mystery of what happened to the princes that everyone is obsessed with?"

"I know! And his reputation before the death of his brother, King Edward IV, was exemplary. He was known to be just, loyal – a man of true principle. He was courageous as well, as is shown by the charge he made to try to finish the battle quickly by confronting Henry Tudor personally. He died alone 'in the thickest press of his enemies' and was cut down from behind – bloody cowards they were!"

"So, what went wrong then?"

"Well, that is the question, isn't it? Most Ricardians would say it was really Edward's fault because of the question of the validity of his marriage to Elizabeth Woodville. He had a reputation as a philanderer and his marriage to Elizabeth was secret so it was quite in character for him to have previously married another woman to get her into bed, the same way he had with Elizabeth Woodville. If only he had… no, there is no point indulging in 'what ifs'. We can only look at all the surviving evidence and judge for ourselves."

Do You Hear What I Hear?

They had followed Richard into Burgundy, listened to his voice through the whole experience, and again when he returned to England, after his brother, Edward, had won the throne. It had been as a result of the Battle of Towton that Edward gained the crown – the bloodiest battle ever on English soil, with about twenty-seven thousand dead in one day. A sobering thought.

They had had every conversation translated until, after several weeks of practice, they had become quite adept at understanding Richard's words, even without the translation. The one exception was Rupert, who could not seem to grasp the mediaeval way of speaking despite all the practice. Eventually he stopped attending the monitoring sessions and was assigned to negotiate the rights of an exclusive documentary with a TV channel. Every time Eve saw him, he was grumpy and rude.

Eve was just about to leave for work, excited to hear what Richard would have to say this time, when she remembered that her cleaner, Shirley, was due back after a long break. She had had some serious family problems, in fact her husband had been diagnosed with terminal cancer and she had given up her cleaning jobs to nurse him. Eve hadn't bothered to get another cleaner, but now Shirley's husband had died and she was asking if she could return, so Eve gladly said 'Yes'. Shirley was a real treasure but the only problem was that she would insist on tidying up everywhere and Eve sometimes liked to leave things to hand, so she wouldn't forget them. Shirley also had a nasty habit of throwing away anything she thought was not essential – and her definition of 'essential' differed markedly from Eve's.

One time she had thrown away some ticket stubs from a special concert by Eve's favourite band. She had been keeping them as souvenirs of the show, but that wasn't the only reason she was keeping them; the stubs had been autographed by the whole band! By the time Eve had realised, the bin men had been and the ticket stubs were irretrievable. Shirley had been mortified when she had found out, although Eve didn't really tell her off, but she wanted to make her realise that she shouldn't just throw anything away. Unfortunately, it wasn't long before her old habits resurfaced and Eve was heartbroken when a ball of fur from her old, deceased cat, Widdy (short for Widdecombe Fur) had been discarded. It had been in a ginger jar on the mantelpiece, a poignant keepsake that was irreplaceable.

"But it was only a clump of dirty fluff!" Shirley had protested when Eve informed her of the mistake. "It wasn't marked or anything... how was I to know it was something special?" Her chin had begun to wobble and she took out an immaculate handkerchief (no tissues for her) and dabbed at her eyes.

"Oh, I know, Shirley, you didn't mean it. But please be a bit more careful in the future."

Eve had smiled and offered her a cuppa and the incident was forgiven, if not forgotten. To be fair, she had tried really hard from then on and Eve had had no cause to complain, but she suddenly remembered the little, sample jar of Richard's DNA that she had put in her desk drawer. She didn't think Mrs M would be going through her drawers, but she couldn't take the risk of her throwing that out! So, she grabbed it from the drawer and put it in her jacket pocket while she fiddled with her keys to lock the front door. She was running a little late. Then she jogged to the car and made her way to the office.

When she arrived, the others were almost ready to begin the day's investigations. They had decided the day before to attempt to trace the events leading up to Edward's coronation, since the date was known, 28th June 1461. They knew Richard was in attendance and they chose a date a week or so before.

After she took her familiar place in front of the machine, she picked up her steaming cup of coffee and blew the surface to cool it.

Stellan flipped the switch.

"Oh Ned! I mean 'Your Grace'," Richard's boyish tone was excited and much more spontaneous and less measured than his usual level timbre. "Are you really going to be crowned king next week?"

"Yes, I hope so, and you need not call me 'Your Grace' in

private, although it would be best to when strangers are present – to preserve the royal dignity, you know?!" He winked at his brother.

Wait a minute! How...? Did I really hear Edward's voice? What's going on? And how did I 'see' that wink, how did I perceive Edward himself, anyway? She glanced at the others, but they seemed to be acting normally. *I'll see if it continues and maybe ask them about it later.*

Another voice cut in, congratulating Edward on his upcoming coronation; a pleasant, rich, young voice, but something about it... it made her feel uncomfortable. She instinctively mistrusted this lad. *Who is he?*

"George, I am going to honour you with the Dukedom of Clarence, the title that once belonged to our illustrious ancestor, Lionel of Antwerp."

Oh, that's who it is, the middle brother, George. How odd that such a – yes, beautiful – voice can evoke such a strong feeling of... what is it? Unreliability? Deceit? Irresponsibility? All three? Whatever, I would never trust him if I knew him.

Edward continued: "You will both attend me for my coronation and ride behind me in the procession. You will be allowed to stay at Court for a few days and then I will see you settled in Greenwich. You can begin to learn the duties and obligations of princes of the realm and George, you will take up the duties of a Duke also in due course."

"So, will I be in charge in Greenwich? After all I am older than Dickon."

"Yes, but Margaret will be there too and she is older than both of you."

"Pfft! She is just a girl though – she does not count!"

"George, do not be disrespectful – you know our father told us always to honour the women in our lives. He always treated Mother with respect."

"Well, I know you have always... honoured... the ladies, Ned." The voice was ingenuous, but the look on George's face revealed his meaning – it was too innocent, falsely so, and Eve remembered Edward's reputation as something of a Casanova. Edward, himself, narrowed his eyes and tilted his head, his gaze never leaving George's face. He raised his index finger and wagged it solemnly at him.

"Hold your tongue now, George, if you value your hide!"

George smirked but remained silent and Edward turned to Richard.

"Dickon, I am planning to send you to another noble household for your knightly education and I am almost sure it will be Warwick's. He has been my most loyal and supportive adherent in all this uproar and madness, both before and after the deaths of Father and Edmund, and it will be a great honour for him to have the upbringing of my royal brother in his hands. You will probably be based mainly in Middleham – that is where he prefers to dwell most of the time. Do you have any objection?"

"Yorkshire! God's blood, Ned – are they not right uncivilised in the North? And... and I was hoping that I would see more of you now you are king. I barely saw you when I lived at Fotheringhay and you at Ludlow." Richard hung his head, looking down to hide his emotion.

"Mind your language, Dickon – we cannot have a young prince of the blood royal using such curse words!"

Richard took a deep breath and let it out again slowly.

"I apologise, your Grace," he whispered.

"Never mind, just do not make a habit of it, eh? And our cousin assures me that Yorkshire is the best possible place to bring up a young knight – a Knight of the Bath?" There was a twinkle in his eye and a gentle, coaxing tone about his voice.

"Knight of the Bath!" Richard's head flew up and he squared his shoulders as he stood as tall as possible before his enormous brother.

"That's right! You and George are going to be made knights – very soon. The day before the coronation, in fact. I hope you will not let me down, but will stay awake keeping vigil all night in the chapel and bear yourself with chivalry and honour. Will you?"

"Oh yes, Edward, I have longed for it, desired it so much... to be a knight of Christ!"

"Well, you will be now and I am sure you will make me and our dear mother proud. And Father and Edmund will be looking down too. Now, come here and let me embrace you, brothers. We must all stick together now, the three sons of York!"

He wrapped his huge arms around his two young brothers and gave them a great bear hug. Richard could hardly breathe but said nothing, happy to be so close to his hero-brother. They celebrated with a goblet of wine and then Edward ushered them out – it was getting late. Richard held back, lingering inside the great, wooden door as George left ahead of him. He pulled tentatively at his brother's velvet sleeve.

"Edward, may I speak with you please?" he whispered.

"Of course, brother, what is it?"

"The ceremony, of the Bath, I mean. I am worried about it. Do I have to have strangers undress me – can I not do it myself?"

"Dickon, you will have to get used to having body servants – you are a prince of the blood and as such you are not supposed to act like a commoner. Especially not when you are about to become a knight!"

"But, Ned, I... I have a problem." He had further lowered his voice and his head in embarrassment. "May we speak in private? I pray you!"

Edward put a brotherly arm around his shoulders and drew him back through into his bedchamber, ushering the servants out and pouring some more wine for his brother.

"Sit, sit! Now what is this problem?"

Richard sank down onto the chair indicated by the king.

"I... I do not think I want to be a Knight of the Bath after all. Thank you for the honour, though."

"What?! But I thought you 'longed for it so much'!" Edward said.

"Well, I have changed my mind."

"Well, you cannot. It is all arranged and I will not be embarrassed by my brother just because he is too shy to have servants disrobe him!"

"But I cannot do it! I just cannot, please Ned!" He was trembling and on the verge of tears. "You do not understand!"

"Then explain, I am listening."

Richard let out a long, trembling sigh. "I am... deformed," he mumbled, avoiding Edward's keen gaze.

"You are what?"

Richard whirled around, his eyes meeting his older brother's, jumped to his feet and shouted: "I am deformed – a crook-back!"

Edward opened his mouth and closed it again, and then burst out laughing.

"You are jesting!"

"Am I laughing, Brother?" Richard's eyes were blazing. There was a long pause.

"Show me!" Edward said.

Richard chewed his lower lip and then tore off his doublet, closely followed by his undershirt. Then he turned his back to his brother.

Edward gasped.

"Dickon, I had no idea. But how long...? You never had this before... when we used to swim in the Nene."

"No, it only started recently. It began by feeling stiff and sore – I thought I had just overdone it riding and shooting the bow. Then Margaret noticed it when we were playing by the moat one day and I fell in – well, actually she pushed me. It was stinking and filthy so I took off my shirt and ... she screamed. She thinks I have been cursed. Ned, do you think God has punished me?"

"No, no, of course not! Although perhaps he is testing you – giving you a special burden to bear. Yes, that must be it – he has chosen you to bear it, marked you out as equal to this challenge."

Richard's expression lightened, "Do you really think so, Ned?" For once his almost perpetual frown had disappeared.

"I do. And, look, I will get only two trusted servants to attend you before the ceremony and let them know what to expect. You and George will not be with the others being invested anyway, as royal princes. All will be well, brother, I promise. I will make sure you are not discomfited." He smiled and Richard returned it.

"Thank you, Ned," he whispered.

Oh, Holy Night

On the allotted day, the one before Edward's coronation, Richard was taken to the room bearing the huge wooden bathtub, where the two specially chosen servants helped him to disrobe and washed him with soft sponges and perfumed soaps. They made no comment, nor did they react when they saw his spine. The washing represented purification.

While he was being cleansed, John Howard, one of Edward's supporters and an experienced knight, quizzed him as to the duties and responsibilities of knighthood. He had learned the code of chivalry from an early age and Edmund, his brother, killed at Wakefield, used to read him stories of King Arthur and his knights. He had always looked forward to becoming a knight. He knew that they had to be loyal to their Lord or King, pious and devout to honour the Church, they had to be courageous in battle, show honour and shun treachery, be courteous and generous and be a gallant defender of women. And they always had to keep oaths made on their honour, or else they were committing treason to their knighthood. As far as the battle element was concerned, he would spend the next years of his life in training for this, learning the fighting skills required to kill the enemy and defend himself. He knew it would be hard, but he embraced it – it would lead to him being a true knight. But he would also be taught more gentle pursuits such as music, dancing, etiquette and games of strategy such as chess. He smiled to himself – already he could beat George nine times out of ten.

When he was finished bathing, he was helped out of the tub and wrapped in linen, then sent to lie abed to dry out. As soon as he was dry, he was dressed in a white vestment, to symbolise purity, a red robe for royalty and black hose and shoes which represented death.

After he was dressed in the simple robe he was led to the chapel, where he, George and fifteen other young men had to keep vigil all night, praying and asking for guidance on how to be a perfect knight. He was escorted there to the accompaniment of sweet music and monks chanting – he saw George also being led out to the chapel and the others following on. A sword and shield had been placed on the altar and blessed by the priest – this was the sword which would be used to dub them 'knight'. But before then they had to remain awake all night and pray while kneeling before the altar the whole time.

Eve suddenly was aware that Richard was utterly determined not to fall asleep. She knew somehow just how important it was to him to be a perfect, chivalrous knight. George and the rest had also been brought in, having undergone the same bathing ritual. After they were left alone in the chapel, George began to whisper to Richard.

"We could have a game of cards while we wait."

"Do not speak thus, George – we must remain silent and contemplate our sins. Then we must pray to the Blessed Virgin to help us be chivalrous, honourable and valiant. Now pray, keep silent – if you do not wish to do the ceremony properly, well, I do!"

And he turned away from George, clasped his hands together and closed his eyes, ignoring his brother until he, too fell silent and nothing could be heard except the distant chanting of monks, coming from the nearby monastery.

As they were hearing nothing but silence for the next twenty minutes or so, and probably would for the next several hours, Eve suggested they move on and Stellan turned the dial.

Hours later, as dawn tentatively slid her fingers of light through the window and illuminated the chapel, while the bells rang out from the nearby churches, the prospective knights' escorts returned to fetch them. They were brought before the priest to make confession. As Richard began to ask the priest's blessing before enumerating his sins, Eve, realising what was happening, stood up.

"Stellan, please turn this off – it's his confession and it's not right to listen to that, it's meant to be private. I don't feel comfortable at all – it's so wrong! Please?"

Stellan looked surprised at first, but as she spoke, he raised his eyebrows and nodded slowly, flicking the switch off.

"Thank you," she said, letting the breath, that she hadn't been aware she was holding, out with a sigh. "I know most people are irreligious these days, atheist and suchlike, but Richard was a devout Catholic and it isn't fair to spy on his innermost secrets. The confessional is sacrosanct."

"I thought that was just the reason we are doing this project; to spy on him and find out his guilty secrets, isn't it?" David was looking smug and she could have slapped him if he wasn't her boss! "Surely a confessional would be the perfect place to discover the truth."

"David, he's only eight years old – what major sin do you think he has committed?" she asked, the tetchiness obvious in her tone.

"Mmm, OK, I'll give you that – I don't suppose it is relevant. But a later one might be."

She decided to ignore that and hoped it would never happen. She didn't think she could stay in that room if they were going to do that. They had a quick coffee break and then Stellan moved the dial on a few minutes and caught the end of the Mass that they had to attend before the actual ceremony. Part of it was a solemn sermon reiterating the duties and obligations of a knight. Then the sword and shield were handed to Edward, who had been present for the Mass. Each young man was then presented to Edward in turn and vowed their sacred oath of allegiance, promising to have no involvement with traitors, never to give evil counsel to a lady but to treat her with great respect and defend her against all and, finally, to keep to the fasts and abstinences of the Church and hear Mass every day, making offerings to the Church. Richard felt like he was in a dream, he was so tired, but stood straight before his brother and king as he said his sacred oath of allegiance.

After watching George be dubbed a knight, his turn came and he knelt there before Edward. His giant of a brother came forward and said: "Dearest brother, go and be thou a valiant knight and courageous in the face of your enemy and be true and upright that God may love thee." Richard replied: "I will."

Then Edward, taking the sword and tapping him on the neck with the flat of it, said: "I hereby dub thee Sir Knight."

Edward then gestured for the boys' sponsors to come forward again and fasten the spurs to their charges' heels and then he himself came forward and buckled the belts on, one around each knight's waist. Finally, the boys were taken back up to their chambers where they were allowed to take their rest after the long night of ceremonies.

Ball of Confusion

Eve could not understand what was going on. Stellan had told her that the machine only picked up the voice of the DNA subject and that had certainly been the case for the first few recordings they had made: the baby Richard crying, the young boy terrified at Ludlow's Market Cross, his journey into exile on the continent and the young Richard singing. But this time she could hear the voices of others, even the ambient sounds around him, and it all seemed so much more vivid, more real. Stellan must have changed something on the machine, improved it and not told them. Yes, of course that must be it – he had wanted to surprise them. After the meeting was over, Alex wandered over to her.

"So, what do you think, Eve. He doesn't give much away, does he? Although it was interesting about his spine – calling himself a crook-back. But generally, he seems to have been quite reserved, even as a child."

"True! It's just as well that Stellan has enhanced the machine's scope, isn't it? It's much easier to follow the conversation when the other people can be heard and the local sounds really add depth to the whole thing. Those bells really made me jump and..." Her voice trailed off as she looked up at Alex's face. His brown eyes were wide with surprise and his brow was wrinkled in puzzlement.

"What do you mean, Eve? Nothing's been changed – nothing at all."

"But the machine is picking up more, isn't it? Not just Richard's voice."

Alex laughed outright then, his expression changing to one of amusement.

"You nearly got me then, Eve, I thought you were serious for a minute."

She opened her mouth to reply but thought better of it and closed it again, grinning back at him and letting him believe she had been pulling his leg. What was going on? Was she the only one who had heard more than Richard's lone voice? She made herself a coffee and went over to Stellan.

"So, Stellan, is there any way you can fine tune the machine so that it could pick up sounds other than Richard's speech? That would be so useful, wouldn't it?"

"Yes, it would," he began. "But no, unfortunately it isn't possible to hear anyone or anything else, or at least not unless I can get hold of somebody else's DNA who was there at the same time and place. Is there anyone like that, do you know?"

She thought about it for a while. Who else who had been present at that time might have accessible DNA? Edward IV and Elizabeth Woodville? Well, their last resting place was known, but the queen had never allowed any royal tombs to be opened – she didn't want to set a precedent – and it was unlikely that Charles would either. There was some of Edward's hair around, but no DNA could be isolated from it – it had been tried before.

It wasn't known where Richard's son, Edward, had been buried. George and Isabel were known to have been interred in Tewkesbury Abbey, but their remains had become mixed up with other bones when the crypt had flooded and so not only would it be difficult to find which bones belonged to whom but their DNA was likely contaminated anyway. Anne Neville's tomb, in Westminster Abbey, was also 'lost'.

Francis Lovell, a figure who would have been fascinating to research, had disappeared and no-one knew where he had died. Even Perkin Warbeck, the pretender to the throne who had claimed to be Richard of York, the younger of the two princes, and had been buried in the Church of the Austin Friars in London after being executed by Henry Tudor, was lost because the site had been bombed in the war and whatever remained of him was destroyed. No, all the possible candidates were either lost, mislaid, or forbidden to be examined.

"No, Stellan, I don't think there is anyone who would be available, I'm afraid. Shame, eh?"

She went back to her desk and sipped on the coffee, letting the bitter drink slide down her throat, hoping it might stimulate her brain enough to work out why it was that she could hear more than the others. She grimaced as she realised there was no sugar in it. She often kept a sachet or two of sugar in her bag or pockets in case of emergencies. As she felt in her jacket pocket, her finger touched the hard plastic of the sample bottle and she had a revelation.

What if, because she had some of Richard's DNA on her person, taken from his actual body, her psychometry skills had taken over and filled in the sounds that he was hearing as well as the words he was uttering? If a piece of metal could absorb such emotion when it was only worn or owned for a relatively brief period of time, surely someone's actual DNA, a part of their essence, should hold yet more of a link to that person, shouldn't it? But why did she only experience this when Richard was speaking? It was true she had occasionally felt a surge of emotion connected with Richard and his remains: the tomb, the feeling when she had first touched the vial of DNA, but nothing as detailed as this. Her only theory was that perhaps the vibrations of his voice resonated with his DNA sample somehow, so that the emotions and sensations he had experienced were brought to life again, like spectres of reality plucked from the far reaches of time. And wasn't that what 'The Fly' was doing too, to some extent?

But how could she tell the others? Well, obviously, she couldn't tell them; they would think she had gone loopy. Not only that but she would have to admit to having stolen some of Richard's DNA! She decided to keep quiet and note down all her visions and feelings as things progressed. After all, perhaps it was simply her own vivid imagination, that she had become so involved in the life of Richard of Gloucester that she was filling in the blanks of his life herself. But how could she check and see if the voices she heard and the scenes she saw were accurate?

Until the Day We Die

They continued eavesdropping on Richard while he was undergoing his training at Middleham, in the service of Richard, Earl of Warwick, the man who would later become known as 'The Kingmaker'. The future Richard III was about twelve years old and they had heard him repeating Latin passages from the scriptures and other works, mainly to do with battle strategies, religious texts, law and the duties of a knight. They had found that Richard was a fierce fighter, using his mobility and speed to defeat boys who were larger and heavier than he was.

They were listening to him now.

A gasp.

"Francis, look out! There's a bull loose in that field. God's teeth! He can't hear me."

Then, louder: "Francis! FRANCIS!!" accompanied by heavy panting. Eve could hear the sound of his boots striking the floor as he ran, could see the field that he could see, with Francis sauntering along oblivious to the bull charging up behind him. He was a tall boy, taller than Richard, even though he was a few years younger, and darker, his glossy, dark brown hair shoulder length and well-groomed, adorned with a deep blue hat with a small, crimson feather in it. She could even see the tip of it fluttering gently in the breeze.

"Hey!! HEY!!" Richard whooped loudly and she knew he was no longer trying to make Francis hear – the wind was tearing his voice away in the other direction – but attempting to distract the bull. The bull was huge, heavy-set and almost as tall as Richard himself. Richard tore his murrey cloak off and flapped it as the bull hesitated and turned its head sharply in the direction of this new intruder into its territory. It struck the turf with its hoof and snorted, its eyes seeming to radiate malevolence. And, all the while, Francis strode on, blissfully unaware. Then, the bull was off, turning its heavy bulk around to face Richard and lowering its head as it charged. Richard flicked the cloak again and then turned and ran, waving the cloak the whole time, while the bull's heavy hoof-beats drummed a rhythm into the ground.

She felt Richard tire and he slowed, turning and holding the cloak out to the side, like a matador. As the bull neared the waving fabric, he dropped it and neatly vaulted over the fence, his costly, velvet cloak trampled into the mud. The bull investigated it with its horns, shaking its head and bellowing, while Richard pelted back down the side of the field, alongside the fence, yelling for Francis. And, at last he heard him and turned his head, a frown of curiosity on his dark brow.

"Richard!" he called, smiling and turning to face his fellow squire. As he did so, his expression changed into one of terror as he spied the bull, which had tired of ravaging the folds of Richard's cloak and had turned its attention once again to its former quarry. Francis sprinted to the side of the field and clambered over the fence to land, panting, at Richard's feet.

"Sweet Jesu!" he whispered. "Thank the Lord you managed to let me know what was happening. There was no bull in that field yesterday! I had no thought of any danger. What an idiot I am!" He paused. "What's that at the top of the field? There's something on the ground." He glanced back at Richard and noticed his cloak was missing. "Is it your cloak? That beautiful, murrey velvet one?" His face was stricken with horror.

"It is a small price to pay to save you from injury… or worse. Did you not hear me yelling at you? I have almost shouted myself hoarse! I had to get in the field and distract the beast in the end."

"No, I heard nothing until a few moments ago. You went into the field with the bull on purpose? To save me?"

"Of course. I was never going to let you get trampled to death in the mud – the sight of blood makes me queasy!" He grinned at Francis.

"Well, thank you…your Grace." As if his fright and Richard's actions had made him suddenly aware of Richard's rank, Lovell made as if to kneel on the grass before him, but Richard stopped him with a wry smile and a hand on his shoulder.

"I told you, Francis, you must call me Richard. We are friends, aren't we?" His voice held a note of doubt and also hope.

"Yes, your Grace… Richard. Even more so now, since I owe you my life. How can I repay you?" He sounded anxious.

"Just by simply that, being my friend. Francis, I have noticed that the other boys… they stop talking when I enter the room and sometimes seem to whisper behind my back. Do you know why?"

Francis shrugged. "Probably because of who you are. You are a noble duke, a royal prince – brother to the king himself. They know not how to behave with you. Maybe some of them also

82

wonder if you will carry tales to your brother about them."

"I never would!"

"Of course not, but… they do not know you properly yet. Give them time."

Richard nodded and they walked off back up to the castle on the hill, side by side.

This Is Me

A couple of weeks later, still at Middleham, Richard was practising swordplay and one of the other boys, by the name of Rob Percy, had sidled around the corner, holding something under his tunic. He spoke to another boy, leaning in so that no-one else saw him and lifted the edge of his tunic. They both grinned. He glanced at Richard, who was so intent on his practice, he had not even noticed, but Francis nudged him.

"Percy's stolen another pie! Cook has made some of her pigeon pies and they are delicious. Let's see if he will give us a taste."

The boys surrounded Percy and he doled out a small piece to each of them. When he came to Richard he paused, then offered a piece to him too, his eyebrows raised. Richard took it and thanked him. It was delicious!

All at once there was a loud shout and a large, angry-looking man, their training master, came striding along and called to Rob:

"Percy! Come here this instant! Cook tells me one of her pies has gone missing and it was you she saw making off in a hurry. What have you done with it, boy? Come on, now!"

Percy hung his head and walked obediently up to the master,

who shook his head at the sight of all the crumbs on the boy's tunic. The master cuffed him round the head. By this time, all the other boys, including Richard, had stopped their various activities and were watching, fascinated.

"Right, it will be a beating for you boy. Report to me at supper time – no supper for you today."

He turned to leave, but Richard spoke up.

"Master Benedict, please do not punish Rob. It was me who told him to do it. I could smell those pies and, well, I sent Rob to get me one. It is me who should be punished, not him."

Rob stared at him in astonishment.

"Really?" Master Benedict sounded sceptical but Richard's gaze never wavered. "Well, then, you had better report to me instead. Do not think just because you are a royal duke and a prince of the blood that you will be treated any more lightly than the rest."

Richard nodded. "Of course not, Sir," he said softly.

Rob heaved a sigh as Benedict disappeared again, without the pie. "He will get away lightly," he muttered to his friend, but he gave Richard a swift nod of thanks.

A few hours later, Richard presented himself before the master. Eve could feel his trepidation, but also knew he was determined to see it through.

"Well, Richard. Why did you take the blame for Percy? I know it was not on your orders he took the pie. He is always getting into trouble whereas your conduct has been exemplary. Admit it, son, and you will be spared the beating."

Richard swallowed but said nothing, staring straight ahead.

"I *shall* give you a beating, lad. Your brother has authorised us to treat you no differently from the others."

"I know that, Sir. Rob stole the pie at my behest."

The master sighed heavily and picked up a switch from his desk.

"Remove your tunic and shirt."

Richard drew in a breath. He would be revealing his secret if he removed the shirt.

"Sir, may I please keep the shirt on?" Something in Richard's steady gaze and determined voice must have affected the master for he paused, his stare boring into Richard.

"You may, but if you do, you will receive double the number of strokes," he said, his lips thinned and his eyes glittering.

Richard nodded and, with trembling hands, he removed just his tunic and turned his back to Benedict.

Eve gasped as the switch was brought down across Richard's back. She could feel every blow, like a razor blade cutting her flesh. Twelve times the switch rained down, until tears filled Richard's eyes, but he gritted his teeth, refusing to cry out.

When it was over, he was ordered to return to the communal room he shared with five other boys, including Rob and Francis. It was deserted, since all the others were at supper. He sat on his bunk and let out a long, shaky breath, gingerly letting his fingers travel to his back and shoulders; his whole back felt as if it were on fire and the shirt was sticking to him, where here and there, blood had seeped from his wounds, but better that than letting Benedict see his deformity. He carefully removed the shirt before it stuck fast and took a linen clout, wetting it from the pitcher of water on the shelf and winced as he dabbed at his back, struggling to reach.

Just then, voices in the corridor heralded the return of his room-mates and he hastily replaced the shirt, unwilling for them to discover his shameful secret. Their excited chatter hushed as they entered and caught sight of him, sitting there, his face still lividly pale from his ordeal, his white shirt stained with red. They all stood around, whistling at the severity of the beating, obvious from the state of the shirt and giving Richard looks of admiration at his stoicism.

"God's nails! That whore-son really did give you a beating!" Rob exclaimed in astonishment. He bit his lip. "I did not really think he would, what with you being, you know, a duke and all."

"While I am here, I am to be treated the same as you."

"Well, thank you for taking my punishment. I appreciate it. I still have not recovered from the last one, you know."

"I realised that."

"Here, let me bathe your back for you, I know it is hard to reach, yourself."

"Thank you, but no. I can manage." He gave Rob a swift smile, stood up and marched from the room in the direction of the garderobe. When he got there, he found that Francis had followed him.

"Why on earth did you take Percy's beating for him? He deserved it, he was the one to take the pie."

"Well, we all partook of it. I wanted to show the others that I am one of them, that they can trust me not to snitch on them."

"Hmm, I see. Do you think it worked?"

"I shall have to wait and see." Richard gave a rather strained grin.

"Come on, let me help you," Lovell said, his tone determined. Richard sighed but didn't move at first, weighing up Lovell's worth with his measured gaze. Could he trust him? He thought he could.

"Very well... thank you. But I must warn you about something. I have a... a... curve in my spine, so do not be shocked. I do not want everyone to know about it, so I trust you to keep your counsel."

"Of course, Richard."

Lovell helped him off with the shirt, showing an admirable lack of surprise or horror at Richard's condition. He bathed the cuts, smearing some special healing cream on it that he said his nurse had given him to bring with him when he was sent to Middleham. Richard gritted his teeth at first, but then felt the soothing action of the cream start to work.

"Thanks, Francis. Oh and, by the way, my close friends call me Dickon."

Shallow

Another friend Richard made at this time was the younger daughter of the Earl of Warwick, Anne Neville. The young squires had to learn other aspects of being a knight than just fighting and training. They studied Latin, Law, and also dancing, etiquette and how to treat a lady. For this they had to attend various feasts and functions, where they served the lord, the Earl of Warwick. There were multiple rules of manners they had to obey and as for the dancing, it was the young daughters of the earl and the ladies who attended the countess who acted as their partners.

Francis was shy and Richard often helped him by tutoring him in the etiquette and the dance steps, so he would at least have those so practiced that he did not need to think too much. Richard, himself, was naturally graceful and musical, so had no trouble with the dancing itself. However, as he was a little shorter than most of the others, he usually ended up being partnered by Anne, the younger of the earl's daughters. This made him feel a little awkward as she was four years younger than him and still a baby in his eyes. Not that he was interested in girls at all really. However, Anne felt differently and her eyes would follow him whenever he was in the same room as her. Of course, the other boys noticed and would never let him forget it.

"Hey, Dickon, your sweetheart is looking at you again!"

"She wants to kiss you, for sure!"

Richard rolled his eyes and tried to ignore them. He found it embarrassing and annoying.

One day, it all got too much for him. Anne had followed him out of the great hall after a practice, asking him if he would go with her to the stables to see the new foal and he saw two of the boys whispering behind their hands and making rude gestures, as if suggesting she was interested in something more than the foal. He found it disgusting and, without thinking, he snapped at her:

"Why would you think I would want to go anywhere with you! You are just a baby. Why do you not leave me alone for once!"

She stood there for a second in silence, shocked and humiliated by his rudeness and hurt by the anger and venom in his voice.

"I know you like horses, that is why I asked you. But it is not compulsory – you may please yourself!"

Then her little lower lip began to tremble and she turned and left the room, not running but in a dignified way, her head held high.

Richard immediately felt guilty for being so nasty to her, as it wasn't her who was at fault, but he knew the eyes of the others were on him and he did not dare go after her.

The next time there was a dance practice, he stepped forward to her, intending to apologise, but she walked right past him and took Lovell's hand. It was his turn to be shocked and humiliated. He bit his lip and scanned the room for another partner, his gaze alighting on one of the countess's ladies, a tall, ungainly girl who had two left feet and blushed red if any of the boys so much as looked her way. She almost passed out when confronted by the Duke of Gloucester. He struggled through the whole dance, feeling as if he wanted the earth to open and swallow him whole.

For the next month, Anne would not even look at him and he began to long for her attentions again. There had been no harm in her, why had he been so horrid? It had been selfish and shallow to treat her so shoddily, just because he could not endure a little teasing.

Finally, something happened to break the tension between them. Richard was grooming his horse in the stables. Even though eventually he would have his own squire to do such tasks, the boys still had to know how to do them themselves. Richard rather enjoyed it, the rhythmic strokes relaxing him and giving his muscles a work-out at the same time. Just then he heard a scuffling noise and raised voices outside. He stopped his work and walked to the door. Outside, a groom was holding a puppy by the scruff of its neck and laughing as he made to dunk it in a bucket of water.

"It is only the runt – Master Benedict will not want it. It might as well be drowned now."

"No! I will keep him and look after him. Do not..." Anne gulped and tears filled her eyes as the groom dipped the little pup in the dirty water. Richard did not hesitate and flung himself at the youth, even though the lad was much taller and broader than he was. However, Richard had the element of surprise and the boy cursed as he was flung from his feet and assailed with a swift fist. Richard scooped up the pup, which was bedraggled but otherwise none the worse for its dunking, and gave it to Anne.

The groom, who had not been long employed as such by the earl, stood up and was about to launch himself on his unexpected assailant, when he realised by his rich clothing who it was and instead bowed and said:

"I am sorry, your Grace. I did not mean to cause offence."

"Really?" Richard asked, his hands on his hips and a frown on his face. "You were being cruel to a young girl. The earl's daughter."

"The earl's daughter?!" the youth squealed. "I had no idea... I mean, she is dressed like a servant girl. I am new here – I did not know."

"Even were she a servant, it was a nasty thing to do."

The lad stared at his boots. "I apologise, your Grace. My Lady."

He bowed to them both and Richard made an impatient gesture, indicating he should go. The boy did not waste any time, glad to escape a worse punishment.

Anne stood there, hugging the little scrap to her and then looked into Richard's eyes.

"Thank you, cousin Richard," she said, formally.

"Anne, you need not be formal – please call me Dickon, as you were wont to do before... before I was so rude to you. I apologise too. I hope you will forgive me and we can return to our previous way of treating each other."

"Very well," she said and gave him a shy smile.

"What are you going to call that little runt of a dog?"

She beamed at him as she replied.

"Dickon," she said.

He laughed loudly.

"Well, I suppose I deserve that!" he chuckled.

So What?

Over the next couple of weeks, they listened to many different religious services, feasts, knightly lessons and hunting. Richard was often on horseback, in church or training in the physical skills needed to be a knight.

But on occasion they discovered something more insightful or interesting.

In 1466 they heard Richard speaking to someone important. Eve knew it was Warwick himself.

"You sent for me, Sir?" Richard was always polite.

"Yes, son. Edward, your brother, has asked that you begin to hear some legal cases. As you are now Admiral of England, you will travel to Southwark for some practice."

"Yes, Sir."

He set off the same day and rode one of the strange 'pacing' horses that seemed to flow over the ground instead of jolting their rider up and down. It made it much more comfortable to ride long distances.

And, at Southwark, he did indeed hear a case as Lord High Admiral. A diamond grinder by the name of Segar Suterman had been accused of being in debt and Richard had to make a judgement on it as Admiral of England.

"That's amazing!" Stellan said.

"Yes, isn't it?!" Eve replied, enthralled.

"What do you mean – why is it amazing?" Rupert asked, his brows furrowed in confusion and his mouth twisted into an expression of incredulity. He still couldn't understand the mediaeval English very well, so Eve had taken to writing out brief notes to give him the gist of Richard's words on the few occasions he attended the 'Fly' sessions. "I thought he heard lots of cases, didn't he? That's what you were telling me the other day."

"Yes, he did, but this is different – look at the date on 'The Fly'."

"1466 – so what's significant about that?"

"Richard wasn't yet fourteen years old."

"What?!! And he had to make the judgement?"

He made a dismissive sound, his eyes so wide she could see their whites.

"Exactly. They had to grow up fast in those days."

"Good God! I have a nephew of that age and he can't even decide what he wants to eat in a restaurant, let alone make a judgement in a criminal case."

"Well, Richard had to – obviously Edward believed in giving his brother early responsibility. He doesn't seem to have trusted George with this kind of thing so early, although it may be that the records are lost – many are from that period. It was known George was considered of responsible age at about sixteen. Maybe Richard was more sensible than George."

She put her head on one side as she continued.

"He certainly seems to have been well versed in the law from an early age – they think he may have been destined for the Church or maybe a career in Law before Edward came to the throne. He had beautiful handwriting; much nicer than Edward's or George's so that could have been true. He seems interested in the law anyway. Or possibly he benefitted – or suffered – because he was given such responsibility at the same time George got it – he would have been sixteen when Richard was thirteen. Younger siblings often gain things straight away that their older siblings have had to wait for, don't they?"

Chapter Three

London, 1467

I Want to Know What Love Is

Their research had moved on a little in time to the next year and Richard was in London…

"But, Sir, won't you please tell me where we are going? Ned might need my services and he will not know where to seek me."

"Do not fret, lad. Ned is fully aware where we are going. In fact, it was his idea. Now, will that satisfy you? You will find out where we are heading soon enough." And with that, he spurred his horse on faster and Richard had to do the same to keep up.

Richard frowned. Although he was only fifteen years old, he was already developing two small lines between his brows because of this habit. He frowned when he was worried, when he was concentrating and when he was angry, so it was not that surprising. On this occasion he was part worried and part annoyed. He liked Jocky Howard, his cousin, but he had not had that much to do with him up until the last few weeks, as Jocky was a lot older than him. He had spent much more time in his company of late, learning about war strategies, Calais and good lordship, since he was Admiral of England and had been now for some time. Warwick had told him to listen to Howard and learn from him and he had done so, listening and watching him closely. He was a quick learner.

Richard noticed Howard beginning to slow down his horse and he paid a little more attention to his surroundings. They were beside the river in London, having taken a barge from Westminster and thence a horse each, which Jocky had arranged to have waiting for them. They were approaching a large building, with lots of people coming and going. No, not people – just men. Richard could see no women at all. Then he did see one or two – they were dressed in rather a lewd fashion and did not stand around outside as some of the men were doing.

"Have you ever been to the bath house before, Dickon?"

Richard's eyebrows flew upwards. "Bath house! Why on earth have you brought me here?"

He was so shocked he entirely forgot to call him 'Sir', as he ought to, since Howard was his elder.

Howard chuckled. "Can you not guess, boy? Most lads of your age would have come here on their own, many times, by now. Ned certainly did. It is a place of great attraction to young males."

Richard frowned again and looked down at his shoes in embarrassment. He knew what kind of thing happened at the bath house. He just had other things to occupy his time and energy, like training to become a knight and learning how to fight properly. He had no time to waste on women. Although he had recently found himself the object of attention for several of the maidservants at Warwick's castle of Middleham, and one or two young noblewomen, including Warwick's younger daughter, Anne. He had hated it at first but, as he matured, he found it quite flattering, but also tiresome when he needed to be concentrating on his studies. The only one of them he really liked was Anne, ever since she had shown such mettle when he had humiliated her. She had reacted in such a dignified way and, when she had avoided him, he had found he missed her. After the episode with the dog, they had become closer, but just as friends. He had known her most of his life, and they had something in common, both being the youngest sibling. But they had never... he had never... Anyway, what was Ned doing telling Howard to bring him here?

"Dickon, there is a young lady here who would like to make your acquaintance."

"What do you mean? I wish to know no-one from such a place."

"Now lad, give her a chance and I am sure you will. Come now and let me introduce you."

He ushered Richard through the entrance where there was a man sitting on a seat and taking money for the hire of a bathtub, linen towels, soap and other luxuries.

Howard leaned down and mumbled something Richard didn't hear, passing the man a bag of coins, and the man called up the stairs and gestured to the two to proceed to the upper floor.

They got only halfway when they were met by a large, round woman with a soft, ample bosom and a hard gaze. Her frown left her when she saw Howard, however.

"Jocky!" she simpered. "You didn't tell me you were coming back again so soon!"

Howard grinned at her and gave her a wink. "I wish I were, good lady, but this visit is not for me but for my dear friend and cousin here. We have an appointment with Madeleine."

"Madeleine! That skinny little wretch! Wet behind the ears – let your friend come with me and I will show him a lot more."

"Nay, Sarah, methinks you would be a little too much for him to handle. Now, where is Madeleine?"

Richard was now certain he knew what was happening and he felt his cheeks flame with embarrassment and shame. He hated the fact that Edward had suggested this, because it meant he would know all about it, and he hated that he was being brought here by Howard like he was a mere child. Would he go in the room with him and watch while he learned the ropes?

"Look, with respect, Sir, I do not think I wish to proceed at all – Ned should not have prevailed upon you to do this. I am uncomfortable and..." He came to an abrupt stop as a petite, doll-like young woman came into view at the top of the stairs. Her hair, shockingly, was loose and cascaded around her shoulders and down her back in a thick wave of glossy ebony curls. Her eyes were a clear, sparkling blue and her lips, painted red and parted in a genuine smile, were so inviting that he felt his own mouth go dry. He had never seen such a beautiful girl. She was older than him, quite a bit probably, but her small frame and innocent-looking face made him feel protective. And underlying that was the sense that she knew life, had done many things in her time and knew secrets she might impart if you were lucky.

"Madeleine! Good e'en – this is my cousin, Richard, whom I

told you of before. Dickon, this is Madeleine, from Calais originally."

Richard could not speak but managed a smile and a polite bow. She giggled prettily, the sound like tinkling bells, and then she smiled at him. She reached for his hand and simply pulled him up the stairs as if she had known him years. He marvelled at her confidence.

"Richard, you are a very pretty boy! Jocky told me you were but I did not believe 'im. I am surprised you need my services. I would 'ave thought there would be many young girls eager to... instruct you!" She glanced at him from under her long, dark eyelashes and licked her pretty lips. Then she opened a door to their left and pulled him inside.

She closed and locked the door and, seeing his look of apprehension, she whispered. "Do not fear – you are safe with Madeleine. And you would not want Jocky or anyone else wandering in, would you?" She took his other hand in hers and stood before him. He could smell a heady perfume – roses and lavender – but before he could protest, escape or even breathe, her lips were on his and he felt the exhilarating thrill of her tongue entering his mouth. Tentatively, he raised his hands and touched her beautiful hair. It was soft and smooth and slid between his fingers like silk. He took a handful up to his nose and inhaled the sweet scent, then bent his head to her neck and let her ebony locks cascade around his face.

He groaned. He was so aroused he was afraid he might embarrass himself by losing control even now, but she gently drew away from him and waited for his heart to settle down a little. She expertly undid his doublet and points, removed his clothing a piece at a time and ran the back of her fingertips sensuously down his upper arm, before she divested herself of her own clothing and stood before him, completely naked. Her breasts were softly rounded and firm, the skin white and unblemished, the rosy peaks of her nipples inviting his touch.

"Madeleine," he whispered, as she drew him down on top of her, parting her legs for him and drawing him in.

Hungry Eyes

Eve glanced, embarrassed, at the others, but of course, although they could hear a few gasps and groans, they couldn't sense everything like she could; Richard was nothing if not restrained in his outward responses. They couldn't know the mixture of joy and guilt he felt, that he was torn between his adolescent hormones driving his instinctive behaviour and his learned piety which made him feel ashamed of those same natural instincts. They couldn't feel those physical sensations he felt as he surrendered his innocence to the sensual Madeleine. They couldn't know the touch of her hair and smell the scent of her body, see the flickering shadows on the wall from the guttering candle by the bed. It was almost as if, during these voyages into the past, she became him, knowing his thoughts and feelings, almost as well as her own. Her own breath was matching his as his arousal peaked and she had to grip the sides of her chair to stop herself from crying out as he did, a deep gasp of fulfilment. She felt someone was watching her and glanced to the left to see Alex's eyes on her, a thoughtful shine to them, and then he gave her a cheeky grin. She was mortified. Surely, he couldn't tell what she was experiencing! Before she could turn away or say anything, Rupert said:

"Bloody hell! Was that what I think it was? Naughty old

Richard, eh? I thought he was meant to be pious and straight-laced."

"Well, he was only fifteen! Boys will be boys," Eve replied, glad the uncomfortable moment with Alex had passed. Then she sensed him behind her.

"Want to come to a musical tomorrow night?" he asked. "I have two tickets for 'Jersey Boys'."

She looked up at him. He was smiling and his eyes were twinkling, fixed on her as if she were the only girl in the world. She couldn't help smiling back.

"OK, why not?" she said.

One Step Beyond

The next day was when Eve was seeing Alex for their date to see 'Jersey Boys'. He leaned across and whispered to her, as everyone listened to the conversation from the past.

"Can't wait for tonight!" He gave her a surreptitious wink and put his hand down next to hers, his index finger reaching across and giving her hand a gentle, tingling caress. She shivered. It reminded her of the scene in Silence of the Lambs, where Hannibal Lecter, the dangerous cannibal, caresses Clarice's finger with his as he hands her the documents through the prison bars. Yikes! Hopefully Alex wasn't like him!

He took her to the show and afterwards they went back to his flat for a drink. She sat on his couch while he fetched the wine, looking at the paintings he had on the walls and the plain, minimal decor of his apartment. The paintings were abstracts; colourful but basically large, overpriced, blobs and splashes that could be claimed to represent anything at all. Not her taste. Nor was she in any way minimalist herself. In fact, she was more of a hoarder. She liked to keep things out that she was working on or that needed action so she wouldn't forget them, and she also liked to have pictures of family, friends and pets on the walls. Either those or beautiful landscapes of Norway and such places. Plus, Alex had no books on display – didn't he read at all?

Alex returned with the drinks on a tray and placed them on the glass coffee table, sliding in beside her on the huge leather sofa. He gave her a glass and opened the wine, a good vintage Bordeaux apparently, though she wouldn't have known either way. He clinked glasses with her.

"Cheers, Eve! Here's to us!"

He smiled and held his glass up to the light, then inhaled the aroma, before swirling the wine around, sniffing it again and then sipped it, savouring the taste, she supposed.

She suppressed a giggle by sipping her own wine. It was fine and she took a larger mouthful, letting the blood-red liquid slide down her throat.

"Like it?" he asked. She nodded, smiled and took another sip.

"Want to go out on the balcony?" he asked, inclining his head toward the glass doors leading onto it.

"OK," she replied, following him out. As they passed one of the paintings, a huge red blob in the centre of an explosion of pinks, purples, blues and greens, he paused and looked at it, his head on one side. "This is meant to represent passion," he said, watching her closely to gauge her reaction. She raised her eyebrows. "You see that pink element there – that looks like a breast to me." His arm was somehow draped casually around her shoulders as he gestured towards the painting with his wine glass. "And that is incredibly phallic, don't you think?" His face was close to hers, his gaze locked to hers, eyes twinkling with mischief, his voice husky. Suddenly, his lips were on hers and she was pressed up against the wall, his eager body pushing up against her. She was still holding her drink and managed to gasp out:

"Wait! Let me put my wine down." She drew back and he took the glass from her hand, deftly placing it on a nearby table along with his own.

He stepped back towards her and she suddenly panicked. As he reached for her, she took a step back, her hands on his shoulders, trying to fend him off. She wasn't ready for this. It felt alien, her sudden vivid image of him making love to her. It felt wrong.

"Alex, please, can we cool things down a bit? I really feel I need to get to know you a little better before…"

She broke off and looked up at him, shaking her head slightly.

He drew a deep sigh. He stood in front of her, one hand on the wall beside her head, the other on her hip. He thrust himself away from the wall, his hand slapping against it in frustration and swept his fingers through his dark hair.

"I'll drive you home," he said, not meeting her gaze.

"Thank you. Look, I'm sorry, it's just…"

"Don't apologise – I'm the one who should be saying sorry. It's me all over. Too impatient."

He gave a mirthless smile and picked up her coat, handing it to her and putting on his jacket. Half an hour later, she was in her own house, wondering if she had made a big mistake.

Goodbye Girl

The next day, Alex barely spoke to her. Did he feel humiliated? Angry? Why were men so difficult to read?

The Fly had moved on a few years and, from the context, Richard, still at Middleham, was speaking to Warwick.

"My Lord, you know full well in what esteem I hold your daughter, Anne, but you also know that I am my brother's man in all things and have pledged my loyalty to him. Therefore, I regretfully refuse your offer of marriage to her and I and Edward both feel it would be best for all if I remove from here forthwith. I thank you for the education and shelter you have provided me these years and I will certainly miss everyone I have come to know, but my mind is clear and I will not be swayed." He didn't meet Warwick's eyes as he spoke.

"But your brother is being unreasonable. I have been more than patient with him, even when he got himself wedded to the Woodville woman. He humiliated me – I was in full negotiations with the French for a marriage to the princess Bona of Savoie. I was mortified when I found out he was already married." Warwick began pacing, punching his fist into his other palm as he strode up and down. "Then he sent me to the continent to carry out negotiations with the French and Burgundians regarding your sister, Margaret's, marriage. I favoured forming diplomatic links with the French. And what does he do?! He lets me lead them on, knowing he has already made a secret deal with the Burgundians! He made me a laughing stock again! And now he is being difficult about allowing my daughters to marry his two brothers. I cannot endure this any longer!"

Warwick's face was furious but Richard was unwavering.

"I am sorry you feel like that, but I cannot in all conscience go against the express wishes of my brother, the king. So, I will take my leave tomorrow, my Lord."

It was only a short conversation, but Eve realised, having just read about this time period, that Warwick had tried to persuade Richard and his brother, George, to wed his two daughters, Anne and Isabel. George had gone along with his plan, but Richard had refused and returned to the side of his brother, Edward, in order to support him.

She explained the background to the others and Rupert, who had made plenty of headway on the TV negotiations now and had returned permanently to listening in on 'The Fly', said:

"Anne was probably an ugly old witch, I suppose. He was probably glad of an excuse to avoid marrying her."

"I don't think so," she replied. "She was a good 'catch' because there were only the two daughters, so anyone who married one of them would end up inheriting loads of land and revenues; they were very rich heiresses. And she was only a teenager."

"But he couldn't have really cared about her, apart from the riches he would be losing. If he did, surely he would have married her, just as George did Isabel."

Rupert looked pleased with himself for working this conundrum out and began making some notes, leaning on his desk with his elbow.

But she realised that she knew this scenario wasn't true and, at first, she wondered why Rupert even thought such things – it was so obvious to her that Richard was sincerely fond of Anne. It didn't feel like passion, but a gentle love, a protective feeling. Why couldn't they see that? Then she realised that what he had said actually gave nothing away about his feelings, apart from the words 'esteem' and 'regretfully' which didn't necessarily equate to love; he could just have been being polite. So why was she so sure that he felt totally torn when he told Warwick he was leaving, that he did want to marry Anne even though his conscience would not allow him to betray his sworn loyalty to Edward?

It was her weird psychic abilities, of course. She hadn't heard or felt anything out of the ordinary until the day she had taken the spare DNA sample to work with her. Since that day, she had been experiencing emotions way beyond those she should have been feeling at the time – and also when Alex had first given her the sample; she had immediately had tears in her eyes. At the time, she had put it down to her recent split with James, but maybe it wasn't that at all. Well, whatever it was, she didn't feel she could tell the men this; she could just imagine the teasing she would get from Rupert.

Just as she was thinking about him, Rupert came over and asked her if she wanted a cup of coffee.

"Oh, yes, please, Rupes. White –"

"One sugar," he finished for her. She nodded, smiling, and he went off. She could hear him clattering around in the refreshment area and then he returned with a cup of coffee for each of them. She took a sip.

"Mmm, thanks – that's just what the doctor ordered."

"So, how was your date the other night?" he asked abruptly, his eyebrows raised.

"Oh, it was OK," she said, taken by surprise.

"Hmm. Is it going to be a regular thing, then?"

"I don't know. Possibly. Maybe."

"I suppose you'll be too busy then," he said, his lips pursed together.

"Too busy for what?" she asked.

"Oh, nothing." He paused, took a mouthful of coffee then continued. "I was going to ask if you...no, it doesn't matter."

"No, tell me, what were you going to ask me?"

"Well, you know the trouble I've had trying to understand the mediaeval English? Well, you're so good at it now, I wondered if you'd give me a bit of extra tuition. I feel rather left out of the project since I missed quite a bit."

"Sure!" she said. "What about tonight?" As she said it, she realised someone had passed behind her and she glanced round. It was Alex.

"Yes, great! Yes!" Rupert said. "Shall I stay behind after school, Miss?"

She couldn't help smiling and they arranged for Rupert to drive over to hers after work. She would meet him there, as she also had her car with her.

When she arrived, she found him waiting on her doorstep, arms folded across his chest.

"What time do you call this?" he joked. "That's what you get when females are allowed to drive."

He gave her a wide grin and she couldn't help smiling as she opened the door. She led the way inside and switched on the light, stooping down to give Samantha a stroke. The cat rubbed against her hand and meowed loudly.

"Are you hungry, Sweetie?" she said.

"Well, I wouldn't say no to a nibble, Petal," Rupert quipped, a wicked twinkle in his eye.

Eve couldn't suppress a burst of laughter. "Oh, you!" she said giving him a playful slap on his shoulder. "OK, is a sandwich alright?"

"Fantastic, thanks!"

"Coffee? I have a latte machine."

"Ooh, how can I refuse an offer like that!"

He sat down on her sofa, seeming to take up most of it with his large frame, and Eve went into the kitchen, fed the cats and then made a ham and tomato sandwich and a latte for herself and Rupert, bringing them into the lounge on a tray.

"Right then, shall we start the lesson and eat at the same time?"

"Yeah, can do," he said as if it wasn't his idea at all.

She brought over her laptop and squeezed in beside him, firing it up while she took a bite out of her sandwich. Chewing slowly, she clicked the mouse and went online. She clicked on a YouTube video of a Renaissance poem, written just after Richard's time and spoken with an authentic mediaeval pronunciation. It was about a parrot. It was quickly spoken, but had subtitles which helped a great deal to associate the sounds with the writing. She thought it would help Rupert to get a general feel for the spoken mediaeval word.

"Bloody hell, that's fast!" he protested, crumbs falling out of his mouth and landing on the carpet. Lucky she wasn't house-proud.

"It is, but if you can follow this, then listening to Richard should be easy, don't you think?

He looked at her ruefully. "Maybe, but I'm rubbish at languages. I was more number-orientated at school and the only language I'm fluent in is gibberish."

"Oh, don't be negative. Haven't you heard of the law of attraction? If you believe you are bad at languages, you will be – you attract whatever you think about."

He didn't reply, just looked at her with his eyebrows raised, a sceptical smirk on his lips.

She continued: "Anyway, let's get started. We can stop and start it and go over it several times. Don't worry – I'll teach you 'mediaeval' if it kills me!"

They spent the next couple of hours working at it and laughing. Rupert was so easy to talk to compared with Alex, whom she felt slightly intimidated by, and Stellan, who was incapable of casual conversation. The sound of her mobile cut through their laughter.

She smiled apologetically to Rupert, picked up the phone and swiped to answer the call.

"Hi Alex," she said, turning away and walking into the kitchen as she listened. She didn't notice Rupert's frown as she put the coffee machine on.

She returned five minutes later with another latte each and sat down again beside Rupert.

"So, where were we?" she said, feeling suddenly awkward. The atmosphere of easy companionship had disappeared.

He ignored her question. "What did he want?" he asked, making it sound as if the devil himself was calling her.

"Not that it's any business of yours, but he wanted to arrange a date for tomorrow."

He grunted and took a large swig of coffee, keeping his eyes on the computer screen.

"And did you accept?"

"Yes, of course. We get on well."

He downed the rest of his coffee and stood up.

"Well, I'd better go. It's getting late. See you in the office…And thanks for helping with the translation."

She was taken by surprise, confused by his abrupt decision to leave.

"Oh, OK then. You're welcome… See you tomorrow."

She followed him to the front door and watched him run through the rain to his car. Then she closed the door and sat back down on the sofa, her home feeling strangely empty to her.

What Do You Want?

Alex had suggested going to the cinema and picked Eve up the next evening, his smart, sporty Jaguar purring as she slid into the passenger seat. He leaned towards her, proffering his cheek for a kiss and she complied, although it seemed rather false and a little presumptive.

He took her to see a romcom, and they shared popcorn. After a while he took her hand, but, although she was wondering whether he would lean in for a kiss, he was the perfect gentleman and never tried anything at all. By the end of the film she had relaxed and he suggested a local tapas bar for drinks and a bite to eat. He parked the car close to his apartment and they walked around the corner to the restaurant. While they were eating, she found the talk flowing quite well – he was a great listener and his recent apparent sullen shunning of her now seemed to be forgotten. He was back to his previous charming self. They chatted about various subjects and the conversation invariably came around to their work and the current project.

"So, do you think we will find out anything valuable about the fate of the princes?" he asked, taking a bite of tomato bread.

"Well, I'm sure we will get something – whether it will be explicitly about the princes, I don't know. I hope so – it would be incredibly exciting, don't you think?"

"Mm, definitely," he mumbled, as he chewed the bread. "Excuse me," he said, his hand covering his mouth.

Eve smiled and picked up an olive with a cocktail stick. As she savoured the salty taste, Alex finished his mouthful of bread and said:

"What was that joke all about, then?"

"What joke?" She looked up into his eyes.

"You know, the other day when you said you could hear other people and sound effects. What was the point? It wasn't even that funny."

She hesitated and, keeping silent, finished eating the olive. Then she shrugged and gave an embarrassed smile.

"I'm not very good at jokes. I just thought it would be funny, I suppose."

She knew she didn't sound very convincing – she had never been much good at lying.

He took a forkful of meatball and chewed it slowly, watching her face with a puzzled frown. He swallowed and ran his tongue around his teeth, seeking out any small morsels of food.

"Anyway, it's a pity that Stellan can't track other people's voices too – it would be invaluable in clarifying the various situations, wouldn't it?"

She breathed a silent sigh of relief and smiled back at him – thank goodness he had let that particular subject drop.

"Yes, indeed it would," she said, helping herself to some patatas fritas.

After a delicious meal and good wine, they left the tapas bar and he hailed a taxi to take her home, paying the driver in advance and giving her a quick peck on the mouth. She wasn't sure whether to be relieved or insulted that he hadn't tried to take her back to his place. Still, he had obviously taken her words from their last date to heart – she had said she wasn't ready, so he was clearly giving her some space and time, trying not to rush her. Relieved then, she decided.

When she got home, she noticed a message from Rupert on her mobile – she must have not heard it arrive in the noise of the bar. She opened it.

Hi Eve, just wondered if you were free tomoz for more tutoring! :D Rupes.

She couldn't help the grin on her face and replied: *Sure, why not? – see you after work. Want me to cook? :) E*

There was a ping almost immediately and she saw a thumbs up symbol and another inanely grinning emoji.

She plugged the phone into her charger – it was getting low – and made herself a cup of hot chocolate. She sat and watched some light-hearted comedy show, Sophie asleep on her lap, Samantha beside her and her furry slippers on her feet.

Written At Rising

Eve had helped Rupert with the mediaeval language lessons again a few nights before and she really thought he could be dyslexic. Only mildly so, but he did seem to struggle with pronunciation at times and his spelling was... creative; he would sometimes transpose letters. But he was eager to learn and with a lot of patience from Eve and perseverance from him, he had finally begun making headway. He was settled back in the group again and seemed to be following most of Richard's words. Alex had been polite and friendly to Eve but they had not had any more dates.

They were using one of Richard's surviving letters to pinpoint him at a time in 1469. He was at Castle Rising in Norfolk.

"So, Dickon, I have received urgent news of a new rebellion in the North and I need you to bring a goodly force of men-at-arms to assist me in quelling it. We must leave as soon as possible. It will be vital for me to have someone I can trust with me."

"But, Ned... Sire, I was not expecting... I mean, I ... I... of

111

course I am at your Grace's disposal, as always. However, to raise enough men to help quell a rebellion, that requires money, lots of it. I am sorely afraid I do not yet have the means to provide for them… their pay, their arming…"

His voice trailed off.

"Well, you will have to find a way, will you not? You must have men who are obligated to you for various reasons. Plus, you are now the holder of lands from the Duchy of Lancaster, are you not?"

"Yes, Sire. I do not understand."

Edward laughed.

"It is obvious. Write to them and ask them to loan you some money for the time being. You have shown them good lordship and they will owe you their support now. Or think about Lancaster and who is Chancellor of the Duchy. But I expect you to attend me north along with your men. We shall go via Fotheringhay, where I have commanded men to muster, and Nottingham. Understood?" Edward lowered his head, not in submission but as an angry bull does before it charges. He was showing his authority and fixed Richard with his steely gaze.

"Of course, your Grace," Richard replied, bowing before his brother.

"You may leave," Edward said and turned back to the game of chess that he was playing against Lord Hastings, his long-time friend.

Richard left the chamber quietly, chewing his lower lip in thought. Who could he write to requesting a loan? He wandered back to his own private chamber a few doors away from the king's. He tried to remember who the Chancellor of the Duchy of Lancaster was.

He sent for a scribe as soon as he had settled himself at his desk, a goblet of wine at his side. As he sipped the cool liquid a name came to him. There was a knock at the door and he called out: "You may enter."

A young man, his hair soft and fair to his shoulders and his beard not yet past the downy stage, entered and bowed low before him. He waved his hand as he had seen Edward do countless times, to indicate the lad should rise.

"A letter please, Giles."

"Aye, your Grace." Giles strode proudly over to the writing desk in the corner, plucked up a trimmed quill and dipped it confidently into the ink. He then selected a pristine piece of vellum and sat there, his eyes on Richard, his quill poised. Richard began to dictate, speaking slowly and clearly so that the scribe could keep up with his words.

"Headed 'the Duke of Gloucester'. Right trusty and well-beloved, we greet you well. And for as much as the king's good grace has appointed me to attend upon his highness into the north parts of his land, which will be to my great cost and charge, whereunto I am so suddenly called that I am not so well purveyed of money therefore as behoves me to be. And therefore pray you, as my special trust is in you, to lend me a hundred pounds of money until Easter next coming, at which time I promise you shall be truly thereof content and paid again, as the bearer hereof shall inform you. To whom I pray you give credence therein and show me such friendliness in the same as I may do for you hereafter, whereunto you shall find me ready. Written at Rising, the 24th day of June." He paused, licking his lips in concentration. "Read that back to me, please."

The scribe did as he was bid, whereupon Richard took the quill to sign the letter with an assured flourish, R Gloucester, and, after a moment's hesitation, added a postscript in his own hand:

113

'Sir J Say I pray you that you fail me not at this time of my great need as you will that I show you my good lordship in that matter that you labour me for.' He then rolled the sheet into a tight cylinder and sealed it with red wax, imprinting this with his personal signet.

Stellan paused the machine. "What was that all about?" he asked, his eyes narrowed in concentration. The language was a lot more formal than most of that they had previously heard, but Eve knew exactly what was meant.

"He wanted to borrow a hundred pounds from Sir John Say. Edward had taken him by surprise with this and he was short of funds." She had said it before she really thought about it. David looked at her quizzically.

"How do you know that, Eve?"

"I can pick up the mediaeval English quite well now, and he was dictating, so spoke quite slowly and clearly, although the language was formal."

"Yes, I think we can all get the gist of the words now, some of us better than others," he muttered, glancing at Rupert. "But how did you know who it was written to? He didn't mention that."

"It was in the postscript he wrote himself at the end."

"What postscript? The last I heard him speak was to ask the scribe to read it back. How do you know there was a postscript?"

"I think I've heard about it from... from Sue," she improvised, feeling her cheeks flushing pink. "That must be it."

"Great, well, let us get this saved, labelled and archived. Eve, can you ring Sue and find out for sure about the letter? You can all go home a little early, but I expect you all to be here sharp tomorrow, OK?"

They all agreed and, as Eve packed up her desk, she wondered what Sue could tell her about this letter, if it still existed.

She rang her as soon as she had got home and made herself a cup of coffee.

"Hiya, Eve," Sue said cheerfully. "Is this a social call or are you in need of my help?"

"A bit of both," Eve replied, taking a large sip of the tea and making herself comfortable on the sofa, beside Sophie, her fluffy, tortoiseshell cat. "Are there any letters that survive that Richard wrote? In particular was there one from 1469, when he was staying at a place called Rising?"

"Oh yes, that's Castle Rising in Norfolk. I have been to visit that castle – it has the hugest moat around it and quite a bit of the castle remains. It's very atmospheric!"

"Oh wow! It sounds amazing," Eve said. "But what about the letter?"

"It was the earliest letter that has been found signed by him, when he was sixteen. He wrote it to the Chancellor of the Duchy of Lancaster, a knight called John Say, it is thought – at least that is what the postscript seems to be spelling out – those original mediaeval manuscripts are pretty difficult to decipher. It looks like 'Sir J Say'."

"He was only sixteen? But he sounds so mature," Eve exclaimed.

"Well, they had to mature quickly in those days, didn't they? He was already Duke of Gloucester and became Constable of England round about then – he had to judge people and pass sentence on them, sometimes death sentences, executions. Then he had to oversee the carrying out of them. At sixteen! No wonder those times were so violent with teenagers being in charge of battles and executions. Incredible really. But, of course, the average life expectancy was only in the thirties in those days."

"Really?! Oh my God!" Eve paused, horrified at the thought of teenagers being in charge. "Anyway, thanks for all the information – is there a copy available of this letter? It would be really useful."

"There might be some available on the internet, and there are some in various books too. I'll have a rake around my bookcase and see what I can find."

"Thanks, Sue, you're a real star!"

Sue changed the subject and began telling her tales of her latest shopping trip and places she'd visited while Eve's mind was wandering; she had basically proved to herself that her 'feelings' were accurate. She had known that the postscript was to Sir John Say and what it said, even though Richard hadn't said it aloud. If she could get a look at a copy of the letter, she could check what she'd thought the postscript said against the real one!

Sue was as good as her word and a couple of days later, Eve was perusing a book which contained most of the significant documents associated with Richard's life. She turned to the contents pages and found a reference to 'Good Lordship' – that was it! The earliest surviving letter written by Richard. With trembling fingers, she turned to the page indicated and scanned the image of the document, her eyes alighting at the end, on the postscript. The writing was indeed difficult to decipher but, luckily, there was a printed transcription: 'Sir J Say I pray you that you fail me not at this time of my great need as you will that I show you my good lordship in that matter that you labour me for.' That was it! It was exactly as she had 'heard' in her

116

head after Richard had signed the document. Or no! Actually, it wasn't exactly what she had sensed because she had 'heard' the full name 'Sir John Say' rather than the Sir J Say' he'd written. It must have been his thoughts she was picking up. She was both relieved that it wasn't all her imagination and rather shocked that her psychometry skills were so accurate. Wow! Perhaps now she could trust that what she 'heard' and 'saw' and 'felt' were truly psychic links to the past, to Richard III himself.

The Ragged Staff

A few weeks later, Richard had been summoned to his brother's private chambers. Eve was glad she had the benefit of 'hearing' Edward too and sensing Richard's perception of him and his surroundings. It was almost as good as watching a film or period drama. She felt sorry for the others, who only heard Richard's words – he wasn't the most loquacious person.

"Curse him! Dickon, Warwick has gone behind my back and married Isabel to George against my explicit orders! God's blood! When will he realise I am the king, not he! He thinks I am still the young boy he steered to take the throne. Does he not realise how this undermines my authority? If I let him get away with this, every other baron or earl will be rebelling along with him – it will end up like the situation King John had to deal with. I cannot have it, Dickon! I cannot!"

"Yes, Sire, you are right. Warwick has become over-mighty – he thinks he can change his mind and depose you, putting George in your place."

117

Richard used the formal mode of address since Edward was on the edge of a towering rage and he had seen how the slightest extra annoyance could tip him over the edge; he didn't want to be the one to do the tipping.

"How dare he!? And do you know what he is saying? He has brought up that illegitimacy story again – that I am the bastard son of a French archer. As if Maman would have lain with a common archer! She will be furious with George for going along with it. But, of course, all he has ever wanted is the crown, even if he has to slander our lady mother to get it."

"What do you intend to do?"

"I will command him to appear before me and apologise – Warwick too, of course – and confiscate some of their lands. They will both have to grovel at my feet before I will forgive them."

Stellan, David and Rupert asked her to explain what had happened. She told them that basically Warwick had become estranged from Edward because he had expected to be the power behind the throne but had been sadly disillusioned after Edward's marriage, when the Woodvilles had become the most influential force around Edward.

What Kind of Man Am I?

On 29th October, Edward charged Richard with three commissions of array, for Shropshire, Gloucestershire and Worcestershire, in order to control the Welsh Marches. This was his first foray into military command, but he was helped by having several older, more experienced advisers, such as Walter Devereux, Lord Ferrers. Also involved in Richard's expeditions into Wales to quell disputes was William

Herbert, the young Earl of Pembroke. Some of the unrest had occurred after Herbert's father had been executed after his defeat at the Battle of Edgecote. Another who attended with Richard was James Harrington, who was famous for having helped to capture the old king Henry VI when he was a fugitive from Edward in 1465. Richard was talking to him now as they rode to Wales.

"So, you contend that your father died after your brother, John, both at the Battle of Wakefield, where my own father was killed, and that his land should have then passed to you, as the next son?"

Richard paused as his mount shied a little at the sudden flight of a bird out of the bushes they were passing.

"Yes, and in any case, John only had two daughters and the estates are held 'in tail male' so they can't inherit." Harrington smiled ruefully. "Of course, Thomas Stanley contests this and has been granted the estates and the marriages of the girls. He even tried to have me indicted illegally. If, as you say, your brother intends to grant you lands in their territory, they will not be happy about it."

"I am sure they will not. But you have managed to hold on to your castle of Hornby despite it being granted to the Stanleys, have you not?" Richard grinned.

"Yes, so far. But the Stanleys are tenacious and will not easily give up what they feel is theirs."

"Well, I can see why you think it unfair. Edward does at times make his decisions based on expediency and patronage, rather than fairness. I will speak to him about it, but he knows his own mind, so do not count on my influence."

"Well, I am grateful for your support nevertheless," James smiled as they rode on.

What's Up?

"What is happening here, do you know?" asked David. "The Stanleys were the ones who betrayed Richard at Bosworth, weren't they?"

Eve had been reading up on this period of Richard's life and answered immediately.

"That's right, and this dispute involving the Harringtons could be at the root of the reason why, not the princes at all. The two Harrington brothers, James and Robert, were retainers of Richard and fought with him at Bosworth. But their father and older brother, John, had both been killed at the Battle of Wakefield, where Richard's father had been defeated and beheaded by Margaret of Anjou."

The others nodded, except for David who looked confused. Eve tried to explain.

"By the laws of inheritance, if the father had died first, his estate would go to John, the eldest brother, and as he then died soon after, John's daughters would be the heiresses. James disputes this because if John died first, then James became his father's heir and would inherit after he died. Even if it was a matter of a few minutes."

"I see," said David. "It's a bit complicated."

"Yes, and also James says the estates couldn't be inherited by a woman anyway. The following March, Richard visited Hornby Castle, which James held on to despite Edward's orders that the Stanleys could have it. He had been granted quite a lot of land and power in the Stanleys' territory and they had to pay him fees from it. They didn't pay them until Edward wrote threatening them, so they were in conflict with Richard even then."

"Wasn't that all sorted out by the time Richard became king, though?" Alex asked.

"Well, yes, but when he was king, he decided to reopen the case and intended to reverse Edward's decision, so the Stanleys went over to Tudor."

The men all looked thoughtful as they contemplated the tangled politics of the late fifteenth century.

Chapter Four

London, Twenty-first Century

Something Inside (So Strong)

Eve was sitting beside Rupert in her lounge and leaning over his shoulder to see the document he was studying, while a recording of one of the Richard III sessions played. The document was a transcript of the session, verbatim, by Mary Mander. They had been working on it for the last two hours and, at last, they seemed to be making some headway with Rupert's ability.

"I actually understood nearly all of that without referring to the transcript!" he said delightedly.

"Great! Want a beer to celebrate?"

"Why not? I could have one and still be OK to drive."

Eve went into the kitchen and took a cold lager for each of them out of the fridge. She handed one of the cans to Rupert and pulled the ring on her own. She became aware of his eyes on her and turned her own to meet his gaze, raising her eyebrows in silent question.

He frowned, took a swig of lager, swilling it around his mouth to savour the taste before he spoke.

"You look tired, girl," he said.

"Thanks for that!" she said, making a face at him.

"No, I mean it – you look exhausted. Are you OK?"

"Yes, of course I am." But she looked down at the coffee table, her finger tracing a circle in a small puddle of spilled beer.

He said nothing, but lowered his head and fixed her with his gaze, his expression stern.

"Is that Alex keeping you up late?" he said, a teasing tone to his voice. She whisked her head up to scowl at him.

"Rupert! That's none of your business! But no, I haven't been out with him recently – it isn't him." She again avoided his eyes and swirled her beer around in the can.

"What is it then?" Rupert asked.

She sighed and shook her head, pressing her lips together.

"I just... I... it's just work taking it out of me. It's draining."

He narrowed his eyes suspiciously.

"It's not just that though, is it?"

She met his gaze and hesitated. Could she tell him the truth?

"Has that bastard hurt you? He has, hasn't he?" Rupert had straightened up on the sofa and looked as if he was about to march out of the door and confront Alex there and then.

"No! Whatever gave you that idea?"

"What is it, then? You are so obviously under stress – tell me, Eve."

His puppy dog eyes pleaded with her and she realised he was genuinely concerned.

"Do you promise not to laugh or tell anyone else, if I tell you?"

"Maybe," he said, cagily.

"Cross your heart!" she said.

He rolled his eyes and dutifully made the sign of the cross over his chest. "OK, I promise not to laugh or tell anyone else – providing you are not being deliberately hurt by him... or anyone."

"OK, well, I'm not, so you can forget about that." She took a deep breath and let it out a little shakily. "You know I have been doing those psychic classes?"

"Ye-es?"

"Well, I have found out I'm really quite good at psychometry – when you hold something and can sense its energy and vibrations. You can tell a lot about who owned the object, what they were like and I sometimes see images in my head which relate."

"What's all this got to do with stressing you out?"

"Well, I have a small piece of Richard's tooth DNA and I found that, if I carry it with me at work, I can hear and see other stuff apart from what Richard is saying – I can even smell and taste things. But it takes some concentration and it does drain me. Plus, I have to be careful not to let the others know what's going on."

"Why?"

"Well, one, because they might think I'm crazy and two, I sort of stole the tooth sample."

He gave a short laugh, then stood up.

"Right, if you don't trust me enough to tell me the truth, I'm going! See you tomorrow."

He picked up his jacket from the back of a chair and made for the door.

"It *is* the truth!" she said, her heart thudding with the shock of his doubting her.

"Yeah, right!" he called as he slammed the door behind him.

Eve couldn't help herself – she went over to the window and sneaked a peep outside to watch Rupert cross the street and slide into his battered old Peugeot. She could see the dent in the passenger door even from her viewpoint behind the curtain in her flat. She saw him sitting in the driver's seat, staring fixedly ahead of him for what seemed like ages.

Then he took out his mobile phone and pressed a few buttons. He was speaking to someone and waving his hand around as he spoke. She smiled to herself remembering how he would often knock things over or whack someone in the eye when he got excited about something, but then her brow furrowed in a frown. Suppose he was telling David or Stellan about her little secret? But he hadn't seemed to believe her, so telling someone else would be unlikely, surely.

She felt a strange sadness as he finally indicated and drew away. Why hadn't he believed her? She recognised that she had been placing quite a lot of hope in his support, but she couldn't count on him now. She watched his car turn the corner, sighed and turned away, deciding to research some more about Richard.

More Than Words

The next day, Rupert seemed pretty much his normal jokey self, but when she ventured to ask if he wanted another mediaeval language lesson that evening, he smiled but said:

"No, sorry, I can't tonight – I've got a date!"

Eve's heart thumped in her chest. Don't be silly, Eve, he has always been just a friend. It's great he has a date. She thought about it and couldn't remember him ever having mentioned anyone before. Oh, yes, he had – there had been a girl, Camilla, whom he had dated for a while in his university days. She nodded to him, smiling,

"Oh, great! Have a good evening."

"I will, girl, I will!!" he said, grinning inanely.

She rolled her eyes and turned back to her screen. She was typing up her account of the last 'Fly' session. David had asked her to keep a record of their progress and highlight any information that might have any bearing on the matter of the Princes in the Tower. Unbeknown to David, she was also documenting her own experiences; the sights, smells, sounds and feelings of mediaeval England. In fact, all the vivid sensations she had known through her psychometry of Richard's DNA sample, including her intimate knowledge of his real feelings regarding the different problems, joys and challenges of his eventful life. She wasn't sure why she wanted to record everything, but she found she had to – it was as if each day's 'eavesdropping' would swirl around in her head unless she got it off her chest and written down in her personal journal.

Their afternoon session was quite important, compared to many of their recent ones, which had involved dry documents, incomprehensible court cases and mundane aspects of Richard's daily life.

They had discussed the time that Warwick and George had captured Edward at Olney, holding him in Warwick's northern strongholds. He had been held at Middleham for a while until Warwick had discovered that ruling the country in Edward's name was not popular. The merchants and people wanted their king back. Orders were resisted and obstructed and, when rebellion arose and he couldn't raise an army to quell it without Edward, he realised he had to give in and allow the captive king to leave. Edward and Warwick had reconciled for a while, but the brief rapprochement hadn't lasted long and George and Warwick had rebelled again, until Edward had pursued them so wrathfully and implacably, they had had to flee to France, taking their families, including the now heavily pregnant Isabel, with them over the narrow sea. It was this period they were witnessing now.

There Goes My First Love

"By God's nails, now Warwick has gone too far!" Edward flung the letter he had just received into the hearth, watched the flames begin licking away at the words reporting his cousin's treason and began pacing up and down like a caged lion. "There will be no forgiveness this time, he will soon see the strength of my wrath, the ungrateful, hell-spawned, roguish knave!"

"What has he done now, Sire?" Richard stood in his brother's private chamber, his forehead lined with worry. He hated this conflict between his adored elder brother and the unholy alliance of George and their cousin, Warwick.

"Guess! No, do not trouble yourself – you would never guess it. He has fled over to France – to the hands of Louis the Spider King – along with his wife and daughters – and George."

Edward sauntered over to the side table and helped himself to a large chunk of cheese and a piece of manchet bread.

"But was not Isabel great with child? Surely she would not have been made to leave their home at this late stage?"

"Well, she was, apparently. She lost the child. It seems Warwick will even risk his daughter's and unborn grandchild's lives to further his march up the ladder of power."

"She lost it? Poor Isabel – she did not deserve that. She was only obeying her father and George."

Richard's nimble fingers toyed with his ring, twisting it round and round as he thought what the girl must be suffering.

"True – as is Anne." Edward said, glancing sideways at Richard as he chewed the bread and cheese.

Richard's restless hands suddenly quieted and his face flushed a bright pink as he tried to regain his composure. He cleared his throat before he spoke.

"Anne? What of her?" Richard asked, attempting to make it sound like a casual enquiry. There was the faintest suggestion of a tremor in his voice and it had risen up slightly from its normal timbre.

"Warwick has married her to the son of that she-wolf, Margaret of Anjou: Edward of Lancaster. Then he intends to put old, mad Harry back on the throne in my place! He has some nerve, I will give him that."

He took a swig from his goblet of Rhenish. Richard was silent, the previous flush of blood drained from his face completely, leaving him ghostly pale. He began to bite his lower lip, but could not trust himself to speak without betraying his feelings.

Edward glanced at Richard, then quickly back to his goblet. He swirled the rich liquid around a little and then downed the remainder.

"Thank the Heavens you are not like George and wisely decided to decline Warwick's offer to marry Anne, eh? Else I might now be preparing to fight two brothers for the crown, instead of just one." He sighed. "I am sorry Dickon, but the deed is done. I know you cared for her once, but the time has come to forget about her now. You should find yourself a willing wench to tumble – another woman would surely divert your mind from Anne."

Richard did not reply at once, but lowered his head and then nodded slowly.

"You are right, Ned. I must forget her now. I just hope that little brute treats her well; she is so delicate, although she has a great spirit."

He pursed his lips and then licked them to moisten them.

"Good! Good! Come now, brother and try this good Rhenish. You have eaten and drunk nothing this evening."

Richard took the proffered goblet and thanked Edward, swigging down the drink in one. Edward refilled it.

"That's more like it. Let us make merry tonight and, on the morrow, we will show the world that the strength and unity of the brothers York are not to be taken lightly."

After an hour or more of downing cup after cup of Rhenish, Richard's thoughts of Anne started to drift away and he even laughed at a few of his brother's silly jokes, but he refused the next refill.

"Thank you, Ned, but I think I would rather retire for the night, if it is all the same to you. It has been a tiring day."

Edward leaned over and clasped his brother's slim hands in his own large ones, making Richard feel like he was a child again.

"Good night, brother. Sleep well – we have much planning to do on the morrow."

Richard bowed and left the room, relieved to have kept control when the news about Anne had come as such a shock. He had somehow always thought that one day they would marry. As he made his way, in a somewhat wobbly fashion, through the maze of corridors to his guest room, he abruptly decided to go outside for a breath of fresh air to clear his head before going to his bed.

And he needed the privy after all that wine. After he had relieved his toilet needs, he went out into the herb garden, knowing he would be unable to sleep yet, and wanting some time alone. However, his need for solitude was not to be met this night.

He had just turned the corner and walked through the stone arch, when he heard voices ahead of him; a male and a female – obviously on some amorous assignation. He sighed, intending to turn back – he didn't need any reminders that he had no special someone to meet with – when the woman screamed and the man raised his voice, yelling at the woman furiously. The sound of a slap resounded through the night air, followed by a bellow of rage and a scuffling noise. Richard hurried into the herb garden to see what was afoot and found a man holding a woman backed up against an apple tree, fumbling with her skirts and muffling her cries with his other hand as he attempted to have his way with her. Richard grabbed the man's shoulder and pulled him away. The man cursed under his breath and veered round to face Richard. It was William Hastings, that notorious womaniser and Edward's partner in sin on many occasions. Richard was unable to see who the girl was, as her face was in shadow and she had lowered her chin in shame.

"William, the wench is not willing, you boor! Leave her be! Can you not find a woman who will agree to your advances? Are you that desperate?"

"Dreary Dickon!" Hastings said. "At least I have some fire in my loins – have you ever even had a woman? Sometimes I wonder how you and the king are brothers, you are so different."

But his words were just bravado; he knew that Richard outranked him and dared not defy him. He gave a short, barking laugh and turned on his heel, marching off through the arch.

"Are you harmed?" Richard asked the woman, who had rearranged her clothes and stood there trembling, as if she believed Richard would simply take Hastings' place. "What is your name?"

"I... I am Alys, Sir," she said, attempting to curtsey and almost overbalancing, her legs were so shaky. He grasped her arms and steadied her. "Are you really the king's brother?"

"Yes, but there is no need to curtsey here. Yet you have not answered my question. Did he harm you?"

"No, your Grace, you stopped him before he could do anything much. It was my own fault – I was foolish. I trusted that he was an honourable man; he told me he would show me where to pick the lavender to help me sleep. My brother stands accused of theft and I am frantic with worry that he will hang. Then he began complimenting me and then touching me and, when I protested, he just... he just... tried to force me."

"Hmm, do you know Lord Hastings? I doubt it, if you trusted he was honourable. He is well known for his liking for women – any women."

"I have never met him before, but he was dressed so splendidly I thought he must be a gentleman."

"Fine clothes do not always make fine character. You would do well to remember that, Alys." He smiled at her and she returned it shyly. "Now, may I escort you – well, where do you wish to be escorted? Do you live within the palace?"

"Yes, my Lord, I am one of the Queen's ladies-in-waiting."

"Come then, I will escort you back and, on the way, you will tell me all about the troubles you have with your brother. You said he had been accused of theft? Who was it who has accused him?"

"It was someone very close to the king himself; Sir Anthony Woodville."

Richard let out a low whistle. "I can see why you are worried. The Queen's family is not known for their mercy. What did your brother steal?"

"Nothing, your Grace! He was caught with Sir Anthony's dagger – Giles saw it lying on the ground and recognised it as Sir Anthony's – he thought he might get a reward for taking it back, only he was caught before he could do so and of course they thought he was stealing it. He has never stolen anything in his life! He says Sir Anthony must have had a frayed thong securing it that allowed it to fall off. Have you any suggestions?"

The girl's fists were clenched and diamond teardrops threatened to fall from her large, blue eyes. Richard's protectiveness was immediately triggered – the girl's eyes even reminded him a little of Anne. Or perhaps it was just that Anne was at the forefront of his thoughts. He stopped and took her by the shoulders, firmly turning her to look at him.

"I will see what I can do, but Anthony has the king's ear and he will not always listen to others, so I cannot promise anything. Do not get your hopes up too much."

"I won't," she whispered and smiled up at him, tears, of gratitude now, sparkling in her eyes.

Let You Love Me

A few days later, they had discovered another encounter with Alys. She had sought Richard out to thank him, for he had managed to persuade Anthony Woodville to give her brother the benefit of the doubt. He had checked his thong and had indeed found it to be frayed, not cut as it would have been had the dagger been stolen.

"Your Grace, I am so grateful to you for helping us – Sir Anthony has even recompensed my brother for the time he spent in Newgate. He has done quite well out of the whole affair, all thanks to you! And you saved me from that horrible man, Hastings!"

"Arise, Alys, there is no need to kneel before me. I am glad I was able to help on both counts."

He raised her from her obeisance and suddenly she was in his arms, embracing him around his waist and resting her head on his chest. He was so taken aback, he did nothing, just looked down onto the top of her head, his arms held stiffly out to the sides. He could see a tiny, fair wisp of hair which had escaped the head-dress she was wearing. It made her seem so vulnerable, like a child. Slowly, he relaxed and his arms went around her, tentatively. She turned her face up to his. Her eyes were wide, sea blue, like Anne's, her chin small and firm. He took it in his hand, caressing underneath it with his index finger. Her mouth was so close to his, he could feel her breath on his skin, smell the aroma of cinnamon, sweet and tempting. Then their lips met and he moaned against her mouth, feeling her warm body press firmly against his.

"Alys!" he breathed, as desire took him out of control and he embraced her soft curves, his breathing quickening. "Do you want?…"

She nodded, her eyes never leaving his. He took a deep breath and walked to the door, shooting the bolt across. He turned, leaning back against it as if to feel its solidity, and murmured: "Are you sure?"

"Yes," she whispered taking a step towards him.

He took her hand and drew her past the desk through another door, which led to his bedchamber. As he helped her disrobe, he sighed and said softly: "How lovely you are, Alys."

Eve switched off the machine.

"That's enough – we don't need to listen to any more, do we?" She didn't really want Alex spying on her as she struggled to control her own reactions to Richard's sexual encounters.

David rolled his eyes but they all agreed it would not further their research.

Stiletto Heels

As Eve left the office that evening, she caught sight of Rupert striding over to a young woman. The woman was dressed in an obviously expensive coat and fashionable hat. Her handbag and shoes matched perfectly, the heels on the shoes so high that it looked as if she might teeter off them at any moment. She wobbled a bit as she leaned forward to offer her cheek to Rupert to kiss and grabbed onto his arm. An obvious ploy to use her ridiculous shoes as an excuse to grab him, Eve thought uncharitably. Then she smiled to herself. What did she care, anyway? But she couldn't help looking again, to try to see who it was that Rupert was going out with.

It's Camilla, I'm sure of it! She said to herself, as she recognised the upturned nose and pert ruby lips of Rupert's ex. She bit her lip thoughtfully. From what she remembered, Camilla had broken Rupert's heart before – she hoped he wouldn't be hurt again; he didn't deserve that. He was basically one of the good guys. Oh well, he was a grown-up – it was up to him to decide whom to date. She turned away to where she had left her car and got in. She threw the remote in the central alcove and started the engine. She gave a sigh, chewing her lower lip as she looked in the mirror and pulled away. She was feeling a little sad as she opened her front door and entered her flat. She picked up the post and absently sorted through it, her thoughts remaining with Rupert and Camilla, until she saw an envelope with a solicitor's address on the top corner.

Oh no! What is this all about? she thought, as she tore it open. She guessed it was something to do with James. Perhaps he was saying how they would divide the flat and contents. She took a deep breath and, with shaking hands, unfolded the letter. She scanned through the words, not fully taking them in, and then re-read them.

"What?!!" she said, aloud. "You bloody bastard! You bloody, bloody bastard!!"

She tore the letter up into several pieces and sent them fluttering to the floor. It was a notice to quit the flat – James was claiming it was his and not a joint asset. It was true it had originally been his and she had moved in when they had decided to live together. True, she had not actually paid the mortgage directly, but she had used her own earnings to pay the household bills and get the shopping. She had thought James was at least going to play fair with her, since it had been he who had left. She had stupidly thought he would give her the option of buying out his share of the flat – now, it seemed, she didn't even have a share!

She sank to her knees in desolation. What could she do? Should she resist and refuse to leave? Could he force her out? Tears of both anger and grief overwhelmed her and she sat where she was on the floor and sobbed.

She glanced round the room seeing familiar objects and patterns through the prism of her tears. The wallpaper they had chosen together and hung, amid laughter, when their first few attempts had gone wrong, tearing and sticking in the wrong place, but they had succeeded in the end. The solid-oak coffee table she had fallen in love with and sighed over, knowing they couldn't afford it, but finding it waiting for her in the living room on her return from work. The sofa he had bought without consulting her, that she had hated at first but grown to love, remembering how he had made love to her on it one drunken night. She put her hands over her head and bent forwards, leaning on the expensive carpet, then curling up into the foetal position as her emotions overwhelmed her.

She lay there whimpering for several minutes, until Samantha came over to see what was happening and Eve sat up, all her tears spent, and hugged the little cat to her heart. Sophie was asleep on the sofa. There was no-one, no-one 'family' she could call; it had always been James whom she thought of as her family, whom she had turned to in a crisis and now he was the instigator of one. Her mother was in a nursing home and she couldn't worry her father with her problems. She dragged herself into the kitchen, her eyes welling up again as she noticed the coffee machine, a birthday present from James to her.

She deliberately ignored it and made herself a cup of tea instead, resolving to call a solicitor in the morning; there was nothing she could do now anyway. She picked up the cup of steaming comfort and, followed by Samantha, went into the bedroom.

Be Alright

"So, does that mean I am going to lose the flat?" Eve asked the junior partner of Sansom and Foster.

"Well, you could take it to court, but technically your boyfriend can sell it because you are not on the deeds. You say it was originally his flat and you moved in. So, as you didn't get your name added to the deeds, you don't have an automatic right to a share."

"I asked him about that and he said it didn't matter once we were co-habiting – that all of our property was jointly owned."

"Well, he was wrong, I'm afraid. As I say, you could take it to court, but if you lose you would be liable for legal costs. You do have a good case for a share, but it will take time. You don't need to decide immediately – take a little while to think it over and get back to us."

Eve put her hand up to her head and rubbed her temples. She had a splitting headache and had no idea what to do. Part of her wanted to fight James tooth and nail, but the other half didn't have the energy for a battle. She sighed and nodded, thanking the woman and rising to leave.

Back at the flat, she suddenly thought of Sue and rang her immediately, bursting into tears at the sound of her friendly voice.

"I don't know what to do, Sue! I don't want to give in, but what if I lose? I will be bankrupt. Maybe I should just let him have the flat."

"Look, why don't you come and stay with me for a while. Get away from things – it might help you to make a decision, eh?"

"Oh, I don't know. I wouldn't want to put you out."

Eve was also thinking that Sue lived outside London and it would be a much longer commute to work for her if she accepted her offer.

"Don't be silly – I would love to have you as a guest for a while – it would be fun. I could show you all my Richard III paraphernalia, now you're interested in him as well."

"What kind of 'paraphernalia'?" Eve asked.

"Oh, all sorts – jewellery, pictures, books, banners, coasters. You name it, I've probably got it!"

Eve laughed and realised she might really enjoy spending some time with Sue – they hadn't really met up in person for ages and it would be great to chat with her again face to face.

"OK, then, I will come. It's the weekend tomorrow, so I'll drive over to you on Saturday morning, if that's OK."

"Yay! It'll be great fun, Eve, I can't wait."

Loyalty Binds Me

The next day, Eve was in her car and setting the sat-nav to Bedford. She looked up at her bedroom window in the little flat and sighed. She had arranged for a neighbour to go in and feed the cats for the time being – she needed some time to work things out. As she accelerated away from the kerb, she wondered when or even if she would ever live there again.

Sue welcomed her with open arms, and it was nice to have someone to keep her company and to talk to in the evenings. They discussed their varied psychic experiences. Eve even plucked up the courage to tell Sue all about her ability to pick up on Richard's emotions and to 'hear, see and feel' the things he did. It was so good to confide in someone who actually believed in that kind of phenomenon. Sue was excited and impressed with Eve's ability.

"You should write it all down, you know."

"I have. I have two notebooks full! And I've been typing the notes up and saving them in the cloud too, just in case."

"Well, that's great but, actually, I meant you should turn it into a book."

Eve looked at her a bit taken aback. A book!

"I don't know. It's a lot to write."

"Well, you've written it down anyway, haven't you? It'll be more editing than the actual content you need to do. And you might make a bit of money; Richard III is really popular, you know?"

"What about the confidentiality though?"

"Well, that will be after the company have published their research. And they can't very well object to your psychic findings because it's personal to you, not part of their stuff. When Richard's remains were found loads of people published books and gave lectures about their part in it. It's nothing unusual."

"Hmm. I'll have to think about it," Eve said, suddenly thoughtful.

She liked staying with Sue's family and their dog, Beauty – a laid-back greyhound who was very calm and placid. She and Sue went for walks, shopped, cooked together and did some psychic exercises.

Sue had a strange gadget called a 'Ghost box' and she told Eve it could be used for communicating with spirits.

"Shall we try to speak to Richard with it?" she asked.

"How does it work?" Eve said, her curiosity aroused.

"It's basically a radio tuner, but it never settles on one station, it just keeps on passing over all the frequencies and picking up the odd word here and there. Sometimes spirit can manipulate it so that they can answer questions."

"OK, let's have a go!"

They sat in Sue's lounge and lit a candle. Sue asked for a

protective shield around them so that no negative energies could enter their circle and they visualised white light surrounding them. Sue switched on the ghost box.

The sound that emerged was a mixture of white noise interspersed with the odd word, half word or snatch of a song.

"We would like to communicate with Richard the Third. Are you there, Richard?"

Nothing dramatic happened, so Sue tried again.

"Please Richard, if you are there and are willing to speak to us, you can use the energy in this device to give your answer. Can you confirm you are there?"

The ghost box hissed, buzzed and a muffled 'Aye' came out.

Sue looked at Eve in delight.

"Did you hear that? He said 'Aye'!"

Eve nodded, unsure, as it had not been particularly clear.

"Richard, are you happy to talk to us?"

A long pause and then a clearer 'Aye'.

Sue's eyes were shining.

"We believe that the Tudors defamed your reputation. Is that correct?"

Crackle, hiss, hum. Then "Treason!" very clearly.

Sue: "Is the experiment Eve is involved with going to clear your name?"

"Fly!"

Sue looked at Eve.

"Is he telling you to flee?"

"No, that's the name of the technology we are using," Eve said, enthralled.

"Richard, will it clear your name?"

The ghost box emitted a high-pitched screech, buzzed and then: "Richard." It was very clear again.

"Oh, he has said his name. Maybe he misunderstood us. Richard, we know your name is Richard, but will the 'Fly' restore your good reputation?"

"Mayhap!"

"He says 'Mayhap', that's the old way of saying 'Perhaps'. Do you think it will clear his name, Eve?"

"I don't know – it is difficult to say. So far it is still pretty ambiguous, because although I can 'hear' and experience what Richard does, the others can't and the 'Fly' can only record his words. So, unless he actually says something that clearly refers to the princes, it still won't be proof."

Sue nodded.

"I see. How exciting though! To actually hear his voice. Of course, this ghost box isn't transmitting his actual voice, only his words filtered through radio stations. What is his voice like?"

"It's very nice actually. He is softly-spoken mostly and has a lovely singing voice. We have heard him join in with Church services and sing along to the music at banquets. We are working chronologically, so we are only up to about 1470 at the moment – it does take a lot of time."

"I bet it does – well, it's just about to get juicy, then!"

"What do you mean?"

"Well, 1470 is when Edward and Richard are driven into exile in Burgundy by Warwick."

"Oh, right! George has betrayed Edward and sided with Warwick, while Richard has stayed loyal."

The ghost box said: "Loyalty!"

They both glanced at each other and giggled.

The Great Escape

Sue was right – the very next week, Stellan had located Richard with Edward at Doncaster.

"Dickon, we must flee! Wake up, brother, or you will be dead before you cease to dream!"

Edward shook his brother firmly and Richard gasped in shock as he awoke abruptly from his rest.

"What? What is it? Edward?" He rubbed his eyes to get rid of the sleep and got out of bed immediately, pulling on his clothes without waiting for the reply; he knew his brother would not be waking him up for nothing.

"Keep quiet, Dickon. We must be swift and silent or else Montagu will have us."

"Montagu? He has turned against you, Ned?"

"Aye – but as I said, we have no time for talk – let us go!"

They joined Anthony Woodville, Will Hastings and several others downstairs and quickly found their horses, mounting up and leaving in the opposite direction to the way Montagu was reported to be approaching, according to Edward's spies. They rode hard, not sparing their horses until they were well away and the possibility of being caught was past. They made for King's Lynn.

"Dickon, I need you to go west and find those who remain loyal to me – you must tell them I have had to flee to Burgundy for a time, but that I will be back with the Duke's aid. Bring any men you can muster to our cause and then find a ship and join us over the narrow sea."

"I cannot come with you?!" Richard said, his tone not appropriate for addressing his king.

Edward frowned, but made no reprimand; after all, he was now to be a king in exile.

"It is better if we split up, just in case… Anyway, it will not be for long. You can meet up with us as soon as you have fulfilled my request. God speed, Dickon." And he bent his great frame down to embrace his brother.

"I will not let you down, Sire," said Richard softly, his manners returning as he remembered his motto – Loyaulte Me Lie: Loyalty Binds Me. He turned his horse and galloped off into the darkness, accompanied by only two retainers. It was his eighteenth birthday.

They moved the time along a few days and found Richard on a ship bound for the Netherlands. He was standing on deck staring into the distance as if he might see his brother waiting for him on the quay. He landed at Zeeland and had to make his own way to where his brother, along with the men who had managed to escape with him, was waiting for the Duke of Burgundy to decide if he would help them. He found Edward in a tavern, his clothes the worse for wear and his purse empty, reliant on the generosity of his brother-in-law. Despite this, he still somehow managed to exude self-confidence.

"We will not be here for long, brother. The Duke will soon see sense and furnish us with men and ships with which to take back my stolen throne. What news is there from England?"

"Warwick has re-crowned old, mad Harry. He wheeled him out from the Tower and paraded him through the streets of London. Poor old Harry seemed as confused as the citizens of London. It was clear who was the real power behind the throne, the true ruler of the country – Warwick."

"Well, not for long! I vow that I will have my crown back by this time next year!"

Richard thought Edward was being a little over-optimistic. It was unheard of for a king to be driven into exile and then return to win back his kingdom. But he smiled and nodded anyway. It helped to think it might be true, to have something to aim for.

In the meantime, Edward and his disconsolate band of followers frequented the taverns, tupped the wenches, played dice and drank. They had to borrow money from Louis de Gruuthuse, the man who had once been a Burgundian ambassador to Edward's court. They waited months, surviving hand to mouth over a freezing winter, until finally, persuaded by the fact that Louis of France had declared war on Burgundy, Charles, Duke of Burgundy gave them money, thirty-six ships and twelve hundred men – not as many as they had hoped, but perhaps enough. They set off from Flushing in March of 1471 and were forced north from East Anglia, finally landing on the east coast of Yorkshire.

Refused entry to Hull, Edward relied on his wits and they turned north to York, where Edward asked to parley with the mayor. Accompanying him, Richard had to smother a smile when Edward, in a voice as sincere as the Angel Gabriel, spoke to York's mayor.

"Look, William," Edward said. "I know I am no longer king – I simply want to claim my birth-right of the Dukedom of York. I will be content with that. So, will you let us in? There are few enough of us here."

Then he had smiled and the mayor had acquiesced. But, no sooner had they entered the city than Edward began recruiting men to his cause.

"William Parr and James Harrington have brought six hundred men with them already. And, Dickon, I want you to talk to George. He is keen to join up with us again, at least according to Mother. But he will have to grovel first of course!"

"So, did Edward get the throne back?" Rupert was like an eager schoolboy, impatient to know the outcome.

"Obviously, or he wouldn't have been on the throne just before Richard became king."

"So how did he do it?"

Eve laughed. "Wait and see! Stellan, can you move the action on to Barnet on…" She looked down, consulting her copious notes. "April 14th, same year – 1471."

Battle in the Mist

"So, Dickon, you will take command of the right battle. Whatever happens hold your line. I intend to deploy the Yorkist army before dawn –"

"In the dark?!" Richard burst out, forgetting himself before his king.

Edward gave him a stern look but didn't rebuke him.

"Our men will move in close to Warwick's front line. I am reliably told there will be a fog this night; it and the darkness will conceal us from Warwick." He almost spat the name of the man who had defected to the bitch of Anjou. "Under cover as we shall be, his cannon will fire right over our heads and once he has spent his firepower uselessly, we can pounce and take him by surprise. We shall have to keep as quiet as possible while we manoeuvre and then, when we are in position, we must stay still and low and hold our nerve. Is that clear?" Edward looked into Richard's eyes which were bright with the adrenaline of the anticipation of battle.

"My Liege, I will not let you down. I will fight to the death

145

before I let my command fail."

"Good man! George, you will be with me, supporting the centre."

Rob Percy leaned over and whispered into Richard's ear: "Where Edward can keep an eye on him!" He gave a short laugh. George had returned to Edward's side when it had become clear that he would never become king under Warwick's regime.

Edward turned to William Hastings, his friend.

"Will, you will command the left battle. Warwick is a formidable foe, but we know his methods – he and Montagu taught us all. Now is the time for the pupils to defeat the masters. Now all go and get some sleep – we will make a start long before dawn."

Richard went back to his own tent and thought through the battle plans again. It wasn't a difficult plan, in theory, but what if something went wrong and the plan had to be modified? He sat at his table with the map of the terrain in the centre, the battle lines drawn on it in his own neat hand. He tried to envisage any possible event and how to best react to it. In the end, his friend, Rob, urged him to rest.

"I know it is difficult to sleep before a battle but we do need our heads to be clear in the morning. Rest is important."

"I know, and Ned always sleeps like a baby the night before, by all accounts. But I know if I do not go over all this now, I will be turning it over and over in my head all night long. Now, just one more time."

He ran through his alternative plans and then folded up the parchment, knelt by the portable bed to pray and then slid under the coverings. He soon heard Rob snoring, but his thoughts were too busy for rest to come easily. He began to mentally rehearse some of the moves he and the others had practised during their training. Closing his eyes to picture it in his mind, he gradually drifted off.

He was woken in the early hours of the morning by one of his squires, Tom Huddleston, who was gently shaking him and calling his name. He came instantly to full alert and sat up abruptly.

"Ned is calling for us to move our line up close to Warwick's. Break your fast, your Grace, and then Tommy and I will get you into your armour."

Richard forced himself to eat some bread and cheese and drink a mug of small beer, although truly he had little appetite. This was the day! His very first proper battle! He glanced over to his gleaming set of harness hanging on the hooks by the tent flap. It was pristine, shining steel, inlaid with chased gold designs of the Rose of York and the White Boar that was his own cognizance. He hoped it would do its job today. His brother Edward, deprived of his rightful throne by Warwick's machinations with the French queen, Margaret of Anjou, had to win this battle or the Yorkists would be bereft of power once again. No king had ever been deposed, exiled and then returned to get back his crown, but if anyone could do it, it was Edward. He was the epitome of magnificent kingship, a Sunne in Splendour indeed. Richard was proud to fight alongside his brother.

"I am ready," he called to the two Toms, Huddleston and Parr, and they began methodically dressing him in his padded arming tunic and then fastened each piece of armour to him, until he felt as if he were encased in a stifling metal coffin. He flexed his gauntlets and accepted the battle axe and sword that his squires offered him. The sun was still to show its head above the covers of the horizon. His banners were flying as he made his way outside, but they could barely be seen in the gloom. He thought they would be limp anyway, with the damp of the fog soaked into them. The mist had indeed materialised and all the normal sounds of camp seemed to be muffled by it, the fog's clammy hands smothering the men's voices. The orders were passed along from man to man quietly and they finally set off, moving as silently as they could towards the enemy lines.

He could scarcely believe Edward's daring – to move up so close to the enemy (and in the dark!) was a clever strategy, but risky. If they were discovered, either by the fog lifting, or by noises giving them away, the carnage would be dreadful. As it was, as dawn broke, he heard the cannon start their firing, about an hour after they reached their position. He jumped at the loudness of them – the enemy must be almost on top of them. The advantage was that all Warwick's precious cannonballs were fired harmlessly over their heads, wasted and powerless, just as Edward had predicted.

The mist was still thick, even after the sun rose, and Edward's army began their move. At first, they had the element of surprise, being so close, and managed to kill many of Warwick's men before they fully realised what was afoot. Once they did, it was a different story. Richard was pitched against the enemy's left battle, but as they advanced, he became confused because it seemed there was no-one where Warwick's left battle should be. He didn't waver but kept to the plan, advancing slowly. He could hear men fighting on his left and further away, but nothing from directly in front of him. Suddenly he realised what had happened. Because of the fog, they had drawn up their lines a little too far to the right, which meant that his battle had overshot Warwick's left side of the army, and Hastings' would find that the commander in charge of Warwick's left flank would have done the same to him.

Well, he could use it to his advantage – he ordered his force to turn to the left, which would mean they would come into contact with the enemy from the flank instead of face to face. It might surprise them. He caught sight of banners in front of him and recognised the cognizance of Henry Holland, the Duke of Exeter. He urged his men forward before Exeter's became aware what had happened and they crashed into the side of Exeter's force, eliciting yells of surprise, pain, rage and fear. The mist hindered his sight and he fought blind at times, using his hearing to locate the enemy and his fellow knights and supporters. He had his squires beside him and they fought together, blocking blows, dealing out death and wounds. His new, shiny armour was soon stained with blood and gore, and had acquired a few dents and scratches. As soon as Holland realised what had happened, his men turned and began to fight in earnest. Richard found his men being pressed back and the terrain to his rear was difficult – uneven, boggy in places and scattered with scrubby bushes and thickets. He knew he had to rally his army and regain the upper hand.

"Do not yield!" he yelled, as a man in Exeter's colours confronted him. He planted his feet and swung his battle-axe, missing the man, who wielded a mace and raised it above Richard's head. He twisted and brought his axe up to parry the blow and the force sent a shock wave through his arm and it suddenly felt dead and useless. He saw the huge dent in his vambrace from the other man's weapon, which had been deflected but not fully parried. The man raised the mace again and Richard suddenly felt a wave of rage envelop him. He screamed wordlessly and brought his sword to bear in his left hand, trying to find a gap in the man's armour. He couldn't find it and stabbed at his face instead. The unexpected change of tactic took the man unawares and he swayed back, giving Richard the chance to raise his axe again. His arm still felt odd, but he could move it and the axe smashed into the man's helmet, killing him instantly. A shower of blood sprayed him and he stepped forward, ignoring the man lying dead on the ground, even though his breakfast threatened to make a second appearance.

Another man had filled the first one's shoes and Richard fought on, calling to his men to resist. The two Toms were right by his side and he was grappling with the new man when he heard a curse from Tom Huddleston as he was sent sprawling on the ground beside him. Richard knew his training so well he didn't hesitate to see what had happened, but continued to fight, yelling constantly to drive on his fellow soldiers and strike fear into the enemy. Tommy Parr stepped in to parry a lethal blow from a second man as Richard finished off the first one with a blow from his axe. Given an instant of respite he turned to help Tommy, only to see him felled by a large knight with a halberd. It was the Duke of Exeter. Tommy glanced at Richard, a surprised look on his face, and then fell forwards, the whole back of his head destroyed. Richard felt bile rise in his throat and spat it out, grief now combining with his fury as he fought on, dispatching the man Tommy had been struggling with and then forcing his way through to Exeter. Henry Holland, who was the estranged husband of Richard's sister, Anne, was much taller and broader than him, but Richard was fuelled by fury and grief. He dealt Exeter a ringing blow before he had even realised he was there and, as he collapsed to the floor, Richard stepped over him and turned his attention to the next assailant.

Richard felt like the fight was never-ending, and he caught a brief glimpse through the damp tendrils of fog of some of Hastings' men fleeing before the five-pointed Streaming Star of Oxford's battle. Oxford would have had the same advantage over Hastings that Richard's formation had of flanking the enemy. Richard now urged his force to greater effort to help Edward, who was struggling against Warwick's command without Hastings' aid. The battle ebbed and flowed with first one side, then the other, pressing forwards. Suddenly, there was a commotion on the left. Richard heard cries of "Treason" and was puzzled to see one part of Warwick's army seemingly turning on another. Oxford had retrieved the men who had chased Hastings' fleeing soldiers to Barnet and, stopping them pillaging and rampaging through the town, he had driven them back into the fray, but by this time the battle had turned, because of the armies not being properly aligned facing each other, so instead of the struggle being in a North-South direction, it was now being fought North-West to South-East and he had approached from the side, coming face to face with Montagu's forces. In the fog, Oxford's 'Streaming Star' banner had been mistaken for Edward's 'Sunne in Splendour' and Montagu had unleashed his archers on his own allies. Oxford's beleaguered soldiers, now being attacked by their own side, had started to yell "Treason!" and this had only served to increase the confusion. The two Lancastrian commanders were doing Edward's job for him and, seeing and recognising what had occurred, Edward roused his men to renewed action, Richard's and George's forces backing him up.

With the three York brothers now all united in the centre of the battle, Warwick's men had lost the momentum and turned to flee. Richard drew to Edward's side and received a huge grin and a solid clap on his shoulder from his brother. Edward's men chased Warwick and his remaining soldiers to where they had tethered their horses and the York brothers all converged on the place. By the time they had reached the Earl, Edward's men had already killed him, along with his brother, Montagu.

Edward was furious. "I told you not to kill him!" he cried, his voice hoarse from the long use of it during the battle. "I ordered him to be taken alive."

He looked at Richard, who returned his glance, both of them sad at the death of a man who once had been a great warrior, a great man and their friend.

"How did it ever come to this, Ned?" Richard whispered. His brother said nothing, but placed a heavy mailed hand on his little brother's shoulder and gave it a squeeze. Richard winced and, noticing his pain, Edward immediately sent him to the surgeon's tent to have it seen to.

Edward ordered the bodies of Warwick and Montagu to be taken to St Paul's Cathedral to be displayed the next day. Exeter, whom Richard had felled and thought dead, had disappeared and Oxford had escaped too. There were still enemies to defeat but the Battle of Barnet was won.

"Wow! That was intense." Rupert's eyes were alive with excitement. "I wish we could hear more of the surrounding noises – other voices, the clang of sword on armour, etc."

"Isn't the sound of Richard yelling, grunting, gasping in pain enough?" Eve asked, feeling slightly guilty since she could hear it all – and see it. She had had to deliberately un-concentrate in some places, so she didn't see all the blood and gore. Rupert would probably have loved it.

"When he shouted: 'Do not yield!' That was fantastic," he said.

David was nodding and Stellan had his usual enigmatic expression; Eve never really knew what he thought about anything, he was so hard to read, even with her fledgling psychic ability. Alex was silent too, but Eve picked up from him a sense of hostility. When she stared at him in shock, he turned and gave her a smile. Perhaps she was mistaken.

"So, what's next, then?" asked Rupert.

"The Battle of Tewkesbury," Eve replied.

Tewkesbury Tale

Richard was almost falling asleep on his horse, despite the drizzle which had quietly but insistently soaked him to the bone. Edward had driven his army mercilessly, knowing it was vital to engage 'Queen' Margaret's forces before they managed to cross the Severn and join up with Jasper Tudor's Welshmen. Even for him, a king renowned for the speed of his manoeuvres, this was a prodigious feat. And so soon after the Battle of Barnet, it was even more miraculous.

They had tracked Margaret's progress north and managed to prevent her taking shelter in Gloucester. Richard himself, as Duke of Gloucester, had sent his messenger to advise the town's Mayor and Council not to open the gates to Margaret, however much she pleaded, threatened or attempted trickery. And they had complied. She and her army had had to turn northward again and try to cross the Severn higher up. Edward aimed to catch her before Tewkesbury, hence the implacable forcing of his army ever faster.

Now they had finally reached Tewkesbury and their quarry

was in sight. She had not had enough time to cross the river and was now forced to stand and fight. Both the armies were exhausted already, so they would rest the night before engaging. Richard walked round the camp as his men pitched their tents, giving them words of encouragement and praise – he believed that this personal touch helped create unity and loyalty in them.

For once, Richard had no trouble falling asleep. He slept heavily and dreamlessly and woke disorientated and aching. He was at first shocked to see that there were two new squires attending him, until he remembered that the two Toms were gone. He tried to be patient with the new boys, but they were not as practised in dressing him; it had to be done perfectly because of the curve in his spine, which the armour was made to support and fit exactly. They were naturally nervous and he could sympathise – he remembered having to learn the duties of a squire and, after all, it was not their fault that his two friends had perished defending him in battle. So, he simply waited for them to finish and then smiled his thanks.

This time Richard was to take command of the vanguard, the most prestigious and dangerous appointment. He was full of pride, but nervous too. He was still haunted by some of the terrible sights he had seen at Barnet, and not only the deaths of his squires. He had seen men screaming as their life ebbed away with their blood. One man just sat on the ground quite calmly, with both his arms severed, another desperately tried to push his own entrails back inside his abdomen and yet another, younger than Richard, sobbed for his mother as an enemy soldier dispatched him. As the attack progressed, Richard had just tried to deal with the enemy surrounding him and forced the evil sights from his memory. Now, he had to put them from his mind once again – he had to be ready for a new battle today.

He marched into Edward's tent for his final instructions and it was just as dawn spread her rosy fingers through the dark sky, extinguishing the stars, that they set up their formation. Clarence was in the centre with Edward again and, confident from Barnet's victorious field, they eagerly engaged with the Lancastrian lines. Richard fought like a lion, or a cornered wild boar, his own cognizance, and it wasn't long before the battle began to swing in the Yorkists' favour. The young prince Edward of Lancaster, in the centre of the field, fought well, but he had no experience. Although he was not much younger than Richard himself, Richard had put down skirmishes in the Welsh Marches and commanded the left flank at Barnet, holding his line despite being almost overrun by Warwick's army. He had grown in confidence and his brothers, older and wilier, were just as indomitable. They all did their part, working together and commanding separately and, finally, the Lancastrians were routed and fled into the River Severn where, for a time, the fast-flowing water was stained the colour of blood. Many who were retreating drowned in their waterlogged jacks and cumbersome armour. And Edward, the young Lancastrian prince, was killed fleeing, by George's forces.

Richard, knowing the prince had been the husband of Anne, his childhood sweetheart, was at first exultant when he heard, his heart leaping at the possibility that he could still achieve his boyhood aim of making her his wife. Then he repented of his jubilation, feeling guilt at the shedding of more young blood. He vowed he would wait a while before approaching Edward regarding Anne. He knew not whether she mourned her husband of so short a time, nor whether she would take him, Richard, as her husband. But even though he kept to his vow, he was restless and desperately wanted to see her again. He wondered if she blamed Edward and him for the death of her father and he wanted to explain that Edward had ordered Warwick not to be killed unnecessarily. Although he thought he could guess Edward's mind on the matter; Warwick had taken a step too far and if he had been taken alive, he would have doubtless been beheaded for treason, a fate which would have been much worse for Anne to bear. No, he was glad she had been spared that, at least. But, with her mother hiding away in sanctuary, her father and husband killed, Anne must surely feel very much alone in the world. And Richard wanted to gain her trust – to let her know that she would never be alone again, if she would agree to wed him.

When he finally saw her, she looked much more mature than the innocent, little maiden he had grown to love. He could see pain in her eyes, uncertainty and, yes, fear. Surely, she couldn't think that Edward would punish her for the mistakes of her father and husband? He found her in a guest room at Westminster. She at least had her own solar and servants. He knocked on her door and waited. He heard a muffled voice and then the door swung open, revealing Anne sitting, straight-backed, in the window-seat, looking out into the garden. The setting sun caught her hair, painting it gold and emphasising the shadows around her eyes, though nobody had seen her weep; she was nothing if not a daughter of Warwick. He felt more love for her in that instant than if she had flung herself into his arms, although he longed for that too.

"Anne," he said, softly, savouring her name on his tongue.

She turned fully from the window and rose, making a graceful obeisance to him. Her formality pierced his heart, wounding him more deeply than the blow he had taken at Barnet. She had never before treated him as anything but her equal, her friend. Yet now she was the daughter and wife of traitors and he the glorious brother of the king. He went to her and took her hands to raise her up.

"You need not ever curtsey to me, Anne. Your blood is as noble as my own, after all."

"But mine is attainted," she said, her voice toneless, wooden. Where was the girl with the vibrant singing voice, the cheeky banter and the romantic declarations of love? Before he could reply, she hurried on: "Richard, what is going to happen to me? Will Edward...?" She lowered her head, biting her lip the same way he did when he was worried. He could not remember who had picked up the habit from whom.

He was still holding her hands and he squeezed them gently, hoping to reassure her. But it must have reminded her he had hold of them for she drew them away quickly and commenced pacing up and down like a caged lioness.

"Will he lock me away in a convent? Or imprison me in the Tower? Or..." She turned petrified eyes on Richard, just for an instant losing her self-control.

Richard put his hand on her shoulder and she turned to him, the blue-green eyes he had known so well suddenly brimming with tears.

"Do not weep, Anne. I will protect you – no-one intends you harm but, if they did, I would defend you with my life. Surely you know that? I intend to ask Edward for your hand. That is, if you will have me. Perhaps, after being Princess of Wales, a Duke seems too lowly for you."

He meant it as a jest, but she stiffened and drew away from him and he realised she must mourn her young husband and see him, Richard, as his killer, or at least one of the enemy who caused his downfall.

"I am sorry – I did not mean to cause you pain. I know you are newly widowed and I understand you need to mourn. I speak not of an immediate marriage. But please say you will think on it."

She shook her head, turning her eyes down, her head lowered.

"I do not wish to speak of him."

A silver tear tracked down the side of her nose and she brushed it away impatiently. At a loss as to how to behave towards a crying woman, as most men were, he decided to ignore it and changed the subject.

"You are to be sent to live with Isabel and George – at least for the time being."

Anne stood there and regarded him coolly from beneath her fashionably-shaved eyebrows. She had never shaved her eyebrows before. How he longed to embrace her, but he couldn't risk her rejection. He would bide his time.

Chapter Five

Demons

Richard knelt in the chapel, his face set in a grim expression. He knew if he once let his control slip, he would collapse into tears and never be able to stop weeping. And he was a man – he had to put away such childish indulgences. He would have liked to thrust his errant thoughts to the back of his overactive mind. To forget all the horror of what had happened at Barnet and Tewkesbury, but his conscience would not allow it. He felt guilty, because he was alive and the two Thomases were not. They had died in his service, protecting him, their Lord. They had died as men, even though they had been but boys. And with them many other men he had known, admired and loved – all had died in his service and it pained him. Not only that – he also had the guilt of blood on his hands. He had killed many of the enemy, but that was in the heat of battle and was kill or be killed. But there was one he felt the guilt of much more; a helpless, insane old man who had done nothing wrong except be weak and be born to be a king.

He thought back to the dreadful night in the Tower, when Edward had sent him to oversee the execution of Henry, the old king. Once Henry's heir was dead, his own death would end the Lancastrian threat. Richard might be just eighteen but he was Constable of England and as such had to oversee executions. To him it was not an execution though, it was murder.

The old man was praying when Richard and the three men chosen to do the deed had entered his spacious cell in the Tower. He had his own altar as he loved to pray; a priest in spirit if not in fact. He rose and looked at Richard and a sudden sadness came into his eyes as if he knew what was going to happen. He looked down and then knelt on the stone floor at Richard's feet, his head bowed and his lips moving in prayer. A priest had taken his confession just that morning and he could go to God clean and without sin. He didn't resist when two of the men took his arms, one each side, and held him still while the third one struck him once on the back of the head with a shovel. Richard would hear that sound in his head for years. Henry had silently slumped to the floor and the deed was done.

As easy as that and yet the hardest thing Richard had ever done. He felt the guilt even though he had protested about it to Edward and tried desperately to change his mind. So now it was something more to pray for.

He clasped his hands together and said the prayer in his mind, enunciating each word separately in his thoughts:

"Dear God, who made us all in your image, forgive the sins of thy servants, Thomas Huddleston and Thomas Parr, John Harper, John Milewater and Christopher Worsley, who died bravely in defence of my own pitiful life. Please shorten their time in purgatory so they may find their way to heaven, forever to dwell with thee there in your gracious love. Comfort their families and loved ones, who have lost their great hearts. Please also look kindly upon me, thy servant, Richard Gloucestre and cleanse me from sin. Help me to resist temptation, uphold truth and justice and defend the weak. I know I am unworthy but show me, dear Lord, the way to reach thy side in the fullness of time, by bearing without complaint the burdens thou hast given to me in thy wisdom and by doing what is right. Forgive me my sins, and at the time of my death, allow me to dwell with thee forever. Thank thee for the sacrifice of thy son, Jesus Christ Our Lord, who died for the sins of us all. Amen."

"**M**ove on a bit, Stellan, this is boring – nothing's happening." David ordered the Swede.

Of course, the others could hear nothing, but Eve had 'heard' it all and found it deeply moving. He was so sincere and so earnest – and so young. Then her attention was attracted by the sound of Richard's voice as Stellan found another location and time.

Rockabye

"**Y**es, send her in," he said quietly to his squire.

The door opened and the woman walked in silently and knelt before him.

"Alys, you know you need not kneel in my presence. Please, arise."

She stood then and Eve could sense her trembling as Richard stood up and came towards her. His own steps were tentative also and there was an unaccustomed awkwardness to his movements as if he was holding himself stiffly.

"Let me see," he said, his voice so soft, Eve could barely hear it.

He stopped at her side and reached towards the bundle she held in her arms. Pulling the covering aside he peered down into the face of a tiny baby, obviously very young.

"There was a soft hissing sound as he drew his breath in sharply and then he swallowed. He cleared his throat, then said:

"She is truly mine?"

"Of course she is… your Grace."

"Richard," he corrected, automatically. "I am sorry, Alys, I did not mean to suggest you… I am just rather overwhelmed. Of course I knew these things happened, but I never somehow expected it to happen to me. I cannot believe I am really a father."

"Well, you are, your… Richard. What do you think of her?"

He smiled. "My first child – she is beautiful. What have you named her?"

"Katherine. She had to be baptised and you… were not available, so I made the choice. It is my favourite saint's name. I hope you do not mind."

"No, of course not… Katherine… perfect. Hello little one," he cooed over the bundle. Then he turned to her mother. "May I hold her, please?"

"Naturally – you are her father, after all!"

He gave a short chuckle as if he still didn't quite believe he was actually a father, then he carefully took the baby in his arms.

"She is quite heavy, is she not?" He gently stroked the child's downy cheek and smiled as she opened her eyes and her gaze met his own. Then she began crying, opening her mouth and letting a sound emerge that seemed far too loud for such a small being. "Oh no – I do not think she likes me," he said, turning to Alys again.

She smiled. "She is just hungry – we have had a long journey today and I wanted to come straight to see you. And she is not new-born, she is now six weeks old."

"Oh, of course," he said, hastily handing her back to her mother. "Er, where do you need to go – will my bedchamber do?"

"It will do perfectly, thank you," she replied and he showed her through. "Um… you can stay if you wish?"

He swallowed, hesitated and then nodded. "If you do not mind."

He watched, fascinated as his baby daughter suckled and Eve knew he felt a mixture of pride, joy, responsibility and guilt. He knew he could not marry Alys and did not, in truth, want to, but it made him feel guilty for her predicament.

"Alys, what is it you want from me? You know I cannot marry you but I want to acknowledge my daughter. You and she will want for nothing."

"That is not why I came, Richard. I thought you had a right to know you were a father and I wanted you to see her. I am grateful for your financial help, but what I really want for Katherine is for you to be a part of her life."

"Of course I will be. Where are you living now?"

"I am about to be moved to Pomfret. I asked Elizabeth if she could find me a position as a wet nurse somewhere and she knows of a lady there who needs one."

Richard nodded. "I will visit whenever I can."

"**H**a ha! So, he wasn't as pious and perfect as the Ricardians claim, was he?" Rupert crowed triumphantly.

"He was a teenager when he conceived the child and they didn't exactly have reliable contraception in those days, did they? At least he supported the mother and even said he would take an interest in the child's upbringing."

Eve found she was getting really irritated with the way Rupert kept on taking the traditional view of Richard. Her face was creased in a frown as she continued.

"He did as he promised as well. He paid an annual allowance to Alys and brought little Katherine into his household when she was older. He even found a good marriage for her when he was king. I think that makes him incredibly responsible – I'm sure most men would just deny they were the father and leave the woman to fend for herself. Richard tried to do what was right, even if he wasn't perfect – he wasn't a saint, he was a man."

Brother's Bane

Richard went to visit Anne at George's London home. Several times. And each time George refused to let him see her. There was a different excuse every time:

"She is tired from the trauma of losing her father and her husband."

"She is unwell, I am sorry, brother." (With an insincerely sad expression).

"She is praying for her father's soul." Then, the latest one:

"Look, Dickon, I am sorry, but she just does not want to see you. I have tried to persuade her and given you excuses to spare your feelings, but I cannot keep on pretending. She does not want to marry you."

"Then let her tell me so herself," he said. "Where is she?"

"She will not see you – she told me to give you her answer." George returned Richard's unhappy gaze steadily. Eve thought his eyes held a hint of deceit but couldn't be sure – she couldn't pick up on George's emotions the way she could Richard's.

Richard stood there fuming, but Eve could tell George had struck a nerve. Richard wasn't sure Anne still had feelings for him and he had the awkwardness of any modern teenager when it came to her, despite his early responsibilities.

"Tell her I will be back until she speaks to me herself," he said and turned to go, while George stood there smiling behind Richard's back.

One Last Time

Edward had ordered Richard north to keep an eye on the Scottish border and generally be his representative there, for the North was notoriously difficult to control. He had made his young brother the Constable of Pontefract and Stellan managed to trace him there, or Pomfret as it was then called.

"Alys, she has grown in the short time since I last saw her!"

"That is what babies do, Richard."

"Aye, but still…" He stood smiling down at his sleeping daughter, her dusky eyelashes contrasting with her pink, peach-soft, cheek. Eve felt the surge of pride in him that he had made this perfect little being and also his gratitude that Alys had been so understanding and undemanding. He thought of Anne and his mood dipped. Perhaps he would never have her as his wife, if what George said was true. Why should she want him

165

anyway? He was hardly as handsome or manly as his brother Edward. He was conscious of his slight build, his less than average height and, of course, his shameful deformity, his burden. He didn't think Anne knew of it, but George did – he wouldn't put it past him to have told her – even to have exaggerated it. No wonder she didn't want to marry him. Then his attention was drawn back to his child. He was surprised at the love he felt for her – he had never been interested in babies, but this child made him feel like a man at last. It had been so easy to be with Alys.

He turned to the woman herself and smiled at her. She was pouring him a goblet of wine and placing some sweetmeats on a platter. She brought it over to him and they drank while watching Katherine sleep, not speaking, but in a companionable silence. She offered Richard the plate of honey cakes and his hand brushed hers as he took one, sending an unexpected thrill of desire through him. Unaware, she smiled and bit into her cake. Then, seeing the look in his eye, she swallowed it quickly and lifted her mouth to his as he stepped towards her and took her in his arms.

He kissed her gently, his hands exploring her curves and she sighed, stroking his hair. Then they were on the bed, their clothes abandoned and their young bodies responding to each other as nature intended.

"Oh!" Eve cried, embarrassed at the intensity of the feelings she was experiencing through Richard. David looked excited – Eve wondered if he was a bit of a voyeur by his reactions. Anyway, for David there wasn't much to see or hear – only Richard's soft groans and heavy breathing. She was managing to control her reactions much better now and could 'tune out' the feelings she didn't want to share.

Come Back My Love

They moved on again and Richard had returned to London. "George! For pity's sake! Tell me where she is or I swear I will…"

Richard's voice trembled with suppressed fury along with an undercurrent of fear. Eve knew he was almost at breaking point. He wasn't just angry, he was in despair.

"I have told you, Brother, that she is not here – she disappeared several days ago, the Lord knows why – I certainly do not! The last I saw of her she was…"

"GEORGE! I know you are lying! Why do you act like this? You are such a scheming, self-serving cumberworld!"

There was a long silence, but Eve could visualise the scenario as clearly as if she were there. George, standing there, his arms folded, head held up in a cock-sure manner. In contrast, Richard, his head lowered, eyes glaring at George from under his scowl, hair falling around his face like a soft curtain, fists clenched at his sides, trembling with the suppressed desire to act. But what could he do, apart from beat his frustration out of his smug, mocking brother?

Abruptly, he turned on his heel and marched off, hand on the hilt of his sword. He was muttering under his breath:

"You bloody miscreant – I will find her, I swear by the bones of Our Saviour Jesus Christ! And you will not get your filthy hands on her inheritance, either, George. I shall search the whole place. Anne! Anne! Where are you?"

His voice was steady if slightly muffled but Eve could feel he had a lump in his throat and an overwhelming desire to sweep his sword, ringing, from its jewelled scabbard and run George through with it. His anger mixed with fear and panic, a turbulent brew which was overwhelming. How he was keeping his emotions under control, she couldn't fathom.

"What's going on here?" whispered Rupert, breaking the drama of the moment. Eve was glad as she had been starting to feel her own emotions mirroring Richard's. "Do you know who he is speaking to?"

"Yes, it's his brother George, again. George had charge of Anne Neville after the Battle of Tewkesbury and Richard wanted to marry her."

"Oh yes, the rich heiress, wasn't she?"

"Well, yes, she was – she was an entirely appropriate bride for him. Anne was a few years younger than Richard, they had known each other at Middleham Castle, he must have felt protective towards her. At least, that's what I think," she finished, lamely. "I think they must have had at least an affection for each other." Of course, she couldn't explain that she absolutely knew he had an affection for Anne – they would think she was a lunatic if she admitted she could pick up his thoughts and emotions through psychometrising his DNA. She would lose all credibility. She had to be careful. She knew the others were listening, as Richard was silent for the moment.

"Well, perhaps we can find out later on when we go further on in his life." David glanced at her with a slightly quizzical look and turned to Stellan. "Can we move on a bit?"

"Of course!" Stellan tapped in some co-ordinates and started the machine once more. It seemed to take an age before it finally settled and displayed the now-familiar 'Subject Found' message.

Rag Doll

"Speak, man! What do you know?"

"There are rumours that there is a new cook's maid in a local tavern on the south bank of the river, your Grace. They say she is fair-skinned like a noble and that her speech is gentle and gracious. And she came to them unknowing of how to even clean a pan."

"Can you take me there?"

"Aye, my Lord, of course."

"Wait outside. I must summon my men and Lord Lovell."

She sensed his urgent steps across the room, his movements graceful and silent as a cat, as he ushered the man out.

"John – go and fetch Francis Lovell, if you will. As quickly as you can!"

"Aye, your Grace."

Then Eve knew, somehow, that he was pacing up and down, up and down, the cat caged and needing to get out – out and doing, taking action, where matters would be under his control, instead of this infernal waiting for news. She also sensed his elation at the news that she might be found, that the waiting was finally over and the time for action had arrived. Then:

"Francis! We may have found her – in a cook house of all places. My poor little Anne. Will you come with me to the place and effect a rescue? The thought of her soft, white hands being plunged into hot, greasy water – her feet forced to stand for hours as she serves rough-voiced rogues with their vittles – fair turns my stomach. I want her out of there, the sooner the better. Well?"

"Of course, Dickon, let me summon a band of men to accompany us and we'll saddle up the horses and be off. Is this the informant?"

"Aye, he will lead us there."

Eve for one, could hear the excitement in his voice, suppressed but still noticeable. He did love Anne, she was positive, but of course, the others weren't hearing the other voices replying to Richard, nor feeling his mental state, which, although on the surface was well-balanced and stable, was fragile and tense on the inside.

There followed a time of short exchanges and long pauses as Richard and his entourage wended their way through the narrow streets of mediaeval London.

"Stellan, can you superimpose a map of London from those times onto the screen and have Richard represented by a red dot so that we can see where he ends up?" Eve asked.

"Hmm, I don't see why not, if such a map is available – it's a fairly simple programming task. Can you get hold of one?"

"I can try – can you pause it for a minute?" She was already Googling it as he nodded and she soon found a site where you could download digital versions of countless maps of different places in the UK and Europe from different times. About ten minutes later she had the relevant one on her laptop and sent it over to Stellan's. He opened the file and spent a further few minutes fiddling about with it while the rest of them got coffees and waited, discussing the situation Richard was in at that time.

"So why did George object to Richard marrying Anne? He was already married to her sister, wasn't he? So, he couldn't have married Anne."

Rupes sounded puzzled.

"No, George didn't want to marry Anne, but he didn't want Richard to either because, if Anne remained a widow or retired to a convent, for example, George would get control of all her inheritance as her closest male relative – he was, in effect, her guardian. If Richard married her, he could claim half of the sisters' lands and wealth. Also, Edward had declared that Anne's mother, the dowager Countess of Warwick, Anne Beauchamp, was to be treated as if she were dead so that her inheritance could be shared between his two brothers."

"That was a bit below the belt, wasn't it?"

"Well, Edward could be pretty ruthless when he felt like it... and she was the wife of a traitor, after all."

"Right, folks, I think I have done the map – gather round and see," said Stellan and they all did as he asked.

The screen now showed a copy of the map Eve had given him and the red dot of Richard was fairly close to the centre. Stellan started the machine working again and they watched in fascination as Richard's dot moved through the old streets, Stellan's programming skills having proved surprisingly accurate, it seemed.

As the dot turned a corner and paused, they heard Richard's voice again.

"Open up! Open up immediately or I shall beat this bloody door down!"

He sounded livid.

"Er... My Lord of Gloucester, please come in. Are you seeking accommodation for the night? Or mayhap a good hearty meal?"

"Nay, nay – I wish to search the premises. Please bring all your servants and employees and line them up here. And take that surprised look off your face. Francis, will you wait here and keep an eye on them, while I take the men and search the whole place?"

"Of course, your Grace," Lovell said, and began ordering the occupants to line up as Richard had commanded.

"Tom, Robert, Hugh, follow me," Richard said as the thump of many feet on the stairs was heard, interspersed with shouting and doors opening and closing.

A woman's voice: "What do you want? How dare you – oh! Your Grace, I had not realised who… I beg your pardon, my Lord. What can I help you with? I hope there is no problem…?"

"Mistress, we are here to search the place – I believe you are harbouring a noblewoman in the guise of a servant."

"Your Grace, I can assure you, we are loyal servants of your noble brother and would never presume to…"

"Aye, but which brother?"

"I… I… we meant no harm, your Grace, we were just doing our duty as we were told of it. Your brother, the Duke of Clarence, informed us the lady was in hiding from an abusive husband and needed shelter in a place she could not be found. We had no reason to dispute it. We –"

"Yes, yes, I do not hold you to blame – it is my scheming brother who is the guilty one, so you have nothing to fear. However, Edward, the king, has decreed that George must hand over the woman, so bring her forth immediately."

"Yes, your Grace. Matilda, go and fetch Nan from her attic room and bring her here to us. Quickly, wench, if you know what's good for you!"

"Thank you, Mistress."

After a few minutes' pause, where the woman offered Richard refreshment, which he refused politely, there was a soft footstep outside the door, a gasp and an even softer voice:

"Richard! Thank the Lord! George told me you wanted nothing more to do with me and threatened to send me to a convent for the rest of my life."

172

Eve could hear the tears in her voice and felt, like a physical pull, the emotions of Richard; she knew he wanted to hold Anne to his heart, but was prevented by the other people looking on. He could not show his feelings in public, it wouldn't be proper. Besides, he was unsure whether she shared his feelings. He felt torn by Anne's distress and, most of all, relief that she had been found.

"How could you doubt me, Anne? You know I want you to be my wife."

"You had not come to visit me and George said you had changed your mind. He told me Edward had granted him most of my inheritance and that you did not want to marry me without my wealth. I felt abandoned!" She choked back a sob.

"He was lying! I did come to see you, several times – George always fobbed me off with excuses. He said you were ill, that you were busy, that you did not want to see me because you were still in love with Edward of Lancaster. When I insisted, he told me you had disappeared. It has taken me weeks to find you."

If not apparent in his voice, which was even in timbre and tone, it was clear to Eve, since her powers of psychometry revealed his emotions all too clearly; he loved her. He couldn't wait to be wed to her.

Got My Mind Set On You

"Anne! I cannot believe he would do this to you! Look at your poor hands..." he took them into his own, but she drew them back, brusquely. Hurt, he took a breath and then said, stiffly: "I apologise. I mean you no harm, my Lady. I will deliver you at once to sanctuary at St Martin's Le Grand. I am not my brother and will not force you to do anything you do not do freely of your own will."

Eve could see his muscles quivering as he resisted the temptation to take Anne in his arms. He said much less than he thought – she knew exactly what he thought – that Anne was revolted by him. She had shrunk away at his touch and he was wounded at her reaction. He loved her, he really loved her! Another question asked by historians for decades was revealed. She knew beyond the shadow of a doubt that he wanted Anne for love, not just because she was a rich heiress who came with lands and titles galore, although that was obviously a consideration. She had also seen the state of Anne's hands and the look on her face when he took them into his own, tenderly and gently. It wasn't revulsion she saw there but shame. Shame at the disarray she was in, the filthy clothes she wore, the roughness of her hands, the dirt beneath her nails. She wasn't used to this squalor and she thought he would be disgusted at the sight of her like this.

She's not repulsed by you, can't you see, you fool? Talk to her!

But Richard stepped back and held the door open for Anne, carefully avoiding touching her at all as she passed by him. Eve felt an almost tangible longing in him, to have this woman as his wife. It wasn't avarice which drove him, nor was it lust, just the desire to protect and defend this woman, to cherish her. He held her in affection, he felt on safe ground with her, this friend whose childhood he had shared, whose father he had respected. She was family, she was home; he needed her.

He helped her onto the spare horse they had brought and held onto the reins as if someone might come and steal her away again. He dared not suggest she rode with him on his horse, not after she had flinched from him. He led her to sanctuary at St

Martin's Le Grand and delivered her safely into their hands. He ensured her room was comfortable, and her needs met – a bath, clean clothes, warmth, food and drink. And then he left her to ride swiftly back to George's house and confront his brother. When George's steward opened the door to his urgent knocking, he pushed his way inside and ran up the stairs two at a time, heading straight for George's solar. The steward shouted out for guards, but Richard ignored him. Hearing the commotion, George himself opened the door to the solar and, without hesitation, Richard flung himself at him like a small ball of fury and managed to bloody his brother's nose before George's guards intervened and separated them. He might be smaller and slighter than George, but he was quick and strong and had taken him by surprise. The satisfaction he had from the copious blood was great indeed.

"What the hell do you think you are doing, you little rat!"

"Paying you back for the ills you caused Anne, you ... you... fopdoodle!" He was so angry, he couldn't think of anything stronger to call him.

"Huh! So, you found her then. I suppose you will marry her now – well, you can have her, but do not think you will get her livelihood!"

Eve thought George meant Anne's inheritance and property by 'livelihood'.

"I *will* get it – for her! I shall see Ned and he will restore her inheritance to her – you are a scoundrel, George. She could have died in that awful place."

George said nothing, but looked down at his boots, dabbing at his nose with a piece of white linen. Eve could tell that Anne's possible death had been a part of his plan, or at least that he didn't care if it turned out that way – then he would be sure to get all the inheritance as her legal guardian. He really was a despicable person, interested only in what he could gain from any given situation. His voice was smooth and oily, compared to Richard's low, earnest tones.

Suddenly all the anger that had flared so quickly in Richard departed and he stared at George feeling only pity for him. He would never feel love like Richard did for Anne. The only love he felt was for himself and that kind of love brought no joy. George would never have enough – his desires would ever be unfulfilled because there was always something more he wanted. Give him an apple and he wanted two, a groat and he wanted a pound, an inch and he took a mile. Grasping, materialistic, bitter. But perhaps it was just his way of dealing with the insecurity that came from them losing their father and going into exile at such an early age – the solid ground of their family, their home suddenly turning to lethal quicksand in one sudden act. Fortune's wheel would turn whatever they did and both of them sought security, a way to bolster up their wealth, their power, in order to survive. However, George did it through making possessions his defence and Richard through loyalty and friendship.

He turned away from George in disgust and went immediately to seek an audience with the king. Edward was busy with one of his many ladies and tried to turn him away, but this night he brooked no refusal, not even from Edward. When he had explained where he had found Anne and what George had tried to do, he asked the king for permission to request Anne's hand in marriage. She might feel repelled by him, but he was rich and powerful and could protect her from harm. Anne was sensible and would see that marriage to him would be of benefit to her too.

"Be careful Dickon. George is sly; if you marry her too quickly, he will claim you abducted her and forced her into it. He will try to have it annulled."

"Claim I abducted her!" he cried, incensed. "He put her to work in that filthy kitchen, he made her do menial work, hard work – she was like a slave!"

"Nevertheless, he could claim it. I suggest you visit her in Sanctuary and discuss it with her. If she agrees to the marriage, I will have a contract drawn up whereby if the marriage is dissolved, for whatever reason, and you do not marry again, her wealth will still go to you – then he will have no reason to try to annul the marriage. But George will not be happy, Dickon. He will fight to get the lion's share – you know what he is like."

"Aye, indeed I do. Thank you, Ned. I will go to Anne in the morning and ask for her hand."

Good Ol' Fashioned Love

When he crossed the bridge and made his way into the holy place of sanctuary, he felt weak at the knees as if he had drunk too much wine and had trouble walking aright. He asked for Anne and was directed to her room. When he knocked, she called out for him to enter and he did, producing some sweetmeats which he had brought for her. They sat silently chewing on them, each lost in his or her own thoughts, each unsure what to say to the erstwhile friend who had now become a stranger, the childhood companion who was now an adult, with the burden of experiences unknown to the other.

Anne gained the courage to begin.

"What is to become of me, Richard? How long must I remain here?"

177

"I have spoken to my brother."

Anne gasped. "To George?"

"No, to Ned. I.. I know you do not still care for me the way you used to, but I am the king's brother and a royal Duke. You could be a Duchess and I could protect you, if..." He swallowed, hesitating to say the words.

"If?"

"If you will marry me. I promise to protect you and cherish you. George will never bother you again."

"What makes you think I no longer care for you? I am still the same Anne you explored William's Hill with. The one you scared by hiding frogs in her shoes. Have you changed, Dickon?"

When she used his familiar name, he knew she did still care.

"Yes, I have changed. I have become harder, colder. Life can do that to you. But my feelings have not. I love you, Anne. I always have. You are my peace, my solace, my home. Marry me and I will do my best to make you happy. Will you?"

She looked deep into his eyes as if she were weighing his words for the precious element of truth. He returned her gaze and she breathed: "Yes! Yes, I will marry you!"

His whole body, taut as a drum skin, relaxed as he heard those precious words. His heart then knew again the joy he used to feel in Middleham when he and Anne could talk for hours about nothing and laugh together and play together with no complications. As he took her in his arms, he vowed that they would go back and recreate those times together. They would live in Middleham again, but this time as the Lord and Lady of the Castle, the Duke and Duchess of Gloucester.

Chapter Six

London, 1471

Take Good Care of My Baby

However, there was a lot to do before they had the luxury of a wedding. Firstly, Richard had to negotiate with George the details of the inheritance shared by Anne and Isabel. Their mother, who was in sanctuary at Beaulieu, had been declared nominally dead, so the whole of her and her husband's lands and titles would go to their daughters and, hence, George and Richard.

The brothers both pleaded their own case before the king and argued for their rights extremely articulately. The Fly's research team were fascinated to hear the clever arguments and cunning turns of phrase that swept backwards and forwards between the two royal brothers.

When Richard related the proceedings to Anne she was appalled.

"You have declared my mother dead?!"

"It is not as bad as it seems. George is being terribly difficult so Ned thought the best solution would be to get your and Isabel's inheritance sorted out now. I have ceded the Earldoms of Warwick and Salisbury to him and in return we have been granted more lands in the north. We have Middleham already - Ned granted it to me before. I have also given George the office of Great Chamberlain. I am content. You have your fair share of the inheritance. I intend to ask Ned to allow your mother to come and live with us – would you like that?"

"Oh yes, Dickon! Thank you!"

"Well, all is well then. We only have to wait for the dispensation from Rome, concerning the relationship formed between us when you married Edward of Lancaster."

Richard was a distant cousin of her previous husband, and their marriage created an 'affinity' which meant they were considered as related.

"What will happen now?"

"I shall continue my work in the north, while you remain in sanctuary. It should not be too long as we already have the previous dispensation because your father and I were cousins."

"Oh yes, Father applied for that when Isabel married George and I still have it."

Richard smiled and they chatted excitedly about the coming wedding until Richard took his leave. He kissed her chastely on the brow and she squeezed his hand before he left.

"I can hardly wait to make you my wife, Anne," he whispered.

He rode to York and visited his lands and holdings in the area. While visiting Pontefract, Richard had gone to see his daughter and Alys again, only to find that Alys was expecting his second child. He was both dismayed and proud. He wanted to be faithful to Anne and decided he must tell her about his base-born children. He hoped she would understand.

Alys, meanwhile was suffering more with this pregnancy, following, as it did, so closely after the first. She was tired and pale, although she willingly accepted the wine that Richard offered her. He made sure to visit her often and so it was that during one of these visits, he arrived to find the castle all of a bustle.

"What is happening, Margaret," he asked the wife of the steward who had been rushing by him.

"It is Alys, your Grace – she has been labouring for the last three days and it is not going well."

"Let me see her!" he cried, distressed.

"Your Grace, 'tis no place for a man, the birthing room."

"It is my child she bears – I would see her now!" he said, raising his voice a fraction and speaking in more clipped tones.

Margaret hesitated and then nodded as she hurried off, with him following. "But let me speak with her first and tidy her up a little – she will not want you to see her that way."

"Very well," he said softly.

Ten minutes later he was ushered into a large chamber containing a bed and birthing stool, a table with wine and sweetmeats. Another with a bowl of water and a pitcher and several lengths of cloth. All the curtain ties were unfastened and the women wore their hair unbraided, which was supposed to help the birth. Herbs were strewn across the floor, giving off a sweet-smelling aroma. This, however, could not disguise the scent of blood and other unmentionable bodily fluids.

Richard took a deep breath of clean air before he walked into the room. Alys was lying on the pillow, her hair spread out all around her and her face even paler than in the early months.

"Richard," she whispered when she saw him and managed a weak smile.

"How goes it, Alys?" he asked, feeling stupid – it was obvious it wasn't going well.

"Badly – I am exhausted and the midwife says I must not push yet. I –"

She broke off and began panting, then screamed for the midwife as a gush of blood stained the bedclothes under her.

"I will wait without," Richard said and gave her a swift kiss on the brow as he turned on his heel and left. He felt rather faint and sat on a chair outside the room for what seemed like days, until finally the midwives hurried out to him and told him he had a son.

"Really? Is he well?"

"Yes, your Grace, a fine lad."

"And Alys?"

The two women hesitated and glanced worriedly at each other.

"Do not lie or conceal the truth from me, I would rather know the worst."

"She has lost too much blood – she will not recover. I am sorry, your Grace."

Without further words, he strode into the chamber and knelt at the bedside. Alys was breathing fast and shallowly and her lips were a worrying shade of blue. He took her hand, cold and clammy, and she gave a groan.

"Alys, it is me, Richard. Can you hear me? We have a son, a healthy lad."

He turned and waved one of the women over, indicating she should bring the child, who was crying lustily.

"Alys, look," he said, taking the child and bringing him close to Alys' face. She stirred slightly and her eyes opened just a crack. She smiled weakly and a tear glistened in her eye. She spoke, but so softly he had to ask her to repeat her words and moved closer so her lips were right next to his ear.

"Name him 'John'," she said. "For my father."

"John," he repeated and glanced for the first time at his son, who was still crying. He felt a sudden, swift clenching of his heart as he realised the child would be motherless, would never know her. He bit his lip and hugged the child to him, planting a soft kiss on the child's downy hair. He handed him back to the woman, commanding her to find a wet nurse and feed him, and turned back to Alys.

"Alys, I will. I –." He broke off as he realised she had passed away as quickly and quietly as a whisper on the wind. "Oh no," he groaned and shouted urgently.

"Call a priest at once. Her soul…"

"She has already been shriven, my Lord, but I will fetch Father Matthew."

She left the room silently and he turned back to the mother of his children and bowed his head down onto her still chest, weeping for her, his motherless son and himself.

"**W**hat on earth is going on there?" Rupert said, with a look of sheer puzzlement. "Isn't a birth normally a happy event? He sounded grim."

Eve always tried to imagine how it must seem to the others who could only hear Richard. It must be confusing at times.

"His… mistress died giving birth. They often did in those days. He asked for a priest to ensure she had been shriven – so the time she spent in purgatory could be shortened."

Rupert folded his lips inwards in an expression of regret.

"Of course – they were tragic times really, weren't they?"

She nodded wordlessly. Alex stared at the floor, David shuffled some papers, coughing in embarrassment, and Stellan made a wry face before shutting down 'The Fly' for the evening.

I'm Not the Man You Think I Am

L ater on, Stellan retuned the machine to the time during the next year when Richard and Anne were about to marry:

"Anne," Richard whispered, his voice taut with tension. He sounded as nervous as a traitor on the scaffold. "There is something I need to tell you before... before we marry."

"Yes?" she asked.

"Yes, well, more than one thing, actually. I want our marriage to be based on honesty – there should be no secrets between us. Do you agree?"

"Of course, my Lord."

"You have no need to be so formal, sweeting. Not when we are alone, at least. Well, firstly, I need you to know that I have two natural children, whom I have recognised and will bring into our household when they are a little older. At the moment, they are being cared for at Pontefract by their grandmother."

"Richard! I thought you loved me all these years – how could you...?" There was a sob and Eve could sense the guilt that Richard was feeling as he went to her and embraced her. She pushed him away but he grasped her shoulders and refused to let her go.

"I do love you, Anne. I... I was devastated when I heard your father had married you to Edward of Lancaster. I thought I had lost you forever. I am so grateful that God saw fit to bring us together again. But, at that time, I was distraught and, thinking I would never see you again, I took up with a young woman. She was some comfort to me in my grief." His face was anxious

184

and the guilt in his eyes was obvious. He lifted her chin so that she had to look into his eyes. "I was very young. I drank too much and well, I found in her some solace. In truth, I think she saved me from madness. She was kind and loving – I needed her comfort then. She bore me a daughter and then, a year later, a son, whom she died birthing. Katherine and John. He was conceived at the time when you were at George's house in London and he told me you refused to marry me. I began to doubt that I would ever win your hand and again she comforted me in my distress. Anne, surely you know I would never have lain with her if I thought for one moment that we could be together. Please forgive my weakness. I swear that I will keep my vows to you, if you will still marry me. Never will I lie with another woman while you live. But please do not blame my bastard children for my errors. Can you forgive me?"

"Well, I suppose it must have been difficult for you. And if they are motherless…" She sighed. "How can I not open my heart and my hearth to them?"

"Thank you!"

"What is the second thing you have to tell me?" She sounded wary, as if wondering what even worse revelation was to come.

He took a deep breath. "I have a... an affliction in my body. A deformity of my spine. I can hide it from casual observers, with tailored clothes and fitted armour, but when you are my wife, you will inevitably become aware of it."

"Where? Can you show me?"

"It is not fitting here in this house of God, but you can feel it through my clothes – put a hand on my spine, here."

There was a short silence and then a muffled gasp.

"Oh, Dickon, does it pain you? I had no idea you bore such a burden."

"It does ache at times, but it is bearable. I manage. I just wanted you to be prepared before our wedding night." He paused. "Do you think it is a punishment from God?"

"Of course not! Whatever makes you think that? What have you ever done to deserve such a punishment? You have always been honest, honourable and kind. Rather God has given you this burden to bear to test you, because He knows you will endure it and still be the good man you have always strived to be."

"Oh, Anne, you know not how glad I am to hear you speak such words of comfort! Ned said much the same thing, but if you think the same... I am truly blessed and I can hardly wait to make you my wife before God."

"Neither can I," she whispered.

Goodnight, Sweetheart, Goodnight

"Anne, you are beautiful."

Eve had never heard such tenderness in his voice before – normally it was so controlled, so devoid of emotion. That wasn't to say he felt none, only that he contrived never to reveal it to all and sundry. She knew this because she felt it along with him, transmitted through the medium of his DNA in the form of a tiny fragment of tooth. How strange it was that she was able to do this, feel the actual emotion of a man who lived so long ago, but she was as sure of it as she was of her own name. Somehow the combined vibration of his voice and the proximity of his actual DNA contrived to transmit the emotions he was feeling to her own heart, even though he gave nothing away through his voice. But on this occasion, he had let his guard down, for Anne. For the girl he had loved since he was a teenager at Middleham under the tutelage of her father.

"Repeat after me: 'I, Richard Plantagenet, Duke of Gloucester, do take thee, Anne Neville, to be my wedded wife.'"

Richard repeated the sacred oath, as did Anne hers, and Eve blinked as tears of pure emotion stung her eyes. They were so sincere. She had heard marriage vows of various kinds spoken before, friends had uttered them in her presence, but she didn't think they had believed them the way Richard and Anne did. In the back of modern minds, ever-present, was the thought that there was always divorce if it didn't work out, that it didn't necessarily mean ''Till death us do part'. But it did for them. The oath was binding and unbreakable and it made the wedding more sacred, more serious and more romantic somehow.

There followed a private feast attended by only close friends and family and then they retired to the bridal chamber.

When the door closed, there was a silence where only Richard's breathing could be heard, faster than normal, as he slipped off his doublet and hose and turned to Anne, already settled into the huge canopied bed. He pulled off his undershirt and slid under the sheets beside her and gently stroked her arm from shoulder to elbow, then bent his head to brush his lips against the angle between her neck and shoulder. She tensed and shrank away.

"Anne? What is it? Am I so repulsive to you? Do you wish me to cover my deformity?"

"No, Dickon, dear heart! Of course not – it is part of you and I love it as I do the rest of you. It is just that... that... I know not what to do, what is expected of me."

There was a protracted pause and then he spoke again.

"Do you mean you are still a maid? Did you not lie with your

187

first husband?"

"No, I did not – his mother would not allow it; she thought me unworthy of her spoiled brat of a son. She forbade him to consummate the marriage unless and until my father won back the crown for her husband, Mad Henry."

"Which he did. For only a short while, it is true, but still..."

"Well, she told me she wanted to be back on her own throne before she would believe it. I felt so ashamed, you know. Obviously, she was making any excuse not to let me be a true wife to Edward. I felt... rejected. She treated me as little better than the dirt on her shoes."

A tear slid down her cheek and Richard leaned over and kissed it away, stroking her hair with his long, nimble fingers. Her hair was honey-blond and so long, when unbound it reached almost to her knees.

"Well, I shall not reject you. And I have to admit, I am glad that I shall be the first man to know you. You are perfect, my Anne. Come, kiss your husband."

He bent his head, his lips meeting hers and ran his hand beneath her shift, caressing her, gently, slowly, waiting for her to respond to his lovemaking.

Oh! This felt so embarrassing – to eavesdrop on such a personal moment, especially since she could feel all that Richard felt. She was aroused and yet repulsed at the same time. It was inappropriate to intrude on their intimate relationship and she leapt to her feet and switched the machine off abruptly.

"What the hell are you doing?" David cried, his brows drawn together in a scowl.

"We don't need to listen to that. It's wrong and it has nothing of historical consequence – nothing that relates to the questions we want to answer. Stellan, don't you agree? Let us move on to something more political."

"Don't we want to explore what he was like as a man as well?" David countered. "It's all relevant, as far as I can see."

"We don't need to be... voyeurs. It's a step too far. There are plenty of other moments where we will be able to see what kind of man he was."

"Eve is right," said Rupert. "It's quite distasteful to listen to that, knowing it isn't just a film or play or something; it's real. And it isn't fair to them. They may be long dead, but in my book, it's still violating their privacy. They have a right to keep their personal relationship between them only."

Eve was astonished at his comments, but delighted that he had backed her up.

David held Rupert's gaze for a while, but then moistened his lips with his tongue and lowered his head.

"Very well, I see your point, I suppose. Move on to the next significant event, Stellan."

Days

Richard and Anne were now settled in the north and Richard was hearing pleas and making judgements in his chamber at Middleham. His solicitor, Miles Metcalfe, was present for consultation if Richard needed to check a point of law, which was rarely, as he had excelled at his law studies during his knightly education under Lord Warwick.

"Your Grace, the next two are come from Newsholme, near Howden, a father and his three sons requesting to join your affinity here."

"Let them approach, Miles."

The four men were ushered into the presence of the Lord of

Middleham. One was short and stocky, about forty, with dark brows and sharp, shifty brown eyes, flint-like in their hardness. The others were taller, younger and slimmer. One, the youngest looking, had the look of many young men who were pretending to be braver than they actually were. His mouth was weak and his eyes softer than his father's, but he had the same dark brows; the resemblance was clear. The other two had their father's shifty eyes but their noses were more prominent and their chins stronger. One had lighter, curlier hair than his father and the other, the tallest one, sported an impressive moustache which hid his mouth. They all made clumsy obeisance to the Duke.

"What are your names?" Richard asked without any preamble.

"I am Thomas Forster, your Grace, and these are my sons, Robert, Richard and John."

"And you wish to enter my employ?" Richard held the man's eyes with his gaze.

"Yes, an it please your Grace. We have come far seeking honest work." It was the father who spoke.

"I see. What skills do you have?"

"We are yeomen, we have been soldiers and we can all fight."

"Very well, we are always in need of good fighting men. You are accepted – go and speak to my steward, John Conyers – he will assign you quarters and see to your instruction."

"Thank you, your Grace."

Richard nodded and dismissed them, then passed onto the next request.

"Who is next?"

"A peasant from over Masham way. He has a complaint about Jervaulx Abbey."

"Oh, indeed? Well, send him in."

190

The man, a small nondescript fellow, dressed in dirty, smelly rags approached the dais, removing his cap and bobbing his head as he did so.

"Your name, my man?"

"John Fletcher, your Grace."

"What is your complaint?"

"The Abbey has set a fish garth in t' river Ure by their fields, your Grace. They are tekkin' all the fish and leavin' nobbut a paltry few tiddlers fer us in Nether Ellington, who bide downstream from 'em. We depend on them fish in times o' scarcity, like. We see yon Abbot all fat and content while we go starvin'. T'ain't fair, tha knows. Them households downriver 'ave asked me t' put their case, like, as their spokesman."

"Hmm, it certainly seems unfair. How many households are affected, do you know?"

"Loads, your Grace."

"Loads, eh? Very well, Master Fletcher, I will look into it and we will sort it out, I can assure you. But it may take some time, as the matter will have to go before the king, since it involves the Abbey. I fear you are not the only sufferers of this offence – I have heard of this elsewhere and I will do my best to put a stop to it, you can be assured of that."

"Thank you, your Grace."

Fletcher bowed and left the chamber.

"Hmm," Richard said. "That is not the only case of fish garths being used illegally in the area, is it? Where was the other one?"

"It was in Goldale, I believe, your Grace."

"Ah yes, that is right. Well, we shall have to bring the matter before the king and get it resolved. Any more petitioners, Miles?"

"No, that is all for today."

"Then we just have to write a few letters..."

"What was that thing about fish garths? What is a fish garth anyway?" Alex asked Eve.

"It was a large trap that spanned most of the width of the river or stream and caught fish as they passed downriver. So, the rich abbeys and monasteries, nobles too, probably, were depriving all the people downriver of being able to catch them. Only the little ones got through and they were no good for eating. I know Richard petitioned for fish garths to be outlawed and destroyed in his domain, and he got Edward to agree and made sure the job was done as well."

"Stellan, perhaps you can see if you can find out more about these cases?" David asked.

So Stellan began listening by himself for a while until he found something he thought might be of interest. Eve sat and waited for the now-familiar internal images to pass through her mind as 'The Fly' started whirring...

As You Turn Away

Richard dismounted and handed the reins to the groom as the guards stood to attention. He nodded and turned away, then paused and turned back again, his head on one side, beckoning one of the guards to approach. "You are the new man – Thomas is it?"

"Aye, your Grace, Thomas Forster, and this is my eldest son, Robert." He pointed out the tall, young man standing beside the gatehouse. Richard nodded.

"Are you and your sons settling in alright, Thomas? Any problems?"

The man's eyes darted quickly to his son and back again. He had a somewhat insolent gaze and a hard mouth but he gave a tight smile that didn't reach his eyes.

"No, no problems, m' Lord. We've no complaints."

"Very good." Richard stood, looking thoughtful and removing his brown leather riding gloves. One of his alaunts, his favourite, Galahad, loped up and nuzzled his hand. Richard petted him absently and then addressed the man again. "Well, you may return to your post."

As the man turned away, Galahad lowered his ears, his hackles raised, and gave a low growl. He was staring fixedly at the man, Thomas. The man glanced over his shoulder and Galahad rushed forward, barking fiercely, his whole body stiff with tension. Forster flinched and then kicked out at the large dog, which immediately leaped for the man. He cursed and kicked out again, causing the alaunt to yelp. Before the dog could resume his attack, Richard called him to heel.

"Easy, Galahad, that is enough."

Richard frowned slightly and placed a hand on the dog's collar. The dog licked his lips and glanced up at his master, his hackles slowly subsiding.

"He will doubtless get used to you soon, Forster."

The man nodded, but his eyes revealed a dark, suspicious glare. He turned back to his guard duty and Richard, followed by Galahad, ran up the staircase to the keep, frown lines appearing as he pondered why Galahad had reacted so badly – he was usually of such even temperament.

Unusually Unusual

It was a week or so later that Richard heard some alarming news about his new employees. A sheriff had arrived from York, accompanied by a small contingent of armed men. When he was brought before Richard to state his business, he made his obeisance and said:

"Your Grace, there is a young widow, Katherine Williamson, who has petitioned for justice concerning the matter of her late husband, Richard, who was robbed and murdered on his way home to Howden from Riccall. He was waiting for a ferry at a place called Hemingborough when he was set upon by three men, named as Robert, Richard and John Farnell."

Richard said nothing, but regarded the man with a steady gaze, his eyebrows raised quizzically. The man shuffled his feet under the azure glare, coughed and continued.

"He was attacked first with a spear, causing him to fall from his horse and then, when wounded on the ground, the men cut off his hands and one of his arms from the elbow, hamstrung him and then robbed him of his goods including his bow, arrows, sword and buckler, and left him there to die of his wounds. The robbers are reported to have fled their homes and are thought to have been heading this way. I am here to enquire if you have any news of them."

Richard immediately narrowed his eyes and turned to his steward:

"John, is there not a father and three sons working in the guard who came to us from that way about two weeks ago?"

"Yes, my Lord, that is correct, but their name is Forster."

"That is an alias they use. If they are here, I would ask that you deliver them into my hands to take them to York for trial," interjected the sheriff, closing his mouth when Richard gave him an admonishing glance.

"First bring them here," he said to John.

Five minutes later they were, all four, standing before him.

"This man accuses you of robbery and murder. What say you to this?"

"I deny it!" exclaimed the elder man. "And my sons too, your Grace. We claim your protection, my Lord, as we are part of your affinity."

"God's teeth! Do you think to run to my protection like a child hiding beneath his mother's skirts? It may be you are innocent, but that is for the courts to decide." He turned to the messenger. "You may take them to York for trial. I will not have it said that the Duke of Gloucester shields men of his own household from justice, just because they are in his affinity." He redirected his stern scrutiny back to the Forsters. "It seems to me you were trying to use the old customs to escape due process, but you will not get protection from me. Justice comes first."

Question

"So why didn't Richard protect those men – they were his employees and would have expected to be under his protection, wouldn't they? Didn't the lord protect his affinity as part of the whole 'deal' of good lordship? The lord would give his protection to them and they would be prepared to serve him when he needed them, etc." Rupert had obviously been swatting up on Richard's times!

"Sue told me about this incident. The thing was they had deliberately entered into his service after the crime to benefit from his protection when they knew they were guilty. It was a 'cunning plan' you might say. Only they didn't reckon with Richard's sense of justice. He believed in the law and was a stickler for due process. He handed them over to the courts in York, obviously happy that they would be judged fairly, but be rightly found guilty if they actually were. They seemed to have robbed and murdered an innocent man. Good for Richard, that's what I say, murdering bastards!"

"Were there any other examples of this kind of justice after he became king?" David asked. "I'm trying to see if he changed at all, once he had got power – some people do, you know?"

"He didn't seem to change that much. I know of a case involving nepotism that he reversed. And he made some great laws in his one and only Parliament. But maybe we should wait and try to eavesdrop on those – they would be very interesting."

"Yes, you're right, of course. Let's be patient – we will find out what he was like as king soon enough."

Castles and Dreams

"Anne, I have an idea," Richard said. "Did you hear the new singer in St Akelda's choir this morning? I was deeply moved by the sweetness of his voice. I wondered if you would like it if we made a choir of our own to sing God's praises in our own chapel? We could engage the best in the land and create a choir to be admired all over Christendom. What say you, wife?"

"What a wonderful idea, Dickon. I would love that! They could be dressed in your livery and we could listen to the choirs wherever we go and choose the best to engage in our service. Oh yes! Let us do it, husband."

Stellan moved the search along a few months and found another reference to the choir.

"Well, Anne, finally I think we have succeeded in creating our choir – I have listened to the latest of our singers, a young man called Matthew, and he is indeed a great talent. The choir master has informed me that they have rehearsed their first psalm and so they will now perform it for us. Pray, sit you down and Ralph here will bring us wine while we listen."

"Thank you, Dickon." Anne replied.

Eve could tell that Richard had reached across and squeezed her hand just before the choir trooped in, all arrayed in tabards that were in murrey and blue, a small boar badge on the front of each.

Stellan was about to switch it off – after all, they couldn't hear the music – but Eve stopped him.

"No, Stellan, leave it for a short while... er... Richard might say something else of interest."

He looked at her with a puzzled expression, but left the machine running. Eve heard the voices of the young boys soar in unison, then split into a beautiful harmony, sending shivers down her spine, it was so moving. No wonder Nicholas von Poppelau, the Silesian courtier, had said that Richard's Court had the loveliest music he had ever heard.

"That was quite splendid, Benjamin, and in so short a time! You have done wonders, man. The boys can all take some time off and be rewarded with a penny."

The whole choir bowed and were led out by the choirmaster. As soon as they were alone, Richard turned back to his wife.

"Now, Anne, shall we commission a troupe of mummers also? They can be hand-picked by us and under our patronage. Do you agree!"

She smiled up at him as she sipped her wine.

"Yes, Dickon! It is a wonderful idea. But what will they do when you are occupied with other matters or when we are at Court?"

"They will have permission to perform elsewhere when we have no need of them. They can earn a little more that way. And others will see what a wonderful troupe we have gathered."

"Perfect!" Anne replied. There was a long, companionable silence as they finished their wine, relaxing in their solar and simply enjoying each other's company.

After a while, Stellan switched the machine off and looked at Eve.

She felt a little embarrassed, so started speaking.

"Did you know that Richard was also known for his architectural commissions? He had many buildings redesigned or built and often incorporated large windows to let in more light. One of them still survives in Barnard Castle in Yorkshire – it has a depiction of his boar above it and looks out onto the river."

"Really?" Stellan asked, all his attention on her.

"That's right – oh, and he also had an extra floor built onto Middleham Castle, with huge windows so that more light would come in – they could afford glass, of course. He obviously liked opening up his buildings to let in the light."

Chapter Seven

Middleham, 1474

When A Child Is Born

They moved on with their research to a time when Richard and Anne had been married for a couple of years.

"Jesus, Mary and all the Saints, please let her live! You must help her, I cannot lose her like this. Please give her strength to survive. I do not care if the babe dies, only let Anne live!"

On his knees, Richard crossed himself and then began again, praying over and over again.

He had been outside the birthing chamber hours ago and the screams and the smells were nauseating. He wanted to go in and comfort his labouring wife but, of course, the women would not let him.

"It is women's work, your Grace. You go off and relax; someone will call you when there is news."

"I will be in the chapel." he had said. But no one had yet come to advise him of her state. Perhaps that was good news? Surely if she had... gone... someone would have rushed to find him?

He left the chapel, but only to pace up and down outside in the courtyard, where they would see him if someone were sent to find him.

As he paced, unable to cease, he suddenly heard a commotion from the upstairs walkway. He watched, terror-stricken, as one of the midwives started descending the stairway. He ran up to meet her halfway.

"What is the news? Speak, woman!"

He realised he had grabbed her by the shoulders and he withdrew his hands and clenched his fists, then put them behind him; it helped to conceal the shaking at least.

The woman attempted a curtsey, a dangerous pursuit on the stairs. "You have a fine son, your Grace."

He felt his heart thump and a strange mixture of joy and fear. "And Anne?" he asked. "Is she well?"

"I would not call it that, but I suppose she is as well as can be expected. She has had a long labour and the child is big, so his passage into the world was difficult. But all is well now. She is exhausted of course, poor lamb, but she was very brave and diligent and her reward from the Lord is a bonny son. What will you call him, your Grace?"

"Edward," he said without hesitation. As if he would call his new heir anything other than the name of his brother, the king.

A few mere minutes later, he was sitting beside his wife on the bed and holding their tiny son, his first legitimate child.

"Is he not beautiful, husband?"

"Aye," he whispered softly, so as not to wake the sleeping child. "Just like his mother." And he leaned over and kissed his wife tenderly on the lips, uncaring what the staff witnessed. "But he definitely has his father's eyes."

She smiled back at the Duke and he knew in that instant that he would never swap one moment of time here in the countryside he loved with the wife he adored and their new baby son, for the hustle and bustle of Court and all the intrigue and plotting that went on. He remembered a time when he and Lovell and sometimes Anne, when she was young, would go together to various haunts around the castle. He knew it like the back of his hand and it would always be home to him. And now, he hoped to his son.

He bent his head, the dark waves falling around his son's face to tickle his little nose. He gently kissed the soft downy hair and whispered.

"Edward, this is your new home. I hope you like it. Know that we will never allow any harm to come to you, if it is in our power."

He handed the sleeping child to Anne.

"Thank you, Anne, for our son."

He smiled at her, his eyes sparkling, and she returned his smile, her own eyes moist.

"So, did he only have one child?"

Rupert looked at Eve, curiosity in his eyes.

"Only one legitimate one – as you know from that previous recording, he had two illegitimate children before their marriage. Nobody knew who their mother or mothers were, although there were a few theories. Now we know that Alys was their mother, don't we?"

Dream

That night Eve had the strangest dream. She was walking on a river bank when she saw a slim, young man, dressed in rich mediaeval clothes and wearing a jaunty, blue velvet hat with a jewelled brooch on it. His hair was light brown and wavy, with slight golden hues where the sun caught it and his eyes were a deep, piercing blue, the kind of eyes that look at you and see right through into your soul. His expression was serious and he nodded as her eyes met his.

She had a deep, irresistible urge to kneel and she duly sank to the grass, but she couldn't tear her eyes from his sapphire gaze. She was trembling from head to foot and then she heard him laugh, a sound so merry and uninhibited that she could not help joining in.

"Your Majesty," she said and he shook his head, causing his hair to ripple like the waves of the ocean.

"Nay, my lady, that form of address was never mine – 'Your Grace' is how I was known. And why art thou kneeling? Thou hast no need to offer me such obeisance, indeed I should offer it to thee, who does me honour and defends my name. Rise, my lady, and know I am grateful."

Of course, it was him, Richard III. In the dream, she had an urgent need to warn him and she said:

"Your Grace, do not charge for Henry Tudor at the Battle of Bosworth Field – you will lose and die."

"Dost thou predict the death of the king, witch?" he said then, his eyes glittering like jewels, but he was still smiling.

"Of course not, your Grace, but I am from the future and your future is my history."

"My lady, then it is unchangeable. What will be, will be – it is ordained by God, so I shall not attempt to change it. If I must die, then so be it – I will die King of England."

And suddenly he was dressed in full harness, his gilded armour glinting in the setting sun and casting reflections across the grassy banks of the river. He was holding his helm and he placed it on his head. She saw the royal coronet fixed proudly and defiantly on top of it. He had a horse, suddenly appearing out of nowhere, and a huge troop of knights were now surrounding him, like an honour guard.

"I do not die alone, my lady, and I do not fear death, for I know my heart is pure and heaven will be my reward, there to meet once more my loved ones; my wife, my son and my brothers. Yet, I am saddened that my honour will be besmirched and I charge thee now, if thou lovest me, to defend my name and try to right the wrongs which have been done to my reputation."

Then he kissed her hand, and his eyes, so beautiful and so sad, met hers again and she knew he could read her thoughts and she blushed. For if, as they say, the eyes are a window on the soul, then this man was the most beautiful and kindly spirit and she knew in that instant that she did love him and would defend him to her dying breath. He gave her hand a final squeeze and then mounted his horse and turned, galloping off into the misty distance without looking back.

She woke, sobbing, her pillow damp from her tears.

As she showered, getting ready for work, she thought over the dream again. She hadn't had such a vivid dream since her childhood, when she remembered dreaming of a rock star, Robbie Williams. Up until then she had disliked him intensely, but in the dream, he had been charming and kind and her judgement of him had changed because of it. After that, she had no longer disliked him and had even been to see him play live once.

She felt this dream had had a similar effect. She had been curious about Richard III before and leaned towards giving him the benefit of the doubt, but now she felt defensive of him, connected to him and personally involved in the project. What had he said? 'If thou lovest me… defend my name.' She did. She would.

To France

"When will this infernal rain cease!?"
Edward heard George's over-loud protest and scowled at him.

"George, the weather is probably just as bad back in England. Anyway, things could be worse. Look at us: we have a huge army and the support of Charles, our brother-in-law. Louis is bound to be quaking in his boots. He knows I have never lost a battle in my life."

Richard kept his silence and simply watched in amusement as his brothers bickered. At least George was now back in the fold of the House of York and no longer acting the traitor to his family and his King. George was difficult – he had always been discontented, never satisfied with his lot in life. He had a naturally ambitious and jealous nature, traits which had got him into considerable trouble in the past. At the moment, he was towing the line, though.

As they continued, they espied a lone horseman approaching them and they drew to a halt and waited to see what was afoot.

The man reined in his sodden horse, sending gobbets of mud flying and causing George to emit a curse as one spattered onto his velvet-covered leg. The man dismounted and reluctantly bent his knee to make obeisance to his King.

"What is it, man, speak up and give us your news."

"Sire, I come from the Duke of Burgundy. He sends his greetings, but regrets that his army is delayed at Neuss and he does not expect to bring them to join your Grace for at least another two weeks."

"What? But he promised to bring his men to back up my army. What use is he if he cannot even keep his word?"

"Well, you can ask his reasons yourself, Sire, since he follows about a mile behind with his entourage. He bids you proceed to St Quentin who will open their gates to you and give you some shelter from the inclement weather."

Edward gave the man a hard, calculating look and then gestured for him to rise, which he did with no small amount of relief.

"Join our company and you may take refreshment as soon as we halt for the night."

They pressed on and, as soon as the Duke caught up with them, Edward ordered his men to set up camp. He soon disappeared into his royal tent with Duke Charles at his heels, whence angry, raised voices could be heard for some time, followed by the Duke storming out and heading for his own tent. Richard requested entry to see his brother.

He was careful to make a respectful obeisance on entering and waited for Edward to invite him to speak.

"What is it, Dickon?"

"I could not help but hear the argument between you and Duke Charles. What are you going to do? I hope you are still intent on reclaiming our French lands. We do not need Charles' help – our numbers are such that we should be able to overwhelm the French easily without him."

"I do not know, Dickon – I have a bad feeling about this whole campaign. We may have a large army, but many of them are green and have never seen a battle. They are undisciplined. And nothing has gone right since we set foot in this damned country.

First the weather, then going astray, Charles backing out of his vow – what next I wonder?"

"The rain cannot last forever, surely, and you know how great a warrior you are. And, you have George and me to help you; the three sons of York back together and invincible."

"Hmm! Well, let us see what happens over the next few days, eh?"

The Gold It Feels So Cold

"Traitorous whore-sons!" Edward roared his disapproval as the cannons of St Quentin sent heavy stone cannonballs hurtling towards his advance guard, followed by a shower of whirring arrows. He ordered them to retreat, leaving several dead and wounded men behind. "When I next see Charles of Burgundy, he will wish he had never met me! How dare he betray me this way!?"

"Edward, Sire, let us press on and engage with Louis' forces sooner – it might even be a better strategy – he will not expect us to move so swiftly!" Richard was keen to engage the French. He still had in his mind the long-ago glory of Agincourt and wanted to see action.

"Hmph! I do not know about that – but we certainly cannot stay here for the night, as planned. We will have to press on for the time being; I will think on it as we ride."

And Edward turned his horse and trotted back to the commanders of his army to inform them of the bad news; they would have to continue to march in the rain without a proper night's rest.

They had continued on for another hour or two when a messenger arrived from Louis, the 'Spider King', himself. He was a nervous-looking man – hardly surprising considering the fearsome reputation of the English king. He made an elaborate obeisance to Edward, who bade him rise and ordered the men to set up camp swiftly. The king's tent was erected first, and refreshments were brought to him and the messenger. Only his body servants and Richard, who hovered at his brother's side, were allowed to remain in Edward's presence while the messenger gave his report. After hearing it, Edward sent him away without making any comment on the news, saying, in perfect French, that he would think about it and inform him of his decision later.

"In the meantime, please avail yourself of my camp's hospitality. I am only sorry that we do not have our usual delicacies and fine wine."

He turned to the nearest squire:

"John, fetch my brother, George, will you? And Will Hastings, Antony Woodville, Lord Howard and Northumberland. Quickly now!" The squire scampered off and a few minutes later the king's other brother arrived.

"Your Grace?" George appeared beside Edward and made a swift, respectful obeisance before his brother, who gestured him up immediately. "You summoned me, my Lord?"

"Aye, brother. I have some news for you – let us wait for the others to join us. John – fetch some wine for my brothers."

Richard and George took one of the goblets each and Richard downed half the wine in his, as he took one of the seats which Edward indicated. Hastings arrived next, followed by the others.

"I have summoned you all here to let you know of a proposal received from the Spider King. He wants us to go home without engaging."

"What?!" Richard leapt to his feet and slammed the goblet down on the wooden table between them. "Is he an imbecile? Why does he think you would even consider it?"

"Because I will, Dickon. He has proposed a tribute of seventy-five thousand crowns for us to return without joining battle. And he will then pay another fifty thousand to me every year and betroth his son, the dauphin, to my daughter, Bess. And of course, you, my chief generals, will also be given gold and gifts."

"But, Ned, what about all the funds given by the people towards a glorious campaign in France – a new Agincourt!? You cannot just... sell your soul to that devil, Louis. For one thing, he will not stick to the agreement, you can be sure. He will wheedle his way out of it as soon as he can. Secondly, you have over eleven thousand men here! When will you get such a great chance to conquer France again?"

"I will not need to – Louis is basically surrendering without a fight. Why should I endanger the lives of those eleven thousand when I do not need to?"

"Well, for one thing, they will not be too pleased to be sent back home without the chance to get loot from the French. And the merchants will be unhappy that you took their money for no reason. To say nothing of what our father would think – I thought you wanted to win back the land you were born in. The land that old Henry lost after Father returned to England. You said we, the three York sons, would return home in glory, that the French would be slaughtered just like at Agincourt, that our fame would be known forever."

"Calm yourself, my hot-headed brother. This campaign has not been blessed with good luck so far. The weather, the desertion of Charles and the treachery of St Quentin. If Louis is stupid enough to want to pay me off, why should I insist on endangering my men?"

"Because it is dishonourable, Ned! I cannot be a party to this – I am sorry." Richard stood up and made as if to leave.

"Be seated!" Edward said, his voice icy cold. "You will be a party to this – there is going to be a treaty with the French to be signed on the bridge of Picquigny in two days' time. I expect you to be there!" he thundered. Their eyes met, both blazing, over the table and Richard jerked his chin upwards as he said: "As you command."

There was a long silence, pregnant with tension, and then Edward nodded and said: "You may go – we will discuss this further tomorrow."

Richard turned and stormed out of the tent and went to his own, where he stomped in and shouted unfairly at his groom for not moving quickly enough to remove his boots. He sent for Lovell.

"My Lord?" Lovell appeared at the tent flap, a quizzical look in his soft, brown eyes.

"Come in Francis. A terrible thing – Ned has decided to sell his honour to the French – to capitulate to Louis' reprehensible demands in return for gold and gifts. What about the men? They will receive nothing and will have to face the shame of it when we return. I cannot believe Ned would do this!"

Francis entered the tent and sat down beside Richard. "Well, he is not getting any fitter, Dickon. Perhaps he is relieved he will not have to fight."

"Nonsense! He is still a formidable warrior. He is just taking the easy way out – doubtless influenced by Hastings. You know, Francis, I used to look up to Ned. When I was a boy, he was my hero. I have modelled my whole life on his – well except for his licentiousness with women, of course. His lordship, his governance of the realm, his tactics in battle. I wanted to *be* him. It is only recently I have come to see that he has feet of clay. But this – this is beyond the pale. My father will be turning in his grave."

He took a jug of wine and poured Francis a goblet. Picking up his own, he stared into it, swirling the red liquid around, his brow creased in a frown as he stood there. He licked his lips and sighed, his hair catching the reddish glow of the candlelight. Francis took a sip and then looked up at his friend.

"So, what are you going to do? Are you going with him to meet Louis and sign the treaty?"

"He has commanded me to, but he also said we will discuss it again tomorrow. I suppose I had better try to get some sleep and see if he will excuse me from witnessing the signatures. Maybe George can do it instead. Thanks for letting me rant. I feel calmer now. Tomorrow will tell. Goodnight, Francis."

Francis gave a short bow and left the tent. However, the next day, he was again at his friend's side when Richard was summoned to see the king.

"Richard, I do not expect you to cross me with others present. I may be your brother, but I am also your king and you must be respectful in public."

Richard bowed his head and nodded. "I know, Sire. I apologise. But I ask that you do not insist I attend the signing of the treaty. I still feel it is wrong."

"Very well, but I expect you to meet Louis and be civil to him at some point. He has specifically requested to meet all the York brothers so if you are not at the bridge, he will wonder what is occurring. I will say you feel unwell. You may go for now and I will keep you informed of developments."

Richard was therefore allowed to be absent at the signing of the treaty on the bridge at Picquigny, but, three days later, he was sitting in the great hall of one of the French castles, where he had been invited to dine with the Spider, Louis. He had been forced into it by Edward and knew that he was expected to do nothing to endanger the damned treaty.

He looked across at Louis, who was seated at the head of the ornately carved table, just one seat away from Richard, wearing a grubby old doublet and dull black hose. He also had on a pointed hat and a chain of office, but his most striking feature was his huge nose, which looked like nothing so much as a puffin's bill. His black eyes darted about noting what was happening in every corner.

"My cousin, the Duke of Gloucester, thank you for accepting my humble hospitality. I hope you enjoy our feast and the entertainments put on just for your pleasure. We have some jugglers and a dancing bear, but also a choir singing French songs – I heard you were particularly interested in music. May I call you Richard?"

Richard turned to look at him again, in shock. Why was he being so friendly? What did he want? But how could he refuse the king of France, especially when he was ostensibly being so polite to him? He inclined his head, gracefully.

"I would consider it a great honour, your Grace."

"Then you must call me Louis, Richard." Louis smiled revealing a row of rotten teeth. His breath smelled of garlic and his clothes of French herbs. "Also, please accept these gifts as a token of the future co-operation between our two lands."

He clapped his hands and some servants entered, struggling with something large and heavy. This was revealed to be a set of gold plate and Richard pursed his lips and frowned; he knew

211

Edward would be furious if he refused Louis but, on the other hand, he felt that accepting Louis' gifts would be almost as bad as accepting a bribe. Louis would think his acceptance a victory but, if he refused, Edward... Edward ... well, he didn't want to push his brother too far. Perhaps he could accept the gold plate – it seemed rather churlish not to, now that he was here. He smiled at Louis and lowered his head in a gesture of acquiescence, saying:

"You are too kind – I accept with thanks."

"Wait, there is more!" said Louis as he flapped a hand to his servant.

A few minutes later the man returned leading two spirited horses. They were young and full of life, tossing their shining manes and prancing their feet. Richard was just about to protest that this was too much, when he saw that one of the horses, the one furthest away, was a pure white colour and his proportions were perfect. The way he held himself was proud and confident, his ears pricked forward and his nostrils quivering as he sniffed the air. All at once, he turned his noble head and seemed to look right at Richard. Then he stamped one of his hooves and nickered softly, for all the world as if he was trying to communicate with him.

Richard had always loved horses – he tried to train them himself, especially any that he wanted to use in battle; you had to be sure that your destrier would obey you without question. You had to gain their respect and Richard always did this by spending time and patience on the training process. He knew of men who left their horses' training to their Master of the Horse or who used violence and fear to force the beasts to obey, but in his own experience that was not the best way. As a result, Richard's horses were renowned for being reliable, courageous

212

and obedient. He had just lost his best horse to a broken leg and this proud creature... well, this horse could be a most suitable replacement. Well, he could at least go and inspect the creatures.

"May I?" he asked Louis politely and the French king inclined his head, raised his eyebrows and beamed in agreement; The 'Spider King' knew he had ensnared Richard in his web.

Richard walked over to the two horses and made a show of inspecting the other one first. It was a mare, beautiful, her coat groomed so well it shone like a burnished chestnut. She had a white blaze down her nose and two white socks, her mane jet black. She was Anne's favourite colour for a horse. How did Louis know? Richard stroked the mare's nose and then up her neck and along her flank. Stunning.

Then he turned to the huge, grey stallion. As the Duke approached him, the big horse pranced and nodded his head up and down, as if he was showing off to him. Richard could not help smiling. He was perfect, the horse of his dreams! How could he refuse this gift? He argued to himself that this was surrendering, just as bad as Edward selling out to Louis, but then he reasoned that he would be pleasing Edward, his beloved brother. He admitted defeat and turned to Louis with a wary smile.

"This is a wonderful gift, Louis. I do not know how to thank you – they are perfect for my wife, Anne, and me. I am honoured and humbled by your generosity."

"No, no, do not mention it, Richard. They are from Syria, you know, of the best bloodstock, of course."

Louis placed a hand familiarly on Richard's shoulder and he forced himself not to flinch back. He hated any such contact anywhere near to his right shoulder which was higher than the other owing to his spinal problem.

"Now what are you going to name them?"

Richard gave a tight smile.

"I shall leave the chestnut for Anne to name, but in England we often name our horses for their origin, so I think I shall call the grey 'White Syrie'. Thank you."

"Splendid. Now are you sure you will not accept a small monetary... tribute in addition?"

Richard narrowed his eyes and cast a sideways glance at the crafty king.

"A bribe, you mean? No, thank you, Louis. I think you are pushing me a step too far."

Louis smirked and then gave a short chuckle, his hands raised in surrender.

"Very well, very well, but you cannot blame me for trying."

"So, he did have a horse called White Syrie! That's one mystery we've solved then. Some people said it was a myth – well, it's true there was no evidence for it before. There is a record of the names of many of the horses Richard owned – there were a lot of them too! And no 'White Syrie'. I think it was Shakespeare who said it first. Well, it seems there was one thing he was right about after all."

"So, did Louis keep to his treaty with Edward?" Rupert asked.

"For a while, but eventually he reneged on it and married his son to somebody else. He stopped paying the pension just before Edward died. One theory speculates that it was partly because he was so upset at Louis' betrayal that he became ill and passed away – he was only forty years old."

To Fotheringhay

"Richard, there is a Royal messenger climbing the stairway. I hope it is not bad news."

Anne's delicate eyebrows drew together in concern and her eyes sought her husband's for reassurance.

"Let us go and see," he said with a grim smile.

After the messenger had knelt and presented him with the ornate, rolled parchment, Richard unrolled it and began to read it aloud.

"'From the king,

My dear, trusted brother, Richard, Duke of Gloucester, we charge you to organise and oversee the reburial of our father, the late Duke of York and our brother, Edmund, Earl of Rutland. The funeral procession to begin near Wakefield, where they have until now been interred and to end at the Church of St Mary and All Saints, Fotheringhay, where our family seat is located. You shall oversee the exhumation of their earthly remains and you shall have the honour of being the chief mourner. There shall be a great feast in honour of our father and brother after the re-interment.

We commend us to you as heartily as we may,

Edwardus Quartus Rex

Written at Westminster, etc.'"

"Well, that is a great honour, my Lord." Anne always spoke formally in company.

"Indeed, it is, my Lady. Well, I must begin to plan the details and reply to my brother, the king, affirming his wishes."

And Richard swept off to his Great Chamber where he spent several hours.

On July 24th he was at Wakefield, where he had overseen the respectful exhumation of the Duke of York's and the Earl of Rutland's remains from the humble tomb where they had been interred. Their bodies were placed on hearses in the chapel until the procession was underway. Richard's father was dressed in a mantle trimmed with ermine and a cap of maintenance, covered with a cloth of gold. He then lay in state beneath a wooden framework or hearse, which was surmounted by blazing candles. His body was guarded by an angel of silver, holding a golden crown to show all who saw it that the Duke had been king by right.

Richard himself was dressed in sombre and respectful black as he and several other lords and officers followed the funeral chariot, which was pulled by six black horses all caparisoned in black, marked with the arms of France and England. A knight carrying the ducal banner went before the chariot.

At every stop for the night, the bodies of the Duke and his son were reverently borne to a place of sanctity and masses said for their souls. People came out to watch, as it was the sort of spectacle that was rarely seen.

Richard did not speak all that much and then his utterances were mainly to do with the services performed at each nightly rest stop. Apart from that, it was mainly pleasantries between him and his hosts and the clerics responsible for the masses. He seemed to be exhausted with all the preparations that had had to be made, which had kept him up late most nights, planning.

However, eventually, the cortege reached Fotheringhay, where the party was met by college members and other clerics. The king himself was waiting for them at the entrance with George (the Duke of Clarence), Thomas Grey (the Marquis of Dorset), Earl Anthony Rivers, Lord William Hastings and other noblemen. When they reached the king, he began to weep and knelt before his father's body, his head lowered in respect. Then he placed his hand on the Duke's body, finally kissing it while his tears still flowed freely.

"Oh Father!" he whispered, then stood back as the procession entered the church and the Duke was taken to the choir, where a hearse was waiting for him. The Earl of Rutland's hearse was in the Lady Chapel. All the important participants surrounded the two hearses while more masses were sung. The King's Chamberlain presented seven pieces of cloth of gold, which were placed on the Duke's body in the shape of a cross.

The next day more masses were sung and a sermon was given by the Bishop of Lincoln. Then, various offerings were made by some of the lords, including the Duke of Gloucester, who presented the Duke of York's Coat of Arms. The other offerings consisted of various pieces of his armour and weapons and Lord Ferrers rode his coursers, clad in his full harness and bearing a reversed axe in his hand.

When the funeral was over, all the people who had attended were allowed into the church to pay their respects and receive alms, five thousand at least. Then the bodies were placed in the vault prepared for them in the chancel. The dinner was served to twenty thousand people and there wasn't room in the castle, so tents and pavilions had been ordered to be set up by the king to take the overflow. The bill for all the food was over three hundred pounds and the menu included capons, cygnets, herons and rabbits.

This was another occasion that Eve watched alone. She thought the pageantry and dignity of the whole thing were performed immaculately and everything went without a hitch, thanks partly to Richard's competent organisational skills.

217

I'm A Believer

While researching the sources and contemporary records of Richard's reign, Eve had joined several Ricardian and other historical groups to try to get both sides of the story. She found that invariably the Ricardians were friendly and kind where those of a more Tudor-loving disposition were harder somehow – they were less willing to give the benefit of the doubt and often resorted to nasty, bullying tactics.

She found a blog with various articles of interest about Richard and his time, and enjoyed browsing through it. She learned a lot about Richard and also the customs of his day. There was a post about the marriage ceremonies and canon law, one about Richard's psychological profile, done by modern psychiatrists and using the evidence of his actions, one about his horoscope and another concerned with his handwriting. It was an eclectic mix of erudite and frivolous articles and she thoroughly enjoyed them.

She was interested to note that his psychological profile concluded that he showed no psychopathic tendencies (unlike Henry VIII) but that he may have been particularly sensitive to and intolerant of uncertainty. That wouldn't be surprising considering the turbulent times he lived through and the terrible experiences of his early life. It meant he was very trusting of those who were close to him, but suspicious of new acquaintances and decisive in action if it was required – these traits certainly seemed to fit with Richard.

Next, she looked at his horoscope – she had enjoyed astrology when she was a student and even made up a few charts for her friends. She was surprised to find – although thinking about it she shouldn't have been – that he had several planets in Libra, the sign of the Scales of Justice. No wonder he was so concerned about the law and administering it fairly to all. No surprise that he was a cultured man of good taste and a lover of music, architecture and luxury either. All these traits were typical of Librans. And, of course, he was also known for his lavish banquets and feasts – an excellent host, as shown by the Silesian courtier, Von Poppelau's, testimony. Ah! She noticed he had his planet Mars in its ruling sign of Aries – this emphasised its influence and made sense of his great martial ability and his skill as a warrior. It also foreshadowed his death from head injuries – Arians, were prone to those. Fascinating how it all seemed to fit his character perfectly.

She particularly enjoyed a post about his handwriting. It was only for fun, but the analysis concluded that he was an open, straightforward person, had a temper at times, was a good communicator and a bit of a control freak! Well, he was a human being, after all. His friends were also analysed and were also found to have well-balanced, open and generally positive traits shown in the writing, but when it came to Richard's enemies, it was even more riveting.

She was wondering what Margaret Beaufort's writing would be like – she seemed to have been the brains and planning behind her son, Henry Tudor's, bid for the throne. She imagined her script would be devious and illegible. When she found a sample, she was pleased to see that she had been right – it was completely indecipherable. But it was also large and confident – which she hadn't expected – and showed violent tendencies. Something about it made her shiver – she would surely not like to meet that woman on a dark night! Completely ruthless! Of course, this article didn't claim to be 100%

accurate, but even she, as a layperson, could see the heavy, slashing downward strokes, like daggers, which were so prominent in Margaret's hand.

All in all, she was becoming more and more convinced that Richard was nowhere near the black figure he had traditionally been portrayed as. All the evidence was weighing up and it was all on the side of his innocence.

Isabel

Richard and Anne's marriage was partly a matter of business and family alliances, but they seemed to be genuinely fond of one another and found in each other a safe haven – it was as if they represented home to their other half. They had much in common as regards their interests – especially music and religion. They were both more than usually pious and loved music and song. They were able dancers too and often could be found joining in with the dancing after their lavish banquets.

Eve and the team were listening to Richard chatting with guests at one of these banquets, part of the Yuletide celebrations, when he suddenly ceased talking. Eve could see him and the whole scene in her mind, of course, and she gasped as she saw a bedraggled messenger who was being shown into the Great Hall. He was spattered with mud and looked exhausted as if he hadn't slept for nights. He was still panting a little from his recent exertions. His livery was only just visible beneath the mud and filth, but Richard obviously recognised it as his eyes went wide and the smile died at the sight of the man.

He stood and waved him to approach the high table and the messenger knelt before him. Richard rose and strode around the table to raise him and offer him a seat and a drink before he asked his news. Eve could tell Richard knew it would be bad news. She felt his heart beating fast and the flutter of fear in his stomach. She wondered if he was being so hospitable merely to postpone the inevitable.

The messenger sat and took a deep draught of the wine Richard was offering but avoided his questioning gaze. Instead he glanced periodically at Anne and finally Richard too followed the man's lead and looked at his wife. She, astute as she was, had also noticed this and her forehead creased as fear laid siege to her thoughts too. She put down the goblet she had in her hand and moved calmly around to stand beside her husband. She said nothing but her eyes were eloquent as she met her husband's gaze. Unable to reassure her, he reached across and gave her hand a gentle squeeze, then he addressed the messenger.

"There is news from my brother of Clarence?"

Ah! thought Eve. *That's what the mud-decorated cognizance is – Clarence's Black Bull.*

"Aye, my Lord. I bring bad news from his household. His wife, Isabel," he said, glancing at Anne and adding: "Your good sister, my Lady. She has succumbed to child-bed fever, God rest her gentle soul."

For a split-second Anne's face crumpled, her chin quivering, as Richard rested his hand on her narrow shoulder. Then she gained control of herself again and addressed Richard.

"My Lord husband, I request the messenger be allowed to deliver the details of this most tragic news in the privacy of our solar," she said softly, no hint of emotion in her voice.

"Of course, my Lady." He nodded curtly to the man, who rose again on legs shaking with fatigue and followed the Lord and

221

Lady of the North out of the Great Hall and across to the Lord's chamber and solar.

On their arrival, Richard pointed out a chair to the man and found a padded one for his wife. He remained on his feet.

"What is your name?" he asked, speaking in a firm, yet soft voice.

"Nicholas, your Grace."

"Well, Nicholas, please relate how this sad turn of events occurred, if you will."

"As you may know, my Lord, your brother, the Duke of Clarence, and Isabel, became parents again in October – a boy child they named Richard, after you and your father. All seemed well at first but then she became ill and gradually worsened over the following few weeks, never rising from her sickbed and unable to eat, barely to drink. She passed away five days ago."

"Five days..." Anne muttered. "We were celebrating and joyful, while she was lying dead and cold. How is it I did not know; did not sense she was gone from this life?"

She let out her breath with a shuddering sigh and Richard turned to her and embraced her, his arms holding her head against his flank, stroking her hair, which had come loose from its coif.

"Thank you, Nicholas – please go you to the Hall and tell Sir John that you are to partake of meat and drink and then he will find you a bed for the night. Anne, we must go and pay our respects to your sister at her resting place." He turned back to the messenger. "You did not say where the Duchess will be laid to rest...?"

"Tewkesbury Abbey, my Lord."

"Thank you, Nicholas. You may leave."

When the man had departed, Richard turned back to Anne and without a word, knelt before her on the floor and took her hands in his. They were frozen and stiff with tension. He drew them to his lips and kissed them tenderly, then stroked her cheek with his finger. At this tender regard, her control broke and she wept, falling to her knees also and going into his waiting arms, where she sobbed silently as he held her.

They set out for Tewkesbury the next day, with a minimal entourage. Their progress was slow because of the inclement weather – there had been blizzards which had made the roads difficult and the cold made frequent stops necessary.

They arrived in Tewkesbury on twelfth night and by that time Isabel had already been laid to rest. They were made welcome in the Abbey and taken to see the last resting place of Anne's sister, where they lit candles and said prayers for her soul, making a handsome donation to the Abbey to ensure she would be remembered in their prayers in perpetuity.

"We should visit Warwick Castle and give our condolences to George," Richard said.

Anne frowned and pursed her lips.

"Look, love, I know you dislike him, but…"

"Dislike him! He had me abducted and kept like a slave, Richard! I cannot bear to even look at him. I am upset enough as it is about Isabel. Pray, do not ask me to visit that man. I know he is your brother, but he is a selfish, over-ambitious coxcomb!"

Richard looked at her, shocked at the vehemence of her words. It was not like Anne to speak ill of anyone. The affronted expression on her face made him burst out laughing. Anne tried to remain serious, but could not help but join in his laughter and the tension of the moment was broken.

"I will not force you to see George. I will send you home with an escort to ensure your safety and follow on once I have seen him. I have to go. He may be difficult but we share the same blood and I feel I must see him."

So, they parted and Richard travelled to Warwick Castle with only a very small group of retainers.

He found George distraught and inconsolable. His eyes were bloodshot and red and his face blotchy and pale. He had lost weight and looked somehow insubstantial compared to the brother Richard had last seen the previous summer. Richard knew he had made the right decision, though, when George realised he was there and flung himself into Richard's embrace, sobbing.

"George, do not weep. She is with God now, brother. You must let her go."

"It is not just Isabel – the babe, your namesake, passed just a few nights ago. I have lost both of them. It is not fair, Dickon, not fair. She did not deserve this."

"I am sorry to hear that. But you must accept it. It is God's will."

"Then I curse God!" shouted George, his face turning red as anger replaced grief and he pushed Richard away from him.

"Shh! Do not speak such terrible words, George. It will not bring them back. Come, let us have some refreshment and try to pull yourself together."

Richard put a comforting arm around his brother and patted his shoulder, whereupon George began to weep again, a sound full of misery.

"She was the only thing I ever loved," he mumbled, tears spilling down his cheeks and making his eyes like shattered glass.

Eve was almost in tears herself as she could sense the grief in Richard at his brother's distress. She felt his helplessness and the heaviness of sadness in his heart as Stellan cut the contact. Alex broke the silence.

"Well, it's five thirty, folks. Home time. Unless you'd like to go to a ballet," he said, his last comment aimed at Eve. "I have tickets for Sadler's Wells for tonight – a friend can't go and asked me if I'd like them. I thought you might like to come."

"I've never been to a ballet before," she said, not sure that she would like it.

"Well, then, you must go at least once in your life. It's that new young principal male dancer, Dmitri Kavalyov."

"Really? I've heard of him – isn't he the one who is a bit rebellious?"

"Yes, he thinks he's the new Sergei Polunin, but he is very talented. What do you say?"

"I say 'Yes', thank you," she smiled.

"Let's go then!" he grinned back at her, and they left together, chatting away.

Rupert looked after them and then lowered his head, sighed and picked up his leather jacket.

The Best You Never Had

Eve sat in Sadler's Wells Theatre beside Alex, supposedly watching Swan Lake, but her mind was wandering. She realised that ballet just wasn't her thing and her thoughts kept drifting to Richard and the sadness in his life and that of his family. She jumped as Alex leaned over to whisper in her ear.

"What do you think of Natalia Krasichova. She is so talented, don't you think?"

Eve nodded and smiled, but hoped he wouldn't ask her anything more, as she had no idea whom he was talking about. In fact, the only dancer she was not only aware of, but also impressed by, was Sergei Polunin, a superstar of the ballet world, but also known as the 'bad boy of ballet', an alliterative and emotive description, cynically designed to appeal to the public – and it worked. She had only agreed to go to the ballet with Alex to see whether this 'new' Polunin was as gorgeous. Polunin was not only physically stunning but his dancing was unbelievably brilliant. He had walked out of the Royal Ballet several years before and worked with David La Chappelle on a modern interpretation of 'Take Me to Church' by Hozier, the result uploaded to YouTube. It had gained millions of views – she herself had watched it about twenty times. She told herself it was because his talent was so amazing, but actually it was mainly because he danced in ripped, skin-tone leggings, so tight they could have been sprayed on, and nothing else. His muscles were like a classical Greek sculpture and his tattoos were impressive too, reinforcing the 'bad boy' image. His jumps were so skilled that he seemed to fly through the air and float at the apex of the arc he made and his dramatic interpretation of the music was moving and mesmerising. However, this new guy was nowhere near as good.

Alex was oblivious to her indifference regarding the other dancers and she suddenly felt tired of trying, tired of pretending to like something she really didn't. She and Alex obviously had nothing in common. His taste in art was dire, in her opinion, and his love of ballet, pretty boring. OK, they both enjoyed eating out and were intrigued by the Richard III experiment, but was that enough to consider having a relationship with him? True, he was charming and good-looking in a self-obsessed sort of way, but Eve had never been the type to view looks as the most desirable quality in a man.

So, when Alex moved in to kiss her in the taxi home, she turned her head away and apologised.

"Alex, sorry, I'd rather you didn't... I don't feel we have much in common – it was a lovely evening and thanks for inviting me, but it really isn't my thing and I don't want to get close to anyone unless I feel it's going somewhere."

He drew back from her, frowning, and replied:

"What do you mean? We have loads in common – what about Italy, eating out, dogs. I'm not letting you go without a fight. Look, I've been patient, I backed off when you asked me to, didn't I? I don't want to give you up. Please, Eve!"

She leaned further away from him.

"I'm sorry. That's all I can say – I just don't feel a spark with you. I thought it was only because I had recently split from James but it's not that. I don't want to waste your time."

His eyes grew hard and his lips compressed into a thin line as he stared at her. Then he sighed and moved away, shaking his head.

"OK, have it your way, but I believe you'll regret it someday, I really do."

She breathed a silent sigh of relief – at least he hadn't tried to insist. She spent the rest of the journey staring out of the window, watching the people splashing through the drizzle, the street lights garishly reflected in the puddles. But she didn't care – it was as if a weight had been lifted from her shoulders.

Chapter Eight

Cambridge, 1477

Sanctus

They had located Richard at Cambridge in April 1477, as Duke of Gloucester. He was being shown around Queens' College or, as it was then known, the Queen's College of St Margaret and St Bernard.

"Yes, this will be perfect – a new chantry here, I think. My wife, Anne, and I are intending to grant the College the advowson of Fulmer, in this county. As you may know, it came to us after it was forfeited by the De Veres. In return for this, I would request that prayers be said for the souls of the De Veres, the Earl and Countess of Oxford. Also, for the good estate of the king, my esteemed brother, Edward, and his queen as well as for the weal of my own family – my wife, our son, Edward, and me. Also, I wish prayers to be said for all those who fell at my side in the Battles of Barnet and Tewkesbury six years ago, in particular Thomas Parr and Thomas Huddleston, my loyal and trusty squires, John Milewater, John Harper and

Christopher Worsley and all other gentlemen and yeomen, servants and lovers of me as Duke of Gloucester, who were slain in my service. I will, in fact, go to your chapel now and pray for their souls myself, if you will kindly lead the way?"

"Of course, your Grace. We thank you and your Lady wife most heartily for the endowment. And we will gladly pray for your family and the king's. As for the young squires and others who died – it is tragic when lives are taken too soon and in violence. You do well to remember them so kindly and we will be honoured to include them in our prayers also."

Richard smiled ruefully and followed the man as he took him by the swiftest route to the chapel, which was part of the front Court, where he knelt and prayed for the souls of his brave young friends, to whom he probably owed his life.

The team heard him as he intoned the prayers for the souls of the dead – something which they were now familiar with. It was clear Richard was every bit as pious as his reputation suggested.

After the chapel visit, Richard asked to see the Library, which was on the north side of the front Court and one of very few purpose-built libraries. It held an impressive collection of manuscripts and books – over two hundred – and Richard spent a good hour perusing the illuminated tomes and manuscripts.

Act

In the same year, 1477, the team also found Richard and Anne acting as prominent members of the Guild of Corpus Christi in York.

They listened in on Richard's attendance at the religious procession which took place the day before the Feast of Corpus

Christi and the York Corpus Christi plays, which were performed on the actual day of the Feast.

It was pretty boring for most of the team, who could only hear Richard himself, because for most of the celebrations, he was silently listening or repeating the litanies and prayers that everyone participated in. But Eve saw it all as if through his eyes and found it awesome.

The celebration started before dawn with a torchlight procession of all the city's dignitaries, both clerical and secular, honouring the body of Christ. The atmosphere was one of anticipation, joy and excitement, and Eve could hear the chanting as they processed, as well as see the flickering torchlight. She enjoyed the gradual blossoming of dawn's rosiness as they solemnly followed the host, held aloft by the Archbishop and trailed by the numerous wagons which would comprise the various scenes of the Corpus Christi plays, to be performed the next day.

The plays took over thirteen hours to perform in total and the rest of her colleagues were completely bored after about an hour, so Eve asked Stellan if she could listen to some of the rest of it later; Stellan often left the machine whirring away, recording everything when there wasn't much to hear, just in case something significant turned up and it was usually Eve who volunteered to monitor these. She enjoyed absorbing the various scenes and she got paid overtime for scanning the recordings at her leisure, carefully encrypted, of course.

She did this for the plays too, because she found them fascinating. There were forty-eight plays altogether, and they were financed by the different guilds, such as the Mercers, Wainwrights, Tanners, etc.

The plays were often relevant to the particular guild that

performed them. She loved that the play concerning the building of Noah's Ark was performed and financed by the Wainwrights, the Wine-sellers did the Wedding Feast of Cana and the Chandlers or candle-makers, the play which included a depiction of the Star of Bethlehem. There were plays showing Christ's birth, Herod's Murder of the Innocents, the Last Supper (this was the Bakers' Guild's domain) and the Day of Judgement. Many of these had special effects such as actors being raised and lowered by elaborate pulley systems and all had music, colourful costumes and singing. She thought it must be similar to the Oberammergau Passion Play. Even though she wasn't religious, she found it deeply moving and wondered if that was due to the very real emotions she was picking up from Richard, to whom it was all of vital importance. She finally began to understand how all-pervasive religion and prayer were in mediaeval times.

But then came shocking news from the south.

Act of Treason

It was the same messenger who had advised them of Isabel's death. This time he was white-faced and trembling as he stood before the Duke and Duchess.

"Yes, spit it out, Nicholas!" Richard said, brusque in his need to know the news.

"It is your brother, the Duke of Clarence, my Lord. He has been acting foolishly, dangerously. We think he must have lost his mind because of his grief. He accused poor Ankarette, Isabel's servant, of poisoning her and his new-born son. Ankarette, who had been a faithful and hardworking servant to them both! He had her dragged from her bed and taken from her home in Cayford, in the county of Somerset, to the Guildhall in Warwick, seventy miles away. There he set up a trial – a mock trial, as it was entirely illegal and unauthorised. The jury were composed of his own men – bought or threatened, so they had no choice but to give the verdict he required: Guilty, guilty of murder!"

Nicholas's eyes brimmed with unshed tears. Anne waved a servant over to pour him a drink, which he took gratefully and then put down on the table.

"Continue, Nicholas," Richard said, his voice almost a whisper.

Nicholas swallowed.

"She begged him to spare her, swearing she was innocent, that she would never hurt Isabel or her child, but he would not listen. He would not soften his heart. *We* all knew she was innocent – she was just a poor, old woman. I think she was more upset that he would even think such a thing than that she was to die. He had her hanged the same day."

Richard sighed heavily. "Oh, George! Why is he so foolish! Is that all, Nicholas?"

"Not quite, Sir. King Edward heard of it and has had Clarence arrested and imprisoned in the Tower. He cannot act like a king when he is not, he said. Oh yes, Clarence had requested – no, demanded – to marry Mary of Burgundy too. The king refused, of course, and Clarence… let his displeasure be known."

"Charles of Burgundy is recently dead, so Mary is the heiress. He wanted to become Duke of Burgundy?"

"Aye, your Grace. He is an ambitious man."

"Ambitious – yes, aren't we all? It is a natural state for the nobility, but George knows not when he goes too far." He sighed. "I can see Edward's point – if George became Duke of

Burgundy, he would have a way in to invade us and threaten Edward for the throne of England."

He stood with his hand on the back of his wife's chair and tapped his bejewelled fingers on the wood, his brows drawn together into a frown. "However, to arrest him…!" He pursed his lips and closed his eyes momentarily as if to block out the thought of it.

"What will you do, my Lord?" asked Anne. She knew her consort disliked conflict and uncertainty.

"Edward will let him languish in the Tower to consider the error of his actions for a while. Then, hopefully, he will relent and release him with a warning."

But his brows were drawn together in worry and it was Anne's turn to give comfort to her spouse. She embraced her husband and whispered:

"Surely Edward will forgive him? He always has before."

"I hope so, Anne, I hope so."

Beggin'

It was not until the following February that they tracked Richard to London, to the Palace of Westminster. He was talking to his brother, Edward, the king. They couldn't tell, but Eve knew, that Richard was on his knees before his brother and had a look of desperation in his eyes.

"Please, Ned, do not do this! Surely you will regret this rash decision – forgive him, he is our brother after all. We are the three sons of York, united against the world."

"Not any more, Dickon." Edward's normally handsome face was set in a determined grimace of anger and Richard knew he was sailing close to the wind. He had to trim the sails carefully to avoid running aground on the rocks of Edward's royal ire.

"But you have forgiven him worse before. I do not understand why he must... why his punishment is so severe this time. Let me speak to him – mayhap I can persuade him to curb his ambition. You have given him enough of a shock by imprisoning him in the Tower for so long. I am sure he expected to get away with a warning. He will not dare go against you again, he..."

Edward flung out his muscular arm and swept the wine goblets and platter of sweetmeats off the table with a crash that made Richard jump. His voice was hoarse with rage.

"Enough, Richard. He sought to marry Mary of Burgundy, which would have given him enormous power. And do you think he would have remained content with that? Of course not! He would have been facing me – and you – across the battlefield. You will speak to me no more on this subject. My decision has been made and it will be done. Do not waste your time or your words on him. He has overstepped the mark for the last time! And you may not speak to him, either."

"But.." Richard's normally even features contorted in his desperation.

"AAAAH!" Edward roared, his face red with his excess choler. "Be silent, unless you wish to join him in the Tower! Now get out!"

Breathing heavily, Richard made his obeisance and left, slamming the door behind him to show he was still defiant, despite obeying his king. He went to his usual apartments in the palace and poured himself some wine, which he downed in a single swallow, refilling the glass again and again. He suddenly had a prolonged coughing fit as some of the red liquid threatened to choke him, making his eyes water as he struggled to catch his breath. Then, as if a dam had collapsed with the weight of water behind it, more tears came, along with sobs, as the stark reality of his brothers' estrangement hit him. He had not always liked George, but he had always loved him.

They had grown close during their exile in the Low Countries, just after their father had been killed. George had made him laugh to banish the melancholy that had plagued him after having been sent far away from home, not knowing when or if they would return. He had often defended his younger brother when older boys had teased him – equally often he would tease Richard himself, but that was different. They were brothers, so he had the right to do it, or so he thought.

Yes, they had disagreed over Richard's marriage to Anne and her inheritance, but they had eventually resolved it... Why could Edward not do likewise? George was their brother, the same flesh and blood. This just was not right! He held his hand to his brow in an effort to dispel the pounding headache which had started to worsen, and groaned. He went into his bedchamber and tried to sleep, but his mind would not quiet and he threshed about restlessly half the night long. In the morning he left Court for Middleham. He could not even bear the smell of the place any more. The smell of corruption. He still hoped Edward would have a change of heart.

But he did not and in the February of 1478, news was brought to him of George's execution. Anne entered the solar to find him slumped in his chair, his face paler than usual and his eyes red and swollen. One look at him and she knew what had happened and went over to give him what little comfort she could.

"It is George, is it not?"

"Aye, he is dead, Anne. They say he asked to be killed by

being drowned in a butt of Malmsey." He passed his hand through his dishevelled hair, so unlike him, and gave a short bark of a laugh, mirthless and bitter. "How typical of George to even die in a singular way."

She put her hand on his shoulder and he turned to her, holding her tightly, burying his face against her gown, but made no sound and did not weep; it was as if all emotion had been locked away inside him.

Don't Forget To Remember

After George's execution, Richard stayed away from Court as much as he could, only riding to London if his presence was required in Parliament or for some special occasion. He tried to take his mind off George by involving himself in other projects and one of his favourites was the founding of Middleham College. For some time, he had intended to have the Church of St Mary and St Akelda made a collegiate Church. They were listening to him speaking to someone else, probably a secretary, formulating the wording of the official document...

"Richard, Duke of Gloucester, Great Chamberlain, Constable and Admiral of England, Lord of Glamorgan, Morgannok, Bergavenny, Richmond and Middleham, to all Christian people concerned, greeting in our Lord everlasting. Know you that where it has pleased Almighty God, Creator and Redeemer of all mankind to enable, enhance and exalt me, His most simple creature, nakedly born into this wretched world, to the great estate, honour and dignity that He has called me now to be named, known, reputed and called Richard, Duke of Gloucester and of his infinite goodness not only to endow me with great possessions and gifts of His divine grace, but also to preserve, keep and deliver me from many great dangers, perils and hurts, for which, in recognition that all such goodness comes from Him, I am finally determined in the loving and thanking of his Deity and in the honour of His Blessed mother, our Lady Saint Mary, and in the honour of the holy virgin Saint Akelda, to establish, make and found a College within my Town of Middleham at the parish church there, in which shall be a dean, six priests, four clerks, six choristers and a clerk sacristan to do divine service there daily, to pray for the good estates of the King our Sovereign Lord and the Queen, and for the good estates of my lady and mother, the Duchess of York and of me, my wife, my son of Salisbury and such other issue as shall please God to send me, while I live; and for the souls of my said Sovereign Lord, the King, the Queen, and of me, my wife and my issue after our decease, and especially for the souls of my lord and father, Richard, Duke of York, of my brothers and sisters and all Christian souls, in part of satisfaction of such things as at the dreadful day of doom I shall answer for. The same my College to be called and named forever the College of Richard, Duke of Gloucester, of Middleham, and to be ordained, established and made as follows: have you got all that down, John?"

Stellan paused the machine.

"What on earth was all that about?" asked Rupert.

"I think it was part of the official statutes for the founding of Middleham College. It sounded as if he was dictating to someone, his secretary, I suppose," Eve replied.

"He believed in long sentences, didn't he?" David said, chuckling. "Do we need to listen to this, then? Is it important or can we skip it?" He directed the question at Eve, his researcher.

"Well, it isn't particularly relevant to the question of the princes, but it does tell us quite a bit about him."

"Do you know about this then?" Rupert asked. "I didn't know he had founded a college."

"Well, it never got completed because he was killed before it could be fully established. As far as I recall, Susan told me that this was a very long piece of legal jargon which went into great detail about which of the priests and other incumbents should sit in which stall of the church and what the various stalls should be called."

"What they were called?" asked David, puzzled.

"Yes, they were named after saints and other holy figures such as 'Our Lady', Saint George, Saint Katherine, Saint Ninian, St Cuthbert, etc. Also, he insisted that only he and his heirs should be allowed to appoint the clergy. He goes into great detail about what learning and skills the priests should have, such as being well versed in literature and also skilled in singing plainsong and other types of singing, and that one of the clerks should be able to play the organ and play it daily. We can see he was a thorough and meticulous man, and went into minute detail about every little thing concerning his College so that every eventuality would be covered."

"Or he was a control freak!" piped up Rupert.

Eve rolled her eyes. "It could be that this shows his need to avoid uncertainty. There was a psychological profile that found that he had intolerance to uncertainty. This attention to detail could be his way of avoiding unforeseen circumstances."

"What else did he itemise?" asked Alex.

"The wages that would be given to each of them, what would happen if someone was absent, that the choristers couldn't remain longer than six months after their voices had broken. That visitors should be courteously welcomed. What saints should be worshipped and which collects should be said. That a chest should be made with three locks whose keys should be kept by three separate people to keep the College's jewels, seal and other items safe. That the priests and clerks should be in the choir by the third peal of the bell or else fined a penny. Persistent offenders to be punished." She paused, a cheeky twinkle in her eye. "He even had added a clause that states he reserved the right to change the terms and conditions – they had that sort of thing in those days too!"

Decision

In 1480, they again came across a dispute that Richard had to adjudicate on.

"Who is next, Miles?" Richard asked his solicitor, Miles Metcalfe.

"A man called John Randson, your Grace, a simple husbandman of Burntoft. He is involved in a land dispute with Sir Robert Claxton of Horden."

"Claxton, yes, I know him," Richard said. "His son and son-in-law are both in my service. He is a high-ranking member of the gentry in Durham. Show this Randson in, will you?"

The man entered and performed a respectful obeisance before the Duke, who beckoned him to come closer.

"What is the problem, Master Randson?"

"Well, your Grace, Sir Robert Claxton is preventing me from working my own land. He claims it is his and that is a lie, your

Grace. We both have an interest in it, but I only want to use my portion."

He bowed again and Richard waved him up with a be-ringed hand.

"Do you have proof the land in question is yours, Randson?"

"Aye, your Grace. I have a deed detailing the ownership and two independent witnesses who will swear part of it belongs to me."

"How is he preventing you from working it?" Richard asked.

"He has let his herd of kine in there and the bull is not happy about anyone invading what he thinks is his territory. I have tried to get him out, but I almost got gored. Bulls are right aggressive this time of year, your Grace."

Richard smiled. "Aye, I remember an encounter I once had with one," he said. "Show Miles here your proof and I will make sure it is sorted out."

The man bobbed up and down in gratitude.

"Thank you, your Grace, I knew you would judge fairly. My wife said I would never win against such a prominent gentleman, who also has relatives in your service, but I knew you were a good'un."

"You are welcome, John."

John Randson bowed once more and left the chamber.

Miles was used to Richard's unique, for the times, form of justice.

"Your Grace, you are right to find against Sir Robert; he is a scoundrel and a chancer."

"Yes, Miles. Such is the world we live in these days. People have been abusing the system of livery and maintenance for too long. It was meant to be based on chivalry and honour, not corruption and unfairness. The bond between a vassal and his lord is supposed to be founded on loyalty, faith and responsibility. Sadly, those days are over. But it does not mean we have to roll over in surrender to the new ways. We can do our part for the restoration of the old ones."

Richard then dictated a missive to Sir Robert, instructing him to make the required concessions to Randson.

A few weeks later, Randson was again before the Duke.

"Your Grace, Sir Robert has done nothing about the land in dispute. His kine are still there and he has not divided it or taken them out."

"Well, that is unfortunate. Do not concern yourself – I shall see he takes notice this time."

After the man had left, Richard dictated a second letter.

"I wish to make it clear that, marvelling greatly that you have disregarded my previous instruction, I expect you so to demean you that we have no cause to provide his legal remedy in this behalf." This was part of the follow-up letter he wrote to the recalcitrant lord.

I'll Be There

"Can you explain that, Eve?" David asked. "I understand it was a dispute, but I don't get the details."

"Basically, again Richard is dispensing justice fairly rather than siding with those who are more powerful or with whom he had an affinity – a relationship between the Lord and his vassals. When the guy, Sir Robert, ignored the first letter, the second is saying basically "Do as I instructed or I will have to come there and sort it out!""

Rupert laughed.

"I bet he was quaking in his boots, wasn't he? I mean, Richard wasn't known for his strength, was he? He was only a little guy and very slim."

"He was powerful though, in that he commanded all the men around that area. He was their lord and they owed their allegiance to him. He could make life very uncomfortable for those who crossed him, you know. Everyone knew their place in those days and most accepted their lot in life. So, if he commanded someone to do something, they did it. It was pretty much only the nobility who aspired to increase their power and wealth."

"Well, he definitely did, didn't he? He could be pretty ruthless when it came to gaining power, influence and land."

Eve tilted her head, considering. "Yes, he did acquire a lot of land and gradually built up his power base in the North. But that was the norm in those days – it would have been very peculiar if he hadn't done that."

"If you say so!" Rupert said, grinning.

Hymn Before Action

They had moved on to the year 1482. Before the Scottish campaign, Richard and his generals all went to pray to St Cuthbert. He and the Earl of Northumberland, Henry Percy, were entertained by the Priory, before the holy banner of the saint was unfurled over the army to bless their endeavour. It would accompany them on the campaign to ensure success just as St Cuthbert had ordered done at the Battle of Neville's Cross in 1346, when he appeared in a vision to the Prior of the Abbey at Durham.

A few weeks later, they had reached Edinburgh.

Richard addressed his generals in a loud, ringing voice, facing them on his snow-white destrier, Whyte Syrie.

"Hearken to me. Edinburgh has capitulated without a fight. The king is in the control of his disenfranchised nobles and we will be negotiating with them peacefully. I know your men are disappointed that there will be no plunder for them. However, I expect them to treat the Scots with respect. That means no pillaging or burning, no killing of those who have surrendered and no raping."

"That certainly will not be popular," Northumberland muttered to him so that the others could not hear. Richard pursed his lips and continued.

"If anyone is found indulging in any of these activities, they will be hanged immediately. Is that clear?"

There was a bit of shuffling of feet and murmuring amongst them, but then a chorus of assent.

"Good!" he said, satisfied. "I will see that you are well paid for your trouble. Keep your men in order and all will go well."

And they set off towards Edinburgh Castle in an orderly fashion, supplicants emerging from their homes as soon as they realised they were safe, beseeching the invading army to give them alms. Richard threw them a few coins and led his army into the Castle, which had been thrown open to them. Richard had been charged to aid the Duke of Albany, the King of Scotland's younger brother, to gain the throne, but now the fickle Duke had changed his mind and wished to reconcile with his brother, King James, after all, in return for being allowed to retain his lands and title. So, Richard's victory was a somewhat hollow one. He had spent time and money preparing for battle, had lost men in the skirmishes along the way and, although gaining Edinburgh without a fight, had not fulfilled his brother's commands.

However, he had laid siege to Berwick-upon-Tweed – a town which had passed backwards and forwards between English and Scottish hands – and succeeded in taking it, leaving Stanley in charge of besieging the castle. He expected the fortress to be in his hands if not by the time they returned there, then very soon after. This was a great achievement, particularly as Edward had vowed to accompany the English army and reneged on his promise at the last minute, leaving Richard in sole command.

When he returned to report to the king what had happened, he was surprised to find that Edward had been praising him to the skies.

"Ah! Here he is: the hero of the Scottish campaign! A Hector reborn! I can always count on you, Richard. My most loyal and loving brother. I have written to the Pope praising your military prowess and I intend to bestow on you the right to any land you can take for yourself in Scotland. What say you to that?!"

Richard thanked him graciously, but privately thought it was most generous of the king to offer him land that was not his to give – and that he had to fight to gain. Still, it would mean his son had an inheritance that was not dependent on other factors.

Perhaps the king felt grateful to his loyal brother for accomplishing that much in Scotland when he himself had been unable to even journey that far. Perhaps it was partly guilt at leaving the whole venture to Richard. Whatever, he was pleased to receive Edward's praise and the promise of an inheritance for his son, even if he would have to take it himself, but there was something different about their relationship now. Whereas, before, Richard had always been somewhat in awe of his shining, giant brother, he now saw him for what he was – what he had always been; just a man with as many faults as any other – more maybe. Edward let himself be led into sin by his bodily desires far too much and not just lust but gluttony too. And he also suffered from the sins of pride and sloth now his famous vigour and strength had been depleted by his inability to restrain himself from excess.

Richard's thoughts wandered back to Picquigny – the first time he had realised his god-like brother was just a false idol. The first time he had publicly questioned his actions. And then to George's execution. Their relationship had never been the same since. Richard just could not comprehend why George was so severely punished for something that was not much worse than the betrayals under Warwick's rebellion, years before. And it had affected Edward too – Richard did not understand why, when it had been in his power to pardon him or commute the sentence to imprisonment. Did he regret this fratricide? Or was there something else, something Richard was unaware of?

Chapter Nine

Middleham, April 1483

Cuts Like A Knife

Richard rode across the drawbridge and through the north gate, looking up to the stairway where he knew Anne and Edward would be waiting for him. She always made sure she was there once the advance message had reached her. Richard loved that she knew how much it meant to him and his heart always lifted when he saw them both standing there. Edward was growing so tall – where had the last nine years gone? His mind drifted back to the day when he had been born, all those years ago. And now it was difficult to remember what life had been like before his son and heir had arrived.

His arrival had not been easy – both the babe and Anne had almost died and it seemed that something had been damaged in her by the traumatic birth – she had bled a lot and he had prayed so hard for her to live. At the time he would have sacrificed the life of his son to have saved her, but the thought of that now was horrific. His boy was very much like him, but with Anne's small nose and hair colour. His eyes, Anne said, were completely Richard's, both in colour and shape. And he had his father's strong chin and mouth. He was intelligent and brave, although not the biggest or strongest child, just like Richard himself had been. But Richard could not have been prouder of him. It was just a worry that they had not been able to have more children, because God could take a child at any time, and often did. It would have been reassuring to have more and Edward would have had a companion as Richard had had George, even though he had sometimes wished him gone. Yet, now he was dead, he missed him. Strange, even though he had seen George rarely in the last few years of his life, knowing he could see him whenever he travelled to London or Warwick was comforting. And now he was gone.

He tore his thoughts away from the past and considered the future instead – Edward had told him, after his great achievements in Scotland, that he could take any Scottish land he conquered for himself and his heirs in perpetuity. At last his family's future was secure and he had felt the weight of care lift at Edward's words. Finally, his unwavering loyalty to his older brother had been vindicated. Anne had at times questioned why he was so fiercely loyal to the king, whenever Edward made unreasonable demands on Richard, or overburdened him with responsibilities. But even she had danced around the room with him in joy at the news. Edward would inherit his Dukedom and much land in the North; he would be the next Lord of the North.

He looked up to see his family, a smile beginning to form on his lips, when he realised Anne was alone. Where was Edward? Oh no! Had something happened? He looked at his wife more closely and his heart froze in his chest; she was wearing black!

He leapt from his horse and ran up the stairs to her, his heart thumping madly and his legs shaking.

"Anne, why is Edward not here? Is he...?" He grabbed her roughly by her shoulders and his hands trembled as he saw the grief in her eyes, but she replied:

"Your son is well, Richard, but I told him to remain in the nursery with John and Katherine. I need to speak with you now – there is news from London. I... I am sorry, husband – it is bad, very bad." She took him by the hand, holding it so tight it was painful. "Richard, the king is dead, Edward, your brother. He is gone and he has named you Lord Protector." Tears filled her eyes as he felt the blood drain from his face and swayed with nausea.

"There is a letter?" he managed to choke out. He felt lightheaded, as if he would faint, as if he were dreaming. This could not be true, surely? His big, invincible, incorrigible brother, dead?

"Yes, come inside and sit down – I have prepared some wine and food to sustain you." She led him up the rest of the staircase and through into the Great Hall, where the high table was set for one. There was bread, cheese, meat and fish and some honey cakes, and a jug of wine with his favourite goblet... the silver one Edward had given him. He took a deep breath, blinking back tears, and sat down heavily in his huge chair. Anne poured him some wine and started to put some food on his plate, but he waved it away, although he took the goblet and drained it in one.

"No, let me read the letter first, Anne." He refilled the goblet as Anne walked over to the side table and brought him a rolled scroll with the seal still intact.

"You have not read it?" he asked.

"Of course not, Richard, but the messenger relayed the main substance of the missive as far as he knew it. It is from Lord Hastings."

Richard glanced up sharply and frowned; he was expecting it to be from the queen. But as he inspected the seal more closely, he could see she was right, it belonged to Hastings. He broke it open with a swift impatient motion and unrolled the top part. It read:

To the Duke of Gloucester,

I greet you well and heartily and hope this letter finds you in good health. I apologise for being the bearer of bad news but your brother, King Edward, has passed to God on April 9th following an intermittent illness, having caught a chill while out fishing from a rowing boat a week before, may God assoil him. He added a codicil to his will just before he passed, naming you Lord Protector. The funeral was three days after at Windsor and I assumed the dowager queen had informed your Grace of his passing, but her son, Dorset, let slip that they had purposely not done so. He said his family had so much power that they needed not any involvement from you. The boy-king Edward V journeys from Ludlow with his uncle Anthony and an accompaniment of two thousand men-at-arms. They had requested more but I threatened them that I would retire to Calais and they knew I could force them to acquiesce if I called on my garrison there. They mean to have the boy crowned in London on May 6th. I urge you to take as many men as you can muster and intercept them before they get to London. Do not delay or they will be in full control.

William Hastings, Lord Chamberlain.

His frown increased as he took another swig of the wine and began swirling the rest around and around in the goblet.

"Hastings says Ned died on April 9th! That witch did not so much as inform me, his only remaining brother and his loyal servant – God's blood! She knew how I loved him." He pressed his lips together, fighting to keep control of his emotions. He swallowed the remaining wine and refilled the goblet. "I cannot believe he has been dead two weeks and I did not feel something, did not sense his passing from this world," he said, echoing Anne's own words when she had heard of Isabel's demise. "He was only forty years old, Anne!"

"I know, my love, I know." She leaned forward placing her small, white hand on her husband's shoulder, keeping silence as they both contemplated a future without Edward. She sighed. "So now we have another child-king. Oh, woe is England! And, what is more, a Woodville."

Richard stared into the firelight of the huge central hearth and continued swirling the wine. Then he slammed the goblet down on the table, the red liquid spilling across the polished wood, like blood, and began to pace up and down like a caged cat.

"It sounds as if the Woodvilles prepare for war. But if I take as many men as they possess, war will indeed be the result. I believe they fear me, that is why she did not inform me, and why they insisted on so many men at arms for the escort. Christ's wounds, what to do for the best?"

He continued to pace but called upon a servant to fetch his secretary and, when he arrived, he dictated letters while he marched back and forth, back and forth.

"To the Dowager Queen,
Your Grace, Sister, we greet you well and join you in your grief following the death of our beloved brother, King Edward, may God assoil him. We send our sincere condolences for your loss and assure you of our loyalty to our new king, Edward V.

We hear that the king is travelling from Ludlow with your brother, Anthony, and we will write to arrange a convenient meeting place whence we will accompany the royal party to London. There we will take up the responsibilities of our appointment as Lord Protector, as decreed in Edward's will.

Richard Gloucester, Middleham Castle.

"Then another to William Hastings:

"To Lord Hastings,

We greet you well and thank you for your timely missive informing us of the death of our beloved brother, Edward, and our appointment as Lord Protector. We will do as you suggest and intercept the new king before he arrives in London, after having arranged for a Requiem Mass to be said for our brother's soul in York Minster. I will consult with you on my arrival in London.

Richard Gloucester, Middleham Castle.

"And a third to Anthony Woodville, Lord Rivers.

"To Anthony, Lord Rivers,

We greet you well and trust you have our new king safe in your keeping. As we understand we have been named Lord Protector by our beloved brother, Edward, on his deathbed, we will travel to meet the king's party at Northampton, whence we shall accompany your escort into London. We should be there by the twenty-ninth day of April, when we may discuss arrangements for the coronation with you.

Richard Gloucester, Middleham Castle.

"Thank you, John. Send them using the relay system and, God willing, they should arrive in a timely fashion. We must also arrange a Requiem Mass to be said for Edward in York and afterwards all present must swear allegiance to the new king, Edward V. I hope he is equal to the task ahead of him. Anne, I will need black mourning clothes for the journey and I have decided not to take more than three hundred men."

"Only three hundred? What if the Woodvilles decide to attack you?"

"I fear they would be more likely to do so should I take a larger army with me; they fear me already, and to take an army would cause them to react with violence and panic, a dangerous combination. You see, if I only take a small escort, we can hopefully resolve this problem peacefully. Do you not think I am right, Anne?"

"Mayhap, yet I worry for you, husband. They bear you little love."

He snorted, "They bear no-one much love whose name is not Woodville."

"Then be careful. I could not bear to lose you and nor could our son."

"Ah, yes! Send the children to me, now, Anne. I need to have some cheer on this ill-omened day."

A few minutes later the children were ushered into their father's presence, where they made their obeisance before running into the weary arms he held out to them.

"Papa, are you well? You look so sad." This was Katherine, Richard's illegitimate daughter, always a caring girl.

He attempted a smile and hugged her to him again, taking each child in turn and reassuring them that he was well and that nothing ill would befall him. John, his tall son, who would, he was sure, outstrip him in height in the next year or two, embraced him solemnly and then withdrew, saying nothing, whereas little Edward clung to his father as if he were afraid he would disappear if he let go.

"Children, something very sad has happened," he began.

"What is it?"

"What?!"

"Your uncle, the king is dead. God rest his soul. I will be leaving for London in a few days, once preparations have been made and a Mass said for Edward. Do you wish to attend the Mass?"

They all nodded.

"Well, that is good. You had all best be off to bed then, as we shall be busy on the morrow. Goodnight now!"

He kissed them all and they were taken back to their sleeping quarters by the nurse. He stood silent and still for several moments, his hands on his hips, head downcast. Then he heaved a great sigh and turned pain-wracked eyes on his wife.

"Anne, I cannot eat this food, I am sorry; I feel no hunger, only grief. I can barely believe he is gone," he said, almost choking on the last word.

She went to him and embraced him, his head resting on her bosom as she stroked his hair as she used to do years before, when they were first married. He wrapped his arms around her tiny waist and pressed her close to him, taking comfort from her warmth. She felt him shake with silent sobs as his grief for his brother finally broke free.

The next day, he received a letter from the Duke of Buckingham, Henry Stafford. He was a cousin once removed of Richard's, because Richard's aunt, Anne, was his grandmother. They had met a few times, but they had never come into contact much, as Richard was seldom at Court.

"Beloved Cousin, we greet you well and assure you of our sincerest condolences on the death of your most high and mighty brother, King Edward. It has come to our attention that the queen's family is attempting a coup and are trying to rush the king to London for the Coronation as soon as possible. I hear the new king will be escorted there by the queen's brother and, if you intend to join the royal party, I would be honoured and happy to meet up with you and accompany the king into London beside you. I offer you my support and as many men as you see fit. I will match the number you bring, up to one thousand. I pray you write back soon to inform me of your acceptance of my help.

Henry Buckingham,

Pembroke Castle"

Richard swiftly sent a reply, urging Henry to meet him and the new king, Edward V at Northampton on 29th, and to limit the number of armed men to three hundred.

Ghost of a Rose

They attended the Requiem Mass at York Minster together, as a family, drawing strength from each other. Following the Mass, Richard solemnly swore allegiance and loyalty to the new king and ensured all those attending the Mass did the same. He had acquired several sets of dark clothing for the sad journey and his belongings had been packed. He was almost ready to leave, when there was another messenger.

The letter was another from Hastings, its tone yet more urgent than the last.

"To the Duke of Gloucester,

We greet you well and urge you to act swiftly. If you tarry, the queen and her family will hold the reins of power in London. They say they will exclude you from your rightful office as Protector, for if they reach London first, the prince will be crowned without you and all will be lost. You must hasten to intercept the royal party as soon as you may. My good wishes go with you.

William Lord Hastings."

"**W**ell, it's all kicking off now, eh?" said Rupert, his eyes wide.

"Yes, but it's getting quite late – let us return to it tomorrow and we will start on this important part of the project with refreshed minds." David yawned as if to prove the truth of his words.

When they had packed up, Rupert invited Eve and Stellan out for a drink. Eve was happy to go as she had been working so hard writing up all her notes recently and felt like she needed a little break. This would be just the thing.

All About You

Eve had gone for the drink with Rupert and Stellan, only to find that Camilla had also been invited and was there waiting for Rupert. He went over and gave his girlfriend a peck on the cheek when he saw her, before buying them all a drink. Eve wished she hadn't come now; she just didn't like Camilla. She couldn't warm to her, she had nothing in common with her and she hated her smarmy comments, which were carefully worded to rile people while being cloaked in a veneer of innocent politeness:

"Oh, I love your jacket, Eve, it makes you look so slim. I could never get away with something like that – it would literally hang on me." Implying that Eve was overweight.

"Oh, Eve I was so sorry to hear about you and James, but really you did well to last as long as you did."

Suggesting she should think herself lucky to have had James for even a few years.

Eve could never think quickly enough to give a suitable riposte and it was useless to give a stinging retort when the moment had passed. So, she sat and nursed her white wine, simmering inside and wondering how Rupert didn't see that Camilla was a bitch.

They were sitting at the bar and Stellan was holding forth on how pleased he was with how the 'Fly' was performing, seated to Eve's right. Rupert was sitting close to Camilla, both of them on her left, and he was toying with her long, blonde hair in a way that reminded Eve of a child showing off his toys. She watched him twirling his fingers through it, round and round. Why was she so annoyed? It was his business whom he went out with and his problem if he got landed with a cow like Camilla.

"I'll get the next round," Camilla said sweetly, opening her Louis Vuitton handbag. "What do you want, Rupie, another beer?"

"Sure, that'll be great, love," he replied, a stupid smile on his face.

Camilla leaned forward so that she could see past Eve and asked Stellan what he wanted.

"A gin and tonic, please, Camilla," he replied, smiling and staring at her cleavage, which had been revealed as she leaned forwards.

She had deliberately ignored Eve, not offering her a refill. Eve was so stunned at her rudeness that she couldn't quite believe it had actually happened. She felt like she was back at school again, excluded from the gang. What was worse, the men seemed to be quite happy with her behaviour. Or they were so busy looking at her breasts that they hadn't noticed.

She got up and went to the Ladies. When she emerged from the cubicle, Camilla was putting on her lipstick while staring at herself in the mirror.

"Oh Eve! There you are – we thought you'd gone home," she said, smiling. "So glad you're still here."

Yeah, right! Eve thought. She didn't reply, just nodded and washed her hands. As she dried them, she found that Camilla was right behind her, grabbing her by the shoulder. Putting her mouth close to Eve's ear, she hissed:

"You just keep your hands off Rupert! He's much too good for the likes of you anyway! I know where you live – you have two pretty little cats, don't you? It's a shame cats don't live very long, isn't it?"

Eve turned to face her, horrified at the implied threat in her words, and saw Camilla had an expression on her face that she had never seen before. Replacing her false smile, there was a twist to her perfect coral-coloured lips and a hard glint in her eye.

Eve took a shuddering breath, pushed Camilla's hand, with its long, elegant nails, away and stepped back from her. Was she crazy? Surely normal, civilised people didn't behave like that.

She looked at the woman, unable to speak, she was so shocked.

Camilla looked at her and smiled. It wasn't a pleasant sight.

"I see you understand me. Don't say you haven't been warned!"

And she pushed past Eve and left the room. Eve was shaking as she finished drying her hands, her thoughts racing.

Why on earth did Camilla think she was after Rupert? She had never once thought of him as anything other than a friend. Oh wait… maybe it was because she had been teaching him how to decipher the mediaeval language. If he had mentioned that to Camilla and she was – as it seemed – a crazy jealous psycho, then that could explain it. A vision of the rabbit scene in Fatal Attraction loomed in her head and tears came unbidden to her eyes.

She sniffed and wiped her nose with a tissue. She wasn't sure what to do. Camilla scared her – she was the kind of person who had no limits. Eve had no doubt she would cross the line if she wanted to. She was dangerous. What to do? She could tell Rupert and see if he would believe her. But if he was in love with the girl, he would take her word rather than Eve's and it would alienate him. She could stand up to her herself and refuse to be intimidated. But she wasn't sure she could bluff her way to that and she *was* intimidated by her – she didn't want to risk the safety of her beloved cats. Finally, she decided she would just avoid her even if it meant she would see less of Rupert – at least she would still see him at work; she enjoyed his friendship but it wasn't worth her cats being harmed.

Lord Anthony Woodville

They all gathered, excited, to listen to what the 'Fly' had in store for them today…

"Sire, we approach Northampton, will you have me go on ahead and secure lodgings for the night?"
"Yes, thank you, Ralph. The Blue Boar is a suitable lodging if I remember correctly. And ask if they can have victuals prepared for us all."

Ten minutes later they rode into the town. The Duke instructed his men to camp outside the walls and took only approximately twenty men with him as he cantered into the centre. There was no sign of any of the Royal party – no horses milling about, no men playing cards or drinking, no Royal Standards.

Ralph saw him and walked up to him to take the horse for stabling and feeding. Richard thanked him and walked into the inn, where the proprietor bowed low, whilst drying his hands on a linen cloth.

"Your Grace, I am honoured that you wish to stay here. You will not be disappointed, I can assure you. We have the best mutton pie this side of the Nene."

"I look forward to trying it in due course. Tell me, where is the king staying? Is he here also, Master…?"

"Patterson, your Grace. Nay, it is true the king passed through Northampton, but he did not stay here, nor any other inn in the town. They passed through without stopping, all in a hurry, like, and rode off in that direction."

He pointed in a southerly direction. Richard chewed his lower lip in concentration. "Hmm, south. Toward London. Thank you, Master Patterson. You shall be rewarded for your help." He slapped the leather riding gloves he was holding into his other hand and drew them through his fingers, restlessly.

He asked the man to show him to his chamber and followed him up the staircase to the first floor. The room was comfortable, but not luxurious. If the royal party had not remained here, what was going on? He poured himself a cup of wine from the flask in the room and took a swig, his thoughts racing. Before he could order them and decide what the best course of action would be, there was a knock at the door. It was Ralph.

"Your Grace, Anthony Woodville has arrived. He is downstairs. I thought you would want to know."

"You did well, Ralph, thank you. Will you send him up, please?"

Ralph bowed and withdrew and it wasn't long before there was a tentative rap on the door. Richard called out: "Come in."

The door opened to reveal the Queen's brother, Anthony Woodville, standing in the doorway. He was sweating, whether from the exertion of his ride or nerves, Richard could not tell. He was, as usual, dressed fashionably, though slightly more subdued than normal, in keeping with the solemnity of the recent events. Richard wore all black.

"Ah, Anthony, good! Do come in and share a drink of wine with me." He proffered another cup, after filling it with wine. Anthony seemed reluctant to take it, but finally did so, thanking Richard and taking a large swallow. He took out a white kerchief and mopped his brow.

"Your Grace, I hope you will forgive me – I have ridden hard to get here to you, to explain."

"Explain?" Richard fixed him with a hard gaze. "Oh, of course; you are going to explain how it is that the king, who was supposed to meet with me here, is in fact elsewhere. Where is it that he is located, by the way?"

"He is at Stony Stratford with his brother, Richard Grey, his chamberlain, Thomas Vaughan and his escort. We decided that Northampton might not have adequate accommodation for all of us and your Grace's entourage too, so we went on a few miles."

"A few miles? I see." Richard said no more but his blue eyes glittered in the candlelight. He smiled, without it reaching those eyes. "Well, all is well then. I was just about to eat – please join

261

us, Anthony. We shall dine along the corridor up here – the proprietor has given us a private dining room."

Rivers bowed his head in acknowledgment and gave a stiffly formal smile. His eyes shifted from side to side and he was still sweating. Eve, listening with the others, knew that Richard did not trust him as far as he could throw him. She remembered Sue telling her that Stony Stratford was fourteen miles away from Northampton, towards London. It was clear that there was some subterfuge going on.

"Your Grace, I thank you for your hospitality and offer my sincere condolences on the loss of your brother. He was a great man."

"Aye, he was that," Richard said, dropping his chin and taking a quick swallow of wine. His hair cast a shadow over his eyes but Eve knew they shone with unshed tears. He coughed and called for Ralph to show Anthony to the dining room. "I will join you directly, with Viscount Lovell and a few others. We can discuss our arrangements for meeting up with the king tomorrow, eh?"

Anthony took a deep breath and nodded, licking his lips and wiping his hands on his doublet.

The Lord Protector

They moved the machine forward an hour and immediately picked up Richard.

"Very... thought-provoking, Anthony. You have a fine turn of phrase. I am afraid poetry was never something I excelled at. Law is where my aptitude lies, of course."

"Thank you, Richard, I appreciate your comments. One never knows for sure how one's talents will be perceived by others.

Ehm, the wine is excellent, is it not?"

"More wine for Lord Rivers, Ralph. No, not for me, thank you. I have some more work to do before I retire and I still have a goodly amount in my goblet. I..."

There was a loud knocking on the door and then it opened before Richard had a chance to utter a word. He whirled around in his chair and Rivers knocked his wine over as a man of medium height and mousey colouring entered the room in a rush, the door banging against the wall, he had thrown it open so violently.

"God's blood, Henry! You fair made me jump out of my skin! And poor Anthony has spilt his wine. Ralph, pray, fill Lord Rivers' cup again and call a maid to clear up the spillage."

Henry Stafford, the Duke of Buckingham, swept off his hat in a flamboyant bow, his eyes never leaving Richard's. He was dressed in the finest velvet doublet and silk hose, dark blue, almost purple in colour. His hat had a long peacock feather and his shoes bore the elongated pointed toes which were so fashionable and yet so ridiculous.

"I apologise for my precipitous entry, Cousin. I had meant to be here to greet you on your arrival, but I had a difficult journey from the Welsh Marches. I was at my castle of Brecknock when I heard the tragic news about his Grace, King Edward, God rest his great soul."

He stood there turning his hat in his hands, his expression so stricken anyone would have thought Edward had been his closest friend, not that he had hardly ever even seen him. Edward had rarely had him at Court and avoided giving him any important appointments. In fact, the only times Richard had seen him as an adult had been at the wedding of the young prince, Richard of York, Edward's second son, and when

Buckingham had presided over the sentencing of George at his trial.

"Never mind, you are here now. Come in and join us at table. There is plenty left. We have been toasting the king's memory and you have just missed Anthony's recital of one of his... excellent poems."

"Thank you, Cousin. It is true I am almost dying from hunger. We decided to press on rather than stop for victuals and my stomach thinks my throat has been cut!"

He chuckled at his own wit and Richard gave a thin smile. Buckingham walked into the room and sat down next to Richard, paying no attention to Rivers, who was scowling at him. Buckingham helped himself to meat and bread and ordered Richard's squire, Ralph, to serve him wine, as if he were his own servant. Ralph glanced at Richard, who frowned, but gave a quick nod of acquiescence. Ralph offered Henry the goblet, which he drained in one and held out for a refill.

"So, Richard, where is the king? I would swear my allegiance to the lad. Has he retired already?"

"He is not here," Richard said quietly, staring into his wine cup.

"Not here?!" Buckingham cried. He had a very loud voice. He had stopped feeding his face, his hand, bearing a chicken drumstick, frozen on its way to his mouth. His eyes, light blue and cool, were wide with surprise. "But was it not at Northampton that we were to join up with him?"

He turned at last towards Rivers, his eyebrows raised in question.

"Yes, indeed. That was the original plan. But his Grace decided that he wanted to press on to Stony Stratford – he thought there would not be enough room for all his entourage and also his Grace of Gloucester's here at Northampton."

"Not enough room?!" Buckingham boomed. "This is a thriving town – surely there is plenty of room."

"The king does have quite a large entourage," Anthony said.

"I bet he does!" Henry said, not seeming to care whether or not Rivers heard him. He glanced at Richard and gave a quick wink.

"We shall all be meeting up tomorrow at Stony Stratford," said Richard. "We shall need to arise early on the morrow. Rivers, I can see you are yawning – get to bed and we will ride out together in the morning. Sleep well!"

As soon as Rivers had left the room with a bow to the noble Dukes, Henry turned to Richard.

"Dickon, what in the name of Almighty God the Redeemer is going on? What does Rivers think he is playing at? Does he think he can just spirit the king away like that, when you, the boy's paternal uncle and Protector of the Realm, are not aware of his plans? I do not like it! There is something fishy going on."

"Mmm," Richard said. "I must say I agree, there is definitely something odd going on. Northampton is not a small town; there are plenty of inns here where the king and his men could find lodging."

"Yet why did Rivers bother to come back? He could just have remained at Stony Stratford... wait a minute! Is not that near to the Rivers estate of Grafton?"

"Yes, it is. I was thinking exactly the same thing, Henry."

"Well, great minds think alike," Buckingham grinned. "And please, call me Harry and I shall call you Dickon. We are cousins after all and both Dukes of the blood royal. We should be close allies, think you not? Eh, Dickon?"

And he nudged Richard's elbow, grinning broadly. Richard smiled, his eyebrows raised, and did not comment that Henry had already begun calling him Dickon.

"So, do you think Rivers has some plan to keep control of the king?"

"Well, I have some shocking news for you – for your ears only, though."

He glanced at Lovell and Percy from the side of his eyes, his bushy eyebrows raised questioningly.

"These are my friends, Henry... Harry. Anything you say to me may be heard by them also. What is this news?"

"Well then, at least the servants...?" Buckingham gestured at Ralph and the little serving maid with his cup.

"Yes, yes. Ralph, you and Sarah go down to the kitchens and see if they have any more of those honey cakes – I cannot stomach anything heavier at this time."

Ralph made his obeisance and ushered the girl out. Henry turned to Richard and gave a belch. Richard winced and turned his head.

"Beg pardon," Buckingham said. "Listen, Dickon. This is big! This news is so big it will astound you!"

He was flushed with excitement, although his face was grim.

"Well, spit it out, man! Tell me!"

Buckingham slid his chair closer to Richard's. Lovell, on the other side of the table, scowled at him, his dark brows pulled together and his full mouth downturned.

"I have a servant whom I took in after he fled to Brecknock from Ludlow. Giles his name is. He had been a stable hand at the prince's household there, until something happened a few weeks ago and he ran away. He was taking a nap in the stable, in with the horses, where it is nice and warm, when two men entered and he overheard their conversation. They were Rivers and his nephew, Dorset. Rivers said that he had checked that he was still entitled to raise an army. 'It is all fine', he said. He also told Dorset that he had drawn up a document passing on the Deputy Constableship of the Tower to him!"

"But that is illegal!" Richard said, sharply, a frown deepening between his fine eyebrows. "Only the king can make changes to such appointments."

"I know! But that is not all. My man heard Rivers ask about the 'phial'. 'Did Elizabeth give you the phial?' And Dorset answered that she had, and that she had made up an extra-large dose because the king was so large. My man assumed they were talking about a physic of some kind – Edward was always having problems with his stomach. As you know, he overindulged and his stomach complained, of course."

He paused in his narration to take a large bite of bread and cheese and wash it down with a full cup of wine.

"Quite," Richard said. "But pray continue – I do not like the sound of this at all."

Buckingham leaned his arm on the table and waved around another chicken leg as he spoke.

"Giles thought nothing of it for a few days, until he heard that the king had died and he suddenly realised that those two could have been speaking of..." He paused for a second or two for effect. "Poison!!"

"Harry! Good God, Harry! Do I understand you correctly? Are you accusing the Woodvilles of murder?!"

"Not openly – I only have the word of a humble stable hand against theirs. But it seems like that to me. Apparently, the announcement of Edward's death reached York a few days before he actually died! How else to explain this but that they had administered a dose of poison, he had become ill and, knowing the usual course of the poison's action, they anticipated that he would die and announced it prematurely? Edward did seem to recover for a day or two, but then finally succumbed for good. That must have been when they gave him a second, stronger dose. Maybe they miscalculated the original dose – they said Elizabeth had given them a larger dose because of Edward's size – mayhap it was not large enough. Edward was ever a strong man."

Richard had gone paler than normal, the fate of his brother being spoken of in such a matter-of-fact way making him feel nauseous. He took a deep breath and let it out through pursed lips as he considered Buckingham's story.

"It does make sense, I suppose. But why would the queen want to murder Edward? He was the source of her power and fortune."

"I wondered that too and made some enquiries. Edward had ceased visiting the queen's bed. He had a new mistress, Elizabeth Shore, and it seems he had fallen for her. He called her his 'merry mistress'!"

"Yes, I have met her. But that has been going on for a while – she was no danger to the queen. Surely Elizabeth would not have let jealousy cut off her nose to spite her face. Elizabeth was his wife – a mistress could never oust an anointed queen. And Edward had had countless more before her."

"There is something else. I heard that Elizabeth resented and feared the growing power that Edward was conferring on... you, Dickon."

"Me? But I have never vied for power at Court – I have kept myself to myself in the North."

"Of course, but Edward recently granted you the right to keep any land you conquer in Scotland, did he not? You have been rising in power and influence for several years now and the Woodvilles' power has been diminishing. The queen sees you as a threat, which is why I suspect they are up to something now. We of the Old Royal Blood need to stick together, Dickon. I am here to back you up to the hilt. You need to get control over the young king or they will rush him to London, have him crowned and then your role of Protector is obsolete and you have been eliminated from influence; they will rule the country as regents through the boy."

"You are right, Harry!" Richard stood up and began pacing the room, back and forth, back and forth. "By God, if I had proof that they had had Ned poisoned, I would... that bitch from hell! She has caused nothing but trouble to my family and the country since Ned was stupid enough to marry her. They are everywhere you turn at Court – that bloody family are allied to every noble line you could think of, there are so many of them. No wonder George and Warwick rebelled. But, Harry, even you are married to one of them, the queen's sister, Katherine. Is it true that you resented the marriage, that you oppose the Woodvilles? Do you not have a... conflict of interest in the matter?"

Buckingham grimaced. "I have grown to tolerate her. She has borne me heirs and it is true she is not as arrogant as the queen, but, still, she is a Woodville and should never have been offered as a suitable bride to me. Me! A Duke of the realm, a descendant of Kings!"

Richard noticed that he emphasised some words that he thought important, like 'Royal', 'Duke' and 'Kings'. Buckingham had stopped speaking, cleared his throat and clapped Richard on the shoulder. Richard froze and glared at

269

his cousin, who hastily dropped his hand. Buckingham went on:

"Anyway, I assure you of my loyalty. I will support you in bringing the king under your influence. But what do you think Rivers is up to?"

"I am not certain, but, as you said earlier, Stony Stratford is Woodville territory. Rivers is planning something." He began pacing again. "I have it! The only good reasons Rivers would have for coming back here to tell me where the king is located are firstly to allay my suspicions – if he had not returned, I would probably have pursued the king's party. Secondly, he can guide our party on the road to Stony Stratford, straight through Woodville lands – perfect for an ambush. He would know where to lead us so that we fell right in their trap. What think you?"

Buckingham nodded. "You are a genius, Cousin. Of course – it all makes sense. What will you do?"

"I will have Rivers' lodgings guarded over the rest of the night and arrest him in the morning. We can then go to the king, while my men seek out evidence of the ambush. Let us sleep now – we will need to arise earlier than usual to carry out our plan of action."

Buckingham bowed and left the room.

In the middle of the night, Richard rose from his bed, unable to sleep for thinking about what might happen on the morrow. He sat by the window in a large chair, in the darkness – he didn't want to bother lighting a candle, so the only light came from the dying embers of the fire.

He awoke, shivering, having dozed off, but instantly stiffened as he sensed somebody was in the room. His skin crawled and the hairs on the back of his neck stirred, but he was a soldier and he reacted well in an emergency. He wondered at first if it was Ralph, come to wake him, but it still seemed to be night-time. All at once, he caught a glimpse of a knife in the moonlight that was streaming in through the window, gripped in a raised hand. Before he could react, the knife came down into the bed whence he had come, where he had been lying a short while before. The hand stabbed frenziedly again and again into the mattress, sending feathers flying everywhere and he called out as he flung himself onto the attacker's back, taking him by surprise and easily overpowering him even though he struggled enough to land an elbow on Richard's nose. Feet came running along the corridor outside and the door was flung open to reveal Francis Lovell and Harry Stafford outside. There was a figure lying inert on the floor just outside his room. It was Ralph, unconscious and bleeding profusely from a deep cut on his arm. "Ralph! Francis, is he...?"

"He has been knocked out, but he will live," Francis said, helping Richard with the intruder. Buckingham lit a candle and, when the light steadied, Richard recognised the man.

"It is Harold, Rivers' servant," he said to his two companions. Then he addressed Harold directly. "Who sent you here? Was it your master, Rivers?"

"Yes, yes, your Grace, he ordered me to do it. He told me he would harm my family if I refused."

"You know that what you do is treason? It is obvious you were attempting to kill me. I am Constable of England and about to be confirmed as Protector of the Realm. I am also the senior adult heir male to the throne and, as such, any assault on my person is treason. Do you know the penalty for treason, Harold?"

"Aye, my Lord."

271

The man trembled and lowered his head. Then with a swift, unexpected movement, he twisted himself free of Lovell and lunged towards the knife. Both Richard and Francis were too slow to stop him and he grabbed the knife and buried it to the hilt in his own breast, sinking to the floor as a spurt of bright red blood fountained out of the wound.

"God's bones!" Richard said. There was a pause and then he added: "Well, at least he has saved us the bother of a trial. It is a pity he did not tell us more before he took his own life, though."

The listening group paused the machine at this dramatic juncture and Rupert's expression was a picture.

"Well, talk about exciting! That was amazing! He said quite a bit that was revealing there, didn't he?"

"Yes, this will be worth a fortune!" David said, delighted. "Let's hope he reveals as much when it comes to the Princes in the Tower, eh?"

Eve couldn't help rolling her eyes, knowing she was out of his field of vision.

Warrior

With Rivers arrested and on his way to the North, his servant dead and Ralph alive, but wounded, the two Dukes were on their way to Stony Stratford to try to catch up with the king's party. Rivers, once arrested, had admitted that their suspicions were correct; he had planned to ambush Richard's party on the way to Stony Stratford, but when Buckingham had arrived, he had been taken by surprise and was unsure whether the plan would work with more men than he had expected to contend with. So, he had ordered his servant, Harold, to murder Richard in his bed and then deal with Buckingham, but he hadn't managed to get that far. He told them the ambush plan had been his alone. Of course, Richard suspected that Richard Grey, Dorset and the queen had actually been involved, but as he had no evidence against her he could take no action for the time being. Rivers, however, was to be tried for treason once Richard had the agreement of the Council.

They sent a group of their men to seek out the weapons that Rivers told them had been concealed in a farm cart to execute the ambush. Some of the cognizances found on the weapons belonged to Rivers and some to Grey. Richard intended to question him closely.

As they cantered into the town, they saw the multitude of Royal standards emblazoned on surcoats. Banners waved from afar and the horses, in their Royal trappings, pranced on the spot, impatient to leave. Richard was at the head of their group and rode right up to the Royal party, bringing his horse to a shuddering halt and making the dust fly up around its hooves. The young king was mounted on his own horse, a fine chestnut, and he turned to see who it was who had arrived so precipitously.

"Uncle... oh! Uncle Richard," he said, searching the faces of those riding behind Richard, as if seeking somebody out. "I was expecting my other uncle, Lord Rivers, to be with you," he said, his eyes wary.

"I am surprised you recognised me, Sire," Richard said, ignoring the boy's last remark. He dismounted in a fluid motion and immediately went down onto his knees in a respectful obeisance to his king. Buckingham, who had been sitting silently on his horse, just behind Richard, hastily did the same.

"Where is our Uncle Anthony?" asked a young man mounted on the horse next to the young Edward. He was Richard Grey, the king's half-brother. His eyes shifted from Richard to Buckingham and then to the men in Richard's entourage and a bead of sweat appeared on his upper lip. His horse nodded its head and stamped a hoof, restlessly, picking up on its rider's agitation.

"I am afraid Rivers will not be attending you, your Grace." Richard ignored the young man and addressed himself only to Edward. "As you doubtless know, I have been named Protector of the Realm by your late father, God rest his soul, and I and my Lord of Buckingham shall be escorting you to London to await your coronation. Before we leave here, I would ask a word with you in private, please. Let us return to your lodgings and I will apprise you of what has happened."

"What have you done to my Uncle?" Grey shouted. "The king will not do anything you say until he is restored to us here!"

Richard walked calmly over to him and took his horse's reins.

"I am afraid I must insist. Please dismount and you may attend us with His Grace."

He spoke quietly but firmly and fixed Grey with a stare so cold it could have frozen the sea. The look was dangerous; a sign of the famous Plantagenet temper. In Richard there was no bluster, as there was in his brother George, rather an icy calm before the storm. Anyone who had known his deceased brother, Edward, would have recognised it and apparently Grey had. The look on his face was one of alarm and even outright terror, but his panic made him rash.

"I will do no such thing and neither will Edward. Release my horse or..."

"Or what, Grey?" Richard's eyes were now glittering.

Grey's hand went to his sword, but Richard was too quick for him. His own sword point was aimed at Grey's throat before the panicking man had even managed to draw his. A commotion on Richard's other side proved to be the chamberlain, Vaughan, attempting to go to Grey's aid and being disarmed by Lovell.

"Arrest these men. Have them brought inside while I speak with his Grace." Richard's men hastened to do his bidding. "Sire, I mean you no harm. Please, come inside – we will not delay overlong."

The new king saw how disciplined Richard's men were and how determined Richard himself was and dismounted rather shakily, handing the horse's bridle to a groom and walking with as much dignity as he could muster back inside the inn they had so recently left.

Richard turned swiftly to the captain of the Welsh army that was accompanying the king and said in a loud, clear voice:

"You men, thank you for escorting your king this far, but now I am here, I hereby take up my duty as Lord Protector and shall see to it that the king arrives unharmed in London. You and your men are dismissed and may return to your families in Wales."

Without waiting to check if they would obey, he turned swiftly on his heel and followed Edward into the inn, gesturing for his close adherents to follow. Lovell, Percy and Buckingham did so.

The captain of the king's Welsh army hesitated at first, but then, glancing at his countrymen, he said: "You 'eard the Duke, look sharpish now, we are back to our green hills and valleys, boys."

With a subdued muttering, the two-thousand-strong army began to drift away, heading back in the direction from which they had arrived the day before.

As the sound of the horses' hooves and marching boots drifted back into the inn, Richard finally let out his breath in a soft sigh, only now aware that he had been holding it.

Be the Man

Inside, Grey and Vaughan were being restrained between two burly guards each and Edward was sitting at a large table, his face pale and his expression wary.

"Grey, we know about the plot you and Rivers were involved in – I bet you were surprised to see us arrive, were you not? You might as well confess – you have committed treason anyway, by attempting to draw a weapon against me, the High Constable of England. Do you have anything to say – anyone else to implicate?"

"That cannot be true! My Uncle Anthony would never have plotted against you – he is an honourable man."

The king sounded more annoyed than nervous now.

"He sent his servant to murder me, Edward," Richard said, his tone regretful and sympathetic. "I am sorry, but it is true. He has confessed it to me and knows he has committed treason. As Constable, I could have convened a Constable's court and tried and condemned him there and then, but I want him to have a fair trial. Likewise, these two. They have all been caught like foxes in a chicken coop.

"Anyway, to happier subjects. We left Northampton without breaking our fast and it would be most agreeable to do so here before we leave. Are you not hungry, your Grace?"

His Grace thought about the question for a few seconds and then nodded. Richard called over the innkeeper and requested meat, ale, wine, bread, cheese, fruit and pies. The man hurried off to prepare the order, grinning – he had not expected any extra custom this day.

As they partook of their breakfast, Richard began to speak to Edward about his father, offered his condolences and then went on to tell stories of some of the escapades he had got up to when he was a boy. Because, of course, Edward had not really known his father that well – he had been sent to Ludlow under the tutelage of Anthony, Lord Rivers, since the age of two and didn't often meet his father in Court because he mostly remained in Ludlow on the Welsh Marches, being trained to be a king. So, to hear Richard humanise his father and describe some of the ordinary things he did, mistakes he had made, enchanted Edward. He began to relax, asking questions about his father's prowess in the hunt, his favourite dog, his knightly training. Richard answered him kindly and if he didn't know all of the answers – after all he was ten years younger than Edward and brought up separately too – he gave his best guess. He also told Edward about the North and his own training under the Earl of Warwick, his ambition to be a knight and his desire to learn about the law and mete out justice to the common people. At the mention of justice, Edward paled, remembering his relatives who were now in captivity and on their way to the North to be tried up there.

Richard noticed him withdraw again and cursed himself for not being more circumspect. He changed the subject, asking him what he had learned about being a king.

"I know that it requires a lot of paperwork and signing things: decrees, judgements, grants and all that."

Richard nodded, smiling – the boy was at least intelligent and observant then.

"Why do you not practice now? Here, I have a scroll; you can decide how you will write your royal signature, Sire."

Edward perked up a little and nodded. Buckingham produced a fine quill pen. The innkeeper sent for a well of ink and some blotting sand and Richard signed the paper first, demonstrating to Edward what to do and adding his motto: 'Loyaulte Me Lie'.

Buckingham was also roped in to sign and then the king himself. Buckingham's signature looked as if it had a crown right in the middle of it.

Eve realised the document was one that still existed and that she had seen reproduced online. How fantastic to witness how it came into being all those years ago!

Feeling Good

The next day, Eve set off for work feeling a little apprehensive, a little excited. She had gone out late night shopping the previous evening and bought herself a smart new blouse – it was a subtle, sky blue with tiny, silver buttons and she knew it suited her. With it she wore a royal blue pair of trousers and a contrasting scarf. She was hoping to impress Stellan; she had found herself becoming more and more attracted to him. He was so tall, his eyes so blue and sparkly and his collar-length hair looked like molten gold when the late evening rays crept through the main window and touched it with their gleaming fingers. She was pretty sure he liked blue as he often wore it himself – it brought out the blue of his eyes. He is so... cool! she thought. She had never been involved with anyone foreign... exotic. Yesterday she had watched him pressing buttons and typing commands and admired the way his muscles flexed under his shirt, not to mention how his trousers looked as he bent forwards over the machine – well, it wasn't really his trousers, she admitted to herself, but rather what was inside them! Her thoughts were wandering when she sensed someone behind her and let out a scream of fright as someone said:

"Eve!"

She whirled her head around and came face to face with Stellan. She placed her hand on her chest, instinctively trying to slow her racing heart back down to normal.

"What is the matter, Eve? I know something's wrong. Do you want to tell me about it? I'm a good listener, or so I've been told."

"No, it's nothing, really!" she said, looking down into her coffee cup and swirling the dark liquid around.

He didn't reply but simply stood there, waiting, his arms folded over his chest.

"Oh alright, yes, I had a bit of a fright the other night. Look, do you mind if I tell you in your office where no-one can overhear us?"

"Of course!" he said.

"You do mind?" she asked incredulously.

"No, I don't. Look, I'm sorry. I make some mistakes in English when I am distracted." He looked down at her and gave a slow smile that transformed his whole face. Instead of his normal, rather austere and cold aura, he suddenly looked warm, friendly and very handsome. "Come, I will make us another coffee and you can tell me all about it."

Holding the cup as if it was the only thing keeping her alive,

Eve started to tell Stellan about Camilla's behaviour. She was standing up, pacing as she spoke – she found it helped her to order her thoughts. She told him how she had never been able to find anything in common with her and admitted that she disliked her but couldn't really pin down why, until she had threatened her in the ladies' toilet.

"She threatened you?"

"Not directly – and not me really – it was my cats. She suggested that they wouldn't live very long if I went after Rupert. Well, I was never intending to anyway. I would be happy for him that he had a girlfriend he liked if she wasn't such a psychotic bitch!" She gasped and covered her mouth in embarrassment. "I'm sorry, Stellan, I don't normally speak like that. I…" She swallowed and bit her lip trying to hold on to her composure. She turned her back to Stellan and closed her eyes, trying to block out all her confusing thoughts. Then she felt his hand on her shoulder.

"Eve," he said, softly. She turned and saw the concern in his eyes and that caused the floodgates to open.

"I'm OK, I'm OK," she lied and then she had turned into him, and clung to his chest, surrounded by a sharp, woody scent and feeling the warmth of his body. She gasped and looked up at him, his eyes so blue and deep she thought she would drown. They gazed at each other for a second and then she stretched up and kissed him, the touch of his lips like electricity zinging through her. He kissed her back, and she groaned as her body responded to his. It was she who reached for his shirt collar and undid the buttons, she who slid her hands down his back and then around to the front to slide his belt buckle open…

Afterwards, she panicked and quickly rearranged her clothing as she heard the muffled sounds of others coming into the outer office. Stellan cleared his throat and glanced at her. He looked as embarrassed as she felt.

"Are you alright?" he asked, turning away to button his shirt.

"Yes, I'm fine," she said, knowing she lied. She couldn't believe she had just had sex with the tall Scandinavian, right there in his office! What on earth did she think she was doing? She had refused Alex's advances, even though she was attracted to him, telling him it was too soon, she wasn't ready and then she does this, with a man she knew even less! Well, it had been great sex, but why had she let it happen? Well, not let it happen – made it happen! It had been she who had initiated it, after all. What a slut she was!

Then, just as she was wondering what to say to him, David knocked on the door and, after a quick glance to check she was decent, Stellan called out for him to enter.

"Oh! Hi Eve, you're in early. Glad to see you're all working hard. Well, we are getting to the nitty gritty now, aren't we? These are the critical times of Richard's reign, aren't they?"

"Yes, they are! These few months are the crucial ones as regards Richard's reputation."

"Let's hope we get some answers, eh?" he said and winked at her.

She blushed crimson – had he guessed what had just happened between Stellan and her? Surely not. They had tidied themselves up well before he came in. She turned and picked up her notes and they left the office to organise the next session.

The King of Wishful Thinking

Richard had not exactly won over the new king, but he was at least regarded with respect by him, which was more than could be said for Buckingham. They seemed to hate each other right from the off. Harry had confided in Richard that he thought the king was a pampered, soft, lily-livered brat.

"Ah! It is a shame your brother could not have lived longer, Dickon... then at least we would have a man as our king, rather than a mere boy – and a weak one at that."

Richard said nothing, merely raised one eyebrow. He knew it was never a good thing to have a minor as ruler, but there was nothing they could do about that. Buckingham was being an idiot – even though he wasn't quite as rude in the king's presence, he still made it apparent that he disliked the boy. Well, he was a Woodville and Harry had despised that family for years.

"Perhaps he will grow into the role," he said, smiling at Buckingham.

Buckingham snorted.

"A Woodville never changes," he said. "They are all ambitious schemers, vain, pompous."

Richard kept silent, thinking that many might describe Buckingham himself as such. Edward had not given him honours at Court and if he carried on like this, neither would the new King Edward.

"I hope he is young enough to mould into a good king. He does have some positive qualities: he is intelligent, his manners are impeccable, he is well-read and understands something of the law; I was speaking to him about it last night. Once he is removed from the influence of his maternal family, I am sure we could make a fine king of him between us, Harry!"

"Good luck! But you never know – he listens to you more than me. Did you hear what he called me the other day – a prancing peacock!"

Richard's mouth twitched as he suppressed the laugh that was threatening to bubble up and emerge from his lips.

"Well, you did speak to him rather rudely, Harry. You must remember that he is the king – he could certainly harm your career if he takes a dislike to you."

"True," Buckingham sighed. "I will try to talk to him more. Mayhap he likes hunting – now there we might have something in common."

"Yes, but not at this moment – he will be rather busy for the next few weeks at least."

Grace

Buckingham grinned at him from the back of his large black horse and then they continued to smile at the crowds who had begun to appear in greater and greater throngs as they approached London. They all wanted to get a look at their new young king.

Edward, for his part, was dressed in a deep blue doublet and hose, a feathered hat on his head and was mounted on his chestnut horse, happily returning the waves of the crowds. Some young girls were throwing white roses to him – most fell short or landed on the horse, but he managed to catch one and grinned at the girl who had thrown it, kissing it and putting it in the ribbon of his hat.

Richard smiled as he watched him – perhaps it would be well after all. He would do his duty, arrange the coronation, serve on the Council to run the country until Edward was of age – only a few years from now – and then retire from Court and go back to his beloved Yorkshire. In the meantime, he would strive to engage the affection of the king to ensure his family's safety.

He only wanted to be left alone, although he would willingly keep the Scots under control for him as he had done for his brother.

They were welcomed to London by the Mayor, who had laid on entertainments and feasting. It was decided that Edward should be lodged first in the Bishop of Westminster's palace, although he would have to be moved to the Tower before the coronation – the traditional place where all kings awaited their crowning.

"Your Grace, a word, please?"

It was Lovell. Richard nodded and leaned towards him as he took a sip of his wine.

"The dowager queen has fled into sanctuary, my Lord. Obviously, she was afraid once she knew the Woodville plot had failed. She fears your wrath but her actions betray her guilt."

"Well, leave her there for the moment – perhaps she will come to her senses soon if we ignore her. What about the other prince?"

"She took him with her, along with her daughters, maids – and half the palace treasures, apparently. She had to have part of the wall removed to allow access for some of the larger pieces of furniture."

Richard scratched his chin with his thumb.

"We need to get the king's brother out of there. I will think on it. Meanwhile, we must arrange meetings to discuss the matter of the coronation. There is much to do."

"Yes, your Grace, indeed there is."

By Hearsay

William Catesby was an excellent lawyer and Richard found him easy to talk to – they had love of the law in common and Catesby, like Richard, was an intelligent man. He had been recommended to Richard by Lord Hastings and Richard happily added him to his affinity. They were, for once, relaxing in Richard's London residence, Crosby Hall, when Ralph knocked on the door and announced that Richard had a visitor.

"I do not wish to see anyone at this hour, Ralph. Have them return tomorrow morning."

"He says it is most urgent, your Grace; a matter of national importance relating to the coronation."

Richard cast a sideways glance at Catesby and sighed. "Who is it, then, who dares to interrupt my, all-too-rare, leisure?"

"It is the Bishop of Bath and Wells, Robert Stillington, my Lord."

Richard always had great respect for churchmen.

"I am sorry, William, I suppose I had better see him."

"I will leave you then, your Grace," Catesby said, rising from his chair.

"No, stay. Perhaps your services might be needed, if this matter is so important to the state. Show him in, Ralph."

Ralph bowed and withdrew, returning after a short time with an elderly man, thin and balding, with wrinkles around his mouth and on his forehead that suggested he was a worrier. He wore the rich robes of a wealthy cleric. He bowed before the Duke, who invited him to take a seat and gave him some wine. As he took a sip, his hands were shaking.

"Now, you say you have a most urgent message for me – pray, let me know your mind, my Lord Bishop."

"Y-y-yes, indeed, your Grace. It is a grave matter that has been on my conscience for many years." He frowned even more, shaking his head slowly from side to side like a condemned man trying to avoid the noose.

"May I suggest you start at the beginning?"

"Of course, of course. Well, my story began about twenty years ago, when you were only a boy, not long after your brother, Edward, became king of England. I was at that time a lowly Archdeacon employed by your brother and favoured by him. He summoned me to his presence one day and told me that he wanted me to perform a particular service for him – a marriage service. He was in love, he said, and she was a widow woman, a gentle lady, who would not deign to submit to his... um... his carnal desires without the benefit of marriage. He was determined to have her, he said, and asked me to officiate."

"This is old news, Father – we all know that Edward married Elizabeth secretly because she refused to give in to his lusts, although I was not aware that you were the officiating cleric."

"No, my Lord, you misunderstand me. This was a good few years before he wed Elizabeth and it was a noble lady of the old blood who was the recipient of his desire. Her name was Lady Eleanor Butler, previously Eleanor Talbot, daughter of Old John Talbot, the Earl of Shrewsbury."

"God's Holy Nails!"

Richard turned to see why Catesby had cursed and found him to be as white as the first fallen snow.

"Sorry, your Grace, but I had heard a rumour in my family about this – we are related to the Talbots – but gave it no credence. It soon subsided and I thought it must have been

286

false."

"Unfortunately not," Stillington said, his eyes darting from one man to another. "The rumours subsided because Edward paid off Eleanor's family, warning her not to speak of it ever again. He gave her some land of her own and threatened that he would deny the marriage if she made it public; her reputation would be ruined. He promised to 'look after her' if she kept her peace, but she was a very pious lady, as pious as you are, your Grace. She considered herself wed and would not forswear her vows in order to marry another, so she retired to a religious house and spent her time in prayer and penitence."

"Wait a minute, do I understand you correctly? Are you saying that Edward and Elizabeth were married bigamously? I... I can scarcely believe such a tale! You must bring this woman, Eleanor, to Westminster to be questioned – she can claim her rights herself."

"She cannot, my Lord. She passed away several years ago."

Richard sighed. "This is a sorry tale indeed. Do you see what this means, William?" he said, turning to the lawyer. "If this is proven, the king is a bastard, as are all Elizabeth's children. He cannot be crowned and the succession is in doubt. But, wait! You said she was deceased, so perhaps, if his sons were born after her demise, the boys could be legitimised."

"No, your Grace, not by Church canon law. When a marriage as sanctioned by the Church occurs, the banns are read three times, giving any injured third-party opportunity to object – for example, Eleanor could have objected on the grounds that Edward was already married to her. If no objections are heard at the time but it later is claimed that the second marriage is bigamous, it gives the Church the power to declare the offspring of the second marriage to be legitimate because the second wife was not aware of the truth of the situation. But Edward and Elizabeth also married in secret, negating the Church's power to intervene. Their marriage is invalidated, as if it never existed, meaning the children were conceived in sin, in adultery, and so cannot be legitimised later."

"Sire," Francis said, frowning in concentration as he attempted to follow the convoluted argument. "Did not John of Gaunt, who conceived children outside marriage with the woman Katherine Roet, later legitimise his children?"

"Yes," Richard replied absently, his eyes unfocused and his face pale. "But that was different. Although both John of Gaunt and Katherine were legally wed to others when the children were conceived, he later married Katherine legally. The children were declared legitimate when the two were in a valid marriage. If the Bishop's story is true, Edward has destroyed his son's succession through his own deception and lust. Young Edward cannot be king. All Edward's children are barred from inheriting anything from him – including the throne. Francis?"

He glanced at his friend, who stood there open-mouthed as the ramifications of this revelation became apparent.

"Sweet Jesus, Dickon!" he said, forgetting to use the formal mode of address in his agitation. "If Ned's children are barred, and Warwick is attainted through his father, George's, treason, then the next in line is...!" He halted his words and simply fell to his knees before Richard.

"No, Francis, do not kneel to me! Father, this cannot be – there must be some mistake. Are you sure this first marriage was legal?"

"Of course I am, your Grace. They made their vows to be man and wife before me and her sister, Elizabeth, Duchess of Norfolk, as witnesses. The marriage could not even have been annulled if it was consummated – and I cannot imagine Edward would not have consummated it, can you?"

Richard sat down, his face ashen and his eyes haunted. He downed his wine in one desperate gulp and turned again to Catesby.

"Is there any way out of this mess?" he asked.

Catesby shook his head slowly. "I think not, your Grace. The only way of avoiding the consequences of this would be to turn a blind eye to it, to ignore the testimony of Bishop Stillington and suppress the truth. Then the country would have a bastard for a king."

Richard put his head in his hands.

"Dear God, help me," he groaned. "What do I do? What do I do? Do I crown a boy knowing he is a bastard and possibly bring down God's vengeance on the realm, or do I reveal this... this web of deceit and betray my brother's faith in me? He entrusted me to oversee his son's coronation."

"You have to forget Edward – this is all his fault!" Francis touched Richard on the shoulder, briefly. "He should not have saddled you with this responsibility, it is not fair."

"Doubtless he expected to live on until his sons were grown and the Bishop here was deceased, begging your pardon, my Lord. He probably hoped eventually everyone who knew anything would be gone and things would sort themselves out. Oh, Ned! What have you done!?"

Chapter Ten

London, Twenty-first Century

Innocent Man

As Stellan paused the machine, Rupert gave a derisive snort.

"Pfft! Well, that was a bit convenient for Richard, wasn't it? Strange how this tale of illegitimacy never came out before Edward died. Seems too convenient to me!" He was beginning to get on her nerves. But she couldn't resist rising to the bait.

"He didn't sound as if he thought it was convenient! He sounded shocked to me," Eve said.

"It could have been a set-up – Richard could have primed Stillington to come to him then with the story and pretended he knew nothing of it. Good God! He must have been planning it for months, years even – he was very ambitious and wanted the throne above all else."

Rupert folded his arms and smirked. Eve continued to argue with him.

"But was he? He had always been totally loyal to Edward. And

Edward had rewarded Richard with immense power in the North of England – he was like a mini-king there – Lord of the North. Just before he died, Edward gave Richard any part of Scotland that he could conquer for himself. He liked it in the North – that was where he and Anne chose to make their home: Middleham Castle in North Yorkshire."

"Even if that's the case, once Edward died, he wanted the throne – it's obvious!"

"Really? And on what are you basing your arguments? What we just heard didn't sound like he wanted to be king to me!"

"Well, what do you think happened after Ed died then? What's the Ricardian spiel?"

She paused, collecting her thoughts.

"Richard was in the north when Edward died. William Hastings, Edward's best friend, told him Edward had named him Lord Protector and warned him that the Woodvilles had the new king and wanted to be in control. He advised Richard to take a large contingent of men and go and confront them. But what did Richard do? The first thing he did was to have a mass said in York for Edward and swear allegiance to the new king. It was a big thing in those days, to swear an oath. Oath-breaking was a terrible sin. Why would he have sworn allegiance – and made everyone else do it – if he was intending to take the throne? Wouldn't it have been more sensible to just 'forget' to do that? Then he sent letters of condolence to the queen and the new king, Edward, and arranged to meet the king and his entourage at Northampton and join with Anthony Woodville to escort him into London."

"He was plotting to take the throne then, though, surely!"

"If that was the case, why did he only take about three hundred men with him? The Woodvilles had demanded thousands and it was only when Hastings threatened them that they agreed to pare it down to two thousand! Two thousand men – that wasn't an honour guard, it was a bloody army! But still Richard only took three hundred and Buckingham another three hundred. Wouldn't he have taken more if he was intending to fight the Woodvilles for the control of the king?"

"Hmm, maybe…" Rupert sounded more doubtful. Good! She was winning the argument.

"Then, when Richard had brought Edward to London, he acted entirely properly and as he should have if he were intending to see him crowned. He arranged meetings to discuss all the arrangements, invited all the right people to the coronation, asked Edward to list all the men he wanted to create knights as part of the tradition, arranged for him to have his coronation robes made and even had coins minted in Edward's name. At first some thought these coins were Edward IV's, but it was found that they had the boar symbol in the corner, showing it was done at this time, so they were definitely for Edward V."

"So, was it likely that Edward would have made this secret marriage to Eleanor?" Stellan asked, sipping his coffee.

"The second wedding with Elizabeth was also contracted in secret, so that may have been his 'modus operandi'. It was said that Elizabeth was too wily to give in unless he married her, but even then, he didn't reveal it for about five months. Edward was the sort of man who chased women and got bored with them once he had bedded them, but he was known to have never forced a woman, he persuaded them. It is entirely possible that the marriage with Eleanor wasn't the first time he had promised marriage, maybe even gone through other secret ceremonies, so that he could have a woman and then denied all knowledge later."

"So why didn't these women speak up?"

"He was the king! Perhaps he bought them off, threatened them or their family. Eleanor's family certainly gained some land from Edward, for unknown reasons. Plus, there was the shame of dragging their name through the courts. Eleanor retired to a nunnery and spent the rest of her days in prayer and solitude."

"But why didn't she come forward when the king announced his marriage to Elizabeth?"

"Well, it was a fait accompli – he had been married five months by then. Presumably, he had long abandoned Eleanor and she may have preferred to keep her dignity and stay quiet. She never remarried, which is interesting."

"So why did the Bishop suddenly choose to come forward after Edward's death? As I said, it was all rather convenient, wasn't it? The Bishop was the only 'witness' by that time." Rupert made the sign for quotation marks with his fingers, annoying her even more. He snorted. "Why didn't Stillington come forward years before, if his conscience was bothering him so much?"

"If he had made it public when Edward was alive, he would have been hung, drawn and quartered probably – or at least flung into the deepest dungeon in the Tower and forgotten about. In fact, Edward did imprison Stillington in the Tower for a while, for vague reasons. Perhaps he had been talking too much? So that was the only time Stillington could reveal it. He couldn't wait until the new king was crowned – it would be too late. But it is entirely likely that his conscience could not allow a bastard to inherit the throne of England. Edward may have been living in sin, but he was himself legitimate as far as Stillington knew, but the new king was not."

Rupert was shaking his head.

"Nah! Richard could easily have made it up – Edward was conveniently dead and so was this Eleanor woman. Maybe he invented the whole thing and bribed Stillington to say it was true."

"Except Richard never rewarded Stillington at all – there is no record of any advancement, promotion or payments."

"Well, Richard probably threatened him then. He was a very powerful noble, wasn't he? The most powerful in the land at the time. And he had Buckingham on his side, another powerful lord. They were like a couple of terrorists."

"Terrorists! I know where you got that from – you have been watching Don James, the hip, young, so-called historian. He is so biased against Richard – he was taught by Donald Straker I think, and he loves the Tudors, so claims Richard was a villain."

"So-called! He is a historian – your mate Sue isn't qualified in history, is she? He's not biased, he just goes with the most probable explanation – Richard needed to make a play for the throne and used Stillington to do it."

Eve was becoming hot with anger.

"Think for a minute! Richard was in London with only three hundred men. Hastings alone was very powerful in London and would have been able to call on a private army to oppose Richard. Plus, there were several other nobles there, ready for the coronation. They were in the South, where he had no power base. Do you really think he and Buckingham, with only six hundred soldiers between them, would have the clout to threaten all those Lords and Nobles, not to mention the London merchants?"

She was really getting into her stride now and her cheeks were flushed. She wagged her finger at Rupert as she continued.

"Plus, you assume Richard wanted to be king. To be honest, I don't think he did, particularly. He was comfortable and powerful in the North and Edward had just granted him the right to any Scottish land he could conquer – he was like a mini-king there already. Look, let me give you an example. Suppose a young woman wanted to be a footballer's wife – go on, imagine you are one. What would you do to achieve your ambition?"

"You're so funny, but, OK, I'll go along with you, girl. If I was a 'Chardonnay' or a 'Tiffany' or something, I would go to the London clubs and flaunt myself in front of them – find out where the richest players go and keep hanging around and try to attract their attention."

"Exactly, so if Richard had wanted to be king from years before, as Shakespeare claims, he would surely have spent more time at Court, where all the political intrigues were going on, and ingratiated himself with the other powerful nobles. But he didn't, he kept himself to himself as much as possible."

"So, if he didn't want to be king, why didn't he just send Stillington away and turn a blind eye?"

"Well, in my opinion, his character was to blame for that."

"Ambitious and greedy for power, you mean?" Rupert was lolling back in his chair, his hands linked behind his head.

Eve rolled her eyes.

"Not at all – he was a stickler for acting lawfully and fairly. Plus, he was a God-fearing man. Once it was revealed that the 'princes' were illegitimate, he *had* to become king; it was his duty because he was the next in line, legally."

She pointed at Rupert with the end of her pen as she enumerated her arguments.

"Also, he was a grown man, and he might have been thinking of the good of the country as a whole – it was never a good thing to have a child king. It could have cast the realm back into civil war as different factions vied for control." She paused to take a breath and order her thoughts and then continued. "And he was very interested in the law. He might have seen it as an opportunity to bring in the sort of legal system he had been employing in the North, to great popularity and effect."

"Well, it wasn't that popular when he tried to do it as king though, was it?" Rupert's voice and expression were triumphant, but she had an answer for him.

"Well, I think he tried to do it too quickly. The nobility felt their power was threatened and Richard seems to have made the mistake of assuming others lived by his own standards. He wanted justice and fairness, but others benefitted from the corrupt juries, the fraudulent land transactions and the loopholes in the bail system."

"Well, I saw an interview with Straker and he says he is ninety-nine percent sure Richard murdered the princes." Rupert's tone was smug, but Eve had seen the interview in question and had her riposte ready.

"Really? Did he say what evidence he has to support that claim?" Eve tilted her head and stared at Rupert.

"Well, yes, he said Richard would have..." Rupert's voice descended into a mumble and his chin came down on his chest as he squirmed under Eve's interrogation.

"Would have what?" She put her hand behind her ear as if she was straining to hear; she wasn't going to let him off the hook.

"Would have been stupid not to."

Rupert wasn't looking smug any more and she laughed.

"Well, that's not evidence is it? He's a fool if he thinks that is enough. There is not even any proof that they died at all."

"Wasn't there a pretender in Tudor's time who claimed to be one of the princes?" Stellan had been listening and now chimed in.

"Yes, thank you!" She beamed at Stellan and Rupert scowled. "Perkin Warbeck – or at least that's what Henry Tudor insisted he was called. But Henry didn't treat him like a commoner – he had him at Court – a prisoner, but still... And the King of Scotland allowed him to marry Catherine Gordon, one of his close kin."

"Pfft! The Scots were always fighting against the English – they would have done anything to annoy the English King." Rupert was trying his luck again.

"Really? I doubt they would have gone that far. And what about Maximilian then? The Duke of Burgundy? He helped finance his invasion and gave him soldiers."

"Puh! He was in cahoots with Margaret, the dowager Duchess of Burgundy, his mother-in-law. And, she, well she obviously hated Tudor – he had killed her brother after all, so she would have done anything to get him off the throne, including supporting a false claimant and saying he was her nephew."

"Maybe, but after 'Perkin' was caught, Maximilian still insisted he was the prince, Richard of York. He had nothing to gain then."

Rupert pursed his lips in a petulant pout but remained silent. She gave a small smile of triumph and turned back to her coffee.

"Is there any evidence to support the precontract theory – a marriage certificate, an entry in a parish record book...?" David had been listening intently to the debate and now asked his question.

"There were no marriage certificates then and even parish records only began in Fat Harry's time."

"Fat Harry?" David looked at her, his face screwed up in a frown of confusion.

"Sorry, I picked that up from Sue – Henry VIII – it's her little nickname for him."

David laughed and she continued.

"It is presumed that there must have been some kind of evidence at the time – enough to convince the Three Estates anyway. But also, Stillington was a very well-respected member of the clergy, he wasn't some little local priest. In those days, a marriage could be privately made between two people even without witnesses. All they had to do was say 'I do marry you' to each other and the deed was done. Or if they said it in the future tense 'I will marry you' they were considered legally married once they slept together."

"What? No witnesses, no priest and no paperwork? But one or the other of them could just deny the whole thing – her word against mine, sort of thing," Alex chimed in.

"Exactly, and that's why the Church disapproved of them, but they still went on and they were still legally binding. All the talk of a 'precontract', meaning a betrothal, not an actual marriage, is wrong. Sue told me that it actually means a previous marriage contract. It would only be called that after a subsequent marriage was contracted of course: Pre-contract."

"Well, all I can say is you certainly know your stuff, Eve." David smiled at her. "But what I don't understand is why you can defend him when he took the throne from the boy – even if he was illegitimate – when he had been charged by his brother to protect him, protect both the princes."

"That's another misconception, David. He was named Protector of the Realm, sort of like Head of Homeland Security is today. He wouldn't have had charge of the upbringing and education of the new king, nor would he have had the power of a regent. The Woodvilles had already been entrusted with the prince's upbringing, although that might have changed after their dreadful behaviour in trying to get total control over him as king. And the Council would have governed the realm with Richard having a high position as first among them. Richard was charged with keeping the kingdom safe, protecting the land, not the princes, both from foreign invasion and from rebellion from within. That's why he was within his rights to stamp down on the Woodvilles – they had been found to have been rebelling against his authority as Lord Protector and that was endangering the weal of the realm – the well-being of the country."

"Phew! Well, thanks for the history lesson, Eve. But it's getting late – let's all get off home and we can continue the discussion tomorrow – it's useful to know the various possibilities – maybe we will be able to shed some light onto some of the controversies, eh?"

"So, I haven't convinced you, then?"

"I have no opinion really one way or the other," David replied.

"You've convinced me, Eve," Stellan smiled, his blue eyes twinkling.

Rupert just scowled. "I'm withholding judgment for now," he growled.

A World Without Love

"It's the infamous Council meeting, Eve! Are you excited?" David asked her, his eyes lighting up – probably with the thought of how much money he was going to make if he could solve some of the mysteries surrounding Richard.

"I didn't know you knew about it – have you been researching then?"

"Yes, a bit. He was supposed to have had Hastings killed without a trial, wasn't he?"

"Well, shall we see? Stellan looks to be finished with the co-ordinates and ready to start."

She glanced at the Swede, but he wasn't looking her way. For the last few days he had acted as if nothing had happened between them. Was he regretting it? She had felt a twinge of regret at first and then relived the delicious feelings he had aroused in her, so that she felt she was no longer boring old Eve, but an exciting, modern woman who could have a casual lover if she wished. What was wrong with having sex when she wanted? That was what men had always done. She began to fantasise about Stellan, planning when she might try to get alone with him again. Then the machine began its characteristic buzzing…

Lord of Lies

"Will, are you sure about this? Hastings has always been an enemy of the Woodvilles. Why should he form an alliance with them now?"

"Perhaps because he can see he will not succeed in retaining the power and offices he held under Edward, if you are king. Perhaps because he would rather join forces with them in the hope that he might influence a young king and become his close adviser as he was his father's. Perhaps because he resents the influence the Duke of Buckingham has with you, my Lord." Catesby often seemed to say things in threes, like Cicero.

"Do you know what they are planning to do? Have your spies any further knowledge?"

"He has been using the whore, Elizabeth Shore, to act as go-between to pass messages to the queen in Sanctuary, although we have not been able to obtain any of these messages – they are always destroyed. But Bishop Morton seems to be involved too, as does Lady Stanley. We think they are planning to get the boys out of the Tower or collude with the bastard, Tudor, who still lurks on the continent, hiding under Brittany's cloak."

"Hmm, I bet Elizabeth loved that! Her husband's mistress used as a messenger!"

"But it is a cunning ploy – who would suspect those two of being in collusion. I barely believed it myself and I was shown it, so I saw it with my own eyes."

"I will call a meeting of the main suspects and confront them with their treachery. In the Tower. We will soon see what is going on and who is innocent or guilty in the matter."

Betrayed

"Where is Richard? He said we were to be here at ten of the clock and he is himself absent. How long is he going to keep us waiting?" Rotherham grumbled to Bishop Morton, but his eyes betrayed his unease.

"Here he is now," Morton said, rising and bowing to the Duke.

Everyone was silent and Richard stood before them, twisting the ring on his little finger.

"Gentlemen, I apologise for keeping you here idle. But there is important business to do today. An evil plot has been discovered which threatens myself and the safety of this realm. What do you say should be the punishment for such as these, who commit treason?"

They all tried to avoid his eye, but he finally met the gaze of Hastings. "Will, what say you? How should a traitor be punished?"

Hastings moved his hand down under the table and looked Richard in the eye. "Your Grace, they should be put to death, of course!"

"Even if you are among their number?" Richard demanded, his eyes blazing fury, and moved towards Hastings, who stood up and backed away.

"Steady on, Richard – surely you know I am involved in no plots?" Hastings' eyes were almost popping out of his head.

"On the contrary, Catesby tells me you have been consorting with Elizabeth Shore and using her as a messenger to collude with Dame Grey."

Dame Grey was now the official name for the old queen, Elizabeth Woodville.

"Catesby? He is lying!" he shouted, desperately.

"He is not the only one to report this. You will be arrested and tried for treason, William Hastings."

Richard was only a couple of feet from Hastings now and was about to send Lovell to fetch the guards when an ornately-jewelled dagger appeared in Hastings' hand, pointing straight at Richard's heart. Edward's loyal friend made a clumsy lunge for Richard, who neatly sidestepped and grabbed him by the wrist, effectively disarming him. He raised his voice so the guards waiting outside could hear him:

"Guards! Treason! Treason!" Richard yelled and they came rushing in to arrest Hastings.

"I might have been persuaded to be merciful to you, William, but not now. You have proved your guilt and threatened the life of the Protector of the Realm, a prince of the blood royal. As Constable of England I convene herewith my court. You, Buckingham, you, Stanley, you, Lovell – you are my jury. What say you? Is he guilty as charged?"

Thomas Stanley spoke up first: "My Lord we have all seen with our own eyes how he drew his weapon on you, with intent to kill. There is no doubt of his treason."

"Agreed," said Buckingham.

The others chorused: "Aye, he is guilty."

"Then I pronounce his sentence to be death by beheading. Guards, find a suitable block of wood, take him outside and strike off his head immediately. With the power vested in me as Constable and Protector of the realm, I so decree."

"Aye, Sir!"

All the blood had drained from Hastings' face and he gasped:

"Richard, you cannot do this, we are old friends. We both loved Edward... please!"

He swallowed convulsively, struggling to escape the two guards who held him firmly between them. Richard raised his hand, indicating for the guards to wait. Hastings let out a shaky sigh of relief, but his reprieve was short-lived. Richard turned his cold gaze onto him.

"Old friends? You were Edward's friend, never mine. And your influence helped to cause his descent into sin and corruption. Tell me, did you know about the marriage to Eleanor Talbot?"

Hastings flinched slightly and Richard knew the reply, even if it was unsaid.

"So, you did. And you would have let a bastard boy ascend the throne, said nothing and brought God's wrath down on our fair country." His mouth twisted in disgust. "Take him away."

He turned to the others and ordered the other guards to take them to separate rooms, so he could question them alone and see if he could get to the bottom of the plot.

He was speaking to Stanley, who expressed shock that his wife could have been involved in the plot and swore he, himself, was loyal.

Richard tensed as he heard the unmistakable sound of an axe thudding into a block of wood and another softer sound as Hastings' head rolled into the grass.

Whoops

"So, he didn't have a trial then," David said.

"No, hold on, Richard gave him a swift hearing of the Constable's Court and because Hastings was caught red-handed trying to attack him, he had the right as Constable of England to declare him a convicted traitor and have him executed."

"But what about an appeal? Surely he could have appealed the decision!" Rupert asked, appalled.

"No, not in those circumstances. The Constable could convict someone of treason without leave of appeal. Not very ethical by our standards, but perfectly legal in those days. There were witnesses to his treason, don't forget, and also no-one seemed to object at all – everyone accepted that Hastings was guilty of it."

"What about the others? Stanley and the two priests?" David asked, taking a swift sip of his tea.

"Rotherham and Morton. Yes, Rotherham was let off and Morton was put into Buckingham's custody in Brecknock Castle. Stanley was given the land and property confiscated from his wife for her part in the conspiracy, but none of them were executed. Unfortunately," she added under her breath.

"What?" Rupert asked. "Did you just say 'Unfortunately'?" Rupert sounded incredulous. "You think Richard should have executed them?"

"Well, if he had executed Margaret Stanley and Morton, he might still be alive today!"

Eve was so intent on defending Richard that she hadn't noticed what she had said until the others all burst into unrestrained laughter.

"Oh! You know what I mean – he might have lived and reigned for longer."

Inside her she had a terrible and yet wonderful feeling that Richard Plantagenet was still very much alive for her. She knew him and she felt what he felt, the same physical experiences and the same emotions.

It was at times exhilarating, at times embarrassing. But how on earth was she going to deal with Bosworth?

Lookin' For a Good Time

Eve lingered behind when the others left that evening, as she knew Stellan would take a while to pack up 'The Fly' and she wanted to speak to him. She had been feeling more and more confused by his lack of acknowledgment that they had slept together. She felt even more attracted to him because of his apparent indifference and had decided to have it out with him.

Once everyone else had left the office, she turned to him and opened her mouth to speak, but before she could say a word, he said:

"Hi Eve, do you want to have sex again? I won't be a moment."

She felt all the things she had been going to say to him such as: "Why don't you want me?" "What are your feelings for me?" "Why are you ignoring what happened between us?" all dissolve away. She didn't know whether to feel pleased – after all, hadn't she wanted to repeat the experience with him? Or offended because he spoke as if he was offering her a cup of tea or, actually, more as if she was the cup of tea!

She spoke without really thinking through what she wanted to express.

"No, I don't."

He paused and turned to her, as he sealed the machine back inside its cover.

"OK."

He turned back to 'The Fly' and then came around the desk, picking up his jacket as he passed his chair.

"Well, at least not unless you want to have a proper relationship. Do you have any... feelings for me?" Eve asked, then kicked herself for being so needy.

He sighed. "I'm fond of you, of course. You are very pretty and I enjoyed it last week. But I can't ever have a relationship with you; I have a wife back in Sweden. We could do something short term though, if you want."

Eve felt herself go cold as the shock of what he said, as well as the matter-of-fact way he said it, hit her.

"You're married? Why didn't you say so before we…?"

"You didn't ask."

He looked at her with a puzzled frown as if she was the odd one here.

"But I would never have slept with you if I had known that. What about your wife? Don't you care about her?"

"Yes, but we have an open relationship."

"You mean you both sleep with other people?"

He nodded and ran his long fingers through his hair. "Look, if you're not happy with it, that's fine."

"No, it isn't! You used me!"

He raised his eyebrows, looked at her over his spectacles and folded his arms.

"Really Eve? And I thought it was you who kissed me first, wasn't it? You who threw yourself at me and started to undress me?"

There was a sound from outside the door, like a soft footstep followed by a door closing. Well, they weren't doing anything wrong – at least not this time. She took a deep breath. She couldn't deny what he said. He was speaking the truth. She looked at the floor and let the breath out with a sigh.

"I'm sorry. Yes, you are right – I initiated it. But you should have told me you were married, Stellan." She could hear the whiny note of reproach in her voice.

"Well, I'm sorry too then. But I don't regret the sex – it was… pretty wild." He smiled, showing the cute dimple and gave a quick wink. Then he put his jacket on and picked up his briefcase, holding the door open for her. She walked out in front of him, feeling let down and guilty all at once and he closed the door behind them.

Framed

E ve was the first in the office the next day. She went to her desk, switching on her PC and setting down her coffee, when she noticed that Stellan's office door was wide open. It was unusual for him to leave his door ajar – he mostly kept it closed, as he was often tinkering about with the equipment (or random women, perhaps) and liked to block out the general chatter and noise in the main office.

She went over to the office and peeked round the door.

"Stellan? Are you in? Stellan, I…" Eve's words were cut off with a gasp as she took in the scene that greeted her in Stellan's office. 'The Fly' was no longer sitting on his desk, snug in its cover, nor ready to start the day's search; its small screen was cracked, the casing smashed and several levers, dials and buttons had been broken off and lay forlornly on the floor with the discarded leather cover. The power lead had been pulled out of the casing and the whole machine had been dropped on the floor.

"Oh no, no!" Eve said under her breath, as she instinctively tried to pick the machine up.

It was heavy and she almost dropped it again, but finally managed to put it back on the desk. She turned around, looking at the debris on the floor and felt a strange heavy weight inside her. She couldn't quite fathom what it meant until she realised that they still had no evidence about the disappearance of the princes in the Tower and that, if 'The Fly' was destroyed beyond repair, they probably never would. And she would never hear the voice of Richard III again.

She started as the door was shoved so hard it crashed against the side desk and Alex marched in, Stellan and David behind him.

"Eve! What have you done?" David shouted, his face like thunder.

"Me? I haven't done anything," she protested.

"So, what are you doing in here when Stellan is not here?" David asked, suspicion clouding his normally bright eyes.

"The door was open and I just came in to see if Stellan... where Stellan was," she finished weakly. She gave a pleading look to Stellan, but he was looking at her as if she was something on the bottom of his immaculate shoe. All at once she realised what he must think – that she had destroyed the machine to get back at him for not telling her he wasn't free to have a relationship with her.

"Why did you do that?" he said, his face contorted in an expression of disgust and disbelief. "You might be annoyed with me but this is crazy – we haven't yet found out what happened to the Princes in the Tower."

"It wasn't me who did this!" she shouted, desperately. "I just came in here because I wondered why the door was open. It was like this when I found it."

"Don't lie, Eve," Alex said. "I only just came in and I heard a lot of crashing and banging coming from here. I thought it was a burglar, so I went to fetch David and Stellan from David's office."

She gazed incredulously at him. How could he have heard crashing when all the damage had been done before she arrived?

"No! That's a lie!" she said. "I was the first in the office and this was already done when I came in. I was just coming to fetch David myself. Why would I destroy the machine when we are – were – just about to solve the greatest mystery in English history?"

"I don't know," said David, his hands on his hips. "Stellan, is there any chance you can fix it?"

"Not today. And I'm not sure if I can do it at all. Perhaps I could use some parts from my prototype machine – I have one at home in Sweden, but it isn't so refined and efficient as 'The Fly'. I'll need to take a look and then I'll let you know."

Then Rupert appeared in the doorway, a big grin on his face, until he saw the tangled mess on the floor.

"Bloody hell!" he said.

Just Another Day

David spoke to Eve in his office and finally believed her when she suggested that it was perhaps a rival company who had destroyed the machine. He brought in some draconian security measures to prevent anything similar happening again.

She was very suspicious of Alex accusing her of the deed. Then she remembered hearing footsteps the night before and everything fitted into place. He must have heard her and Stellan discussing having slept together and Stellan saying it was she who initiated the encounter. By destroying the machine and blaming her, he could get revenge on both of them. Unfortunately, she had no proof it had been him, but at least there was no proof it was her either.

As the project was on mandatory hold, Eve now spent her time researching more of Richard's life. Rupert was still going out with Camilla and occasionally invited Eve and the others out for a drink with them, but Eve always refused now.

Stellan was missing from the office as he had flown to Sweden to fetch the original prototype and any other components that he thought might be needed in his attempt to repair 'The Fly'. Eve was glad he was away, because she felt rather ambivalent towards him now. On the one hand she couldn't really blame him for responding to her advances, especially when he and his wife were OK about having an open relationship. But on the other hand, she was angry that he hadn't thought it was important to tell her he was married. Not that she was in love with him, but she had let herself get rather fonder of him than was wise, with hindsight, and, obviously, he was gorgeous physically. She did feel quite lonely, as she had also distanced herself from Rupert, who had always been the one closest to her at work. And, of course, James wasn't at home. In fact, she wasn't at home herself, but still staying with Sue. She was so grateful to her Ricardian friend because at least she had company after work and also someone to talk to about Richard. She was becoming more and more knowledgeable and also more of a Ricardian.

Stellan was gone for three days and when he got back, he was non-committal about whether he would be able to repair the machine. He retired to his office and they could hear banging, buzzing and drilling coming from there as he worked on the repair. He finally emerged after a week of almost constant work to say he had done what he could and it was ready to test.

They all went into his office and took their customary seats.

'The Fly' was sitting on the desk in its usual spot, but looked very different from the previous version. There were some parts that seemed bulkier and larger than the previous equivalent components, with some that were different in colour. The whole impression was makeshift.

"I realise the machine looks rather odd," Stellan said. "But that is only because the previous prototype was a different design – the functionality is the same and it shouldn't make a difference to its efficiency."

"That's fine, Stellan, let's get on with it. Fingers crossed, eh?" David gave a mirthless grin to them all, waving his crossed fingers in the air.

Stellan took a deep breath and plugged the machine in, flicking on the power. Then he pressed the 'on' switch. There was a humming – it was quite different from the buzzing of 'The Fly', more like an annoying mosquito. Stellan pressed a few more buttons, adjusted a dial, pulled a lever and tapped in the date and place co-ordinates for the next agreed attempt.

The whine became more high-pitched and there was also an underlying warble as they all held their breath.

Then a red light appeared and Stellan smiled.

"That means the subject is found!" he said.

Crowning of the King

Eve's ears were filled with mediaeval music and voices cheering. They had been listening in on Richard's and Anne's coronation – she knew the others couldn't hear or see what she could, but she had said they should listen nonetheless so that they didn't miss anything Richard said, since it was such an important historical event. In the end, they had agreed that she could listen alone and note anything important which they could hear later. Of course, they did not know she was noting all the sights, smells, sounds and feelings of the celebration too, as she experienced them. So, she could relax a little and enjoy the coronation as an unseen spectator.

Richard and Anne had already processed from White Hall to Westminster Hall, stepping all the way on a carpet of bright red fabric.

Now the ceremonies themselves had begun, with the royal couple walking barefoot from Westminster Hall to the Abbey for the double coronation – the first for one hundred and seventy-five years and only the fourth in England's history. Richard went first, of course, following the large, ornate cross carried by the clergy. Eve had researched the coronation while Stellan was repairing the machine and had noted which nobles performed which duties, so that she could tell who was who.

Thomas Stanley carried the Lord High Constable's Mace. Eve looked at him with interest – he was an arrogant-looking man, slim, with a peculiar beard and calculating eyes. She disliked him immediately and knew that Richard didn't trust him. The reason he had been so honoured was to try to win his loyalty by bestowing gifts and titles on him. She sighed; all Richard's efforts would prove to be in vain.

There were four swords carried in the ceremony, two sharp (the swords of justice), the sheathed sword of state and one blunted, which was the sword of mercy. The latter was carried by Henry Percy, the Earl of Northumberland, another possible traitor to Richard. He was quite good-looking, although his mouth and chin were weak. His eyes were large and beautiful, but had no spark of intelligence in them. The two swords of justice were borne by Viscount Francis Lovell and Edmund

Grey of Ruthin, the Earl of Kent. The Earl was a good thirty years older than Lovell and rather fleshy in the face, with a long nose and a confident gaze. Lovell was resplendent in blue velvet doublet and crimson hose, his dark hair shiny and well-groomed, his eyes bright with excitement as he proudly held the sword before him. The sword of state was carried by Thomas Howard, Earl of Surrey.

Holding the sceptre was Richard's brother-in-law, John de la Pole, the Duke of Suffolk, who had been married to Margaret Beaufort in his youth, although the marriage had been annulled and he subsequently married Richard's sister, Elizabeth. Their son, also called John, bore the orb. He was young, only about twenty, but had a determined chin and a clear, direct gaze.

John Howard, the Duke of Norfolk, had the honour of bearing the crown and had been named Earl Marshall and High Steward of England by Richard. He was stocky and strong-looking, with a proud expression as he solemnly carried St Edward the Confessor's crown. This was interesting as it was destined to be destroyed in the English Civil War, replaced when the monarchy was restored with a new St Edward's Crown in a different style.

Richard himself was sumptuously dressed in purple velvet and ermine, escorted by two bishops. A decorated canopy was held over him as he walked. The Duke of Buckingham himself carried Richard's train, dressed even more elaborately than usual, his eyes glinting as he enjoyed all the pomp and ceremony.

Following Richard, the queen's attendants walked, with more members of the nobility carrying the queen's regalia and Margaret Beaufort herself bearing Anne's train. She was a tiny woman with a pinched expression as if she disapproved of all the extravagance. Her clothes were plain but obviously expensive and of rich fabric. Her lips, pursed, and her eyes, narrowed, gave her a stern air which served to make all give her a wide berth.

Following her was the Duchess of Suffolk, Richard's sister, Elizabeth, and then yet more nobles and high-status notables.

They entered the Abbey to the sound of a choir singing a joyful melody, and the ceremony began. There were many prayers, further singing and the coronation oath.

Richard took his oath in English – the first king to do so.

The Archbishop of Canterbury, Thomas Bourchier, said:

"Sire, is your Grace willing to take the oath?"

In a clear, strong voice he replied: "I am willing."

"Will you solemnly promise and swear to rule the people of England according to their laws and customs?"

"I so swear."

"Will you, to your power, cause law and justice in mercy, to be executed in all your judgements?"

"I will."

"Will you, to the utmost of your power, maintain the Laws of God and the true profession of the Gospel? Will you maintain and preserve inviolably the peace of the Church, and the doctrine, worship, discipline, and government thereof? And will you preserve unto the Bishops and Clergy of England, and to the Churches there committed to their charge, all such rights and privileges, as by law do or shall appertain to them or any of them?"

"I will."

Then the Archbishop turned to the congregation.

"Do you, the people, wish to accept such a ruler?"

They all shouted:

"Aye, we wish it and grant it."

The new king and queen then moved forward and, shielded from public gaze by a canopy and seated on the thrones of England, they were partially disrobed. Then the Archbishop anointed Richard with the holy oil, on his hands, breast, shoulders and arms and finally his head was anointed with the consecrated chrism. Anne was also anointed in a like manner. They were then clothed in rich cloth of gold.

Then, Richard was approached and girded with the sword of state, symbolically showing that he was defender of the Church and protector of the weak. The ring of state was placed on his finger, he was given the rod and sceptre and finally crowned with the golden crown of St Edward the Confessor. He sat on the great throne which had the stone of destiny within it. Anne was given her regalia and settled beside Richard on her throne. Blessings were asked and received.

They were then presented to their subjects amid universal acclamation.

He looked proud and solemn as he went through all the elaborate ceremonies and finally allowed himself a small smile of reassurance to his queen consort as they accepted the homage of all the nobles gathered there. A 'Te Deum' was sung and a High Mass was said. Eve was surprised to note that she had a lump in her throat during much of the proceedings. What an honour to be able to witness the coronation of a mediaeval king!

Pomp and Circumstance

Later, the Coronation Feast began. Back at Westminster Hall, Norfolk was in charge of clearing the Hall of spectators by riding in on a gaily-caparisoned horse. The Hall was decorated with flags and banners which proudly displayed the arms of the new king and queen. Richard and Anne were led to a marble table on the dais and Anne sat on Richard's left. Two noblewomen stood behind the queen holding a cloth, ready to position it over her head whenever she ate or drank and two squires sat at Richard's feet ready to provide anything he needed. On Richard's right was a place reserved for Bourchier, the Archbishop of Canterbury, but he had been tired by the long coronation and his place was taken by the Bishop of Durham. Four other tables were placed in the hall for the other noble guests. As they entered the Hall, they all in turn pledged their loyalty to the King and Queen. The Hall was filled with the noble guests, which included judges, clerics and the Mayor of London. One of the four long tables was for the queen's ladies, including Margaret Beaufort. Others were served elsewhere and there were about three thousand guests in all.

Behind the high table were two small platforms where the musicians and heralds were. The musicians included trumpeters and minstrels.

With everyone seated, the first course was served, announced by a fanfare of trumpets. The high table was served by members of the nobility who included, in this case, the Dukes of Norfolk and Buckingham, the Earl of Surrey, Viscount Francis Lovell, Sir William Hopton and Sir Robert Percy, who was Marshall of the Hall. The king's food was served on a gold plate and the queen's on a gilt one, while the Bishop of Durham had a silver platter. The seventeen men who had just been made Knights of the Bath served the four long tables. There were fifteen different dishes in all, including such delicacies as pike in a sweet and sour sauce, venison frumenty with cinnamon and sugar, roasted heron, cygnet and crane, beef and mutton, stuffed capons in lemon, sliced jelly and a pheasant with its tail feathers displayed as if alive. The course was finished off with a 'subtlety' – an elaborate sugar or marzipan confection made to look like a symbolic object. In this case it was a crown.

During the second course, which had even more dishes and was just as elaborate, with some of the dishes decorated with gold and silver strips and another subtlety at the end, a dramatic interlude occurred when the king's champion, Sir Robert Dymoke, rode into the Hall and stopped before the High Table. He was fully armed and wearing gilt spurs and clothing of crimson damask. His horse wore red and white silk trappings which almost reached the ground. He issued the traditional challenge:

"Whosoever will say that King Richard is not the lawful king, I shall fight at the utterance." And he threw down his gauntlets and waited.

There was a pause when all were silent and then everyone shouted: "King Richard!"

A goblet of red wine was given to Dymoke, who drank some and spilled the rest onto the floor, keeping the cup as his payment and leaving the Hall.

Then the eighteen heralds on the platform came down and stood before the king. They included the four Kings of Heralds, who all wore crowns. These were the Garter King of Heralds, Norroy, Clarenceaux and Gloucester. The Garter King proclaimed:

"King Richard III is King of England and France and Lord of Ireland!" at which the heralds all shouted: "Largesse!" three times and then returned to their stage.

The serving of the feast had been interrupted because Richard wanted to speak to many of the nobles and guests and the feast was halted every time this happened.

"How is your charming wife?" "I hope your family is well." "Delighted that you could come." "Congratulations on your new arrival." "Thank you for your support." "We must meet and discuss the matter you are concerned with – I am sure we can work something out." And to Margaret Beaufort:

"Be sure, madam, we have not forgotten your son." Very ambiguous!

After all the conversation, there was no time to serve the third course, so only wafers and hippocras were served to the royal couple by the Mayor of London in covered cups of gold. These the Mayor kept as his fee. Following which, they all paid homage to the new king and queen, who then retired to their private chambers.

"Richard, I have never felt so exhausted – or so exhilarated! I can scarcely believe I am Queen of England. It has been like a dream."

"Yes, Anne, I know. I was reluctant to take the throne at first – there are those who will always think I had not the right. Yet now it is done, there is so much I can do to make the realm better. Improve the laws, bring justice to all, as I have in the North, stop some of the corruption and impiety which had become the norm under Edward. Oh, Anne, I have such plans!"

His blue eyes shone and he had a gentle smile that softened his face. It was as if it had been lit up from within. Eve's heart ached, knowing he would not live long enough to achieve his dream.

Chapter Eleven

Oxford, July 1483

These Days

This time, Richard was on progress after the coronation and they found him at the University of Oxford. It was just over two weeks after the ceremony and Eve listened with interest as he was received firstly outside the University by the Chancellor; following this, they processed to the College of the Blessed Mary Magdalene where he was welcomed by its founder, Bishop William Waynflete.

"Your Grace, I thank you for accepting my invitation to visit us and reside in our college. I hope you will enjoy your stay with us. Pray, please follow me and I will conduct you to your chamber where you may rest and take sustenance after your journey. Tomorrow, I would like to invite you, if you are interested, to attend a debate. We will be having one on theology and one on moral philosophy and you are most welcome to attend either, or none, as you wish."

"I would be most keen to attend both, if that is possible."

Richard inclined his head graciously as he replied, while following the Bishop to his designated chamber – the most luxurious one available at the College, which was relatively new.

"Of course, Sire, of course – it is a great honour that you would deign to grace us with your presence for both. I look forward to welcoming you and introducing you to our most talented students on the morrow."

Bishop Waynflete bowed and left Richard and his attendants to their ease.

"Are you really going to attend both debates?" Francis Lovell asked when the king had eaten and drunk his fill.

"Of course, Francis, it is an interesting way of learning and understanding a subject – to debate it, or failing that to listen to other learned fellows do it. You should listen yourself, you know. I remember how much you loved the Latin classes at Middleham."

There was a wicked twinkle in Richard's eye and Eve got the impression Francis wasn't the world's most accomplished scholar. Francis said nothing, but gave a wry smile and said:

"Well, I hope you will not expect me to put on a debate for you when you visit my home next week!"

Richard chuckled and then grew serious.

"My friend, the only entertainment I shall need at your home is the company of you and your lady wife. It will be a relief to relax for a few days. You would not believe how tiring it is to be king and expected to feast and watch mummers, hear musical recitals and talk endlessly about the same things. I even prefer hearing petitions and signing documents to all the pomp and ceremony. There is no respite."

"Aye, I know not how you endure it. I could never wish to be the centre of attention the way you must be wherever you go. It is enough for me to attend you and be unnoticed in the background, ready to serve you in whatever fashion I am able."

"Ah, Francis, do you remember when we met at Middleham. That day the bull chased you and the times we rode out to William's Hill and explored the countryside."

"I remember the day you got yourself a beating when it was actually Rob who earned it."

"Oh, that is hard to forget, my friend. You were kind and helped me smear on a healing salve. You were very gentle and I have never forgotten how you never commented on my spine."

"I knew not what to say, in truth. How is your back, Dickon?"

"It pains me at times and at others I am barely aware of it. Although, I think it tends to worsen as I age. It is very stiff most of the time and especially when I first awake. Still, I do not let it stop me doing anything. It is just a burden I must bear – a penance from God or a test perhaps."

"Well, Dickon, you always do what you think is right – I am sure God knows you are pious and just."

"I hope so, Francis, I hope so."

Our Kind of Love

The next day, they only listened to part of the debates because, as Richard wasn't speaking, only listening, it was pretty boring for the others (and Eve wouldn't have been able to understand them either, as they were in Latin). They heard Richard exclaim in delight at the end and thank William Waynflete heartily, giving the winners of the debates prizes of venison and money. After that, they skipped on to Francis' house, Minster Lovell at the end of the month, where Richard spent a few days relaxing from his royal duties.

The first thing he did when the royal party arrived was to ask Francis for a tour of the house, and his friend showed him the new buildings he had commissioned and his extensive gardens where they could relax for a while.

He and Francis spent a couple of hours walking in the grounds, where Richard told him of his plans for the country, and they then came in and relaxed in the beautiful solar and feasted on the supplies Francis had ordered in to entertain his royal friend. He wanted him to be impressed, of course, but more than that, he wanted him to feel welcome.

"Anne!" said Richard when Francis' wife, who had the same name as the queen, appeared in the solar, her face wreathed in smiles.

"I thank you, your Grace, for the honour you bestow on our humble house. I hope you will enjoy your stay with us. May I send for anything for your pleasure? Some meat and bread? Honey cakes? I see you already have wine."

"I would love a small beer and a couple of your famous honey cakes, Annie. I have had a surfeit of feasts these last few weeks. And please do not feel you have to address me as 'Your Grace' in private, I beg you. I am still the Richard you have known all these years."

She went to Francis who kissed her softly on the cheek and held her close to him with his free arm. He brought his wine goblet to her lips and tipped it for her to sip some. She giggled as the wine dripped down her chin. Her husband wiped it with a linen clout and smiled down at her, his eyes full of love.

"I must go and see to the honey cakes, husband," she said, smiling and left the room in a flurry of silk and velvet.

"She is still as lovely as ever, Francis. Is there yet no sign of…?" He paused and glanced at his friend, who pressed his lips together in a moue of regret and sighed.

"No, Dickon. She is still not with child. She has never even conceived, let alone brought a child to term. She feels she is letting me down and yet I do not know… I suspect… Ah! But who knows God's will."

"You suspect what, my friend?"

There was a long pause while Francis swirled his wine round and round in the goblet.

"I suspect I am the one who carries the blame. I know the accepted wisdom is that the woman is responsible for the conception of a child, but… well, I have known women who never conceived during years of marriage and yet, on remarrying after their first husband's death, are with child almost immediately and go on to produce child after child. It seems to me obvious the first husband must be the barren one. So, I wonder if the fault lies with me. Look at you – you have two bastards and a true born child."

He looked down, seeming suddenly embarrassed at his confession.

Richard put his hand on Francis' shoulder and gave it a squeeze.

"It may be that you have just not been together enough – I know you have pledged your service to me, but perhaps you should spend more time here and… give the problem your full attention. And pray, of course. God works in ways we mere mortals cannot always comprehend, eh?"

Francis nodded without looking up.

"Aye, you are right, of course. Thank you, Dickon."

When Love Takes Over

"**M**y goodness! Look at this! I have received a letter about my solicitor general, Thomas Lynom. You will never guess what he has done. He has fallen for the Shore woman." Richard was shaking his head as if he had trouble taking it in. "You remember she was sent to Ludgate Prison and had to do penance through the streets of London, as the Church ordained, and Lynom was sent to interview her about the Hastings plot. However, it seems she has entranced him. By God, she must be some special woman if she can have such a hold on my brother, Edward, William Hastings, Dorset and now Lynom also. He wants to marry her! The man must be blinded with lust!"

He gave a short laugh.

"You will not allow it, Sire, surely? She is a traitor and a harlot. It would be a kindness to him to forbid it, would it not?"

"Hmm, I am not so sure, Francis. I will see if Russell can dissuade him, but if he cannot, then I shall allow it. After all, when you think about it, she has only been trying to survive and if she makes him happy, who am I to forbid it? I will gain the gratitude of them both in the process, perhaps. I will write a reply now, John."

John Kendall got his implements ready to write what his king dictated.

"'By the King

Right reverend father in God etc. Signifying unto you, that it is showed unto us, that our servant and solicitor, Thomas Lynom, marvelously blinded and abused with that late wife of William Shore, now being in Ludgate by our commandment,

325

hath made a contract of matrimony with her, as it is said, and intendeth, to our full great marvel, to proceed to effect the same. We for many causes, would be very sorry that he should be so disposed. Pray you therefore to send for him, and in that ye goodly may exhort and stir him to the contrary. And, if ye find him utterly set for to marry her, and none otherwise would be advertised, then, if it may stand within the law of the church, we be content, the time of the marriage being deferred to our coming next to London, that upon sufficient surety being found for her good a-bearing, ye do send for her keeper, and discharge him of our said commandment by warrant of these; committing her to the rule and guiding of her father, or any other, by your discretion in the mean season.

To the right Reverend father in God etc. The Bishop of Lincoln our chancellor.'

"There. I shall sign it immediately."

He took up his favourite quill and signed his name with a flourish.

Eve could tell he was still enthralled by the fact of being king and actually signing 'Ricardus Rex' instead of his previous 'Richard Gloucestre'. She sensed pride, duty and disbelief in equal measure and wondered if he had that strange affliction, the 'imposter syndrome' when someone felt like they were not really equal to the job they were doing. On second thoughts, she didn't think so – he was a very able administrator, arbitrator, negotiator and warrior, all essential qualities for a medieval king. He was assured and confident and the disbelief was just because everything had happened so quickly.

Eve looked at her notes again – she had written down the contents of the letter and re-scanned it. She smiled as she re-

read the part where he called Lynom 'marvelously blinded and abused' by the famous Elizabeth Shore. She could see again the incredulity on his face as he read what his solicitor general, a supposedly learned and intelligent man, wanted to do. And the expression 'to our full great marvel' was eloquent and revealing of Richard's opinion of the matter. He clearly thought the man was mad!

The Mystery of the Princes

Stellan had located Richard on his progress and his henchman, James Tyrell, had been ushered into his presence. "Sire, I have worrying news, I am afraid."

Richard frowned and gave him an appraising look.

"Speak then, James, the sooner I know, the sooner I can devise a solution."

"It is your nephews, your Grace. There has been an attempt to take them from the Tower – we are not sure who was behind the plot but we suspect it to be the Woodville faction, although they deny it. They surely want to raise a rebellion and need the boys to be the focus, of course."

"Oh no! My nephews are certainly a problem. What have you done to prevent another attempt?"

"Brackenbury has questioned all the guards and has dismissed any who have acted in any way suspiciously. The boys have been moved to more secure quarters in the White Tower. Their own retainers and their physician have been dismissed and new guards and medics engaged who are loyal to you. Spies are working to discover the origin of the plot and any new ones that might be hatching. The boys are forbidden to leave their quarters for the time being."

"This is indeed troubling, James. Although they are innocent children, their parentage makes them a danger to the lawful ruling of the realm. I have my own idea of what needs to be done, but what say you? You have always been a source of good advice to me."

"We have to remove them. Permanently. You have a difficult enough job as king without the added threat of rebellion. Since they are the target of the rebels, they are the means to prevent it too. We must thwart them by removing the boys. I have discussed the matter with Brackenbury and we think the boys should be separated and sent away to different locations. But not just once – they should be moved from place to place for a while to ensure any spies will not be able to discover their final destination."

"Yes, it is agreed. Go ahead and do the deed. I will form an exact plan of action and inform you in due course. It must be done with the utmost secrecy. I entrust the job to you – you have my full confidence, James."

"Thank you, my Liege, I will not let you down. They will soon disappear and no-one shall know whither they have been taken."

"Yes, and they will no longer be available as a focus for rebellion. Thank you, James."

Tyrell bowed and left the room. After he had gone, Richard sat down, his head resting on his right hand, his fingers massaging his temples. He had not been alone for more than two minutes when there was an urgent rapping on the door.

"Yes, you may enter," Richard said, forcing himself to an alert posture. It was Harry Stafford, the Duke of Buckingham.

"Dickon! I apologise for bothering you – I know how busy you are – but I am about to leave for my castle of Brecknock and there is a small matter I would like to discuss with you before I depart."

"Of course, Harry. Come, be seated and have some refreshment. What can I do for you?"

"Sire, you know I have supported you fully and completely in your endeavour to acquire the crown."

"Well, I would not call it my 'endeavour' – I see it as a duty, a necessary evil. I never wanted to be king, but no bastard may inherit the throne. The land needs a strong king, a grown man, preferably. I can see that I may be able to make England a land to be envied for its justice. So, I accepted the throne as my duty. But it is true I could not have achieved it so easily without you by my side."

"Of course, Dickon, and I too would rather be away in Wales with my family than involved in the intrigues of Court. We have so much in common, Cousin." He smiled his cat-like smile, which did not reach his eyes. "I only regret that we did not grow to be close before this tragedy of your brother's death. Still, we can continue to grow closer now, can we not? I hope you see me as a friend as well as a supporter."

Richard's eyes narrowed as he replied. "Well, yes, of course I see you as a friend. You have been invaluable for your counsel and support and your wit and intellect are immense."

"And family too, we are family, are we not?" Harry was now looking his king directly in the eye.

"Clearly, Cousin."

"Well, what could be better than to ally our two branches of the royal tree in a marriage alliance?" Harry beamed as if he had given Richard the best news in the world.

Richard's brow immediately formed the frown that created two small lines between his eyebrows and he took a deep breath, avoiding Harry's eyes. Seeing his reaction, Buckingham flushed a deep crimson, yet ploughed on regardless, determined to persuade Richard to his viewpoint.

"Your son, Edward, is still young, I know that, but I was married when I was not much older and my daughter, Elizabeth, would make a perfect wife for him, do you not agree? What could be better – our friendship sealed forever in a family marriage alliance?"

He grinned at Richard, the cat-like smile again. He seemed sure of his influence over the new king. But Richard was no pushover and was well aware of who was the king and who the subject in this relationship.

"Hmm," he said. "I can see why you think this would be a good idea. However, as Edward is my only legitimate child and heir, he must marry in an alliance with a foreign power. We saw how much trouble it caused when an English king failed to do this. Ned caused much discontent and resentment when the Woodvilles were raised to power. I will not do the same thing, even though yours is old blood. As it is, there are those who murmur at your sudden rise to power. You must be patient, Harry. There is much time in which we can become closer in many ways. But I am afraid your request cannot be granted. I am sorry to disappoint you."

"But, Dickon, surely you do not equate the Woodville blood with my own? We are cousins. And you, yourself, are married to an English woman." He now sounded petulant and petty.

"Anne and I were married when I had no thought or hope of becoming king. But Edward is the heir – the only heir. I cannot choose to marry him to your daughter – who is half Woodville herself, do not forget!"

"You taunt me with that?! It was none of my choosing to be

married to one of that terrible brood. I have endured years of being set aside by Edward, married to a woman I despise and with no hope of rising in influence. And now you, too, push me aside. How wrong I was to think you were my friend!"

"Henry!" Richard snapped, purposely using the more formal name. "That is enough! I have made my decision and it will not be changed. You overstep the mark. I am your king and I will not be spoken to in this way. I have no need to justify my decisions to you. Now, leave my presence before my temper becomes completely frayed."

Buckingham opened his mouth, thought better of it, closed it again and then turned on his heel and swept out of the room, slamming the door behind him.

Inside, Richard twisted the goblet in his hands and then flung it at the wall, where it shattered and the wine dripped down the wall like blood on a blade.

Whatever It Takes

Richard summoned Tyrell to him when a maidservant had cleared up the spilled wine and broken glass. He had calmed himself down now and had all but forgotten Buckingham and his outrageous demands.

Tyrell knelt before him. "Sire, you wished to see me."

"Aye, James, we have to act swiftly regarding the boys. I cannot have another attempt to abduct them. Have you everything you need to… complete your task?"

"I do, your Grace. I have the pretext of fetching cloth for the investiture of your son as Prince of Wales, so no-one will question why I am in London. Brackenbury has been informed and stands ready to allow me access."

331

"Take this purse, James. You may need to... buy the silence of witnesses. You have my letter of admittance to the Tower. Now, you had best be on your way – the sooner you leave, the quicker this messy business will be concluded and I can get on with governing the realm."

"Thank you, Sire – I have prepared for their arrival in Gipping – my wife is the only other person to know the truth. They will be disguised as common squires and housed with my own family. Elizabeth will be permitted to visit them periodically. That may persuade her to leave sanctuary with her daughters and things may finally return to normal."

"I hope so James, I hope so."

James bowed and left the room, his step silent and swift.

Don't Mean Nothing

"Well, well, well!" David sat back, his hands linked behind his head and a huge grin on his face. "So now we know – he did have them done away with! It was true all along – he murdered the Princes in the Tower. The Ricardians will be bleating that there is some mistake, you can be sure of that!"

"What do you mean, David? It is obvious he had the boys moved."

"How did you get that interpretation? OK, he didn't say 'Murder them' in so many words but 'Go ahead and do the deed... It must be done with the utmost secrecy... I entrust the job to you... they will no longer be available as a focus for rebellion... this messy business will be concluded.' What else could it mean?"

Eve was appalled. Although she knew full well Richard had

only ordered their removal to Gipping, she now realised that, because the others could not hear Tyrell's side of the conversation, the meaning was ambiguous and all too easy to twist into some kind of confession of guilt. What could she do? She couldn't reveal that she could hear both sides of the conversation – how could she prove it? They knew she was tending to favour the Ricardian line and would think she was making it up, or mad? She decided to argue logically.

"Well, it could easily mean that they were being moved elsewhere. Those words could still apply and would still make sense. Why assume immediately that they were going to be killed?"

"Because it was the only way he could be sure they were no longer a danger to him. They would grow up and rebel against him, if he let them live. Kings always killed their predecessors in those days."

"But Edward V was never crowned, never anointed, so he wasn't technically Richard's predecessor."

"Oh, now you're just splitting hairs!" Rupert rolled his eyes.

"Well, actually they didn't always kill their predecessor anyway. Henry IV – a Lancastrian king – let the Mortimer children, the Yorkist claimants, live, although he did keep them under his close control; he just moved them around to different strongholds of his. And they were legitimate – they had more right to the throne than the so-called 'Princes in the Tower'.

She took a breath and continued.

"Plus, Richard wasn't the same as the other kings of the period. He wasn't 'a man of his time' as so many say! He was way ahead of it! His laws, his championing of the poor, his enlightened judgements, his promotion of education."

David was staring at her open-mouthed.

"So basically, you mean we haven't solved the crime of the millennium? There are still two interpretations of the situation and all our efforts have not helped at all? Damn! All our investment of time and money is for nothing!"

"Not necessarily. Look, we have done so much and have Richard's actual voice on record now. We have got to know him much better than anyone else ever has and it must help research into his times to have all that information. It will still be worth a fortune, don't worry!"

Eve knew David's primary concern was the profit to be made from their research. He was basically a philistine and didn't really care about the history. But Eve was disappointed that she couldn't prove Richard's innocence. She sighed.

Smile

They were listening to Richard after he had received a message from Louis XI of France. Eve explained to them that Louis had reneged on his treaty with Edward and had since been harassing English trade ships in the Channel. When Richard came to the throne, Louis sent an acknowledgment and greeting.

"Ha! Listen to this Francis, it is from Louis the Spider. He calls me his 'cousin' and his missive has such a flippant tone, I cannot but reply in kind. Listen: 'Monsieur mon cousin, I have seen the letter that you sent me by your herald Blanc Sanglier and thank you for the news you have given me and if I can do you any service, I will do it very willingly for I want to have your friendship. Adieu, Monsieur mon cousin'. Who does he think he is!? John, please write a letter for me as follows…"

The secretary, John Kendall, took a scroll and quill and dipped the end in the ink.

"'Monsieur, mon cousin,
I have seen the letters you have sent me by Buckingham herald, whereby I understand that you want my friendship in good form and manner, which contents me well enough; for I have no intention of breaking such truces as have previously been concluded between the late King of most noble memory, my brother, and you for as long as they still have to run.
Nevertheless, the merchants of this my kingdom of England, seeing the great provocation your subjects have given them in seizing ships and merchandise and other goods, are fearful of venturing to go to Bordeaux and other places under your rule until they are assured by you that they can surely and safely carry on trade in all the places subject to your sway, according to the rights established by the aforesaid truces.
Therefore, in order that my subjects and merchants may not find themselves deceived as a result of this present ambiguous situation, I pray you that by my servant this bearer, one of the grooms of my stable, you will let me know in writing your full intentions, at the same time informing me if there is anything I can do for you in order that I may do it with a good heart.
And farewell to you, Monsieur mon cousin.'

"There! Let us see what he thinks about that! He shall know that the king of England will not take insults without retaliation."
Richard was in buoyant mood and he had found the letter from Louis entertaining and stimulating.

335

"What did he mean by that?" asked Rupert
"Well, Louis insulted him by the offhand way he referred to him and the way he signed off the letter, so he replied in kind. Louis had sent his letter by Buckingham herald, so Richard went one better – or worse – and sent his by a groom of his stable. It shows he had a sense of humour, don't you think?"

"I guess so," said Stellan.

You Raise Me Up

Eve heard the music before there was any evidence of Richard's voice. It was a fanfare of trumpet-like sounds and the low moan of bagpipes, all to a background of exultant cheering.

She heard a chuckle, a sound of pure joy. She had rarely heard Richard chuckle; he was generally so serious. There was also the bell-like timbre of Anne's laughter and the higher-pitched sound of a child giggling.

"Edward, you must stop the giggling now – I know it was right amusing to hear the Archbishop belch so, but you will have to try to forget about it as we are going out into the crowds again and you are expected to behave like a prince – as you are. A prince is dignified and regal and what else?"

"Gracious, Father. I will try. Do I have to wear this crown all the time? It is very heavy."

"Yes, son, you have to wear it so the crowd can see you are truly the Prince of Wales, the heir to the throne of England."

"Ned, it will not be for much longer. We only have to walk a short distance to the Minster and there we can sit and listen to the service and thank the Lord for his blessings on our house, this day. I know you will behave impeccably, will you not?" Anne smoothed his hair down and rearranged the coronet on his head before they stepped out into the view of the citizens of York.

"Stellan, can we go back a little bit? It seems like the investiture is over, and they are just going to do the service of thanks and walkabout. I would dearly love to eavesdrop on the actual ceremony."

Rupert burst into laughter.

"Eve's drop, ha ha! Good one!" She glared at him. He could be so annoying sometimes.

"Sure, I can go back – how long do you think, an hour?"

"Give it an hour and a half; that should do it."

Stellan fiddled with the controls and entered in some digits on the display, then he pressed the 'on' button.

Stately music filled Eve's mind and she saw the little prince walking solemnly up to his father, King Richard, who was seated on a throne beside his wife, Queen Anne. Both were attired in rich fabrics, which she couldn't name, but they were shimmering and soft looking. Their cloaks were trimmed in ermine and the colours were vibrant and strong – she loved them, but then she had always loved bright colours. She supposed some people would consider them rather garish, but she knew that in mediaeval times the brighter the colours, the richer you were. Even their churches were decorated with biblical scenes depicted in the brightest of hues, so Sue had told her. And she had always thought they were white.

When Edward reached the king, he knelt down solemnly before him and Richard stood up and strode towards him. He took the ceremonial sword from the altar and said the words by which his son became a knight. Then he raised him from his obeisance and took another, smaller sword from the attendant nearby, girding it on around Edward's waist. He placed a ring on his finger and set a fine golden coronet on his head.

He then moved to one of the figures standing beside Edward and slightly behind him. He also stepped forward and knelt before the king. It was all so vivid to Eve that she could see the boy's knees trembling as he remained there, waiting for the king. Richard approached him and, taking his own sword again, also knighted this boy, who was Edward, Earl of Warwick, the son of Richard's brother, George.

Finally, the third figure, a taller, older boy, was also knighted. Eve could feel the emotion in Richard as he beamed at the boy, his own bastard son, John. His pride in his sons and his nephew were almost tangible, but the love he felt for them was also obvious – she felt the pull in her solar plexus as if it were she, herself, who was experiencing the emotions. Feeling this made Eve realise that Richard was human; he might be a king and have the reputation of being ruthless, fierce and cunning, but he still felt the same basic human emotions that every person in the world feels.

Core 'Ngrato

The messenger crashed into the great hall and made straight for the high table. Richard stopped mid-anecdote, the smile frozen on his face as he noticed the wary expression of the man. The Hall became hushed as one by one, the guests, too, became aware that something was afoot. Richard stood up, everyone else following suit respectfully and he gestured for them to be seated, walking around to the front of the table and indicating for the messenger to follow him into his private chamber. They were in Lincoln Castle, on their way back to the capital after Richard had invested his son as Prince of Wales in York.

Richard turned his back on his desk and perched on the edge of it, his hands supporting some of his weight, tense with anxiety.

"Well?" he barked, when they were alone, apart from his secretary, John Kendall.

The messenger dropped to his knees and produced a scroll which he handed to Richard. He broke the seal, which was that of his friend, Rob Percy, and unrolled it with nimble fingers. He scanned it, his lips pursed, then re-read it.

"No!!" he yelled, and flung the scroll onto the floor, his eyes blazing. "I cannot believe... I know he was disappointed, but this!!"

He left the desk and began to stalk the room, like a caged animal, his furious eyes resting on the hapless messenger, who was trying to blend into the decor. Richard's livid gaze came to rest on the servant's trembling countenance.

"Arise, arise!" he ordered. "'Tis no fault of yours that you bring ill tidings. Take you to the kitchens and get refreshment. Then return here for I shall have a reply for you."

When the man had left, Richard turned to John, who had already prepared parchment, ink and sand.

"I need to lay hands on the Great Seal – so a letter to John Russell, Lord Chancellor, please John. Begin with the usual pleasantries and request that he brings me my Great Seal, so that I can be sure to have the means of ratifying any orders officially."

John said nothing but his eyebrows lifted in surprise.

Richard grunted. "It is Buckingham – he has defected to the Lancastrians and is behind the rebellions in Kent and the southern counties. He who had most cause to be loyal to me – I have raised him higher than anyone and yet he is still not content. Well, we shall see who is content soon! Once I have the Great Seal, I shall muster my loyal retainers and squash him like the insect he is!"

"I cannot believe it, Sire! Buckingham is untrue?"

"Aye, John, he must be the most untrue creature living. But, never mind – he will soon regret his treachery."

Richard did not show it, but Eve could tell he was feeling tortured inside. She could sense an almost physical ache in her heart, because this betrayal was from a man he had thought his friend. As John wrote the letter Richard dictated, the king paced up and down like an angry tiger. When the letter was done, Richard thanked John and dismissed him. He picked up the parchment and perused it before taking up a quill and adding a postscript himself. As he penned it, sitting at his desk, his other hand was clenched into a fist and his writing was jagged and untidy, some of the words blurred because of the tears he could not prevent falling.

"What happens about the rebellion, Eve, do you know?" David asked her.

"Stellan – can you track Richard to Salisbury or thereabouts towards the end of the month?" she said, not answering David's question. "It will be much more interesting if Stellan can pick up some of what occurred."

"Of course, I will attempt it now," Stellan smiled. In a few minutes, the machine was buzzing again.

Hell or High Water

Eve suddenly felt cold and could hear heavy rain pattering in her mind. Richard was inside a huge tent, which was decked out in royal splendour and he sat at a small desk. A man was kneeling before him, mud-spattered and soaked to the skin. A drip of water had collected at the tip of his nose and his hair was plastered to his head. A small pool of rainwater had collected around him and he was kneeling in a puddle.

"Well?" Richard barked out to the man.

"The Duke has fled – all his soldiers have long since gone – they can see the weather is set against his endeavour and most of them were probably coerced into supporting him as it was. He has no-one left at all. We have proclaimed a reward for his capture – mayhap your Grace may wish to set the price?"

"Of course – let it be set at one thousand pounds – someone will be tempted to give him up while gaining coin for their own advantage. What of Morton? He was with the Duke in Brecknock – do we have any news of him?"

"He sloped away at the first sign of Buckingham's failure. He was thought to have gone east, but will probably make for the continent, if he has not already."

Richard grunted.

"It is a pity he was allowed to slip through our fingers. But never mind him for now – Buckingham is the one we must find."

Stellan moved the time on again a few days.

"Sire, the Duke of Buckingham has been captured and is being held in Salisbury. His 'loyal' retainer, Bannaster, in Shropshire, tipped off one of our search parties and has claimed the reward."

"Hmm, I hope he enjoys his thirty pieces of silver. The wheel of Fortuna turns full circle – Buckingham betrays me and is now betrayed in his turn." He appeared controlled, yet bitter.

"Sire, he requests permission to appear before you. He wants to speak to you personally – he says he has important information for you and will impart it to no-one else."

"Oh, does he? Well, he will know what it is to want, then. I will not see him. He will be executed straight after his trial, which must be concluded with all haste – I wish him gone from my realm. I will not be there to hear him, but I am sure justice will be served."

"As you command, my Liege," and the man bowed and was dismissed from Richard's presence as were all of Richard's servants.

After he was left alone, he sat down in the window seat of his solar and picked up an unfinished goblet of wine, which he sipped while gazing out over the city of Salisbury.

Eve thought he seemed weighed down by the burdens of kingship, tired and sad somehow. Her own heart felt heavy for him and yet she could also sense his determination, his conviction that he was right, his disappointment and anger towards Buckingham and his being unable to bear the sight of him.

She knew that Buckingham had died without his request being granted and she wondered what he had wanted to tell Richard. It seemed that they would never know.

Bitter End

"My Liege, I have news from Salisbury."
"Yes, Francis, what is it?"

"Buckingham's sentence has been carried out. However, he must have bribed someone or mayhap a loyal servant helped him – he had a dagger concealed on his person as he was taken from his cell. He almost escaped – wounded one of his guards, but the others were alert and soon had him under their control."

Richard's gaze hardened and he asked: "The guard – will he survive?"

"Aye, he is well enough."

"Hmm!" Richard grunted his approval.

"It seems he had been plotting to murder you, Dickon. He was complaining the whole time that he would have had his revenge if you had allowed him an audience."

Richard's head whirled up to meet Francis's worried countenance. His lips thinned as he pursed them, shaking his head, his expression hard and a frown appearing between his brows.

"Then it is well I refused. Well, the untrue creature is gone. There is no more to be said. Let us hope we can have some peace for a time, eh?" He gave a bitter smile and clapped Lovell on the shoulder.

Chapter Twelve

Gloucester, November 1483

Make You Feel My Love

"Sire, we approach the fair city of Gloucester, your own namesake. The mayor and aldermen will be before the city gates to greet you."

"Thank you, William, the queen and I are pleased to be visiting this fair city on our progress and look forward to praising God in the cathedral. I remember a time when I sent my herald here to warn the city not to open the doors to the Anjou woman on her flight to Wales."

"Aye, your Grace, the city and people were ever loyal to you – you have always shown them good lordship and the special favours that come from the fact that you were their Duke. Now, as you are their king, they will serve you even better, I am sure, particularly since you granted them the right to elect their own mayor."

William Catesby, the king's solicitor, had risen greatly to favour with Richard ever since he backed up the assertion of the Bishop of Bath and Wells that Edward, Richard's brother, had been secretly married to one Eleanor Butler, formerly Talbot, before he had undergone another secret wedding with Elizabeth Woodville.

They approached the city gates, the dust rising from the hooves of their horses as they reined them in to await the welcoming committee. The contingent was large, befitting the King of England and every city, religious house or noble home that was planned to be visited on their route would have to pay a large sum to feed and water them all, along with their horses.

Yet, as the mayor, John Trye, and his noble colleagues emerged from the gates to greet their new king, they carried before them a large purse of purple velvet laid on a tray of silver, inlaid with precious stones; rubies, emeralds, diamonds and pearls, which glinted as the golden rays of the autumn sun caressed them. As they approached the royal procession, the mayor stepped forward and abased himself before Richard.

"Arise, arise, John. We thank you for this welcome to your great city and the service you have given us in the past when we were your Duke. We do not forget such things and will ensure that the city is appropriately honoured and rewarded according to our will. And we hope you will continue to be loyal to us, now that we have been anointed as your sovereign Lord."

John Trye rose and discreetly brushed some of the dust from his robes of office.

"Of course, Sire, the city of Gloucester will always be loyal to you and your family. You have ever treated us fairly and justly, nay generously, and we will endeavour to ensure that we remain worthy of your future consideration."

He bowed his head and a group of musicians who were

standing behind him and to one side, began to play a merry tune, a man and woman singing the words to a song which celebrated the fruits and rich harvest of autumn. When they had completed their song, the man holding the velvet purse on the silver plate stepped forward and, bowing low, offered it to Richard.

"We humbly offer you this gift of gold and this silver plate to celebrate your accession to the throne of England."

Richard smiled and leaned down from his horse to accept the gift, but when he felt the weight of gold in the purse, he handed it back.

"The City of Gloucester owes no tribute to us, although the thought is appreciated. We pray you keep the gift for the town coffers, for we would rather have your love than your treasure."

"Your Grace is generous and you do indeed have the love of the city, even more so now that you have acted so. Yet we would insist you at least accept the plate as a token of our continued loyalty."

The man proffered the plate, minus the purse.

Richard inclined his head in a gesture of acceptance and received the plate with a smile of thanks.

"We shall treasure it as a reminder of your loyalty," he said.

"Thank you, Sire, and now will you please pass through the city gates and join us in a feast to celebrate your accession."

"We accept gladly," replied Richard and, the formalities over, they all trooped beneath the great arch of the city gates and into the Palace of the Bishop of Gloucester where the feast was to be held.

The king and queen were taken to private rooms where they were able to wash and change from their travelling clothes, sumptuous as they were, before entering the great hall, hand in hand, wearing slim coronets of jewelled gold.

The king and queen naturally sat at the head of the top table and were served first – dishes ranging from pigeon pies, roast peacock, stewed eel, frumenty, a multitude of meats such as wild boar, venison, beef and lamb, as well as fish and fowl of all shapes and sizes. These included perch, tench, pike, trout, lamprey and carp and the fowl were grebe, avocet, pheasant, grouse, song birds and swan. There were sweetmeats of honey cakes, fruit tartlets and marchpane subtleties.

Eve was enthralled because everything was so vivid to her and all her senses were alive. She saw it all in her mind, heard all the noises from chatter and laughter to the chimes of church bells, from the clatter of the plates to the barking of a dog and the mediaeval music of the lute and psaltery. And overlaying it all, Richard's voice, soft and yet clear, a note of lightness in it, of genuine fun and even the occasional ring of his laughter. She knew that this was the only thing the others heard – Richard's voice alone was picked up by the machine. How lucky she was to be able to experience all this.

She even experienced, at times, the taste of the items eaten and drunk at the occasion. She 'knew' what each flavour was somehow; she loved the honey cakes and the roast boar – in fact most of the meats, but the fish were rather tasteless and full of bones. No wonder the mediaeval clergy had decreed that other creatures, such as otters, were also counted as fish, to give more variety to the meals on the days when eating meat was forbidden. Sue had told her this and she had thought it hilarious, but now she had tasted the fish, practical.

The Joker

"So, this was during the king's progress soon after he was crowned, wasn't it?" asked David.

"Yes, and you note he refused the gold they offered him. Sue told me he refused such gifts in several places – I think it was London and Worcester as well as Gloucester – it was lovely that he said he would rather have their love than their treasure, wasn't it?" Eve replied.

"Well, it was pretty clever. He was probably trying to appear to be a kindly and generous king to start with anyway. Isn't it thought that he acted so well to try to win them over after the rumours of his murdering the princes got about?" Rupert's eyes were twinkling; she knew he was winding her up.

She gave him a hard stare.

"Actually, it is quite possible the princes were still alive then. There is evidence they still survived in the Tower at the time when Richard's son was invested as Prince of Wales – that was September 8th that year, 1483. And there is actually no evidence that they were ever murdered at all. Not a shred!"

"Ha! She's converted you! You're a Richardian!" Rupert was smirking annoyingly.

She placed her hands on her hips and let out her breath in a loud sigh.

"I think you mean 'Ricardian'. And so what if I am? I have done more research about him than any of you and the more I find out, the less I think he murdered his nephews."

"Can you give us some examples of the things you have discovered that have made you feel like this?" Stellan asked, his eyes eager and bright with interest.

"Yes, of course. Firstly, his previous reputation. He was famed for being fair and just – we have seen, for example, that he handed over four of his affinity to be tried for murder when it was discovered that they had joined his household expressly so that he would protect them."

"I'm still not clear about why that is significant. If they were murderers, then surely anyone would have handed them over?"

"Not in those days, actually. The Lord would protect and defend all those who were in his service. It was part of the give and take that represented good lordship. But it was corrupt; criminals could use it to escape the punishment they would otherwise expect and Richard wanted to stamp out this sort of thing. And that other thing he did, we heard it before, was to forbid the large monasteries and nobles to set fish garths in the rivers of land overseen by him."

"What are fish garths again?"

"They are like traps that block the fish from passing further down the stream or river – a bit like a trawler works as opposed to a fishing rod. They caught nearly all the fish so that no-one further down the river could get any. Richard forbade the use of them."

"Hmm, he sounds like a pretty decent guy. But what about the way he took the throne? OK, no-one knows for sure about the fate of the princes, but he usurped the throne from them, didn't he? Not a very kind uncle, was he?"

"Well, there are two sides to that story too. In fact, it could be persuasively argued that Richard is the only king who possessed a genuine parliamentary, that is, legal, title to the crown in the whole of mediaeval times. If you look up the word 'usurp' in the dictionary – I have – you will find that it means 'to take something illegally or by force'. Richard did neither, something that can't be said about his brother Edward IV or

Henry Tudor who both became kings by conquest. Likewise, Henry IV, the first Lancastrian king, claimed the throne using lies, basically, about his bloodline."

Familiar

"OK, guys – Richard is at Winchester. The date is the twenty-second of November, so not long after the rebellion of Buckingham was put down."

Stellan fiddled with the controls of 'The Fly' and pressed a few buttons. Richard's voice, sounding annoyed was immediately heard.

"John, I have just received a letter concerning my clerks of the Privy Seal. It seems some impudent fellow has attempted to bribe his way to a position among them. This cannot be permitted or it shall encourage others to do likewise and the whole system will become corrupt and useless. Besides which, the other clerks who have spent their lives working their way diligently up the ladder will become disillusioned and discouraged. It simply is not just. I am writing to the Keeper of the Privy Seal, John Gunthorpe, forthwith, if you will be so kind as to take it down…"

"Of course, your Grace." John Kendall, Richard's secretary, shuffled the papers around on his desk until he found an unused sheet of parchment and took one of the half dozen or so trimmed quills which were stored in a small jar. He dipped it into the inkwell and held it poised over the scroll. Then he wrote the usual formal headings on the letter indicating to whom it was addressed and that it was from the king. Richard waited until he raised his head and then dictated, speaking slowly and clearly so that his secretary could keep up:

"'To our right trusty and well beloved Clerk and Counsellor, Master John Gunthorp, Keeper of our privy seal. Whereas, contrary to the old rule and due order of admitting clerks to the office of our privy seal, one Richard Bele, by means of giving of great gifts and other sinister and ungodly ways, lately caused it to be that he was admitted into our said office and so occupies it to great discouragement of the underclerks, who have long worked there to gain experience, to see a stranger never brought up in the said office take precedence over them in this promotion. And this precedent if it were thus allowed should be likely to lead to the utter destruction of the running of our said office within a short time. We, not willing any such abuse to be had in our said office, nor the underclerks who have spent the flower of their ages there to be utterly hereby discouraged, charge and command you that you utterly discharge the said Richard Bele of any longer occupation in our said office. And over this we will that no stranger not brought up in our said office shall not accede or occupy in the same hereafter. And these our letters etc. given etc at Winchester the twenty-second day of November the first year of our Reign.'

"I will appoint Robert Bolman to the office instead – he has provided me with good, diligent service and is worthier of the appointment than that scoundrel, Bele. I will write another letter about that in a moment, when you are ready."

Stellan paused the machine.

"Do you want to carry on with that? It's pretty boring, isn't it?"

"It sounds familiar to me – I've heard something about this before from my friend, Sue. It is definitely an indication of his form of governance, and his ethics. Basically, he's stopping someone bribing his way into a good job and bypassing those who have been working hard all their lives to work their way up. He is showing his justice and fairness, don't you think?"

"He writes very long sentences, doesn't he?" Rupert looked rather confused.

"They all did in those days – doesn't seem to be a great deal of punctuation either! But I love the expression 'flower of their ages' about the clerks who have worked hard. And did you notice all the negatives: 'we will that no stranger not brought up in our said office shall not accede'. It just reinforced the negative then, I believe, and didn't turn it into a positive. "

"Huh!" Rupert grunted. "It's all Greek to me, I'm afraid. I'll take your word for it."

From Now On

Richard's first (and what would prove to be his only) parliament was finally convened on 23rd January 1484. Thirty-seven Lords and ten judges comprised the Parliament and there were also two hundred and ninety-six members of the Commons. They met in the Painted Chamber of Westminster with Richard in attendance.

Chancellor John Russell, the Bishop of London, opened the proceedings with a sermon based on I Corinthians xxi.12 which began: 'We have many members in one body, but not all have the same function'. This led on to him urging unity and warning them against dissent and self-interest.

Then Richard addressed the assembly:

"The proper order and political rule of the realm has been perverted so that the rights and liberties to which every Englishman is entitled have been subverted against all reason and justice. This land was ruled by self-interest and pleasure, fear and dread, so that all reasonable and equitable laws have been ignored and despised. I intend to change this sorry state of affairs for the better."

The first piece of legislation passed was Richard's title to the throne, known as 'Titulus Regius'. This was the Royal Title that confirmed Richard's right to the throne of England, by the invitation of Parliament, because of Edward's 'pretensed marriage'. Richard was declared 'very and undoubted king of this realm of England'.

Then there were several attainders, including those of Henry Stafford, Duke of Buckingham, and Margaret Beaufort, Countess of Richmond. There was also a statute granting the King the power to dispose of the lands belonging to the attainted 'at his pleasure'. However, Richard was not as ruthless as might have been expected when it came to women. Margaret Beaufort's lands were merely given into her husband, Lord Stanley's, hands. And Harry Buckingham's widow was granted an annuity.

Next there were some private petitions granted.

But the most interesting items in the proceedings were the laws which Richard's Parliament brought in.

"These are the new laws and statutes that will be enacted during my reign," Richard began. "There will be a minimum property qualification for jurors, which will give more weight to those of greater standing in each community and ensure they are less likely to be susceptible to bribery."

There was a general nodding of heads.

"The 'Piepowder' Courts will be reduced in their area of influence to their original remit of dealing with offences committed at fairs."

This was a court which had begun to have increased power, which was being abused by the local sheriffs and bailiffs, so their power was being cut back again.

"Suspected felons will be granted bail and their goods will not be confiscated unless and until they are found guilty."

Some had found they were wrongly accused and their property taken – this may have included the tools of their trade – and when they were declared innocent it was too late and their goods were gone.

"All estates, feoffments and gifts of land will belong to the one given the land and not the original seller and all property transfers must be proclaimed in court and notified to the appropriate officials."

This was to prevent sellers re-selling property which had already been partly sold elsewhere.

"The importation of silk, lace and ribbons, scissors, bells, nails and other minor goods will be prohibited and imported wines and oils must be properly measured and their price controlled. Italian merchants must sell in gross, not retail and spend their profits locally. And with every butt of malmsey imported, Italian merchants must also import and supply ten good bow staves."

This was to protect English merchants against cheap foreign imports and increase the power of the navy.

"The length, quality and dyeing of cloth to be exported is to be regulated and checked by experts. Importation of goods by aliens is to be prohibited or restricted, excepting the importation and selling of books and printed materials by natives of any country or realm, who may also abide within this realm for that purpose."

Richard was the king who devised the first legislation for the protection and nurturing of the art of printing and the spread of education by books.

"The subjects of this realm shall not be charged with any benevolences. Such charges and any like charges, shall be damned and annulled forever."

At this there was a great cheer. Edward had used this practice extensively – a benevolence was supposedly a voluntary 'gift' to the king, but was actually an enforced one.

Drag You Down

"So why was Richard's Parliament so great?" asked Rupert.

"Well, he did more for justice and helping the common man in his first (and only) seven hundred and seventy-seven days than any other monarch before or since."

"What did he do, exactly? I didn't catch all those complicated laws," Stellan said, his blue eyes fixed on hers. She felt her cheeks flush as she said:

"Before his rule, people could be unjustly accused and even have the tools of their trade taken away, never to be returned again, even if they were subsequently found to be innocent. So, they could lose their livelihood because of a mistaken or malicious accusation. And he tried to stamp out corruption of the juries by ensuring only men who held some wealth were allowed to serve on them."

"Huh! How did that help?" Rupert asked.

"Well, they were less likely to be susceptible to bribery as they didn't need the money."

"What else did he do?"

"He introduced a primitive form of legal aid for the poor; if they couldn't afford a lawyer they could appeal directly to the king's Court of Requests."

"Hmm!" Rupert said, raising his eyebrows and pushing out his lips while inclining his head as he weighed up the evidence. Eve continued.

"He exempted the printing trade from taxes levied on foreign tradesman, so encouraging reading and education."

"Well, that isn't the action of a tyrant," Stellan said. "A tyrant would tend to suppress education and knowledge – try to control it."

"Exactly!" Eve said, delighted. "And he also founded the College of Arms, which shows he was concerned about the establishment and maintenance of standards, in matters of inheritance and chivalry."

"Hmm, maybe he wasn't such a bad guy then."

"He wasn't. He was a reformer and his government was as honest as he could get it. He tried to help the poor people and encourage education. He protected England's trade and encouraged learning."

"You love him!" Rupert said, grinning. She whacked him on the shoulder.

"So, you really think he would have been a good king if he'd lived?" David asked.

"I do. I think he would have been a great king. He improved the 'common weal', the well-being of the common people. Another thing was, he had his laws written in English so more people could understand them and he was the first king to swear his oath of allegiance in English. In fact, he was our most English king because he, both his parents and all his grandparents were born in England. Edward IV was born in Rouen, France, Henry Tudor in Wales (and he had French blood from his mother's side). Even our own queen had German grandparents. Prince Philip was born in Greece, so it isn't until Prince George that we find the same thing again."

"Our most English king, eh?" said David.

"Right!" she grinned. "Oh, and another thing – he outlawed the fraudulent sale of land that wasn't legally owned by the vendor. People had been selling off land and then selling it again to someone else – the same piece of land – with no comeback. That was no longer tolerated. He also standardised the weights and measures of cloth and suchlike so it could be more fairly sold."

"He seems like a bloody saint!" Rupert said. "But I heard he did all that to try to ingratiate himself with the people after they turned against him because of the murder of the princes."

"What have you been reading?" Eve asked.

He grinned at her.

"I've been doing a bit of research of my own – on Facebook."

"Oh, bloody hell!" she said, rolling her eyes. "I bet it was one of the anti-Ricardian groups. Sounds just like the sort of thing they would say. They insist he was a usurper and child-murderer. Some won't even allow that he was a courageous and skilful warrior. One even said he was built 'like a girl'! Ridiculous!"

"Well, where did they get that from then?"

"Oh, the documentary where they found him. Some – and I stress 'some' – of his bones were described as 'gracile'. That is, slender for a man, more typical of female bones. And one feature of his pelvis, the sciatic notch, was wider than usual for a man. But there were other bones, such as the skull and other parts of his pelvis, that were typically male; they conveniently ignored that. He was just a slim male."

"You haven't addressed the point though, have you?" Rupert persisted.

"That he brought in good laws to counteract the hostility about the so-called murder of his nephews? OK, if that was true, why did he act just the same as regards justice and fairness before he became king, before Edward IV died?"

"So, if he was such a great king, why did all the nobles desert him at Bosworth? It must have been because of the princes."

"Why? In fact, his laws empowered the common man against the nobles and this may have alienated them – perhaps he tried to change things too quickly or naively judged others by his own high standards. In any case, only two, possibly three, nobles betrayed him at the battle: the Stanleys had an old grudge against him. While he was a teenager, he sided with the Harrington brothers in a land dispute against the Stanleys. Edward judged for the Stanleys, because they were too powerful to upset, but Richard was going to reverse that decision. So, they had a personal axe to grind. Plus, Thomas Stanley was Henry Tudor's stepfather – married to the Beaufort Bitch."

Stellan laughed.

"You certainly seem to have all the answers. But we also have to be objective. We have to look at the evidence we can find and base our conclusions on that."

"True," she said. "But I do feel I have got to know him. That's why I have got a bit emotional, I admit. He seems like an old friend now."

"Yes, over five hundred years old!" Rupert snorted.

Young at Heart

"What about me, Father? I am older than John, after all, and he is a knight now."
This was Katherine, the king's illegitimate daughter, now fifteen herself and a beautiful young woman.

"Kate, I have not forgotten you, never fear. I have arranged a prestigious marriage for you to William Herbert, the Earl of Huntingdon."

"Oh!" she said, her face falling into a small frown.

"What is wrong? He is a wealthy man and will be yet more so after I endow you both with grants and lands."

"But he is so old, Father!"

Richard laughed loudly.

"He is two years younger than me, and a loyal friend to our family. He may be older than you would like, but he is still in his prime and a mature man who will be able to protect you if anything should happen to me."

"What is going to happen to you?" Katherine asked, concern showing in her face.

"Nothing, I hope, but we never know what is God's will. And William is a good man. He will treat you kindly and with respect. You will be married this year."

"Thank you, Father."

"You always liked William, did you not, child?"

"Yes, but I never thought to marry him!" she said, firmly, blue eyes flashing.

"Come here, Kate."

She went to her father and he gave her a warm hug, encircling her with his arms and stroking her hair.

"Listen, I know best for you in this matter. You are still very young and need someone who can guide you in the running of a household – your own household. You are also a great prize. Many would love to take you to wife and become the king's son by marriage. But William is also a trusted friend and adviser to me, so I know he will do for you the best he can. He is valiant, honest and loyal and he will be rich and powerful too, all qualities important in a husband. Do you agree?"

He stared into her eyes, like looking into a mirror, they were so similar. She broke the hold of his gaze first and looked down at the tiled floor.

"Yes, of course, Father," she said, hugging him back.

Katherine was a dutiful girl and seemed resolved to make the best of her marriage. She knew William Herbert and he was a nice man, after all.

Eve explained to the others who William Herbert was - he had accompanied Richard when he was a youngster, on his first commissions of array on the Welsh Marches. He was a loyal Yorkist and a friend of Richard's so it seemed the king was thinking of his daughter's future welfare by marrying her to a man he knew and trusted. Stellan said he would scan through the next few months and try to track down the wedding ceremony, which he managed after a couple of days.

Katherine looked adorable in the deep blue silk dress she wore at her wedding to William Herbert. And Herbert, the Earl of Huntingdon, was very handsome, Eve thought as she contemplated the scene. The wedding was a rather low-key affair, considering Katherine was the king's daughter, she thought. Although, she was only his illegitimate daughter, so maybe that was why. There was a small congregation of friends and family, including the king and queen, but they were taking a back seat and allowing Richard's daughter and son-in-law their moment as the centre of attention.

The ceremony was formal and, of course, very religious. The young couple said their vows clearly and sincerely and afterwards there was a feast.

Eve always enjoyed 'attending' the feasts of the day and this was no exception. There was sumptuous decoration of the hall, course after course of excellent food, many of which Eve had never even heard of let alone tasted. She was pleased she could try them at second hand, because a fair few looked grotesque, like the lamprey. There was plenty of alcohol also and music provided by Richard and Anne's choir and minstrel troupe.

They heard Richard greeting William as his son and giving them the gifts of grants of land and money, as he had promised.

He danced with his daughter and Anne danced with William. However, instead of the traditional 'bedding' of the new couple, they slept separately, as Katherine was still very young for the marriage to be consummated yet.

"I shall not expect you to do your wifely duty for another year or two, my dear," William whispered to her, and she blushed to the roots of her hair, she was so embarrassed, but managed a soft:

"Thank you, my Lord."

"Child, I have chosen a man who will respect you and protect you, will you not, William?"

"Or course, Sire. I am honoured that you considered me worthy of taking your lovely daughter to wife and I will always show her honour and love, as I do her father," he smiled, showing small, neat teeth.

"Good!" Richard said, collecting his wife and leading her back to the high table, where they continued with the revelries until late in the night.

Benedictus

They had found Richard dictating a document to his secretary in the presence of Catesby (at least Eve knew it was in his presence, she wasn't sure about the others).

"I am continuing my brother's plan for the completion of the chapel at Towton and I am granting an annuity to the parish church of Saxton in our county of York."

She noted down the main points of the annuity, which was a regular kind of legal document that they had often come across before, but then Richard added something much more interesting. The others were about to move the 'Fly' forward, but Eve asked them to wait. She listened intently as Richard mentioned the dead of Towton, the battle that had won the throne for his brother, Edward.

Richard dictated:

"The people of this kingdom in a plentiful multitude were taken away from human affairs; and their bodies were notoriously left on the field, aforesaid, and in other places nearby, thoroughly outside the ecclesiastical burial-place, in three hollows. Whereupon we, on account of affection, contriving the burial of the deceased men of this sort, caused the bones of these same men to be exhumed and left for an ecclesiastical burial in these coming months, partly in the parish church of Saxton in our said county of York, and in the cemetery of the said place, and partly in the chapel of Towton, aforesaid, and the surroundings of this very place."

When Stellan halted the machine, Rupert was looking puzzled.

"What was that all about?" he asked Eve, because she was now the expert on the period. "Why did you want to listen to that?"

"He was talking about the Battle of Towton and said he had moved the bodies of the dead so they could be reburied in consecrated ground. He planned to finish the Chapel of Towton that his brother had begun and he may have done, or at least built quite a bit of it. I remember there was a documentary about Richard III's Lost Chapel – they decided it must have ended up being incorporated into Towton Hall which still exists."

"What's so special about Towton?" asked Stellan, his expression one of interest.

"It involved about ten percent of the adult male population of England at that time and around twenty-seven thousand men died in one day! That's more than those who died on the first day at the Somme. It's a staggering number of corpses! Can you imagine trying to bury that many dead bodies? There must have been heaps and heaps of them."

"But why is it surprising – maybe Richard lost some of his men, like in the Battle of Barnet?" David asked.

"No, he didn't, because he didn't fight in that battle."

"Not so brave then, eh?" Alex said. "Too much for him, was it?"

"Well maybe it was, considering he was only about nine years old at the time!" Eve shot back.

"OK, that is quite impressive, I suppose." Rupert conceded.

"It is. He cared about the souls of those people, even though he wasn't involved in the battle. He was genuinely pious and tried to do the right thing – do you see that from all we've learned about him so far?"

"I do," Stellan smiled and David and Rupert nodded.

Only Alex said nothing, a scowl of annoyance on his face.

What Becomes of the Broken-Hearted?

They had moved on to April 1484 at the castle of Nottingham…

The castle was dark and cold; the spring sun was not yet strong enough to warm the cold stone and the new shoots had only just started to poke through the frozen ground. Nottingham was in the centre of Richard's kingdom and therefore was often a place where he stopped on his many journeys across his realm. It was bright today, though, if not warm. There were few clouds in the sky and those were white and fluffy, like unruly sheep flocking across an azure pasture. There was a light breeze and Richard felt restless, as if there was something he had forgotten to do. Something niggling at the back of his mind. He had just decided it might be a good idea to retire to his chamber and go through the papers he had signed once more, when a commotion arose in the main courtyard. He frowned – surely not news of another rebellion. Perhaps the Tudor had finally made a move – all the better if he did – the sooner he invaded Richard's realm, the sooner he could be swept from it, swatted like a pesky fly.

The sharp rapping on the door to his solar made him jump it was so loud. His squire of the body, Ralph, immediately went to answer and Richard stood up and waited to see who it was. It was Francis. As soon as he saw his friend's face, Richard knew something terrible had happened and he felt his face drain of colour, his heart pound and a tickling at the back of his neck where his hair was trying to stand on end.

Francis almost flung himself into the room and onto his knees in front of Richard. His head was bowed as if he was afraid to meet Richard's gaze.

"Sire... Sire... I do not know how to tell you... I..." he gave a strangled sob and then sniffed, finally looking up at his king. Richard felt his heart thud again as he noticed the tears on his henchman's cheeks.

"Tell me, Francis! What is it?"

"It's Prince Edward... he has passed to the Lord, Richard. He had a mild fever, but took a sudden turn for the worse. Doctor Hobbys could not help him. A messenger from Middleham has just arrived. I am so sorry to be the bearer of such news. Sire?"

Richard had staggered back, his hands balled into fists, the knuckles white, his face paler still. He made no sound, he just stood there swaying for a few seconds and then clutched at the chair he had been sitting in and sank into it, trembling.

"Sire, have some wine – it may help."

"Wine? Wine? How can wine help me? Can it bring my son back to life? Can it mend my heart?" His words seemed to break through the veneer of calm and he reached his hands up onto his head, hugging himself and rocking back and forth, a sound like a damned soul in terrible torture emerging from his lips which were drawn back to bare his teeth in a mirthless grin. "Edward! Edward, my son, my son, no, no, no, no, no, no...!"

He began sobbing then, tears of agony running down his face into his mouth and he dropped from the chair onto his knees as if too weak to hold himself up.

Lovell ran to Richard then and, without hesitation, knelt beside his friend and embraced him, a touch forbidden without invitation. Richard turned and laid his head on Lovell's shoulder as his sobs slowly subsided and he gained strength from Francis' silent support.

As his thoughts became less confused, he suddenly struggled to his feet, gently pulling away from Lovell.

"Anne! Anne – I must tell her myself. She is asleep."

"Do you not think it better to let her sleep and wait until the morning?"

"No... perhaps... but no, I think she would want to know as soon as possible. Come with me, Francis – I fear how she will react. Her only child is dead. How do I tell her? How do I comfort her?"

"You can only be honest, Richard. Just be there to support her."

"You are right, as usual, my friend. I shall be there for her, as you have been for me. You are the most loyal and dearest friend a man could wish for."

And, his expression once more composed, he walked swiftly through into the passageway and on into the chamber where his wife slept. He knocked softly and then entered without waiting for a reply, closely followed by Francis.

"Anne, sweetheart, you must awake. I am sorry, so sorry – there has been bad news, terrible news."

Anne sat up, her hair loose and wearing her nightgown. Her eyes were dark with fear as they saw Richard's expression.

"It is Edward, is it not?"

Richard turned his face aside and Anne let out a wail.

"Is he dead? He is dead, is that what you are saying?"

As Richard nodded, catching his bottom lip between his teeth, she leapt out of bed and immediately collapsed onto the floor, sobbing so much that she couldn't speak or stop. She began pulling at her hair and Richard dropped to his knees beside her, grabbing her hands and forcing her to turn towards him. He held her to him in a desperate embrace and tried to caress her hair, but she struggled and twisted away from him, running to the heavy wooden door and attempting to open it. Richard took her by the shoulders and tried to stop her, turning her to embrace her again, but she fought him, beating her fists on his chest as if she were imprisoned.

"I have to go to him. If I can just get to him... perhaps Hobbys is mistaken... I have to get to him, Richard!"

"No, Anne, there is nothing we can do. He is gone... he is with the Lord now. Our Edward..." As the reality hit him again, fresh tears flowed freely down his cheeks and Anne was sobbing again, both of them clinging to each other like shipwrecked victims to a plank of wood.

Eventually, Francis managed to get them to take a drink of wine and helped them to the chapel where they both knelt and prayed for their beloved, lost prince. Although Eve could hear his lowered voice intoning the normal prayers for his son's soul, his thoughts told a different story; in his head, he was begging God to take his own life in exchange for returning little Edward's.

Eve was also in tears when Stellan finally switched off the machine. She had felt Richard's pain, like a physical one; it was as if she had been stabbed through the heart and she could still hear the echo of Anne's sobs and Richard's cries of anguish in her mind. She felt dizzy and sick with grief for a boy she'd never met and who had died hundreds of years before – it was crazy! She dreaded to think what David and the others would think of her. She glanced at Rupert first and was amazed to see him dabbing at his eyes with a white hanky.

"Rupert?" she said.

"I'm OK, I just got some dust in my eye," he said sheepishly.

She looked at David, who was just sitting there, looking shell-shocked, and Stellan, who was as pale as a ghost. Alex looked his usual composed self.

"Well, I think I should go and get my Cognac so we can all have a drink," David said. "It really brings it home to you doesn't it, hearing them 'live' so to speak. It's like it's all happening right now. Emotional."

Chapter Thirteen

London, April 1484

Because You Loved Me

"How is the queen, Sire?"

Richard turned red-rimmed, tired eyes to his friend, Lovell, and rubbed his hand over his face as if to clear away the grief which he had been wearing like a mask for the last few weeks.

"I do not know, Francis. She will not let me… I cannot…," he sighed and shook his head. Then he paused, closing his eyes and pressing his lips together before he spoke again. "I think she is refusing to eat. She does not want to live without him." He saw Francis' appalled expression and waved his hand dismissively. "No, she will not endanger her soul by self-murder, but she hopes for death, I think. She keeps to her chambers or is in the chapel praying. To be honest, Francis, I do not know her any more. She is silent and withdrawn and unlike the Anne I have known all these years. It is as if something has died inside her with the death of our son. She has changed."

He sat and stared into space for a moment and then smiled and took a deep breath, saying: "Anyway, I must get to work – we have the visit of Von Poppelau next week and I have letters to write, papers to sign."

He was being falsely cheerful, Eve knew because she could sense his actual emotions. He was screaming inside, but felt he couldn't show it. He did not know how to come to terms with his boy's death.

Just then, there was a knock at the door and Francis' secretary came in, bowing reverently and addressed his master.

"My Lord, your good sister, Frideswide, has deigned to visit you. She is in your chambers."

"Thank you, Robert. I will be there in a moment. Your Grace, is there aught I can do for you?"

"No, thank you. I must carry on as normal. The business of the realm continues as ever."

He gave a wan smile and turned to his desk where a huge pile of documents teetered on the edge.

A few minutes later, Francis returned, followed by a young woman, who was obviously close kin to him; they had the same firm chin and direct gaze. However, where Lovell's hair was dark and glossy, his sister's was a shade fairer, a deep chestnut colour, and had more of a wave to it. It was invisible at that time though, as it was enclosed in a neat head-dress. Frideswide was slim and petite, where her brother was tall and broad-shouldered.

Richard looked up from his desk at their tentative knock and his squire, Ralph, announced them immediately. Richard nodded, smiling as he saw Frideswide. It had been years since he had last seen her and then she had been a young maid of just fifteen. Now she was a wife and mother and had blossomed from a skinny waif of a child to a mature and beautiful young woman. And she had brought a tray of food and drink for him.

"Sorry, Dickon, she insisted," said Lovell, grinning wryly. "She says you need some nourishing fare at such a time, not the worry of duty and work. She ordered the kitchen to see to it."

Richard gave a bark of a laugh and threw down his quill.

"Well, you are even more welcome then, Frideswide."

He stood up and, after stretching out his back with a low groan, emerged from behind his desk and went over to her, embracing her and kissing her on the cheek.

"Please, have a seat, both of you. Will you have some Rhenish?"

And he walked over to the side table and took three goblets from a shelf and poured them all some of the rich wine. He was just about to hand Francis his, when there was another knock on the door. It was Kendall, Richard's secretary.

"I'm sorry, your Grace, but I need to consult with the Lord Chamberlain."

"Can it wait, John? He is just about to join me in a drink."

John Kendall hesitated but Lovell rose, waving his goblet away.

"I do not mind, Richard, there is much to do at this time. We shall speak later. Anyway, I am sure Frideswide will be happy to catch up with you without me interfering."

The two men left and Richard took a sip of the wine, then a mouthful of bread and the excellent cold venison that Frideswide had brought him.

"How do your husband and children fare, Frideswide?" he asked, when he had swallowed the first mouthful. She had been married to a man called Edward Norreys when she was just sixteen and they had two sons, John and Henry.

She glanced at her hands holding the goblet and then back to Richard, who noticed her hesitation and frowned.

"What is it? Have I spoken out of turn? Is something wrong?"

She took a swift peek up at him and then lowered her eyes again and sighed.

"I try to avoid my husband when possible as we do not get along very well. We have different... allegiances. And he is not a kind man."

Richard looked at her, appalled.

"Does he hurt you, Frideswide? You know I can do something to help? May I?"

"No, really, he does not hurt me, at least not physically. But he is a cold man and shows me little affection – nor any more our sons. That is what hurts me the most, that he does not seem fond of them. And they are such perfect little boys."

She drew in her breath sharply and a look of distress clouded her pretty face.

"Oh, Richard, I am so sorry... I did not mean to..."

He had turned his face away because the tears he had held in for so long threatened to burst forth. He felt anger towards Norreys, who had two healthy sons and valued them so little, whereas his only legitimate son was gone. He felt such a heaviness in his breast, like a stone and, to his shame, his chin began to wobble and tears burned his eyes.

He walked to the window and Frideswide ran to keep up with him, horrified to see his distress. He placed his hands, balled into fists, on the sill, as if he could hold back the grief physically, and she tentatively put a hand on his shoulder. She felt him tense, but he did not move away and she softly rubbed his shoulder as she whispered:

"Forgive me, Richard. I am such a fool. I hope you know I would never willingly cause you pain. I have always…"

She broke off as Richard turned towards her. His eyes brimmed with tears and his mouth was downturned in an expression so bleak it tore at her heart.

"It is not your fault," he said in a strangled voice.

"Oh! My dear," she breathed and touched his face tenderly.

At her touch, featherlight and yet burning a trail across his skin, something in him broke and he sobbed, clutching her to him, his tears wetting her neck. Intuitively, her arms enfolded him, stroking his hair and making soft, soothing noises.

They remained so for what seemed forever, yet must have been merely a few moments. He finally brought his sobs under control and drew back from her.

"What were you about to say?" he asked her, holding her shoulders and staring into her eyes.

"What? When?" she asked.

"You said 'I have always…' You have always what?"

She took a shaky breath and met his gaze.

"I have always loved you, ever since I was a little maid," she whispered. "And I always shall."

His face softened and warmed and he gave a strangled sob as he bent his head and kissed her. He felt her heart fluttering against his chest as he held her willing body to his. She seemed to melt into his embrace and he knew a sudden, irresistible rush of desire consume him. She returned his kiss and he moaned as his tongue slid inside her soft, warm mouth. His hands strayed down to her firm rump and he pressed her against him hard, hearing her indrawn breath as she felt his arousal.

Her eyes, when he looked at them, shone with love and desire, such as he had not seen in a woman for years, maybe ever.

As if in a torrid dream, he undressed her as he led her into his bedchamber. He knew what happened next was as inevitable as the turning tide and he did not want to resist. He needed this release more than he had ever needed anything before. Just for a moment, lost in the joy of possessing her, he forgot his grief.

Afterwards, guilt assailed him. He might have known it would. He thought inevitably of Anne – cold and distant from him. Why could it not have been she who offered him such unconditional comfort? What a poor excuse for a husband he was – his wife grieving and possibly ill and he was bedding a nubile, young woman, breaking the vow he had made to be faithful to Anne. And with a woman who was not only also married – a double adultery – but the young sister of his best friend. This was not someone he could simply forget about or avoid.

He turned towards her. She was glowing with fulfilment, sleepy and warm in his bed.

"Frideswide," he whispered, caressing a strand of dark chestnut hair away from her face. "I am sorry. I should not have let this happen. I am more thankful to you than I can express, but we have committed a grievous sin."

"I do not care." She stretched her arms above her head, causing her breasts to emerge from the covers and not seeming to notice – or care? "I know what we have done is wrong, but I have longed for it so much and I will treasure the memory of you forever."

Her words evoked a memory of a small boy who longed to be a knight: I have longed for it so much.

As if she suddenly realised she would probably never be with him like this again, tears filled her eyes and he felt his gut twist in pain. He had caused her this hurt to assuage his own selfish needs.

"Oh, Frideswide, do not cry," he said, drawing her once more into his arms and succumbing to his desires all over again. They made love with bitter-sweet abandon, both knowing that there could be nothing permanent between them.

Afterwards, he simply blocked everything else from his mind and held her nestled against his chest, feeling her soft breath on his flesh and trying to forget all the troubles and sadness in his life. He brushed her head with a kiss and drifted off into a deep sleep for the first time in weeks.

When he awoke, she was no longer beside him. He looked around the room and saw her reading, sitting in his chair. She turned when she realised he was awake and smiled.

"Frideswide, what hour is it? I must get up. I have work to do."

"Hush, Richard. Francis has been and…"

"What? Does he know…?"

"I think he probably suspects, although I just told him you were exhausted… well, that much was true!"

She smiled again.

"Frideswide, you should know I never intended this to happen. I am weak and you are so beautiful. But it can never happen again, sweet though it has been. You know that?"

"I do. But never say never. Who knows what the future will bring?" She caught his look of alarm and added: "Do not fear. I will not hope too hard. I am content with this one day. I know you love your wife."

"Aye, although I fear she no longer loves me."

"Of course she does, Richard. She is just too consumed by grief to show it at this time."

"But she will not allow me to comfort her – she will not even speak to me!"

"It is just the way she deals with it. Everyone is different. Some hold it in, others will need to let it out. She will come back to you."

He looked at her steadily for several seconds, then smiled.

"You are wise beyond your years, sweetheart."

He left the warmth of the bed, wrapping a sheet around himself, and poured them both some wine. He kissed the top of her head affectionately and then dressed swiftly. He held the door open for her to pass through and as she did, she raised her hand and stroked his face.

"Thank you, my sweet love," she murmured and she was gone.

Eve was cross with them because they had listened in on Richard's private life, but David had insisted, saying it was relevant since he was now king and still married, so it affected the assessment of his character. She had found the scene almost tragic in its poignancy. What a sad life he had had really.

In the Summertime

In May, Richard was at Middleham entertaining a foreign guest. He looked at the strange little man in puzzlement. Nicolas von Poppelau was shorter then him by almost a hand's breadth, but doubtless weighed a lot more. Not that he was overweight – he was just extremely stocky – almost as broad as he was tall. He spoke no English but a little French and they had managed to communicate thus. A native of Silesia, he was the ambassador of Frederick III, Emperor of the Holy Roman Empire and, therefore, an important contact for future relations in Europe.

At least entertaining von Poppelau took his mind off his poor, dead son for a short while. Anything that did that was welcome, so he threw himself into the feasts, mummery and music as much as he could. Von Poppelau obviously did not know about little Ned's death and Richard would not tell him. It would be less painful that way. Condolences had their place, but he had heard so many in the last few weeks that he never wanted to hear another. Anne was still grieving too much to attend any celebrations and Richard told von Poppelau she was indisposed, but he was the king and could not allow himself the luxury of any more time to mourn.

Von Poppelau attended mass with the Court at Middleham and heard Richard's renowned choir. As they emerged from the chapel, the Silesian declared: "That was the most beautiful music I have ever heard."

Richard smiled graciously, a feeling of pride swelling within him at the compliment. He had invited Nicolas to perform a Latin oration and the strange little man had thoroughly enjoyed himself being the centre of attention. Richard's courtiers were polite in their praise for the performance and Nicolas beamed with pleasure, bowing and smiling at everyone who approached him. Richard requested a livery collar from one of his nobles and presented it to Nicolas with thanks.

"I hope you will accept my invitation to dine with me at the high table," Richard said and the Silesian accepted with alacrity. Richard spoke to him at length as they ate. He found he liked the man, although he was certainly strange. He told

Richard about Hungary's war with the Ottoman Turks and Richard's eyes lit up.

"I wish that my kingdom bordered on Turkey; with my own people alone and without any other prince's help, I should like to drive away not just the Turks but all my foes."

"Ha, King Richard – you have a great heart indeed."

Von Poppelau stayed at Richard's Court in Middleham for nine days and on the final day there was to be a demonstration of how he handled his lance – notable because it was supposed to be enormous! Richard had ordered a simple jousting area to be set up with a 'royal box' or viewing platform and a quintain was placed in the centre. There were several other knights who wanted to show off their skills but everyone was waiting for von Poppelau. His lance was legendary.

After the display of skills by Richard's knights there was a great fanfare to announce von Poppelau's turn.

"Here he comes now!" Richard said, grinning. "I can hardly wait to see this!"

He was sitting on the edge of his seat to get a better view and von Poppelau's servants staggered in with his lance, carrying it between three of them. It was certainly impressive. It was not just the length of it that was out of the ordinary, but the girth too. Nicolas had huge hands like spades, and was obviously strong, which helped him to wield the weapon.

He solemnly took the lance, which he gripped carefully under the crook of his arm, his fingers holding it firmly as he spurred his horse to a canter and then a gallop.

The lance hit the quintain with a crack that split it into kindling and the throng cheered their approbation. Von Poppelau was inordinately pleased with himself and issued a challenge to all, saying he would reward anyone who could lift it and take more than three steps.

There was no shortage of takers and one of Richard's knights, Rob Percy, was the first to try. He gripped the massive lump of wood in both hands and staggered one step before it tipped and the point dug in the ground. The crowd guffawed their amusement and there were several bawdy quips.

Richard himself was desperate to have a try himself, but it would not do if he, as the king, was unable to rise to the challenge so he had to content himself with watching.

Von Poppelau had found out about the death of Richard's son halfway through his stay, and had immediately expressed his condolences. As he was taking his leave Richard said:

"If you ever come to visit us again, you can be sure I will be able to enjoy it much more, for obvious reasons."

Nicolas nodded and smiled.

"I hope to do so, King Richard," he said.

Eve felt a strange kind of wistfulness, knowing that his hope would never be fulfilled, because Richard would die in little over a year.

Guilty

Francis walked into Richard's solar and bowed smartly. Richard waved his hand to indicate he should approach.

"What is it, my friend?"

"There is another petitioner," he said, a puzzled frown bringing his dark eyebrows close together.

"Let them return tomorrow, then. It is late."

"It is Frideswide," Francis said, the uncertainty in his voice betraying his bewilderment.

Immediately, Richard became alert.

"Well, in that case, please send her in."

Frances left the solar and returned a few moments later with Frideswide, before bowing and withdrawing. She looked pale and thin compared with the radiant, healthy girl Richard remembered.

"Frideswide! Are you unwell? Is your husband treating you ill?"

"No, your Grace."

Richard made an impatient gesture.

"You know you need not 'Your Grace' me. Just tell me what you need from me."

She gave a rueful smile.

"What I need you cannot give," she said, lowering her head. Then she raised her gaze to his, lifting her chin proudly. "I am a little unwell – because I am with child."

Something about the way she said it caused him to know the child was the fruit of their illicit passion. He felt a strange mixture of dismay and joy at the thought.

"Your husband – does he know?"

"I think he suspects. He is not well pleased, as you may imagine."

"What do you wish me to do? I will, of course, provide for the child. Do you wish me to speak to Norreys?"

"Will it help, do you think?"

"I can but try. And Francis – is he aware?"

"No. Do you think he should be told?"

Richard nodded.

"Although I doubt he will approve. An old man like me seducing his baby sister."

She clicked her tongue. "You are not old and I am not a baby."

380

He smiled. "Indeed, you are not!"

Later, he summoned Francis to him. He felt more nervous than he was wont to on the eve of a battle.

"Welcome, Francis, please have some wine."

He poured it out, having to concentrate to stop his hands shaking. Then he bade his friend sit and cleared his throat.

"It is about Frideswide," he said, deciding to take the direct approach.

Francis raised his eyebrows but said nothing.

"She has requested my support as she is with child."

Francis frowned, obviously wondering why Richard should be involved when she had a husband. Richard helped him understand.

"It is *my* child, Francis."

He waited, holding his breath. He saw the play of emotions cross his friend's face: disbelief, disgust, anger, reproach.

"You seduced my sister?!"

"It was not like that... she... I ..."

"What? I hope you are not accusing her of seducing you!"

"No, of course not." Richard closed his eyes. "The blame is mine. I did not intend it to happen. It was... it took me by surprise."

"And you exploited her innocence. You, who have always spoken out against sin and lechery. You are a hypocrite! And you are both married – it is a double sin! And she is my sister!! I thought you valued my friendship but I see I was mistaken."

"No, Francis, you do not understand. Of course I value your friendship."

He rose and went to stand beside Francis, who had also stood up. Richard placed his hand on Francis's arm, but he shook it off angrily.

"No! My little sister, Richard! How could you betray me so?" And he turned and left the room without looking back.

Richard leaned on his desk, his head bowed, and sighed. The word 'betray' had cut him to the quick.

Several hours later, Richard had dictated a decree granting an annual grant of one hundred marks to Frideswide. Kendall had completed it and Richard had just signed it and affixed his seal, when there was a knock on the door. Kendall answered it and announced Francis. Richard nodded and Lovell entered, his face impassive. He made a formal obeisance.

"Your Grace."

"Francis, there is no need…"

"Your Grace," he repeated, with more emphasis. "I wish to request to return to Oxfordshire."

There was a long pause.

"For how long?"

"Indefinitely, Sire."

Richard leaned forward with his elbow on the table and pinched the bridge of his nose. He was beginning to get a headache.

"Very well," he said, and pursed his lips.

"Thank you, your Grace," Lovell said, and left the room. Richard dismissed Kendall and sat with his head in his hands.

And he still had to speak to Norreys.

Last Storm

Eve had pretty soon realised that it had been Alex who had destroyed the first machine. She had decided to confront him about it, and his reaction told her she had been right. He totally ignored what she had said and instead hissed:

"I know you slept with the Swede. How could you, Eve? Why him and not me?"

"I don't know, Alex. It was just a spur of the moment thing with Stellan. He was there when I was upset and... it just happened."

"That's pathetic! You don't have sex by accident! You're just a slut – you don't even know him at all!"

"Hey! It's got nothing to do with you whether I sleep with Stellan or the whole of the London Philharmonic bloody Orchestra. It's none of your business!"

He grabbed her by the arm and she pulled away, leaving her jacket sleeve behind, pulled off her shoulder. He let go of it and the jacket swung half off her and something tinkled on the hard floor as it fell from her pocket. The vial of Richard III's DNA! She went to pick it up but he was too quick for her and had it in his hand before she could get to it.

"What are you doing with this?" he said, suspicion clouding his eyes.

"Nothing, give it back to me," she said, holding out her hand.

"No! Do you think I don't know what it is? This isn't yours – you must have stolen it."

"No... I didn't." She felt herself flush to the roots of her hair – she had never been any good at lying.

"David needs to know about this." And he marched off to David's office, despite her desperately trying to grab the vial back.

She let him go; there was no point in trying to dissuade him. A few minutes later David appeared and beckoned her into his office, his expression grim.

"What is your explanation for this?" he asked, twisting the little vial in his chubby fingers.

"I didn't think it was important. I just wanted a souvenir."

"A souvenir! This is a priceless sample of a king's DNA!"

He looked appalled and she had to admit it sounded bad when he put it like that.

"It didn't affect the project at all. And it was my idea in the first place and I sourced the DNA too."

"But it was my money that was paying for all this. Plus, there is the issue of the destruction of the machine. You were the one who was there – I gave you the benefit of the doubt that time, but this suggests I was wrong. You are dismissed. I'm sorry but I have no alternative. Collect your things and go immediately. We will pay you for the month's notice."

He turned away and she left the room, her face burning with embarrassment, anger and shame. Silently, she packed her meagre belongings into a couple of carrier bags and took a last look around the office.

Alex was grinning at her, a satisfied glint in his eye. What a bastard! Stellan was intent on reading a journal of some kind and hadn't even noticed she was packing and Rupert was out of the office that day; he'd taken annual leave to spend the day with Camilla. Eve felt her throat burning as she thought about never seeing him again, as they had always got on well and worked brilliantly together.

She left the office and walked to the car park, hardly able to comprehend that she was now homeless and jobless. She sat in the car in tears for a few minutes before she managed to get herself together enough to drive.

It wasn't the loss of her job she was upset about as much as the fact she was never going to hear Richard III again.

Run To You

In her room at Sue's, Eve had a glass of wine in her hand and was trying to watch the TV when the bell rang. She heard Sue answer it and then a tentative knock on her door. She got up and opened it, astonished to find Rupert standing there.

"Hi Eve – I'm sorry to barge in on you like this, but I had to speak to you. I'm furious with David. It's ridiculous sacking you when what you did wasn't harming the project at all. You're the mainstay of the whole thing. Well, you and Stellan. You are the best interpreter of the meaning of the scenes. It's almost as if you can..." He stopped speaking abruptly and stood there with a puzzled frown on his face. "Wait a minute! That time you told me you could hear everything – it was true, wasn't it? I had almost forgotten about it. Was it true?"

Eve nodded and held the door open for him to come in. She indicated for him to use the chair and she sat on the edge of the bed.

"Do you want some wine?" she asked, but he shook his head.

"No thanks, I'm driving, but I want to tell you that I am going to get David to take you back. I've told him I'm resigning too if you go."

"Oh Rupes, that's really nice of you but there's no need, really. I don't want to cause any trouble. And I did steal that DNA sample. I don't even know why."

"Nevertheless, I have done it. If you go, I go. By the way, I confronted Alex too – he is a little shit! He finally admitted that he was the one who told David and that he had destroyed the machine and tried to get you blamed."

"Finally? What did you do to him?"

"I threatened to cut his balls off."

Eve stared at him aghast.

"No, I'm only joking. I told him there was CCTV footage of him destroying it. That Stellan had a built-in camera in the machine which was triggered when the circuits were damaged. The idiot believed me and spilled everything."

He paused and stared at the ground. Then, looking up again, he said:

"He told me you slept with Stellan." His voice was filled with reproach. "Is it true?"

Eve sighed and ran her hand through her hair.

"Yes, it's true. So? What's it to you?"

He looked at her as if she'd kicked him and she immediately felt guilty.

"Nothing. It's just you've slept with Stellan and dated Alex. I'm the only one in the office you haven't had a relationship with."

"Hey, please! I haven't had a relationship with David. Perish the thought."

"He doesn't count – he's the boss. But Eve, why not me?"

"You never asked me."

He stared at her, his normally cheerful expression serious.

"What if I ask you now?"

Eve was completely taken aback, but before she could harness her thoughts well enough to think of a reply, her phone rang. It was David.

"Eve, Rupert has asked me to reconsider. He showed me proof that Alex was the one who destroyed the machine. And you have worked extremely hard over the last year. Will you come back? Please?"

She knew that 'please' was the hardest word ever, for David. Apart from 'Sorry', which she was aware he would never say.

So, she said:

"OK, I will come back."

After agreeing to go in the next day, she hung up and turned to Rupert to tell him the good news.

"David's offered me my job back."

"Yes, I gathered that. I knew he would."

"Did you? How?"

"Oh, just a feeling." He grinned at her and then grabbed her by the shoulders and kissed her full on the lips. She was shocked at first, but then let herself relax in his arms. She felt warm there. Warm and safe.

Agnus Dei

E ve was back in the office and noticed Alex was absent.
"He's been sacked," Rupert whispered in her ear, as if he had read her mind. "I'm sorry David refused to let you have the DNA sample back. He's given it to Stellan in case he needs a backup."

"I know. It won't be the same though – I won't be able to hear or see anything else."

The day before, she had discussed with Rupert the details she had sensed about Richard and he finally believed her. He also revealed he had had a huge row with Camilla after she had badmouthed Eve and had finished with her.

"I convinced myself I was in love with her, but I think I just dated her because she was there and I wanted to make you jealous. Shame it didn't work."

She said nothing but experienced a warm feeling of contentment that she had not had before. They sat down together and waited for Stellan.

When the machine started, Eve picked up her notebook and listened...

"I wish for the king's remains to be removed and re-interred in Windsor alongside my brother," Richard said. "His tomb in Chertsey is not good enough for a king, even a Lancastrian one."

"Very well, Sire, I will arrange it for you as soon as is practicable."

Eve's eyebrows shot up and she gasped as she realised she could still hear other voices and noises. A chill went up her spine – what was going on?

Stellan moved on a few weeks and found Richard at Windsor overseeing the re-interment of the old king, Henry VI.

After the service, Richard lingered for a time, going to look again at Henry's tomb. He was lost in his thoughts when he heard a soft footstep behind him. He turned and saw John Kendall, his secretary.

"What do you think of the new tomb?" Richard asked Kendall.

"It is most appropriate, your Grace."

Eve could see the tomb, a typically elaborate mediaeval one with the effigy of King Henry in full armour. He was depicted as bearded and clasping his hands as if in prayer. His head wore a crown and two of his devices were at his feet, namely the antelope and the leopard. On the side of the tomb was an angel carrying his shield which bore the royal arms of England and France. She quickly began sketching the design so she could remember it.

"Do you like the way I have had his tabard, sword and gauntlets suspended over it, along with his shield and crowned helmet? I thought to mirror the tomb of the Black Prince in Canterbury. His spurs are kept separately for they are original and actually belonged to him, so can be regarded as relics for the pilgrims to see."

Kendall nodded with an admiring smile.

"Unfortunately, the old king's right arm is missing," Richard said in a low voice. "The exhumation was rather hurried, as was the original interment, and the body was not in good condition, despite what the rumours say about it being uncorrupted. The bones were found in the earth with nothing to protect them from decomposition. His skull is in several pieces too." He sighed. "His relics were brought from Chertsey by barge, in a small wooden box, but I ordered his bones to be laid out reverently in a full-sized coffin this time."

"I see there is a collection box for the donations of the pilgrims."

"Yes, I commissioned my master blacksmith, John Tresilian, to fashion it from iron and it is marked with a letter H, for Henry."

"It is an excellent idea – allow those who revere him to continue to worship him, thus gaining their approval, and profit from them at the same time."

Richard gave a short laugh.

"To be fair, there is already a valuable set of relics here, which brings in much needed revenue."

Kendall regarded him quizzically and Richard grinned, then explained:

"We also have the relics of Master John Schorn, a vicar from North Marston, which lies nearby. There was a drought and Schorn struck the ground with his staff, whereupon a spring of fresh water burst forth – it had healing properties too, apparently. But he is famed most of all because he trapped the devil inside a boot. He would bring the boot out during sermons and allow his congregation to catch a glimpse of the devil to encourage them not to sin. Edward had his remains transferred here in 1478 to help with his building costs. He added one other feature. Do you see that little hole there?"

He pointed to the ceiling of the chapel, where a hole went through to the inside of the tower that was above that part of the chapel, named the Schorn Tower, after the holy vicar.

"It is a spy hole. The Dean and Canons can keep an eye on the pilgrims to ensure both the relics and the offerings are safe."

Bridge Over Troubled Water

He was due to travel on to Nottingham the next day and, after partaking of a modest feast to mark the occasion, he thought to spend a few minutes paying his respects to his illustrious brother, Edward, after the crowd of participants in the re-interment ceremony were gone. He liked to pray for his family's souls alone so he could really feel the sanctity and peace of the sacred space.

He was on his knees before the altar, praying for Edward's soul, when he sensed someone else had entered the chapel. He was not concerned, for his guards were excellent and would not have allowed anyone in who would be a danger or nuisance to Richard. So, he did not look up, but continued his prayer and then slowly stood up, pressing the small of his back, which was aching after being on his knees for half an hour.

He glanced to his left, where the newcomer was also kneeling and praying. It was Francis.

He had been away from Court for a month, and Richard had not summoned him back. If he did not want to be near Richard, he could not blame him and would not force the issue. So, he was surprised to see him now.

He paused and then turned to leave, but Francis stood up and rushed to catch him up.

"Your Grace... Richard! May I speak with you, please?"

"Of course. Come with me to the privy chamber and we will talk there."

There was a slightly awkward silence as they walked. Richard hated this – it had always been the way that he and Francis could talk about anything and any silences were companionable, but that had changed.

Once they were inside Richard's chamber and his body servants were sent away, he sat down and indicated that Francis should also sit.

"How was Oxfordshire?" he asked, offering him some wine.

"It was good. Nice to spend some time with my Anne, you know. She sends her love."

"Is she well?"

"Yes, although still not breeding. Talking of which, I wish to apologise. I was... over hasty in my anger about you and Frideswide. She has come to stay with us until the child is born and she told me... She said she had been as much to blame as you. That you had made her happy. And that she has always loved you – I knew she had a childish adoration of you, but I thought she had grown out of it."

"I never knew that, you know. It was just that she was so... she was kind to me and she reminded me of Anne in her younger days. Edward had only just died and I was lost. I needed someone then and Anne was... absent from me. Frideswide helped me find myself again, brought me back to life. It seems I cannot do without the Lovells."

Francis lowered his head, a gentle smile revealing a dimple in his cheek.

"I am glad. Because the Lovells cannot do without you either!"

Chapter Fourteen

London, Twenty-first Century

I Run To You

"Guess what? I can still hear and see everything! I was sure I would only hear Richard, the same as everyone else, but no!" Eve's eyes were shining as she whispered into Rupert's ear.

"That's weird!" Rupert said, looking at her with an expression half of admiration and half of fear. "How is that even possible?"

"I don't know for sure but I wonder if it's because I carried the DNA around with me for ages and so it's somehow created a permanent psychic link to Richard. They say everything is energy so…" She shrugged.

"Well, tell me all about it later – let's listen to the next instalment, eh?"

He squeezed her shoulder as they sat down.

Richard was hearing petitions at his Court of Requests in York. His secretary, John Kendall, gave him a summary of the first case.

"This is a woman, Mistress Katherine Bassingbourne who asserts her right to a house claimed by her stepmother Ellyn's, family. Her father, Thomas Worcester of York, passed away thirty years ago without leaving a written will, but Mistress Bassingbourne asserts that her father made a nuncupative will which said that although Ellyn should have the house until her death, thereafter it should go to Katherine, and any children she might have. However, Ellyn contests that she can leave the house to her new husband, Henry Faucet's children. Mistress Bassingbourne is now a widow and has need of the security this house could provide in the future."

"Let her approach."

A woman of middle age and attractive mien approached the dais, her fists clenched tightly at her sides and her steps tentative. When she was still several feet away, she knelt on the floor and remained there, her head held low. She was trembling from head to toe.

Richard got up from behind the table and approached her. She jumped when he touched her on the shoulder. He said, softly: "Please, Mistress Bassingbourne, arise and come closer – we do not want all and sundry to know your business, do we?" He smiled as she turned terrified eyes to meet his and her cheeks pinked prettily in embarrassment. "Now what has happened? Tell me from the beginning."

He led her to a chair in front of the dais, but moved it to the side of the great table before having her sit.

"Oh, your Grace, I am ashamed to trouble you with my small problems. I know you are a very busy man."

He smiled again and said:

"Never too busy to hear the problems of those under my jurisdiction and protection. I am interested in justice and if I can help, I surely will. Never be afraid to ask – if it is within my power and serves a just cause, it shall be granted."

"Thank you, your Grace. My father died thirty years ago, may he rest in peace, and he was too ill to make a proper will so he had two neighbours come in to witness his last requests. He said he bequeathed the house in North Street to Ellyn for the rest of her life, but on her death, it should come to me and my children, should I have any – I have, your Grace – I have five children now. Ellyn and I have never really been friends although neither did we have any major disagreements before my father's death. That house rightly should belong to me when Ellyn passes away, Sire. I know you are a fair man and I hope you can help me. Can you, your Grace?"

"We shall see, Mistress Bassingbourne. Now, did you remain on good terms with your father right up until his death?"

"Oh, of course, your Grace. I barely left his side except to tend to the house and garden."

"Are there witnesses to the will still alive? Can they testify before the court?"

"I believe so, your Grace."

"Well, I will summon them to my court to give their evidence and make a judgement as soon as possible. Do not worry, Mistress Bassingbourne. I am sure we will have an outcome that is agreeable to you."

"Oh, thank you, thank you, your Grace!" She knelt on the floor in front of him again and he had to get Miles to help her out of the chamber.

"John, I wish to dictate a letter before any other claimants are seen, because this is rather complicated."

"Of course, Sire."

John took up a trimmed quill and a pristine piece of parchment.

"To Thomas Wrangwysh, mayor of York and aldermen. We greet you well and will you to adjudicate impartially in a dispute between two citizens, one being our poor subject, Katherine Bassingbourne, widow, who makes a grievous complaint against a certain Henry Faucet over the matter of the nuncupative will of Katherine's father.

We enclose a copy of her petition and charge ye to dispense justice in accordance with our laws and good conscience. We will and command that the two disputants, as well as any relevant witnesses, be brought before you that you may hear their several statements.

Ricardus Rex Tertius."

"What is a nuncupative will?" asked Stellan.

"I just Googled it," replied Rupert. "It is a verbal will which is only valid if witnessed by at least two people, usually used if a person on their deathbed is too ill to make a conventional written will."

"Thanks, Rupert," said David. "I was wondering that too. This woman who claims her father had bequeathed her the house – what happened to her?"

"I don't know – maybe we can find out more. What was her name, Katherine something?" Eve said.

"Yes, Katherine Bassingbourne. And her father was Thomas Worcester," said Stellan.

Hard To Say I'm Sorry

Francis had been at home for the Yuletide season, but appeared unexpectedly at Westminster in the middle of January, emerging from a blizzard and frozen almost to his bones. He was still brushing the snow from his shoulders when Richard walked into the room, his brows drawn together in a frown of concern.

"What is it, Francis? More bad news? What has the Tydder bastard done now?"

"No, well, nothing to do with Tydder. It is Frideswide."

The blood drained from Richard's face.

"What? Has something happened?"

"Aye, she has made you a father again. You have a daughter, born on 10th."

"But that is far too early! The babe was not due until next month. Are they well?"

Francis winced and took a deep breath.

"At the moment. The child is very small, but seems strong enough. Frideswide is exhausted, for the labour was a long and difficult one. She lost a lot of blood but I hope she will survive."

"Francis, I will come and see her. There is not much Court business going on so soon after the seasonal celebrations."

"What about your wife?" Francis paused and then added: "Does she know about Frideswide?"

Richard's expression became pained. He bit his lip and then said:

"I was thinking to tell her – I believe in honesty where possible. But I decided not to in the end. It would be too cruel.

How could I tell her I was going to be a father again when her son… when she cannot…"?

He took a shaky breath and rested his head in his hand, rubbing his temples. He shook his head slowly.

"She is ill, Francis. You have not seen her of late. She seemed to rally a little at Christmas. She was more animated, she even smiled a little and ate more than she has done since Edward died. But she has a cough. She thinks I do not know, but she coughs blood, more and more. I fear she is dying. Her physician has forbidden me to share her bed, for fear of contagion, so even if she was able to conceive it is now impossible. They have not told me, but I am sure it is the white plague."

His voice broke and he sat down abruptly, the muscles around his jaw working as he struggled to hold on to his emotions.

"To be honest, I would be glad to get away, just for a few days. It takes a toll to try to keep cheerful, to carry on at all sometimes."

Francis placed a tentative hand on his friend's shoulder while he took a deep breath.

Sweet Child of Mine

Richard had let it be known he was going to Windsor for a few days, but in fact he travelled to Minster Lovell with Francis.

They went straight in to see Frideswide. She was asleep when they arrived and Francis went to order some refreshments for Richard and his retainers, while Richard stayed at her bedside.

When Francis returned, he was holding a tiny bundle of linen, so small it did not seem big enough to contain a baby.

Richard rose and met Francis in the middle of the chamber. He gently drew back the cloth and a tiny, perfect face appeared, rosebud lips and a small shock of dark hair. At the disturbance, the babe moved her mouth as if to suck, and a soft, moist noise emerged, making Richard smile. He extended a finger and softly stroked the downy cheek, withdrawing it abruptly when the child began to blink, revealing sleepy, blue eyes. She sighed and settled herself down again. Francis extended his arms and Richard carefully took the little bundle. She stirred at the change of carer, but then nestled against his breast.

Francis silently left the room.

Richard rocked his daughter slowly, moving back to the chair and sitting down. He looked from his child to Frideswide, pale but peaceful in sleep, then back again. His heart felt battered from dealing with his worry and grief for Edward and Anne, but this girl had given him some hope. It was empowering to know he was truly loved, even if they would never be together. And their one night of passion had resulted in this wonderful child. A small miracle.

"Is she not fair, Richard?" Frideswide whispered, her voice hard to hear, it was so weak and husky, as if she had been screaming. She managed a smile though.

"Like her mother," he said. "Thank you, Frideswide."

"I thought to call her Anne," she said, causing a sharp stab to his heart and his conscience. "She has been so kind to me, allowing me to stay here during my pregnancy."

Of course. Francis' wife, Anne, had always been close to Frideswide.

He said nothing, simply nodded, but something in his expression must have alerted her for she added:

"Unless you have any objections, of course?"

"No, no objections."

He wondered suddenly how it could be that a man could love more than one woman and cause pain to them both in different ways. Well, perhaps it was appropriate that she be called Anne, as it would ever remind him of his guilt and his joy.

He stayed for several days and then returned to Westminster. Numerous grants and petitions had been signed as if from Windsor, including one for another one hundred marks to Frideswide, for 'certain special causes and considerations', backdated nine months. He also granted funds to Francis towards the child's upkeep.

Children

Richard was speaking to his illegitimate son, John. Eve and the others had come across him often when they were listening in on the everyday life of the Duke and Duchess at Middleham Castle and Sheriff Hutton, because Richard had taken both John and his natural daughter, Katherine, into his household from quite a young age. Although Anne had been ambivalent about this at first, she soon realised they were innocent children and would also make excellent companions for her own son, Edward. John was now almost fifteen.

"John, I sent for you to inform you that I am going to officially make you Captain of Calais."

"Really, Father? That is wonderful. But does that mean I shall have to live there?"

"Yes, for some of the time, but Jocky Howard, the Duke of Norfolk, will accompany you and see you right. He is an experienced sailor and commander and will help you to learn all you need. I am sure you will be diligent and dutiful for me?"

"Of course, my Lord Father. I will not let you down."

"That is well, John. You may leave now, and I will draft the document endowing you with this appointment. Goodnight, son."

"Goodnight, father."

He came and knelt before his father, who kissed him on his head, placing his hands on either side of his face in a gesture of affection.

After he had left, Richard sat down at his desk and began to draft the wording for the official appointment. Eve was able to 'hear' his thoughts as he wrote a draft of his intended letter.

"By the King, to all to whom, etc, greeting. Among all, our dear bastard son, John of Gloucester, whose liveliness of mind, activity of body and inclination to all good customs, promise us by the grace of God, great and certain hope of future service. Know that we by our special grace, and out of certain knowledge and our mere motion, ordain and appoint the same John captain of our town and castle of Calais and of our Tower of Rysbank and our Lieutenant in the Marches of the same. Excepting and reserving wholly to us the gift and grant of offices during the minority of the same John, before he reaches the age of twenty-one years. Having, occupying and exercising the posts of Captain and Lieutenant aforesaid, the said John himself or through his sufficient deputy or deputies from the fourth day of March last past for the term of his life with all rights, honours and profits, fees, wages, rewards and prerogatives, in all full power and form according as any other captain of the said town had before this time, excepting and reserving as is aforesaid…"

"Hmm!" he grunted, sounding satisfied with his wording. Eve thought he must have had some education in the law as he seemed to draft out such complicated grants and decrees quite easily.

He summoned his Secretary and handed over his draft for him to write it out formally and then return it to him for signing.

When John Kendall had gone, the king sat at his desk, his hands linked behind his head and sighed, a small smile on his face.

P lease explain what was going on there, Eve? Do you have any idea?" David was looking bemused.

"Well, from the date, I think he was formulating his grant of the Captaincy of Calais for his bastard son, John," she said, unable to reveal all she had heard.

"Oh, I'm sure poor, old John wasn't as bad as all that!" Rupert grinned.

"Well, he wasn't old, for a start," said Eve, rolling her eyes. "Because the grant says there are some powers reserved until he is twenty-one, and we know now that he was born in 1472, don't we, so he was only about twelve or thirteen."

"What!?" David said, stunned.

"Well, remember, they had to grow up fast in those days. Richard was acting in judgement as Admiral at thirteen, wasn't he?"

"Oh yes," said David, frowning. "What a way to carry on!"

Everybody Hurts

It was the sixteenth of March 1485 and Richard was sitting next to the window looking out over the city. He was describing the sight to Anne, who was lying in the great bed, looking swamped by the covers. She was pale, very pale, and her eyes were tired and red, her breathing laboured.

"Can you hear the bells, love? I can see them all going to mass. There are some blossoms out in the castle gardens and two sparrows are courting."

He paused, watching the scene, as Anne said nothing, lying there still and wan.

"It is not a very bright day. In fact, it is becoming more and more grey and drear. Still, the spring is coming, Anne, and we can go out in the gardens when the weather is warmer. We could take food and drink out with us and relax as we used to. I think it is going to rain; look, the sky is looking threatening now; perhaps there will be a storm. What is that? Is someone screaming? There are people massing outside – Sweet Jesu! The sun is growing dim! I know there are logical explanations for this kind of thing, but it is eerie nonetheless, think you not? Anne?"

He turned to look at her and gasped, rushing to her bedside and dropping down onto his knees as he grasped her limp hand.

"No, oh no! Not yet! Do not leave me yet, my love! Stay!"

He rushed to the door and yelled along the corridor.

"Hobbys! Hobbys! Come quickly!"

Then he ran back to his wife and patted her hand desperately. The doctor arrived and gently led him away.

"She is gone, Sire, I am sorry."

Richard made a noise, half groan and half strangled sob.

Francis came into the room at a run and taking in the scene with a glance, sat down beside his friend and then led him gently out of the room.

"I am being punished, Francis. Because of Frideswide. God has punished me by taking Anne."

"No, Dickon, you have been faithful to her all these years – just one slip… surely He would not be so cruel."

"I vowed to her I would be faithful. I said 'Never will I lie with another woman while you live'. I betrayed her!"

Francis did not know what to say so he simply embraced Richard, who at that moment was a friend in need rather than his king.

Anne's funeral took place in the same location where she and Richard were married, Westminster Abbey.

There was little room there so she was buried on the southern side of the Abbey's High Altar, in front of the Sedilia and the ceremony was a lavish one, appropriate for a queen of England.

Richard did not officially attend as it was not the custom for anointed monarchs to be present at the funerals of other anointed monarchs, but he knelt in a private section, curtained off from the congregation.

He prayed for the soul of his poor, lost queen and wept copious tears so that his eyes were red by the time the ceremonies were over.

"I shall have a magnificent tomb made for her in York, in the Minster," he told Lovell after the funeral was concluded. "I plan to have our family mausoleum there once the chantry chapel is finished. I shall move Anne and Edward, our son, there so they can rest together for all eternity."

"Of course, Dickon," Francis said. "I shall help in the planning of the re-interments. Do not worry, we shall make it a fitting tomb for her and Edward. Come, let us play a game of chess – perhaps it will prove a distraction for you this sad day."

Testify

After arriving at the office a little late, having overslept and left Sue's in a rush, Eve got herself a coffee as soon as she entered the office, sitting down in her usual seat to await the day's live history lesson. She glanced at her notes from the day before: this was supposed to be Richard's speech at the Guildhall concerning the death of Anne and his supposed plans to marry Elizabeth, his niece. It was one episode where the date and place were well documented.

"Your Grace, people are commenting on the matching clothes worn by the queen and your niece, Elizabeth, at Yuletide. They are saying she intended to be queen even then and that you must have encouraged them to wear the same clothes to show you favoured her."

"I know, but it was not like that at all – Anne ordered the dress for her – it was one of about a dozen she had had made for her and some of them were made of the same material as Anne's. It was simply a coincidence that they both chose dresses of the same stuff to wear at the celebrations."

"So, what about the rumour that you intend to marry Elizabeth? Is it true?"

"No, of course not! She is illegitimate and half-Woodville, not to mention her being my niece. Why, has something happened?"

"The Duke of Norfolk was given a letter from Elizabeth that urged him to speak to you about 'the marriage'. She also commented that she feared the queen would never die. That is why the rumours have again reared their heads."

"Yes, yes, William! John Howard informed me of the letter. It was just a misunderstanding. I have arranged a probable double alliance with Portugal; I will marry Joana and Elizabeth will marry Manuel de Beja. But there is also a possibility of a Spanish alliance for me, which would leave Bess with no match, or at least no match of equal status to Manuel. The marriage of which she was urging John to speak to me was the one with Manuel. But she knew it had to wait until Anne... until she passed to God. She did say some very selfish and hurtful things regarding the queen, it is true, but that is just her youth – I remember myself at that age. I was quite heartless when I turned out the old Countess of Oxford from her lands – although, to be fair, she was the mother of a traitor and I did offer her a pension in compensation."

"Well then, Sire, that is well. You have given your explanation."

"Nevertheless, I wish to publicly deny this rumour."

"Your Grace, you have just lost your wife – do not put yourself through this stress and pain. You do not need to deny such scurrilous words."

"I know, but I feel I must do it. There are enough false rumours flying around concerning me. If I can scotch this one before it takes hold, I can limit the damage to my reputation."

"In that case, may I accompany you to the Guildhall?"

"Thank you. I would be pleased for you to attend me."

There was then just the sound of their feet walking along the halls and Stellan moved the machine on an hour or two. They were in the Guildhall and Richard was standing at a lectern before all the merchants and members of the public. Then, he cleared his throat and spoke, his voice raised as he spoke much more loudly and clearly than usual.

"I am here of necessity to deny publicly the scurrilous rumours pertaining to my dear, late wife and my niece, Elizabeth. I do swear on the Holy Bible that it never entered my mind to marry my niece, Elizabeth in such a way. Nor was I willing nor glad of the death of my queen, but I am as sorrowful at her loss and as heavy in heart as any man might be. Any man or woman who is proved to have been perpetuating this cruel and untrue fabrication will be sorely punished and any who report them rewarded."

Stellan paused the machine.

"That is his denial of the rumours which he was reported as delivering in 'a loud and distinct voice'. I think we can all agree that is accurate. But do you believe he was telling the truth or was he just a clever liar?"

"He sounded under strain to me. That could mean he was lying," David said.

"Why always think the worst? It could also mean he was simply just that: 'under strain'. For God's sake, the poor man had lost his brother, whom he hero-worshipped, his only legitimate son and then his wife, all within two years! Then he gets accused of all sorts of terrible things, he's betrayed by people he thought he could trust and he has to prepare to defend his kingdom against the bloody Tudor. No wonder he was bloody stressed!"

Eve didn't normally swear, but her frustration at her boss was making her short-tempered.

"Hey! There's no need to get all emotional about it. After all, the guy has been dead for over five hundred years." David gave a wicked grin and sipped his hot coffee.

"So, he was still a human being! Doesn't he have the right to be given the benefit of the doubt: innocent until proven guilty and all that? Especially since he actually promoted the concept in a way – he strengthened the bail laws so that if someone was accused of a crime, he couldn't have his goods confiscated unless found guilty."

Eve's voice had risen in volume as she defended Richard. She found she could no longer tolerate any unfairness at his expense.

"And I'm not being emotional!" she said, feeling tears of anger prick her eyes, even as she denied them.

In the ensuing silence, David coughed, avoiding her gaze, Rupert pretended to be writing some notes and Stellan fiddled with the machine's controls. Men!

"Alright, maybe I do feel a bit emotional about it, but I've researched him and I can see how unjustly he has been treated by history. It's so wrong! We have to try to find out what happened to the princes and clear his name. All the good things he did in his life before becoming king and the excellent laws he made in his single Parliament are always overshadowed by those bloody bastards!"

"Hey, steady on! It was hardly their fault, was it?" Rupert said, his eyebrows raised in surprise as she rarely swore.

"I mean it literally – they were illegitimate – the term 'bastard' was a simple matter of fact in those days. It wasn't a term of insult."

"Well, it's time for lunch now. We will resume this afternoon."

After lunch, they listened to many more instances of Richard giving orders, signing papers, mustering troops and dispensing justice. They noted everything down and one significant thing they discovered was that Richard had ordered Francis to the South coast just before the Battle of Bosworth, or Redemore as it was then known. However, they found out nothing else about the princes. Then, they came to the final day – the twenty-second of August 1485.

Shining Knight

"Norfolk is down, Sire!"

Richard said nothing, but his jaw muscles tightened as he thought of his old friend, gone. He held Syrie's reins firmly as the great horse tried to fight his control.

"Send Northumberland the order to advance and cover Norfolk's line. Has Stanley responded to my order to engage?"

"Aye, Sire. When I said you have his son and you ordered him to join the battle, he laughed and told me to inform you that he has other sons, your Grace."

The messenger did not look at his king, but kept his gaze averted – he knew full well that Stanley was making a deliberately cruel jibe at Richard, who had lost his only legitimate son just over a year before. If he had looked, he would have seen Richard's lips tighten and his eyes narrow. White Syrie snorted and stamped a foot, picking up on his master's mood.

"Well, we shall have to do without the traitor – and he without his son. Bring him out and execute him now!"

The man turned to go to fetch Lord Strange, Stanley's unfortunate son, but Richard called out to him before he had taken five steps.

"Wait! Leave him for now – we have more important things to do. Strange can wait until after the battle." He took the drink offered to him by his squire and then a scout arrived and knelt before him. "Yes, lad, what news?"

"Look, Sire, over yonder – the Tydder is separated from the main part of the army. He looks to be approaching William Stanley's lines. But he has only a couple of hundred men-at-arms with him."

He pointed across the plain before them, over to the eastern side. A small group of mounted men, accompanied by a guard of pike-men, running to keep up, were halfway to the Stanley force.

"Good work, Tom!" He stood tall in the saddle. Then, in a loud voice, he called his household knights to him. "Men! Tydder is separated from his main force – we can charge now and kill him quickly. We can end this battle and prevent any more bloodshed. You remember the plan for the charge – form up! We ride together for England and St George!"

He waved his squire forwards and took his helmet, which had the gold coronet of kingship mounted atop it. In fact, all his armour was gilded as befitted an anointed king of England. He wore his royal surcoat over it.

"Sire, would you reveal your identity to the Tydder army and risk them targeting you, our sovereign king? Perhaps it would be wiser to let them wonder where you are – that way you will not draw their fire."

Rob Percy was frowning, his eyes concerned. Richard would not have let just anyone question his judgement, but Rob was a friend, a close friend of many years' standing.

"I understand your concern, Rob, yet I would not have them think me craven, valuing my own safety above that of the realm – the blessed realm of England that I rule as God's anointed king. Let the bastard mark me well and quake in his boots! Are you with me?"

He drew his sword with a ringing sound as the soldiers cheered and then he placed the shining helm on his head, slamming his visor down and turning Syrie in the direction of the Tydder's cluster of men. In a few moments they were off, galloping across the battlefield, their armour shining in the late August sun and their horses' hooves kicking up a fog of dust. He led the charge, forging ahead of the rest as his horse was so much faster. They galloped at full pelt across the battle lines aiming to catch up with Tydder's small party before he reached the Stanleys. The ground trembled as the hooves thundered over it and the yells of the men, screaming their defiant battle cry, carried over to the group surrounding Tydder's banner of the red dragon of Cadwallader. Richard's own standard bearer was just behind him, valiant Sir Percy Thirlwell. His friends, Percy, Brackenbury and the Harringtons were there, his secretary, John Kendall, too, insisting on riding with him. He knew them all personally, knew their courage, their loyalty and their love for him. He felt mighty, invincible and proud of all of them. No-one could have more honourable and loyal friends.

He let out a yell of rage at the gall of the Tydder, daring to try to wrest the crown from him. He would slay him now and it would be over. There were several horsemen ahead of him, including Tydder's standard bearer, William Brandon, whom he felled with one blow of his battle-axe, his horse screaming in panic as it fell over, pulled by the force of the man keeling over to one side. Brandon lay still on the ground and now another knight took his place. Richard dealt blow after blow, his arms aching and his head ringing with the noise of the axe hitting helms and the frightful screams of the dying men and horses. Suddenly there loomed before him a man he recognised – Tydder's champion and body guard, John Cheney, a man who stood more than a foot taller than Richard, even bigger than his brother Edward had been. He yelled his defiance, jeering at Richard, who felt his rage burst up at the man's treachery in supporting the upstart Tydder. He spurred Syrie on and swung his axe once more, with all his strength and the speed of his mount behind it. Cheney was hit and fell from his horse with a dull, booming thud. He did not wait to see if he yet lived, but rode on – now there were only foot soldiers surrounding Tydder.

Then he saw the group of men encircling Tydder turn to face outward and stick their long pikes in the ground pointing forward, aimed at the horses. If he continued his headlong attack into the group, the horses would be slaughtered. So, he swept Syrie around to the north slightly, aiming to attack from the side of their formation, spurring him on again and glancing behind him to check the others had realised his adjustment – good! They had.

As he reached the area just beyond the edge of Tydder's force, he felt Syrie falter and his pace slowed suddenly. Glancing down he cursed – he had forgotten the ground down here was marshy and Syrie whinnied in panic as his hooves were mired in the heavy, clinging mud. He heard other horses screaming and struggling in their desperation to escape the bog's treacherous hands. He dismounted and led Syrie out, letting him find his own path to safety without the hindrance of a heavily-armoured knight on his back, before leaving him and running at the Tydder's lines, his battle axe in his hands and yelling at the top of his voice. He knew the others would follow his example and did not hesitate to even glance behind to make sure, but wielded his axe against the pike men. The pikes shattered into kindling as his axe swept through them and into the bodies of the men, who screamed in terror at the sight of him, his crown still glowing in the sunlight and his gilt armour now covered in blood and gore. His loyal men were there backing him up and he heard Percy cursing and the ringing of steel on steel. Some of the enemy turned and ran back towards their main army and, without hesitation, he stepped into the gap, his sword now in his hand, dealing death to every man who stood in his way.

He heard a scream behind him that made his blood run cold and he glanced around to see Percy fall, his life taken from behind by a French pike man. To his horror, he saw Thirlwell hesitate a fraction of a second and miss seeing a sword that came sweeping from just beside and behind him to sever both his legs. He fell but somehow kept himself upright, his face white with shock, still clinging to the banner he had been entrusted with. He held it aloft in defiance even though his life was ebbing away into the mud with his valiant blood. Richard's rage bloomed again and he hacked and hewed his way forward, the enemy falling back to allow his path. Tydder was only a few yards away, his face livid with fear as Richard caught his panicked gaze. He would pay for the precious blood shed on this cursed day. But even as he made his way towards him, he heard a rumbling and felt the ground tremble beneath his feet. Turning, he saw Salazar, his Spanish mercenary, cantering up to him, leading a fresh horse.

"Sire, you must withdraw! Look – Stanley's forces are joining the battle against us. Take this horse and flee now – you can regather your supporters and get back your realm another day."

"God forbid I yield one step. I will win now or die King of England."

And he turned back to where Tydder had been, but he was gone – further back again and protected by more pike men. Richard again plunged into their midst, but felt his head ring with noise and pain as a blow from the point of a halberd forced him to his knees. His vision was blurring and everything seemed to slow down as he struggled to get back up to his feet. He sensed someone behind him and heard harsh words in Welsh as his head was grabbed roughly and a dagger sliced along his jaw and the leather strap of his helmet. He cursed as his head was suddenly light, his helmet, with its precious crown gone. He slammed his elbow back and heard a satisfying scream as the attacker's nose was crushed and he managed to get to his feet at last and stood there swaying, trying to get his breath.

His sword was still in his hand, although his axe was gone. He had to turn then as someone was there behind him and he felt a glancing blow whirr across the top of his head and a searing pain. He whirled and swung his sword, slicing off the attacker's arm at the shoulder. Again and again, he swung and stabbed, killing man after man, but more came to fill the space. He forced the deadly blade around again and saw a face he recognised. Rhys ap Thomas! The Welshman who had promised he would prevent Tydder from entering England through Wales. Richard yelled again, his teeth gritted, his hair plastered to his head with blood and sweat, and swept the sword towards the Welsh traitor. Ap Thomas staggered back, his eyes wide with fear, his sword-arm frozen. "Treason!" Richard cried as he stepped forwards and saw, to his satisfaction, a dark stain spreading in the man's groin. He cried a second time: "Treason!" But as he opened his mouth to yell it again, he stumbled in the mire, sprawling to his knees once more and took a massive blow from behind. He could only manage "Trea–" before another, still heavier, strike from a halberd turned his vision black.

Eve was shaking and sobbing uncontrollably like a child who has cried for so long and so hard that she can't stop, great gasping sobs of despair. She felt dazed from the blows she had felt along with Richard, furious at the treachery which had so cruelly betrayed him, as he was hacked to a bloody death in the mud. As soon as the last breath had left his body, she could feel nothing more and the sudden emptiness of her mind, which had become so used to the thoughts and feelings of the last Plantagenet king keeping hers company, was disorientating and distressing.

"No! No!" she sobbed, tears wetting her face and her nose running. She heard an incoherent moaning noise and realised it was the sound of her own misery. "Richard!" she whispered.

After hearing the terrible sounds of the battle, after 'seeing' Richard's courageous death and 'feeling' the blows that felled him, Eve felt as if she had just witnessed the murder of a friend. She had to run from the room, pleading too much tea, to hide the emotions she felt. That was the trouble with her ability; if she connected well, the negative emotions really floored her.

415

She sat in the loo and wiped her eyes and nose, trying to still her racing heart. But her mind kept replaying the last scenes of the battle over and over: Richard's charge; his last stand; Thirlwell, his standard bearer, holding the banner of the white boar aloft even after having had his legs hewn away from under him; Richard's rage when he could not reach Tudor, his scream of despair at the treachery of the Stanleys. She could still hear his voice, hoarse and desperate, yelling: "Treason! Treason!" the sound cut off as the blows rained down on his unprotected head. She tried to block it out, but she couldn't. She felt as grief-stricken as if it had happened only today and she had known him personally, a loyal friend and a good man. She finally gave in to the tears, hoping they would wash away some of the emotion, that they would cleanse her spirit.

Mr Right

When she emerged from the toilet, still a little tearful, she felt a warm arm around her shoulders and Rupert hugged her close to him.

"Are you OK, Eve?" he whispered, his eyes showing their concern.

"It's like it just happened," she choked out. "I feel lost. I have lived with him in my head for so long. It feels… empty now."

"I've never thought you were empty-headed, love," he grinned and she couldn't help giving him back a watery smile.

"Shall we go and have some lunch, and a chat?"

"OK," she said.

He released her from his embrace enough to look down into her eyes. Then he kissed her and she tensed. He leaned back away from her.

"Sorry, Eve. If you don't want…"

"No! I do want…"

She smiled shyly up at him and he tried again. This time, more prepared, Eve let herself melt into his arms and returned his kiss with equal enthusiasm.

He broke off and held her close, taking a deep breath.

"You do know I love you, don't you? Always have."

His words filled her with joy.

"Likewise," she said softly.

"Hey, not in office hours, if you don't mind!" David was looking very annoyed.

Eve looked at Rupert and then they both looked back at David.

"We resign!" they said, in unison.

Then Rupert put his arm around her and they marched out into the sunshine, ignoring David's astounded protests.

When they got outside, she said:

"I don't know what I'm going to do now. I have no home, no job, no man…"

"What about me? Aren't I a man?" he said, giving her a squeeze.

"I think you're just an overgrown child!" she giggled.

"Well, I have a home; you are welcome to share it. Only if you want to, of course. No pressure."

She laughed. He looked rather affronted.

"I'm not joking, you know. There's plenty of room if you don't want to share with me."

He steered her into a cafe and they ordered coffees and sat down.

"Where do you live, Rupes?"

"I have a flat in Islington, but I also have a house in Wiltshire. This is a bit embarrassing. You know I told you that I didn't get on with my parents. That I hadn't spoken to them for years – well, my dad, anyway."

Eve frowned as she struggled to remember the conversation. She did vaguely remember it, from way back.

"Well, it was my dad really. He wanted me to take over the family business – antiques. I didn't want to do that and I didn't want to work with my dad. We always clashed – too alike, I s'pose. I knew it would end in tears if I agreed. I would resent not doing what I wanted to do and he would expect me to obey his orders, I'd have no say. So, I left and got a job. Dad was furious. Disowned me. Eventually, I got the job with 'Future Tech'."

"Where you met me," she said, batting her eyelashes at him.

"Quite! I did see my mum occasionally, but on the sly. My dad didn't know. Anyway, I got a letter two weeks ago. He died. All quite sudden." He stared down at the ground and moistened his lips. "Heart attack."

"Oh Rupes, I'm so sorry. That's terrible."

"The funeral was last week and I nearly didn't go, but I thought if I didn't, I might regret it. So, I went. Mum was distraught of course. Rex, my brother, was the same as always – boasting about how much he'd made on the stock exchange. Abbie was nice, a bit scatty but affectionate – my little sis. Then they gave me a letter from him. It changed everything. Here."

He took a dog-eared envelope out of his jacket pocket and handed it to her.

"I can't read that – it's personal."

"Yes, you can. You have my permission. I'd like you to."

She unfolded the cream paper and began to read.

Rupert,

I know we haven't always seen eye to eye, but you're my son, my first-born son. I wish I could say what I feel, but it comes hard. It wasn't the way I was brought up. 'Keep a stiff upper lip' and all that.

I am proud of you, son, you have courage, I can't deny that. You struck out on your own and made a success of it. In the heat of the moment I disowned you, but I never really meant it. I suppose I'm trying to say: 'I miss you.' I wish you would come back to visit at least, if you really don't want to take on the business. I don't know if you will ever read this, if I will ever even post it.

But if you do, I have one piece of advice for you. If you love someone, don't let them go. Tell them you love them. Keep telling them, and showing them. Otherwise you might lose them, the way I lost you and end up a lonely old man, like me.

I am leaving you the business anyway. Sell it if you don't want to run it. But it is yours to do with as you will.

I hope you forgive me, son.

It was signed with an illegible squiggle and printed with 'Sir Ralph Asheton-Williams' underneath.

She noticed the notepaper was headed with a crest and motto. The crest was a boar's head and the motto was 'In Domino Confido'.

"Wow!" she said. "Your name is really, Rupert Asheton-Williams?"

He nodded.

Your family crest is a white boar's head – there's a coincidence."

"Oh, Richard III you mean? Yes."

"What does the motto mean?"

"I trust in the Lord."

"That could relate to him too."

"My dad's letter was the main reason I finished with Camilla. I never loved her. It was always you. So, I decided to do what he told me for once. And tell you how I feel."

She smiled, reached over the table and took his hand.

"So where do you live in Wiltshire?" she asked.

"Well, it's actually the family seat but Dad left me a cottage not far from the business. I think I'll sell the business though. I know nothing about antiques."

"Oh, let's go and have a look first, eh? I could psychometrise the antiques!"

"Hold on, girl, I don't think that's such a good idea, do you?"

She laughed. Perhaps he was right about the business, but she liked the thought of living in a cottage.

Epilogue

Bosworth Battlefield Site, Twenty-first Century

Bright Blue Eyes That Shine

Over the next few days, she tried not to think about the knowledge she had of Richard. She had all her own copious notes of what she had 'witnessed' but she knew it wasn't evidence that would stand too much scrutiny – any scrutiny. It was only her own mind, they would say, filling in the blanks. None of his actual words had conclusively told them what had been the fate of the princes. He was a man who spoke only sparingly, unfortunately. But she felt like she had to do something. The project seemed unfinished, somehow.

When she confided in Rupert, he suggested going to the re-enactment of the Battle of Bosworth, wondering if it might 'lay the ghost' so to speak. Perhaps she could get closure there.

But that was months away and Eve was sitting at her computer one night, when she realised what she had to do. Whether people believed her or not, even if they thought she was crazy, she had to put the version of history she had experienced down on paper. She might not publish it – she would ask a few trusted friends to read it first and get their opinion – but at least it would be recorded for posterity. She retrieved her notes and set about transcribing them, including all the descriptions of the sounds, sights, smells and tastes of mediaeval Britain. By the time the weekend of the re-enactment was approaching, she had almost finished it. She had only to edit it and get it proofread.

Rupert had agreed to go with her and they parked the car and walked into the area where all the stalls were – there were some great ones – leather goods, mead, weapons, clothing, food – all as authentic as the vendors could make them. She had to admit, she was really enjoying the day. They bought and ate some pies washed down with ale. Eve watched the jousting competition, imagining one of the knights was Richard, although they had not found any evidence that he had ever taken part in such tourneys.

When it came time for the re-enactment part, she became very nervous. It was actually the exact anniversary of the Battle and there was something eerie about the clanking of the armour and the shouts of the men as they fought one another. She soon realised though, that it was nothing like the real battle. There was no obvious blood, no death, no standard bearer spilling blood from the stumps of his legs. And the commentary was designed to lighten the mood, jokingly delivered by 'Thomas Stanley'.

After about ten minutes, once the cannon fire had ceased, the horses and riders entered the field, banners flying along with the manes and tails of the horses. Her eyes naturally gravitated to the man who was playing Richard. He looked splendid on a large chestnut horse, his armour almost as impressive as Richard's own had been, gold details glinting in the sun. It was a blazing sun, too – a sun in splendour. She knew, of course, that it had also been hot on that fateful day, long ago.

'Richard' had his helmet on, but the visor up and she could see his face clearly. He was a big man, broad of shoulder and his face was slightly chubby, his eyes dark as he glared out at the 'enemy'. The crowd cheered – "A York! A York!" It seemed Richard was more popular than Henry Tudor. She was glad – a small piece of vengeance for Richard. But as the horses cantered in, it began to drizzle, the rain becoming steadily heavier and heavier. And when the action demanded that 'Richard' fall from his horse and be slain, there was a loud clap of thunder and flash of lightning at the exact moment he fell. Feeling stupid, she brushed away her tears again. She couldn't see how this would help her. Rupert put his arm around her and gave her a squeeze.

After 'Tudor' was crowned (the crowd booed!), she turned to leave, Rupert silent beside her. There was no need to speak – they both felt the same sadness. It was wonderful how close they had become over their shared experience with Richard Plantagenet.

"I think I had better go to the loo, before we leave," she said, catching sight of the gap between the tents that led to the Portaloos.

"OK," Rupert said, adding: "I'll nip over to the hog roast stall and get us a roll each, shall I?"

Eve nodded her agreement and made for the loos. When she got there, they were all occupied and there was the longest queue she had ever seen, waiting. She sighed. Then she saw the field of horses, just beyond the row of Portacabins and decided to go and see them, hoping the queue would reduce after a little while. The horses were so beautiful, contentedly cropping the grass after their exertions in the battle. It was quieter here, and she realised that this was the area reserved for the performers. She was about to return to the queue, but then one of the horses came trotting over to her and she stood there and patted his quivering neck. He snuffed at her hand and nodded his head up and down, making her giggle.

When she turned to leave, she found she was being watched by a man. It was one of the re-enactors and he came over to her, still wearing his armour, although he held his helmet in his hand. The glint of gold attracted her eye as the sun caught the golden coronet set atop the helmet. It was the man who had played Richard! She felt suddenly shy, her heart fluttering, and told herself off for being an idiot. He was only a man after all. As he approached, she saw he moved with grace and ease as if the armour were weightless. She suddenly felt vulnerable – this area was completely deserted and here was a strange man approaching her. She backed so that she was against the fence, the horse starting to investigate her hair. She moved forward again and decided to brazen it out – she was sure showing fear would be the worst possible thing to do. She raised her gaze to his face, expecting to see the dark eyes and chubby cheeks of the re-enactor. But this man was different. His cheekbones were chiselled and lean, his mouth firm, his hair shoulder length and dark brown. But it was his eyes that made her gasp – they were the most piercing blue eyes she had ever seen, seeming to bore into her soul and know her innermost thoughts.

"Do not be afraid. I will not harm you. I come to thank you," he said.

"What for? I haven't done anything to deserve your thanks – I don't even know you."

He smiled then, his blue eyes crinkling up at the corners, his teeth glinting in the sun.

"Oh, you know me!" he said, softly.

Then she recognised his voice, the voice that had become so familiar to her over the last year. Her mouth fell open in disbelief and she began to tremble all over. Her breathing was coming in little gasps and tiny dots filled her vision. He took her by the shoulders and kissed her once on each cheek, still smiling.

"I value your loyalty and your courage, Eve. Your written testimony will help restore my reputation."

She dropped to her knees, not even aware of what she was doing, and looked up at him, meeting his azure gaze, so intense it made her heart pound.

"My Liege," she whispered, trembling.

He stood upright, his bearing noble and full of grace and then he proffered his hand to her. She took it instinctively and pressed her lips to the gold and finely jewelled ring of state he wore. He brought his other hand around hers and raised her up, his eyes boring into hers. She felt that he could read her mind. He gave her hands a swift squeeze and spoke once more.

"You bear my standard now. I know you will not fail me."

She stared at him as he released his hold on her hands and stepping back, gave her a nod of approval. She wanted to follow him, but she was frozen to the spot and could only watch as his form faded from her sight and disappeared.

She felt the tears again, coursing down her cheeks, but this time she was smiling as she turned to where Rupert was waiting for her.

"Are you OK, love?" he asked, anxiously, as he noticed her tear-filled eyes.

"Yes, I am. I'm great in fact. I'm going to publish – by order of the king!"

FINIS

Author's Notes

I had the idea for this book after I listened to an album of Ricardian music by The Legendary Ten Seconds, in particular a song called 'Sheriff Hutton'. The song described visiting various sites which were important to Richard and imagining the time when he was actually there. The chorus had the lines: 'Where distant echoes still resound, that which was lost may still be found.'

This resonated with me and took me back to when I was a teenager and had read a science fiction book in which the friendly aliens could 'pick up' the visual echo of previous actions. They laughed about two earthlings tripping over in the woods, but the earth people were puzzled because the aliens had not been present at the time. They were told the aliens saw their 'shadows' – meaning they could still see the echoes of something that had happened in the past. I know scientists say that sound waves and light waves continue expanding into the universe, so what if those sound waves could be recaptured...?

I also wanted to include incidents from Richard's life which are not widely known. He made various judgements as Lord of the North and later as King, where people brought their grievances to him to decide on. Apart from the scene where Richard helps Alys's brother with Lord Rivers' accusation, all the cases described in the novel are real, although I have fictionalised them to make them more accessible. I have also mentioned most of the new laws and statutes that he brought in during his first and only Parliament.

Obviously, many of the incidents and happenings in Richard's life are unknown, and have led to numerous different theories regarding them, e.g. the mystery of the princes, who the mother(s) of his illegitimate children was/were and when and for how long he was under Warwick's tutelage. I have chosen the theories I prefer and aimed to fill in the gaps logically and plausibly.

For example, one of the women suggested as Richard's mistress and mother to one or both of his illegitimate children was Alys Burgh. She was paid an annuity by Richard 'for certain special causes and considerations' and was located at Pontefract, where it was thought his son, John, was born. Apart from the name, her story here is fictional.

As regards parts of his life that were better documented, I have generally kept to any facts that are known.

One example of not sticking with the accepted view is regarding Richard's scoliosis, which probably began to become noticeable when he was aged ten to thirteen. I have made it appear a couple of years earlier, so that I could use it to illustrate his possible attitude to it during the Ceremony of the Bath.

There has been some new research regarding Francis Lovell and his family by Michèle Schindler, and I have consulted her blog and used some of the information regarding a possible, previously unknown, illegitimate child of Richard's by Francis' sister, Frideswide. If you are interested in Francis and his family, look out for Michèle's book due out later in 2019: 'Lovell our Dogge: The Life of Viscount Lovell, Closest Friend of Richard III and Failed Regicide', to be published by Amberley.

There is actually a video of the mediaeval poem about a parrot. You can find it on YouTube – it is called John Skelton's Speke Parott.

Trying to speak in Richard's voice is difficult, as no-one really knows much of what he said in various situations and so I have utilised at times his surviving correspondence, which does give us a clue to his character. The letters to Louis XI and regarding Thomas Lynom and Elizabeth Shore show his humour and his tolerance, and the appointment of his son, John as Captain of Calais expresses his pride and love for him. Then there is the postscript regarding Buckingham's betrayal where the Plantagenet rage rears its head! I have tried to keep them as he wrote them although some were in Latin, so these are obviously translated as accurately as possible.

I hope this method works to give the reader some idea of the real Richard III, one that is vastly different from the Richard III of Shakespeare.

You can follow My Writing Blog at:
www.joannelarner.wordpress.com and you can also email me on jrlarner@aol.com. I am on Facebook and my Pages are called: 'Joanne Larner – Author' and 'Richard Liveth Yet'.

Follow me on Twitter - JetBlackJo

The Legendary Ten Seconds website is:
www.thelegendary10seconds.co.uk/

Finally, if you enjoyed this book or any of the others, please consider writing an Amazon review. These are invaluable to self-published authors like me.
Thank you for reading.

About the Author

Joanne Larner published her first novel, Richard Liveth Yet, in 2015. She had wanted to write a novel since the age of thirteen but was never able to finish one.

However, inspired by her fascination for Richard III and time travel, she combined the two and found she could write more easily than ever before. She has now completed two sequels, making Richard Liveth Yet a trilogy - a sort of 'Back to the Future' with Richard III!

Then she was approached by Susan Lamb, another Ricardian author, to collaborate on a humorous collection of anecdotes about Richards's escapades at his castle of 'Muddleham', along with his wife Anne, his son Edward and his friend Lovell, among many others. They published the book, Dickon's Diaries, in 2017 and the sequel, Dickon's Diaries 2 in 2018. The books are not to be taken seriously and a taste of the humour in them can be found on our Facebook Page, 'Dickon for his Dames', www.facebook.com/dickiethird/

Joanne appreciates the predominantly fantastic reviews the books have received - she finds it very heartening to know that others enjoy reading her work! And she notes any critical comments as well.

Also by Joanne R Larner:

Richard Liveth Yet: A Historical Novel Set in the Present Day
Richard Liveth Yet (Book II): A Foreign Country
Richard Liveth Yet (Book III): Hearts Never Change

With Susan Lamb:

Dickon's Diaries: A Yeare in the Lyff of King Richard the Third
Dickon's Diaries 2: Another Yeare in the Lyff of King Richard the Third

Anthologies containing original stories by Joanne R Larner:

The Box Under the Bed: An Anthology of Horror Stories from 20 Authors
Grant Me the Carving of my Name: An Anthology of Short Fiction Inspired by King Richard III

All available on Amazon at: www.amazon.co.uk/Joanne-R-Larner/e/B00XO1IC4S

Playlist

As in previous books, I have used song titles to represent the scenes - just the title is relevant, not necessarily the rest of the lyrics. Here are the songs I used, with the artists, in case you wish to explore them further.

Prologue:
Mars, the God of War - Gustav Holst, The Planets

Chapter One:
I'm So Excited – The Pointer Sisters
Moments - Westlife
Goodbye to Love – The Carpenters
The King in the Car Park – The Legendary Ten Seconds
Make It Happen – Mariah Carey
My Prayer – Frankie Valli & The Four Seasons
Say What I Feel – The Overtones
Don't Give Up – Peter Gabriel
Help Yourself – Tom Jones
History – Megan McKenna

Chapter Two:
The Voice – Ultravox
Singing You Through – All Angels
One Step Forward – The Delta Line Dance Band
Mama – Il Divo
House of York – The Legendary Ten Seconds
Cast Your Fate to the Wind – Sounds Orchestral
Propaganda – Sparks
Do You Hear What I Hear? – Whitney Houston
Oh, Holy Night – The Four Seasons
Ball of Confusion – The Temptations
Until the Day We Die – Pagan Fury
This Is Me – Keala Settle and The Greatest Showman Ensemble
Shallow – Lady Gaga & Bradley Cooper
So What? – P!nk

Chapter Three:
I Want to Know What Love Is – Foreigner
Hungry Eyes – Eric Carmen
One Step Beyond – Madness
Goodbye Girl – David Gates
What Do You Want? – Adam Faith
Written at Rising – The Legendary Ten Seconds
The Ragged Staff – The Legendary Ten Seconds
What Kind of Man Am I? – Jimmy Nail
What's Up? – 4 Non Blondes

Chapter Four:
Something Inside (So Strong) – Labi Siffre
More Than Words – Westlife

There Goes My First Love – The Drifters
Let You Love Me – Rita Ora
Stiletto Heels – Sailor
Be Alright – Dean Lewis
Loyalty Binds Me – The Legendary Ten Seconds
The Great Escape – London Festival Orchestra and Stanley Black
Battle in the Mist – The Legendary Ten Seconds
Tewkesbury Tale – The Legendary Ten Seconds

Chapter Five:
Demons – Bryan McFadden
Rockabye – feat. Sean Paul and Anne-Marie
Brother's Bane – Tyr
One Last Time – Ariana Grande
Come Back My Love – The Overtones
Rag Doll – Frankie Valli & The Four Seasons
Got My Mind Set On You – George Harrison
Good Ol' Fashioned Love – The Overtones

Chapter Six:
Take Good Care of My Baby – Bobby Vee
I'm Not the Man You Think I Am – Bryan Adams
Goodnight, Sweetheart, Goodnight – The Overtones
Days – Kirsty MacColl
As You Turn Away – Lady Antebellum
Unusually Unusual – Lonestar
Question – The Moody Blues
Castles and Dreams – Blackmore's Night

Chapter Seven:
When A Child Is Born – Johnny Mathis
Dream – Imagine Dragons
To France – Mike Oldfield
The Gold It Feels So Cold – The Legendary Ten Seconds
To Fotheringhay – The Legendary Ten Seconds
I'm A Believer – The Monkees
Isabel – Il Divo
The Best You Never Had – Leona Lewis

Chapter Eight:
Sanctus – Karl Jenkins
Act – Ephemera
Act of Treason – The Iscariots
Beggin' – Frankie Valli & the Four Seasons
Don't Forget to Remember – The Bee Gees
Decision – Goldfinger
I'll Be There – Mariah Carey
Hymn Before Action – Karl Jenkins

Chapter Nine:
Cuts Like A Knife – Bryan Adams
Ghost of a Rose – Blackmore's Night
All About You – McFly
Lord Anthony Woodville – The Legendary Ten Seconds
The Lord Protector – The Legendary Ten Seconds
Warrior – Paloma Faith
Be the Man – Rag 'n' Bone Man
Feeling Good – Escala
The King of Wishful Thinking – Go West
Grace – Rag 'n' Bone Man

By Hearsay – The Legendary Ten Seconds

Chapter Ten:
Innocent Man – Rag 'n' Bone Man
A World Without Love – Peter & Gordon
Lord of Lies – Tyr
Betrayed – Frankie Valli & the Four Seasons
Whoops – The Overtones
Lookin' For A Good Time – Lady Antebellum
Framed – Los Lobos
Just Another Day – Jon Secada
Crowning of the King – Blackmore's Night
Pomp and Circumstance – Royal Philharmonic Orchestra

Chapter Eleven:
These Days – Rudimental (feat. Jess Glynne)
Our Kind of Love – Lady Antebellum
When Love Takes Over – David Guetta (feat. Kelly Rowland)
The Mystery of the Princes – The Legendary Ten Seconds
Whatever It Takes – Leona Lewis
Don't Mean Nothing – Richard Marx
Smile – Lonestar
You Raise Me Up – Westlife
Core 'Ngrato – Luciano Pavarotti
Hell or High Water – Passenger
Bitter End – Rag 'n' Bone Man

Chapter Twelve:
Make You Feel My Love – Adele
The Joker – Steve Miller Band
Familiar – Liam Payne & J Balvin

From Now On – Hugh Jackman and The Greatest Showman Ensemble

Drag You Down – The Pierces

Young at Heart – The Bluebells

Benedictus – Bud Johnston, Karl Jenkins, London Philharmonic Orchestra

What Becomes of the Broken-Hearted? – Jimmy Ruffin

Chapter Thirteen:
Because You Loved Me – Celine Dion
In the Summertime – Mungo Jerry
Guilty – Blue
Last Storm – Kurt Nilsen
Run to You – Bryan Adams
Agnus Dei – Karl Jenkins
Bridge Over Troubled Water – Simon and Garfunkel

Chapter Fourteen:
I Run to You – Lady Antebellum
Hard to Say I'm Sorry – Chicago
Sweet Child of Mine – Guns 'n' Roses
Children – Robert Miles
Everybody Hurts – REM
Testify – M People
Shining Knight – Bloody Meadows
Mr Right – Leona Lewis

Epilogue:
Bright Blue Eyes That Shine - The Legendary Ten Seconds

Bibliography and Research

These are a selection of the books and other sources I have referred to while researching 'Distant Echoes':

Richard Duke of Gloucester as Lord Protector and High Constable of England – Annette Carson

Richard III: A Royal Enigma – Sean Cunningham

The Itinerary of Richard III 1483-1485 – Rhoda Edwards

The Children of Richard III – Peter Hammond

Richard III: Loyalty Binds Me – Matthew Lewis

The Ricardian Bulletin (June 2017) pp 39-41: Richard III and 'Oure Poor Subject Katherine Bassingbourne' – David Johnson

The Ricardian (Journal of the Richard III Society) Volume XXVI 2016, pp 41-85: Richard of Gloucester 1461-70: Income, Lands and Associates. His Whereabouts and Responsibilities – Anne F. Sutton

I have also used the internet and taken advice from other Ricardians. Some links to sites used to research the book:

The Richard III Society – www.richardiii.net

Richard III's Loyal Supporters – www.r3loyalsupporters.org/

Michèle Schindler's Blog about Lovell - http://francislovell.blogspot.com

Acknowledgements

I have many people to thank for helping me to finish this book, 'Distant Echoes'. Among them are:

My sister, Lynne Lawer, for her meticulous proof-reading, editing and sensible suggestions; I really couldn't have done it without her.

My friends, Viv and Robert Taylor, for inspiring my vision of Eve and Rupert and Susan for inspiring Sue and being a beta reader.

Dr A J Hibberd, who is the fount of all knowledge regarding obscure documents and facts about Richard.

David Johnson for pointing my research in the direction of The Ricardian Bulletin

Michèle Schindler, whose research on Francis Lovell and his family is ground-breaking. Her book about Francis, "Lovell our Dogge: The Life of Viscount Lovell, Closest Friend of Richard III and Failed Regicide", will be out in 2019, published by

Amberley, and her blog page has many facts and intriguing theories.

Ian Churchward of The Legendary Ten Seconds for the inspiration of his songs, without which this book wouldn't exist.

Philippa Langley, John Ashdown Hill and Wendy and David Johnson, who were behind the research which found Richard's remains, without which I might never have become a Ricardian.

All my Ricardian friends on Facebook, especially my fellow writers/artists: Susan Lamb, Alex Marchant, Marla Skidmore, Janet Reedman, Jane Orwin-Higgs, Sandra Heath Wilson, Maire Martello, Frances Quinn, Linda Lowery, Riikka Nikko, Richard Unwin, Michèle Schindler, Karen Oder, Stephen Lark, Judy Thomson, Barbara Gaskell Denvil, Joan Szechtman, Matthew Lewis and Brian Wainwright, who are all very knowledgeable, supportive and fantastic!

All the ladies from the Women in Business Network for their help and encouragement.

My dogs, Jonah and Hunter. My husband, John, for putting up with me writing into the early hours.

Last but not least, Richard III of England, for inspiring me and firing my imagination.

And anyone else I forgot.

38079172R00257

Printed in Poland
by Amazon Fulfillment
Poland Sp. z o.o., Wrocław